THE SILK MAKER

As Richard walked back to The Grange, his mind filled with questions. What was the true reason behind his willingness to work for the Harcourts? Was there still at the back of his mind a desire for revenge? Had he been so bewitched by Sarah Harcourt that all his common sense had left him? Or was it simply an opportunity to do the kind of work he knew and enjoyed?

And why had the Harcourts been so willing to offer a job to a young man without references, who had even confessed his hostility towards them?

He could find no satisfactory answers, and decided that his best course might simply be to let fate sweep him along to whatever lay ahead . . .

The Silk Maker

MICHAEL LEGAT

SPHERE BOOKS LIMITED

First published in Great Britain by
Souvenir Press Ltd 1985

Published by Sphere Books Ltd 1986
27 Wright's Lane, London W8 5TZ

Publisher's Note

All of the characters in this book are fictitious, and any resemblance to actual persons, living or dead, is purely coincidental.

TRADE
MARK

Set in 10/11 pt Plantin

Printed and bound in Great Britain by
Cox & Wyman Ltd, Reading

For
TEDDY AND KAY

The Silk Maker

CHAPTER ONE

'See who it is, then, Richard.'

The knock on the door was repeated, falling threateningly into the dimly-lit, silent room. Richard ran to open the door, and sunlight flooded in.

'Is your mother at home, boy?'

'Aye, missus.'

'Call me by my name, boy. You know who I am, surely.'

Richard knew her well. Her fashionable bonnet blocked his view every Sunday in church, and when the congregation left after the service, sometimes she would glance at his parents in distant acknowledgment of the little bow that his father always gave. She was Mrs Charlotte Harcourt, wife to the owner of the silk mill where Richard's father worked . . . had worked.

'Please enter, ma'am,' Richard's mother called. She was standing now, her knuckles gleaming white as she gripped the back of the hardwood chair.

Mrs Harcourt fastidiously gathered in her skirts so that they should not brush against the doorway. Richard could hear the rustle of her silk plaid-patterned dress, and the many petticoats she wore beneath it, as she walked into the room. 'I come to offer you my condolences, Mrs Goodwin.'

'You are very kind, ma'am. Will you not take a chair?'

In the light of the single candle which illuminated the sparsely furnished room, Mrs Harcourt could not be sure that the seat was clean. She gave a little wave of the hand to indicate that she would not sit, and drew her shawl about her shoulders. Her gaze settled on the dozen or so books which stood on the mantelshelf, and she sniffed in disapproval. Books! A family like the Goodwins had no business with books – except, of course, the Bible . . . 'Your husband's death must have been a great shock.'

'I still find it difficult to believe.'

There was a strange tone in his mother's voice, and Richard looked at her, wondering if she were going to weep again; but her eyes, though still red-rimmed, were clear. He glanced at his sisters. Mary and Frances were huddled together by the fireplace. He knew somehow that they felt the same uneasiness.

'How old was he? Do you know when he was born?' So few women of Mrs Goodwin's class bothered with such details.

'He was born on the twenty-fourth of March in the year of our Lord eighteen hundred and five.'

Mrs Harcourt looked at her sharply. Was the woman trying to be impertinent? She decided to ignore it. 'Forty-seven is no age, no age at all. Had he complained of feeling unwell?'

'He was in good health and spirits as he left for work that day,' Elizabeth Goodwin replied. 'Then they came and told me that he was dead.'

'A seizure of the heart.'

'So they say.'

'It is unusual in someone so thin. He was very thin, your husband. Undernourished, perhaps.'

'My husband never wanted for food.'

'You cannot deceive me, Mrs Goodwin. Oh, if only people would think before they bring children into the world! You have three, alas – three hungry mouths to feed – and no doubt you and your husband starved for their sake. Such folly! Look at you – you are just skin and bones yourself.'

Richard glanced at his mother again. True, she was thin, but why, he wondered, should Mrs Harcourt say so in such an angry way. She was skinny herself, but whereas his mother's thinness was somehow friendly and comfortable, Mrs Harcourt's was hard and . . . spiky. He decided suddenly that he hated Mrs Harcourt, with her brightly rouged cheeks, and her scent which filled the cottage with its unnatural, pungent smell.

'It is all very well for us women,' she was saying. 'Our

constitutions are so made that we can accept privation – but men require adequate nourishment.'

'William was well fed.' Elizabeth's voice was still the same monotone, as though she dared not allow herself to express any emotion. 'It was work that killed him. He gave his life to the mill.'

Mrs Harcourt bridled. 'Mr Harcourt is the most generous, the most considerate of employers.'

'I know that, Mrs Harcourt.'

'I should hope so. Too generous, too considerate. Besides, hard work never killed anyone.'

Richard saw his mother's eyes flash briefly, but she said nothing.

'Ah, well, the Lord giveth and the Lord taketh away,' Mrs Harcourt declared magnanimously. She bowed her head for a moment, and then continued in a brisker tone, 'Now, we must be practical, Mrs Goodwin, and consider your future. You own this cottage, I understand, but clearly you will not be able to live here without any income. We are fortunate in this part of Essex – the workhouse in Franton is quite excellently maintained. I have had a word with the matron, a most respectable and kind-hearted woman, who fortunately has a place available and who will be prepared to receive you.'

'No,' said Elizabeth.

'What do you mean? Oh, I realise that the idea may be repugnant to you, but there is no alternative. You cannot hope to provide for yourself and three children. How old are they?'

'Mary is eleven, Richard nine, and Frances is four.'

Mrs Harcourt glanced at the children. The girl called Mary would capture a few hearts when she was older, she thought, and the boy was well-favoured too, with his golden curls and that wide-eyed look; the youngest child seemed plainer, and somewhat peaky, though of course it was difficult to tell at that age. 'H'm. I suppose the older girl and the boy could find work, but it is much better that all three should go to the orphanage. They will be taught to read and write. Not that I approve of that – it will only give them ideas above their station. Later, suitable employment . . .'

Richard could not restrain himself. He wanted to say something which would show Mrs Harcourt that she did not know everything about them. 'I do read and write already!' he burst out. 'And so do Mary!'

'You must not interrupt, Richard,' his mother told him quietly.

'You see!' Mrs Harcourt's black curls bobbed in indignation. 'Manners is what they should have been taught, Mrs Goodwin, not reading and writing. Children should be seen and not heard. However, the point is that the orphanage is the best place for them.'

'No, Mrs Harcourt. That is not my intention. I know what such places are like, and –'

'Oh, I have no patience with you people! You refuse to face the facts before your very eyes. Why I trouble myself, I do not know.'

'You are very kind. But I beg leave to decide my own future, and that of my children.'

'It is your sorrow talking,' Mrs Harcourt declared, 'and I must get some sense into your head.' She decided, after all, to sit down, flicking her handkerchief over the seat of the chair before she did so.

This small action seemed to epitomise all that Elizabeth resented in the visit. Richard was not so young that he could not recognise the pain and anger in his mother's eyes, and suddenly he could stand the tension of the room no longer. He felt his eyes filling, and without asking leave, ran to the door. Outside, the bright sunlight made him blink, and the tears spilled over and ran down his cheeks. In front of him was Mrs Harcourt's trap, the bay gelding standing patiently in the shafts, the driver sitting with the reins slack in his hand, and nearby a boy, a year or two older than himself, was whipping a top.

Richard tried to brush away his tears. He recognised the boy as Tom Harcourt, the youngest of the mill-owner's children. He had seen him in church too, fidgeting, tweaking his sisters' hair, tearing a page from his prayer book to make a paper dart, unchecked by his mother unless he made some kind of noise, when she would pat his arm gently, and he would look up at her and give her a special, almost conspiratorial smile.

Tom gazed with interest at Richard. 'Look, Dawson,' he said to the driver. 'He's blubbing.'

'I a'n't.'

'Yes, you are. Boys don't cry, do they, Dawson? Only silly girls cry.'

'Right you are, Master Tom.'

'Then he must be a silly girl, mustn't he? A silly girl with pretty curls.' He was as dark as Richard was fair, and his own straight hair fell lankly about his ears. He looked at Richard expectantly, but when his taunt produced no response, brandished his whip. 'I'll give him something to cry for, shall I?'

Richard turned back towards the cottage, ashamed of the tears that were pricking at his eyes again, and unable to understand why Tom Harcourt should attack him in this way.

Tom gave a shout of triumph, and waved his whip. 'Cry-baby! Off to tell your mam all about it, eh? Can't tell your dad, can you? He's dead. Dead! Cry-baby! Cry-baby!'

Richard spun round and charged towards his enemy, kicking the spinning top far into the rough grass as he went. Tom lashed at him with his whip. The string curled harmlessly around Richard's neck, but the stick itself landed with a crack on his cheek. He did not feel the pain as he hurled himself at Tom, arms flailing wildly, bare feet kicking at his opponent's legs. His strength was no match for the older boy's, and in a moment he was lying flat on his back, with Tom kneeling over him, banging his head on the ground. Thrashing his arms, his fist connected with Tom's face. The older boy gave a howl of pain and anger, and a murderous glint came into his dark eyes.

The driver, who had been watching with an amused grin on his face, decided that the fight had gone far enough. Any more, and the young master might get himself hurt. He jumped down and separated the boys.

At that moment the cottage door burst open, and summoned by her son's cry, Mrs Harcourt appeared, followed by Elizabeth and the two girls.

'Just parting 'em, ma'am,' the driver said hastily.

'Tom!' Mrs Harcourt shrieked. 'Oh, my poor lamb.' She tried to pull him to her, but the boy broke away angrily, trying now to hide his own tears. 'What is this, Dawson?'

'This young varmint, ma'am, 'e suddenly went for Master Tom.'

'Richard!' Elizabeth exclaimed.

'For what reason?'

'No reason at all, ma'am,' the driver said. 'I was too slow in getting down to stop 'im. It was all so sudden-like. I don't think there's much 'arm, begging your pardon.'

'Richard!' Elizabeth said. 'How could you? You will apologise to Master Harcourt.'

'But, Mama, he called me –'

'I do not wish to hear, sir. Apologise at once.'

Richard looked at his mother in desperation, but saw no hope in her angry gaze. 'Sorry,' he mumbled.

'Very well. Now go inside. Your father . . . I will speak to you later.'

Richard hung his head and went back to the cottage. His head was throbbing, and the weal on his cheek was a searing pain, but the worst hurt was in his heart.

Mrs Harcourt listened with pursed lips as Elizabeth herself apologised. 'I can only assume that grief has turned your mind, *and* caused you to lose control over your son. You must, you certainly must reconsider your position, and quickly too – the matron cannot keep a place for you for ever. If you persist in your folly, there is little I can do to help you, though I will speak to my husband about the possibility of employing the older girl. As for the boy, I am sure Mr Harcourt will be disinclined to take him on after this. Nevertheless, I will do my best for him. Why I should do so is beyond me, but then I was ever of too kind and generous a nature.' Assisted by Dawson, she climbed into the trap. 'Come, Tom. Leave that silly top. Mama will buy you a new one.'

Back inside the cottage, Elizabeth called Richard to her. She looked closely at his tear-stained face and softly touched the weal that the stick had left. He flinched. She said nothing, but poured warm water into a basin from the kettle on the hob, took a cloth and gently bathed his face. 'What happened, Richard?'

He told her, haltingly. 'It weren't fair, Mama,' he finished.

' "Wasn't", Richard, not "weren't".' Elizabeth tried constantly to correct the errors which the children picked up so readily from their playmates in the village, and which they had heard all too often from their poor, dear father, who had never been able wholly to discard his strong local accent and rough manner of speaking. She sighed. 'Life is seldom fair, my dear.'

'It weren't – it wasn't fair of God to take Papa away,' said Mary.

'Oh, we must never think that,' Elizabeth said. She pushed back a strand of her faded blonde hair. 'We must never question what God does. We may feel sad, but we must try to rejoice for Papa. He is happy now, with Jesus.' She saw disbelief on their young faces. Well, she could understand how difficult it sometimes was for the young to believe that God knew best, that He truly loved His children, but she had to try to convince them of that truth. 'Come, my dears,' she said softly, 'let us kneel and say a prayer together.'

Richard looked at her surreptitiously as he knelt with the others. Her face had that special look on it, of joy and confidence mingled with humility. It was all very well, he thought. Perhaps she was right about not questioning the ways of the Lord, but Tom Harcourt's ways were a different matter. One day . . . one day he would get his own back.

Later, while they were eating their midday meal, he asked, 'What *will* 'ee do, Mama?'

'I don't know. All I know is that we are going to stay together. I'll not be separated from my family, and I'll not have you and Mary and Frances sent to the orphanage. I would not wish that for anyone.' She thought of the misery of her own childhood, the unwholesome, inadequate food, the harsh and cheerless surroundings, the cruelty of the master and his wife. She would die sooner than let her children suffer as she had.

The unhappiness had lasted until she was twelve. Then a

clergyman and his wife visited the orphanage, seeking a maidservant, and she was fortunate enough to be selected. For the first time in her life she experienced kindness and comfort. The Reverend Percival Norton and his wife were childless, and this waif that they had rescued soon touched their hearts, so that they treated her more like a daughter than a servant. Mrs Norton showed her how to sew and bake, and her husband found great joy in teaching her to read and write and in sharing with her his own love of literature.

Although originally expected to stay with the Nortons for no more than a year or two, she became a permanent part of their household. Like any young girl, she dreamed of marriage, but no man really attracted her until, when she was already past thirty, she met William Goodwin.

The son of a farm labourer, William left the land when he was sixteen, determined to better himself, and worked in Harcourt's Mill, rising to become an overseer in the weaving department. Long before he met Elizabeth he took pains to educate himself, encouraged by the Rector of Brentfield, who led him to a knowledge of the three R's. When the Rector moved to a larger parish and his successor declined to share his library or his companionship with a common weaver, William started attending the church in nearby Stenning, where Mr Norton welcomed him not only as a worshipper but in due course as a frequent visitor to his Vicarage. And there William met Elizabeth, and fell in love, and she, recognising the worth beneath the rough exterior, yielded her heart, and the Reverend Mr Norton gave them his blessing, and eventually married them.

Elizabeth was thirty-two at the time of her wedding in 1840, and William was three years older. She never regretted her marriage in any way. Even as an overseer, William earned little enough, and it was something of a struggle to clothe and feed and bring up their family, but they managed. One of their greatest blessings was William's ownership of their cottage, which he had built himself on unfenced, unclaimed land.

Elizabeth brought her thoughts back to the present, and

smiled at each of the children in turn, trying to keep their spirits up.

'Mrs Harcourt said as we'd starve,' said Mary.

'We shan't starve. I shall take in washing perhaps, or offer myself for cleaning work. Most women in Brentfield work in the mill, so the gentry must be hard put to it to find servants.'

'Someone must be doing for them now,' Mary insisted. 'Supposing they got nothing for you.'

Elizabeth smiled. 'Have faith. The Lord will provide. He always does, if only you have faith in Him. If I cannot earn enough, then perhaps you will. Mrs Harcourt promised she would ask her husband to find a place for you in the mill – and for Richard too.'

'I couldn't never work in the mill!' Richard cried. 'I hate them Harcourts!'

'Hush! They are good, kind people.'

'Tom a'n't.'

'Perhaps,' said Elizabeth gently, 'he has not been brought up in the fear of the Lord. But in any case, you were at fault too, Richard. You lost your temper, did you not?'

'He be my enemy, Mama.'

'I will not have such talk in this house,' Elizabeth said sharply. 'What would your father have said, could he have heard you? Have you no respect for him? And even if it were true, you must love your enemies, as Jesus commanded you.'

Richard bowed his head. 'Sorry, Mama,' he muttered. But he was not. Nothing could destroy the hatred he felt for the Harcourts, nor his repugnance at the idea of working in the mill they owned, the mill which had killed his father. Yet if Mr Harcourt should offer him employment, how could he escape it?

He was silent for much of the rest of the day, wrestling with the problem, until Elizabeth lost patience with him, and told him that if he was going to sulk, he had better go to bed. He lay awake, puzzling over the idea which had come to him earlier that afternoon, trying to remember all that he had heard his father say about the employment of children in the mill, imagining what difficulties he would encounter and working out how he might overcome them.

Richard's opportunity came sooner than he had expected. Elizabeth announced the next morning that she intended going to market in Great Luckton, taking Mary and Frances with her. 'You, Richard, must be the man of the house now, and stay here in case any messages come. There may be word from Mr Harcourt.'

'Aye, Mama.'

Once his mother and sisters had gone, Richard found two pieces of paper and wrote his letters. The first was easy: 'Dear Mama, I be going to Franton to work in the mill. Do not send to bring me back. A kiss to you and Mary and Frances. Your son, Richard.' The second letter was much more difficult, and he spent a long time in composing and penning it to his satisfaction. He felt a frightening guilt as he did so, almost expecting the hand of the Lord to reach down from Heaven and strike him for his wickedness.

Breathing a sigh of relief when he had finished, he placed the letter to his mother on the mantelshelf, gathered together his few clothes into an untidy bundle, wrapped a crust of bread in his handkerchief, and left the house, shutting the door carefully behind him.

When he reached the road, he turned to take a last look at his home. Like so many cottages in this part of the country, it was low-built, with whitewashed walls and a roof of thick thatch. Most of the workers in Harcourt's Mill lived in the heart of the village, their dwellings crowded higgledy-piggledy on the slopes surrounding the green, looking down on the little river which supplied power for the mill, but William Goodwin had built his home a mile away to the east, on the road to Franton. Richard was glad of that – he did not have to go through the village, where he might have been recognised.

He took a deep breath and set off. At first he was anxious, often looking behind to see if anyone were following, but gradually he was able to relax and even to enjoy the warmth of the fine summer's day and the beauty of the countryside. He remembered his mother saying how fortunate they were to live in a part of Essex that was not flat, but which had gently rolling landscape, the low hills wooded, the fields sloping at different angles to lend variety to the scene. The ripening crops glowed in the sunlight, the trees that sometimes lined the track gave welcome shade, and in the distance he watched a heron flapping its measured way along the river. Surely what he was doing must be right, or God would not have sent so beautiful a day.

In some of the fields men were working, and he bent low as he passed so that he was hidden by the hedges. But then he heard behind him the slow clopping of a horse's hooves, and turning, saw that a hay waggon was coming his way. There was nowhere to hide. He waited anxiously.

As the waggon drew level, the driver, an old man with a kindly, weather-worn face, called to him. 'Where be goin', boy?'

'Franton,' Richard replied.

The waggon stopped. 'Jump up. I'll gi' 'ee a ride a couple miles.'

'Nay, thank 'ee.'

'Please 'eesen. Room at back.'

Richard considered. If he got on at the back, the driver would hardly be able to talk to him with that load of hay between them, and if he were to start asking awkward questions, Richard could always jump off the waggon, probably without the man even noticing.

'Thank 'ee, then.' He slipped round to the back of the waggon and scrambled on, and the horse began its slow plod again. The smell of the hay was sweet in Richard's nostrils, and it was good to rest his legs. God must indeed be smiling on him, he thought.

When the driver turned off the track towards a farm, he stopped the waggon again. Richard jumped down, thanked him, and hurried on his way. The driver watched him. 'Runnin' away. Won't get far, poor little sod.' He flicked the reins and drove into the farmyard, Richard already forgotten.

Three hours later the boy reached Franton. He was tired, but the bread had answered his hunger, and a stream had quenched his thirst. He had little idea of where he would find the silk mill that was his goal, but barely had he entered the outskirts of the town when he saw it, lying at the foot of a hill beside a large old church, the two buildings dwarfing the nearby cottages. Painted on the wall of the mill in large white letters was the name 'PRIDEAU'.

He had often heard his father talk of Prideau's. 'It be the largest silk mill in Essex, and probably in England. 'Twould make three or four o' Harcourt's.' He also remembered him saying once, 'They be Huguenots, the Prideaus. Huguenots be French people who come to England so as to have their own religion. That were a hundred, hundred and fifty years ago. They was goldsmiths and silversmiths and paper-makers and silk-weavers, and they settled and now they be English like you and me, even if their names is French, like Prideau.'

'Are the Harcourts Huguenots too?' Richard had asked.

'I dunno. Mebbe, a long time ago. I know that Mr Frederick Harcourt, our Mr Harcourt's father, worked in a shop afore he founded the mill. He weren't educated, but by his own efforts he made hisself a rich and powerful man.' And his father had then launched into one of his little homilies on the twin subjects of diligence and ambition, the latter of which could be a virtue or a peril, depending on how well it was kept in check. In later life, Richard would smile tenderly at the memory of his father, who had certainly been diligent, but who was almost totally devoid of ambition, and could never have experienced much of its virtues or perils.

Richard now straightened his clothes, brushed some of the dust from his boots, felt for the letter in his pocket, and made his way to the entrance to Prideau's Mill. The great door stood open. High up on it was a knocker, which Richard had to stand on tiptoe to reach. Presently a man came, and looked down grimly at the fair-haired boy.

Richard had rehearsed the words. 'Please, sir, I seek work.'

The man did not speak. Seizing Richard roughly by the shoulder, he pulled him inside and along a corridor until he came to a door, which he opened. He pushed the boy into the room, then turned and disappeared.

Richard's first thought was that he had never seen so much paper in his life. It was everywhere – piled on desks, heaped on the floor, much of it thick in dust. At one of the desks, almost obscured by a stack of ledgers and yet more papers, sat a small man wearing metal-rimmed spectacles. He glanced at Richard briefly, then bent his head down again to complete whatever he was writing. All that Richard could see of him was his rumpled, mouse-coloured hair. At last he laid down his quill, and looked up. He had a small, round face. 'What have we here?' His voice was high and thin, and his manner of speaking very precise. 'A stranger in a strange land?' Richard did not know what to reply, and after a moment the little man went on, 'Well, my boy? Cat got your tongue?'

Although he did not smile, and the question was abruptly put, Richard felt that he was not unfriendly. 'Please, sir, I seek work.'

'Do you indeed? What sort of work?'

'Anything, sir, in the mill.'

The man's eyes twinkled. 'Anything, eh? Such as overseer in the crape department, perhaps, or maybe you have it in mind to replace me. Is that it?'

Richard was not sure how to take his mockery, gentle though it might be. 'Nay, sir,' he said solemnly. 'Just ordinary work.'

'Ah, a discerning boy, who recognises that my work is far from ordinary. A boy who will go far. And what is the name of this highly intelligent boy?'

'Richard Goodwin, sir.'

'Well, Richard Goodwin, you will kindly desist from calling me "sir". My work may be far from ordinary, but my position in this company is, alas, insufficiently exalted to warrant such a form of address, even from so respectful a young man as Master Richard Goodwin. You may call me "Mr Hill". Now then, Richard Goodwin, how old are you?'

'Nine, sir – Mr Hill.'

'And where do you come from?'

'Brentfield.'

'Dear me, that's a long way. You have walked here today? Well, no matter – you are here, and that's all that signifies. Do you have your parents' consent to work in the mill?'

'Aye, sir. Aye, Mr Hill.' Richard drew the letter from his pocket, handed it over, and waited anxiously. He had known from hearing his father talk of the employment of children at Harcourt's that parental permission would be necessary, but would Mr Hill be satisfied by what he had written?

Mr Hill unfolded the piece of paper, and read its message. 'Sir, I give my permishun for my son Richard Goodwin to work in your mill. Yrs. Eliz: Goodwin (Mrs).' Neither the childish writing nor the misspelling surprised him – indeed the only wonder was that the mother should be sufficiently well educated to have penned the letter at all. But something bothered him. 'I see,' he said.

'Be it right – the letter? I thought . . . Mama and me, we thought 'twould be all right.'

The boy's wording almost confirmed Mr Hill's suspicions. 'Tell me about your family, Richard Goodwin.'

'There be Mama, and my sisters, Mary and Frances.'

'And your father?'

'He be dead, Mr Hill.'

'When was that?'

'Last week. He were overseer at Harcourt's.'

'Of course, Harcourt's Mill at Brentfield. I am sorry to hear of your loss. And why did you not apply for work at Harcourt's?'

'Because –' Richard could think of no reason that he could give. 'My sister Mary be to work at Harcourt's.'

Mr Hill waited for more, but when Richard remained silent, he smiled and said, 'And one Harcourt employee in the family is sufficient, is that it?'

Richard nodded.

'Tell me, Richard Goodwin, can you read?'

'Aye, sir. Aye, Mr Hill.'

'And write?'

'Aye, Mr Hill.'

'H'm. I must go and speak to my superior. You must stay

here, and you must not touch anything. Do you understand? If you stir so much as a finger, I shall know instantly, and shall summon a fearsome dragon to swallow you in one bite.'

Leaving Richard in his office, Mr Hill went to see Mr Leadbetter, the general manager. 'I've got a young boy, sir, looking for work.'

'Can we use him?'

'I think so, sir. He seems quite bright. The trouble is this, sir.' He handed over Richard's letter.

Mr Leadbetter glanced at it. 'What's the matter with it?'

'I think it's forged, sir.'

'Forged? By whom?'

'The boy, sir.'

'Does he come from a well-to-do family? Has he been to a school?'

'I don't think so, sir.'

'Then don't talk nonsense, Hill. How could an uneducated boy forge something like this? Take him on if you think he'll be of use.'

'But what if it is a forgery, sir?'

'Then presumably the parents will be along to claim their son back. But we shall be in the clear. This is an entirely acceptable letter, Hill. Nothing to worry about. Hire the boy.'

When Mr Hill came back into his office, Richard looked at him apprehensively. The threat of the dragon had not alarmed him, but he was well aware that his letter was under suspicion.

Mr Hill sat down at his desk, looked at Richard, and smiled. 'Are you sure you want to work here, young man? Would it not be better to return to your home?'

'Nay, Mr Hill. I got to work here. I got to earn money for my mother, and I can't work in Brentfield – honest, I can't.'

'But you will not be able to go home at night and come back in the morning. If we do offer you employment, have you somewhere to live in Franton? Some relative with whom you can stay?'

'Nay. I thought – I thought mebbe I could sleep in the mill.'

'T't, t't, t't. What strange ideas they put into boys' heads these days! Well, we shall have to see if we can find some kind person who will take you in. You will have to pay, of course, but you will still have a few shillings to take home to your mother now and then. Will that be acceptable to your lordship?'

'Aye, Mr Hill.'

'Very well. Now I have to enter up your name and particulars. Sit down quietly, and dream of the day, if you so desire, when you become an overseer like your father, or sit in my place and interview ambitious young men desirous of serving this illustrious company.' He picked up his quill, opened another ledger, and began to write.

Richard waited happily. It seemed that he had managed it, though he was almost certain that Mr Hill had known the truth about him. It was strange – Mr Hill did not look in the least like his father, nor did his high, fluting voice have any resemblance to William Goodwin's slow, deep tones, but at times it had almost been as though his father were talking to him. Perhaps it was the way Mr Hill spoke as though he were conversing with a grown man, or perhaps it was just his kindness.

Finally, Mr Hill put down his pen. 'Right, Master Goodwin, we shall give you a week's trial. You will be paid two whole shillings for the week, subject to a satisfactory report on your work from your superiors. Of this vast sum, you will have to pay one shilling and sixpence for your board and lodging.' He saw the dismay on Richard's face. 'Ah, you hoped to have more to send home to your mother, eh? Well, if you work hard you'll soon be earning better than two shillings a week, and that will be all right, won't it?'

Richard nodded.

'Then come with me.' Mr Hill led the way out of his tiny office, along a maze of corridors and into a vast room. It was not the first time that Richard had been in a weaving shed, and the deafening clatter of the looms, as the shuttle flew to and fro, came as no surprise to him. What he was not prepared for, however, was the size of the place, or the number of machines, crowded closely together, with dozens of workers, mostly women, busy at them. As his father had said, it would have made three or four of Harcourt's. The shed was as big and as lofty, he thought, as the church at Brentfield, but much lighter, because of the tall windows on either side.

At the end of the room, a broad-shouldered, powerful-looking man was bending over the shoulder of one of the weavers, checking her work. Mr Hill waited until he straightened up, and then, shouting to make himself heard above the noise, said, 'Another captain of industry, Mr Renshaw. Name of Richard Goodwin. Starting tomorrow, usual terms, usual duties.'

Mr Renshaw looked at Richard sourly. ''Ope 'e's better than the last one you brung me. All right, lad – mind you're on time.' He turned back to his work.

When they had left the weaving shed, Mr Hill said, 'That was your overseer, Mr Renshaw. Henceforth he is to be your God. Serve him with the devotion you would offer to the Lord Almighty, and you will be all right. And be not dismayed – Mr Renshaw has a fearsome bark, but it is worse, much worse than his bite.'

Back in his office, he sat down at his desk and rang a small hand bell. After a few moments, the door opened and a boy a little older than Richard appeared. 'Ah, Master Harris. Allow me to introduce you to Master Goodwin. I wish you to convey Master Goodwin to the house of Mistress Plackett. My compliments to that good lady, and will she accept this splendid specimen of young manhood as a lodger, on the usual terms. You may say further that my advice would be to feed the young gentleman and pack him off to bed instanter, since he has to be here at the mill, booted and spurred and in his right mind, at five minutes before six of the clock tomorrow morning, and not a second later.'

The boy looked at him blankly, and dropping his ironic tone, Mr Hill said, 'Take Goodwin to Mrs Plackett's, tell her he's a new lodger for her, and to make sure that he's on time tomorrow morning. Is that clear?' When the boy nodded, he turned to Richard. 'I don't know what the world is coming to,

Richard Goodwin. I shall soon be reduced to words of one syllable.'

Richard somehow recognised that this strange statement was his dismissal. 'Thank 'ee, Mr Hill,' he said, and held out his hand, as his parents had taught him.

Mr Hill shook hands gravely. As the boys left the office and he bent back to his work, he wondered whether he would ever learn the truth about young Richard Goodwin. That letter was certainly forged, and it was more than likely that his mother would appear tomorrow to rescue her little lost lamb. And that would be a pity – he was an attractive boy, a cut above the usual sort, and Prideau's could do with a few more youngsters of his calibre.

The boy looked better with something to eat inside him, Mrs Plackett thought. When he had first arrived, he had been scared out of his wits, poor little mite, and fair worn out too, so that she'd considered packing him straight off to bed. But she had offered him some stew and he had perked up a bit, and now the last of it was rapidly disappearing. 'More?' she asked.

'Aye. If you please.' The words were barely audible, and the child's blue eyes gazed at her solemnly, as though he did not really believe that there would be a second helping.

She took his dish and spooned a little more stew into it. She was daft, she told herself – give him seconds once and he'd always expect it. 'Don't think you'll get that much every day,' she said harshly. 'I don't take you little perishers in for love. I got a living to earn, same as anybody else.'

Richard's appetite suddenly vanished. He took another mouthful of the stew, chewed and chewed, swallowed at last with difficulty, and laid down his spoon.

Mrs Plackett looked at him grimly. 'Not going to waste it, are you?'

Frightened, he nodded.

'Go on like that, and you and me won't be friends!' Then, as he began to toy with the food again, she added angrily, 'Oh, leave it, leave it! Come on!' She seized his hand and pulled him roughly across the room to what looked like a cupboard.

Opening it, a curving flight of stairs was revealed, leading to a small room under the roof. She pushed him towards one of the cots. 'That's yours. Get to sleep – quick as you can. You got to get up early in the morning.' She went back to the stairs, and turned. 'Don't you dare wet the bed!'

As she went down, she wondered why she had spoken so roughly to the boy. He was a nice enough lad, but some demon had made her want to show him that angelic blue eyes and golden curls would not save him from the realities of life. She might make it up to him later, she thought.

Richard, alone in the room, looked around it in desperation. He needed to relieve himself, the more so after Mrs Plackett's last words. Tears came to his eyes, and he began to whimper, and even when he had discovered the chamber pot in the corner of the room, and had used it, and then had taken off his boots and lain down on the bed, pulling the thin blanket over his shoulders, he could not stop the sobs. He wished with all his heart that he could be at home with his mother and Mary and Frances.

Richard Goodwin, aged nine, a new employee of Prideau's Mill in Franton, cried himself to sleep.

CHAPTER TWO

When Elizabeth Goodwin and her daughters reached home that evening, they were astonished to find the cottage empty. The fire had gone out, the broth which was to be their evening meal was cold, and Richard was nowhere to be seen. Angrily, Elizabeth set about rekindling the fire. It was Mary who found the letter.

Elizabeth read the few words with shocked dismay. Her first impulse was to go after Richard, but it was already dark, and she could not leave Mary and Frances alone in the cottage all night. Where could she turn for help? Almost without thinking, she seized her bonnet and shawl, told Mary to see to the broth, and hurried out.

The Grange, the imposing mansion where the Harcourts lived, was situated half a mile to the west of Brentfield. As Elizabeth walked swiftly through the village and along the winding road, her mind was full of self-reproach. How could she have left the boy on his own? How foolish she had been not to see, after their conversation the previous day, that something of the sort was in his mind.

'Ask the master if he will kindly spare me a few minutes,' she said to the maidservant who opened the door to her. 'It is Mrs Goodwin, and I am in desperate need of his help.'

The girl went away, and returned a few moments later to say that Mr Harcourt was dining, and could not be disturbed.

'Then I will wait,' Elizabeth said. She was left standing in the hall, her mind filled with the image of a small boy wearily plodding the endless miles to Franton, perhaps even now lying down to sleep in some field, shivering in the chilly night air, hungry, thirsty, afraid.

After an eternity, John Harcourt appeared. He was short

and slight. His heavy beard and his dark hair, long enough to touch the collar of his frock-coat, showed no hint of grey, but his sallow face was deeply lined and the cheeks were sunken, making him look almost elderly.

'Well, what is it, Mrs Goodwin?' His voice was testy.

'I am sorry to disturb you, sir. It is my boy.' Conscious of his stony gaze, falteringly she told her story.

John Harcourt shrugged. 'And what do you expect of me?'

'I thought perhaps . . .' Elizabeth's voice trailed off. She had been a fool to come. She might have known that she would get no help here.

He sighed, as though the whole business was tiresome. 'I am sure you have distressed yourself needlessly. The child will come to no harm. If he has reached Franton, he will be taken care of at Prideau's. If he has not, a summer's night in the open will not hurt him, and he will probably have the sense to find a bed of sorts in a haystack or a barn. There is certainly nothing to be done at this moment, Mrs Harcourt.'

'I am sorry to have troubled you.' Elizabeth turned to go.

Hearing the bitterness in her voice, Harcourt said, 'Pray do not act with undue haste, Mrs Goodwin. Mrs Harcourt told me of her visit to you yesterday. I am willing to offer your older daughter employment in the mill, and indeed might also find work there for you, if you wish. But I fear that, even for your late husband's sake, it would be difficult for me to behave with equal charity towards your son. If he is taken on at Prideau's he will be well looked after, and will earn sufficient to relieve you of responsibility for him. It might be for the best. I advise you to consider that most carefully, Mrs Goodwin.'

As Elizabeth walked slowly home, she was overwhelmed with a feeling of helplessness. God, in His great wisdom, had taken her husband from her, and now perhaps intended her to lose Richard too. She felt weary, unable to struggle any longer. She could only resign herself to His will. She thought of what Mr Harcourt had said, and was forced to admit the sense of it. If Richard had found work at Prideau's, would it really be wise to bring him back to Brentfield, where no certainty of employment awaited him? And if Prideau's had refused to take him on – surely they would not do so without her consent – then he would soon come home again, of that she felt sure. Perhaps God was testing her, almost as He had tested Abraham, and like Abraham, she must put her trust in the Lord, committing Richard to His care, confident that all would be for the best in His great plan.

Three days later, Elizabeth was much relieved to receive a letter from Richard, which set her mind at rest, brief though it was. Then, some six weeks after he first left home, he appeared suddenly one Sunday, arriving just as his mother and sister returned from morning service. There was great rejoicing, and Elizabeth was delighted to see that he seemed contented and did not look as though he were underfed or had been beaten or deprived of sleep. The work, he told her with a serious air, was somewhat wearisome – a word he had picked up from Mr Hill.

'When do you have to be at the mill?' his mother asked.

'Five to six in the morning. Mrs Plackett wake us at half past five, and give us a hunk of bread and a cup of buttermilk.'

'And when you get to the mill . . .?' Elizabeth prompted.

'I go to Mr Renshaw, my overseer, and he do tell me what to do. Sometimes he tell me to carry things, or take messages, and sometimes I help when they undoes the bales of raw silk and I fold the wrappings up careful, and sometimes one of the weavers tell me to call Mr Renshaw if one of the machines be broken down, or summat like that. But most of the time I sweep the floor. Mr Renshaw do say as he don't want to see a speck of dust on it, and if I keeps it really clean, as he'll make a weaver of me one day.'

'Good. And what time do you leave the mill?'

'Six o'clock. Mrs Plackett give us our dinner, and then we goes to bed. There be four of us lodges with her.'

'Is she a kind lady?'

'She be a woman, Mama – she a'n't a lady. Felton – he work at Prideau's – he be thirteen – he say never to confuse women and ladies.'

' "Isn't", Richard – not "a'n't". And Felton is wrong. All women are ladies if they are treated as such.'

'I didn't like her at first, but she be all right really. But I wish as it weren't always stew . . .'

'And what do you do on Sundays?'

'We goes to church, of course.'

'I am glad to hear it.'

'And in the afternoon, Harris – he do lodge at Mrs Plackett's too – we goes for a walk, or if it be wet we stays indoors and talks.'

'I would have hoped that you might read some suitable book, Richard. Does Mrs Plackett have any books?'

Richard laughed. 'She don't read or write.'

'Make sure you do not forget how to do so yourself. Each time you come here, take one of your father's books back with you. Read it, and then bring it home and exchange it for another. Books are an education.'

'Aye.'

'And do try to remember your grammar, and to say, "yes", Richard. "Yes" is more polite than "aye".'

'Yes, Mama.'

In his first days at Prideau's, Richard quickly realised that Mr Renshaw, who often roared angrily at him, using strange, ugly words which he had not heard before, was in fact an amiable man, eager to train any youngster who showed interest, and that not only was his bark worse than his bite, but his approbation was greatest for those at whom he shouted the most.

He could always find time to answer Richard's questions. 'Why's it called "throwin' " the silk? Tell you the truth, I don't rightly know. 'Cept it ain't spinnin'. Now, cotton or wool 'as to be spun, taking short fibres and twistin' 'em together to make a thread, but silk's a thread already, spun by the silkworm, see? More than 'alf a mile long, some of them are, but so thin that when they're unreeled from the cocoons, an 'ole bunch are put together, and they stick to each other, 'cause there's a sort of gum on the thread when it comes out of the worm. Well, that's raw silk, and it gets to us in skeins packed in bundles called "books".'

'Why "books", Mr Renshaw?'

'Don't ask me. I don't know that, neither. Anyway, then we 'as to wash it to get rid of the gum, and wind it on to bobbins and then throw it, which means twistin' it, so the threads will stay together. D'you follow so far?'

'I think so, Mr Renshaw.'

'Think so! Think so! You ought to be bloody certain, stupid young bugger! Oh, you're enough to try the patience of a bleedin' saint, you are! I'll go over it again, and this time bloody listen!' When he had repeated the first part of his explanation, he continued, 'Now, sometimes the thread what we've thrown ain't thick enough, dependin' on what cloth we're goin' to weave, and then we take a couple o' thrown threads – "singles" they're called, because they've been twisted just the once – and we twist 'em together in the opposite direction to make "doubles". See?'

Anxious to avoid another torrent of abuse, Richard nodded firmly, and Mr Renshaw took him into the throwing room to watch the silk being wound on to one bobbin from another, the latter whirling round so that the thread acquired its regular twist.

After a while, they returned to the weaving shed, and the overseer's good humour seemed to vanish as he gazed at the floor. 'This place is a bloody pig-sty!' he shouted. 'You ain't swep' that floor since last bloody Tuesday – not properly, you ain't! I want to eat me dinner off o' them boards – unnerstand?'

Richard sighed, and trotted off to find his broom.

Although the hours he worked at the mill, day in and day out, were long, Richard began to find his labours less 'wearisome' than he had at first. His one regret was that he was still too young to be allowed to acquire the skills of throwing and weaving and the other mysteries of the silk maker's craft. But he watched and learned wherever he was in the mill, storing up knowledge against the day when he would be old enough to use it.

* * *

As the months and years went by, Richard's life settled into a routine. Other young boys came to work at Prideau's, and though his own duties remained largely menial, he began to enjoy a position of seniority over them, and no longer spent so much of his time in endless sweeping of the floor – except when Mr Renshaw, dissatisfied with the efforts of the latest recruit to his department, would say, 'Call that clean? It's bloody filthy! Show 'im 'ow to do it, Goodwin.' The overseer still shouted and swore at him, but rarely, if ever, was his anger genuine, and Richard would grin and be told he was a cheeky young bugger, and that his wages would be docked at the end of the week. 'Best little worker you ever brung me, that young Goodwin,' Renshaw told Mr Hill, and, knowing that the little man was in the habit of having a friendly word with the boy whenever he saw him, added, 'Don't you bloody tell 'im I said so – don't want 'im gettin' too big for 'is bloody boots.'

Whenever he went home on a Sunday, Richard was happy to see that his mother and sisters were not suffering too much hardship. Although Brentfield was a large village, its growth having taken place during the bygone days when wool was the staple industry of that part of Essex, most of its inhabitants now worked at Harcourt's Mill, and as Mary had once suggested, there were few families prosperous enough to employ the likes of Elizabeth Goodwin to undertake casual washing and cleaning. However, the few shillings she earned were supplemented by Mary's wages and Richard's own contributions, and the family contrived to live modestly, but contentedly. Before long Frances would be old enough to work in the mill too, and that would ease their financial burden.

Richard enjoyed his visits home. His mother fussed over him, and Frances hero-worshipped her big brother, and Mary had always been a friend. Although she was now growing into womanhood, they remained close, and spent hours together, whispering and laughing and sharing their secrets.

In June, 1857, when he had been at Prideau's for some five years and was approaching his fourteenth birthday, Richard was summoned to Mr Hill's office. It could only mean that he was about to be dismissed. Boys employed at Prideau's were usually sent packing once they had reached an age when their wages would exceed those paid to girls, who in any case were usually better at the precise, monotonous work involved. Richard dragged his feet as he went along the corridor.

'Ah,' said Mr Hill. 'The Adonis of the weaving shed. And how are you, Master Goodwin?'

'All right, thank 'ee. I mean,' Richard corrected himself, since Mr Hill could be as finicky as his mother about the way he spoke, 'I am well, thank you. And you, Mr Hill?'

'As well as can be expected, given the arduous nature of my duties. And now that we have observed the courtesies, to business. You arrive at the ripe old age of fourteen in a week's time, do you not?'

'Yes, Mr Hill.'

'There is no need to sound so gloomy about it. I dare say you will see other birthdays, and one day you might even become as ancient as I am.' He gave his customary little chuckle. 'I must not tease you. It is not birthdays, but dismissal that you fear, am I not right? Oh, be of good cheer, Master Goodwin, for I bear glad tidings. Mr Renshaw appears for some inexplicable reason to think highly of you, and has said as much to Mr Leadbetter, who in turn has spoken of you to Mr Prideau himself, and that august gentleman, for whose health and prosperity we must ever pray, has graciously agreed to retain your services for a further period. Moreover, your wages are to be increased to the truly princely sum of three shillings and sixpence per week. There now, what do you say to that?'

Richard could not speak.

'What, not a word? No doubt you are dumbfounded at the prospect of further years of unstinting labour in return for the merest pittance. No? You are gratified?'

'Yes, Mr Hill. Thank you.'

'Don't thank me, Richard. Let me tell you what lies in store for you. You have already learnt much of our trade, and now you are to learn more. You are to work at throwing and dyeing and weaving, you are to help to make camlets and bombazines and simple silk ribbons and all manner of other materials. And if you work with unflagging zeal and outstanding intelligence, you will be rewarded in a few years' time beyond your dreams. You will work . . .' Mr Hill paused for a second to give emphasis to the words. '. . . You will work on – *crape*.'

'Crape, Mr Hill?'

'You know what it is, of course, and that the secrets of its manufacture are guarded more closely than the Crown Jewels of England. What you may not know is that the whole prosperity of Prideau's rests on crape. The demand is unceasing, and can barely be satisfied. Mark my words, young Goodwin, in the next few years Prideau's will expand, and it will all be due to crape.'

'How do you mean, "expand", Mr Hill?'

'Why, bless you, Richard, we shall start making crape in other places besides this. We shall build new mills, and we shall buy existing mills and convert them.'

'Mills like Harcourt's?'

'Why not? Why not indeed?' Mr Hill looked at Richard for a moment, his eyes twinkling. 'But what am I doing, filling your young head with all kinds of information that has no place in it? You are to go now to Mr Leadbetter's office, to sign your indentures.'

The general manager read aloud to Richard a document which bound him to a five-year apprenticeship, during which he would work every day of the year except Sundays and Christmas Day. It enjoined him, on pain of instant dismissal, not to reveal his employer's secrets nor to bring disrepute upon Prideau's by the taking of strong drink or by any licentious behaviour. In return, he would be paid three shillings and sixpence per week, which sum would be increased by sixpence per week at the end of each year. When he had finished, Mr Leadbetter asked, 'Do you understand that?'

'Yes, sir.'

'And you accept the terms thereof?'

'Yes, sir.'

'Then make your mark. Here at the bottom.'

Richard quickly read the document and then signed his

name with the quill that Mr Leadbetter had handed to him.

The general manager looked at him angrily. 'Are you trying to make a fool of me, Goodwin?'

'No sir.'

'Then why did you not say that you could read and write?'

'I did not think to do so, sir.'

Leadbetter glared at him. 'I don't like workers who have ideas above their station, Goodwin – just you remember that.'

Although he had incurred the wrath of this important man, Richard returned to his work in a glow of happiness, determined to seize the opportunity he had been offered, and never to give Mr Leadbetter cause for complaint. He would have more money to give to his mother, and perhaps even some to spend on himself. And there was no reason why his progress should stop once he got to the crape-manufacturing department. If he worked hard, anything could happen. He might even get transferred to Harcourt's, in his father's old position as overseer, when Prideau's bought them up, as Mr Hill said they might. And after that . . .

Three years passed. At the age of nineteen, Mary Goodwin had developed into a beauty. She had her mother's colouring, but whereas Elizabeth's hair, even in her youth, had been a somewhat faded gold, Mary's was the colour of ripened corn – just like Richard's. When they were together, now that Richard was almost seventeen and as tall as Mary, they looked like twins, as handsome a couple as you could wish to see, and Elizabeth wondered at the strange ways of Nature in producing such striking children from parents neither of whom could boast of exceptional good looks. She had given Mary her own clear skin and eyes of brightest blue, but how had her beaky nose been transmuted into the perfect shape of Mary's, and where had those full, curving lips come from?

Mary could not help being aware of her good looks, but had been brought up to be shy and modest, and though she sometimes dreamed of a romantic lover who would woo and win her, he would be a man like her father, quiet and gentle, who would treat her with respect and with none but honourable intentions. She therefore repelled the rough advances of the young men of the village, so effectively that they thought her stand-offish and hoity-toity. And the reputation for giving herself airs was increased since Elizabeth's training had at last cured Mary's worst habits of speech and made her sound more ladylike, even if the Essex accent had not been entirely eradicated.

Then she attracted the attention of George Harcourt. The eldest of John Harcourt's children, he was twenty-three. For the past two years he had been at Oxford, but in 1860 suddenly re-appeared in Brentfield. It was rumoured that he had been sent down, and though the Harcourt family remained close-lipped, a dozen scandalous stories were soon circulating. Whatever the truth of the matter, there was apparently no question of him returning to Oxford, and he began to work at the mill.

Like the other Harcourts, he was short and dark, and rather sharp of feature. His eyebrows sloped downwards, giving him a sad expression, until he smiled, showing his small, even teeth.

Attending the mill every day with his father – it was said that the two of them were frequently at loggerheads – walking regularly through all the sections of the mill, watching the throwing and the weaving, the dyeing and all the other processes which turned the raw silk into ribbons and materials for scarves and dresses and undergarments, he soon noticed Mary, and was immediately interested in her. He needed a woman badly – a young one for preference, just coming into full bloom. The girls of his own class might have been willing to supply his wants, but a liaison with any one of them held the threat of marriage, and George was not ready for that. Mary Goodwin, beautiful and ripe for love – and obviously a cut above most of her workmates – was a perfect target.

It was easy enough to fall into step with her one day as she went home after work. Mary was shy, answering his questions in monosyllables, her head bowed. They walked together for only a few minutes, but it was long enough for George to know exactly how he would proceed. Seeing her in the mill, he had thought that Mary would be easy meat, and would not have been surprised to find that some lout of a weaver had tumbled her already, and more than one, and more than once. But after talking to her, he knew instinctively that patience and finesse would be required. He smiled to himself, and entered the lists.

At first Mary was bewildered and more than a little uneasy at his attentions, but he behaved meticulously towards her, always raising his hat and calling her 'Miss Goodwin', and taking no liberties. He never brushed against her 'accidentally' on their walks, and when he helped her over a stile, made no attempts to retain her fingers in his. Above all, she was enthralled by his conversation: he spoke often of her father and of how much his own father had valued William Goodwin's faithful service, he always asked after her mother and sister, and he shared her delight in the flowers and birds and animals of the countryside.

Before long, the lover of Mary's dreams had George Harcourt's face. She had not expected that he would ever ask her to marry him – men of his class did not wed girls of hers – but she was surprised that he seemed barely to recognise the fact that she was a woman. She asked him once why he bothered with her.

'Because I like talking to you,' he replied. 'None of the other girls I meet can keep a conversation going for more than a minute without bursting into giggles or expecting me to make them silly compliments all the time. They're all stupid – stupid and ordinary. And you're not.'

Mary's instincts told her not to breathe a word of his attentions to her mother, or to anyone else. George too had taken pains to impress on her the need for secrecy. 'Just because we like being together, there's no need to give the village busybodies anything to gossip about.' But Mary looked forward eagerly to Richard's next visit home. She knew he would understand and that she could trust him. When they were alone she poured out her heart to him.

Richard listened sympathetically. Over the years it had

become his habit to tramp to Brentfield and back once a month, but he had discovered the pleasures of female company, and on the Sundays when he did not go to Brentfield, would often walk out in the afternoon with one of the girls from Prideau's. He was popular at the mill, and almost all the young women were head over heels in love with him, so few of them ever refused his invitations. He might not be willing to spend his money on them, but he put himself out to please, and was always ready to laugh, and being with him was fun. Besides, he was tall and broad-shouldered, and the golden good looks of his boyhood had been strengthened by the determination in the firm jaw and the curving, rather thin lips, and by the lines already etched between his eyebrows by his habit of frowning as he concentrated on his work.

He understood Mary's feelings. On the other hand, there was all the difference in the world between his interest in the mill girls at Prideau's and Mary's liaison with the owner's son. 'You'd better watch yourself,' he said.

'What do you mean?'

'Don't let him get you in trouble.'

'He's not like that,' Mary said indignantly. 'I told you – he hasn't even tried to kiss me. Anyway, I can look after myself.'

'Mind you do. He won't ever marry you, whatever happens.'

'You don't have to tell me that. You're spoiling everything, Richard. I wish I'd never said anything about it.'

'If he ever hurts you, I'll . . . I'll kill him!'

Mary was near to tears. 'Promise you won't say anything to anyone, especially Mama.'

Although genuinely alarmed by what she had told him, Richard could see that there was little point in trying to get sense into her head. He just hoped that she could indeed look after herself. 'All right,' he said. 'I promise. Now, come on – I'll race you home.'

Richard's willingness to work hard and to learn all he could about the manufacture of silk had not escaped the notice of his superiors at Prideau's, and even Mr Leadbetter had been forced to acknowledge his industry and ability, though he could not find it in him to like the young man. Richard, had, however, been disappointed that the goal of working on crape had come no nearer. He had asked Mr Renshaw about it.

'Crape? What d'you want to mess about with that for? Ain't this department good enough for yer bleedin' lordship?'

Richard realised that Renshaw was himself jealous of those who worked on crape, but in any case the overseer was clearly in no hurry to lose his best apprentice, and would presumably therefore not recommend any change in Richard's position. However, shortly after his seventeenth birthday, he was called to Mr Leadbetter's office.

'You are to be transferred to the crape department, Goodwin. I hope you understand the privilege that is being granted you. I will not hide from you that I am far from convinced of the wisdom of this move, and I warn you that you will have to exercise the utmost diligence to satisfy me. Do you understand?'

'Yes, sir.'

'Your apprenticeship will be renewed on an annual basis for the next two years, provided that your work is satisfactory. Thereafter, if you have met our standards, you will become a fully-fledged member of the crape department. First, however, you must sign this paper. Since I recall that you pride yourself on your scholarship, I shall leave you to read it for yourself.' He passed the document to Richard.

'I solemnly declare,' it read, 'that I will not reveal, by word of mouth or in writing or in any other form, to any person or company whatsoever, the processes used, or any detail thereof, in the crape-manufacturing department of J. Prideau & Son, silk makers, of Franton, in the county of Essex, England, unless authorised by a Director or the General Manager of the said Company so to do.

'I understand that any breach of this undertaking will render me liable to instant dismissal and the forfeiture of any wages at that time owing to me.'

Richard looked up. 'May I ask a question, sir?'

Mr Leadbetter frowned. 'Surely it is perfectly clear.'

'Indeed, it is, sir. But why is crape-making so secret?'

The general manager gave a long-suffering sigh. 'Because crape is not only the most saleable commodity that our industry produces, but is also made by a strange, complex process, of which few mills are capable – but only because they do not know how. If our secrets became available to every Tom, Dick and Harry, before long our hold on the market would have been broken. Everyone at Prideau's, including you, young man, would suffer. Do you understand?'

'Yes, sir. Thank you, sir.' Richard signed the paper.

'Right. Go to the crape-making department. Ask the boy to find Mr Jolly, and report to him.'

To get there, Richard had to pass Mr Hill's office. He put his head round the door. 'Don't tell me,' the little man said. 'I am the eyes and ears of Prideau's. I knew before you did. Well done, Richard. Did you know that your wages go up yet again? To five shillings and sixpence a week, and you just turned seventeen. Was there ever such generosity?'

'I'm worth every penny,' Richard grinned.

'Doubtless. But what people are worth and what they get are usually two highly different matters. Oh, by the way, you'd better mind your p's and q's with Mr Jolly. Keep on the right side of him. He's not a good enemy to have.'

'I'll remember. Thank you.'

The door of the crape department was kept permanently locked, and a boy was always on duty outside to make sure that only authorised persons should enter. Around his neck were two loops of string, one carrying the key and the other a whistle, which he was to blow if anyone tried to force his way in. The boy looked at Richard with great suspicion, but eventually agreed to fetch Mr Jolly. Leaving Richard waiting, he unlocked the door, slipped in, and relocked it from the inside.

Eventually, the door opened again. Standing there was a man of medium height, whose somewhat surly expression was intensified because he had lost all his top teeth, so that his upper lip had vanished, while the lower was clamped up over it in a pugnacious way. Moreover, his left eyelid drooped. Richard found himself staring at the almost closed eye, and then was startled when it suddenly shot open to glare at him.

'I'm Goodwin,' he said. 'Mr Leadbetter told me to report to you.'

Jolly grunted. 'Renshaw's blue-eyed boy. I've heard about you. Come on, then.'

He marched off, and Richard followed. At first sight, the crape-making department seemed little different from any other part of the mill. There were throwing machines and looms, and the same clatter and noise. However, there were also some pieces of equipment the like of which Richard had not seen before and at the use of which he could not guess, and the shed was steam-filled and hot.

Mr Jolly led him to a cubby-hole at one end of the long room. 'What do you know about crape-making?'

'Nothing.' Richard was tempted to add that he could not possibly know anything about it since it was so secret a process, but felt it might be unwise to try Mr Jolly's sense of humour.

'Christ!' said Jolly sourly. 'Then we'd better begin at the beginning. The first thing you need to know is that crape is made of a yarn with a very high throw. What's that mean, then?'

'That it's more tightly twisted – has more twists per inch.'

'Right. Thank Christ for that – at least you know something. Come and look.' He led Richard to the far end of the room, and began his initiation into the recondite craft of crape-making.

George Harcourt's instinct, infallible as always, told him when the time was ripe. He had been patient for more than two months now. It was a warm summer's evening, and Mary had escaped from home on the pretext of visiting a friend. He led her to a clearing, softly carpeted with pine needles, in a small wood. 'Let's sit for a while,' he suggested, and then began to speak of poetry, quoting verse to her in his rich voice. 'Do you know these lines of Herrick's?' he asked.

Thou art my life, my love, my heart,
The very eyes of me,

And hast command of every part,
To live and die for thee.

He looked at her then. Her eyes were turned on his, with such adoration and longing that he waited no longer, but took her in his arms.

Mary almost fainted at the touch of his lips on hers. She was aware of the roughness of his beard, the taste of tobacco on his breath, but above all of the strength of his arms around her and the soft, sweet pressure of those lips. She dared greatly, and put her arms around his neck, drawing him more closely to her, and when she felt his tongue probing at her mouth, opened it, responding to him more and more feverishly. Suddenly she was lying on the ground, and he was above her, his mouth still kissing, kissing, kissing. She did not seem to be herself – she was floating somewhere in a haze of love, her body taut and yet simultaneously slack with desire, ready for him to do what he liked with her.

And then he was fumbling at her skirts, drawing them up towards her waist, and his hand was on her legs, caressing, slowly gliding upwards.

She came to her senses. 'No!' she cried. 'No! No, you mustn't!' He took no notice, and she began to struggle to break free, turning her head aside, clamping her legs together to trap his roving hand.

'Don't stop now, you little fool!' he said angrily, and forced his knee between hers.

She thrashed more violently, terror replacing ecstasy. He hit her – a blow on her jaw, hard enough partially to stun her – and she lay in a daze, powerless to fight against the weight on her body, the relentless ripping of her undergarments, the searing pain, and the thrusting, driving movements into her flesh. And then he groaned and arched his back, and she could feel the throbbing deep within her.

She pushed against his shoulders. To her relief, he moved, and his weight suddenly was gone. She lay still, sobbing, dimly aware through the blinding tears that he was standing now, pulling his trousers up and buttoning them, and then, as though from a great distance, she heard his voice, no longer loving, but cold and contemptuous. 'My God – a teaser! A bloody cock-teaser! And to think of all the time I've wasted on you!' He turned and strode away through the wood without a backward glance, and she wept again, knowing that she had lost her dream along with her maidenhead.

Slowly she gathered her wits, wiped herself with her torn underwear, and threw the cloth away. Thank heaven, he had not ripped her dress, but even when she had brushed away the pine needles, it no longer looked fresh and clean. She touched the tender place on her jaw where he had hit her. It was beginning to swell. What could she say to Mama? Perhaps she could pretend she had fallen and hit her face. That would explain any dirt on her clothes, and would be reason enough for the tear-stains she felt sure were on her cheeks. She stood and tried to walk. It became easier after a while. What she could not overcome was the misery in her heart. How could she have thought he would go with a mill-girl for any other reason than to use her? How could she have allowed herself to be so defiled? She trembled with shame and self-pity, and anger at her own stupidity.

Richard found the whole process of crape-making quite fascinating. Grudgingly, yet patiently, Mr Jolly showed him each step along the way, never failing to impress on him the need to guard the secrets. 'I've been approached more than once,' he confided, sucking on the unlit pipe which was always clamped between his lips, except when Mr Leadbetter was in the crape shed. Smoking was strictly forbidden to all below the rank of manager, and that was a sore trial to Joe Jolly. As soon as the whistle blew to signify the end of the day's work, he would take out his tobacco pouch, fill the pipe, and light up as he left the building. 'I been offered bribes and all,' he went on.

'Who by?'

'Men from other mills. Prideau's is the best crape going, lad. They'd all like to know our secrets. 'Course I didn't tell 'em – not any of 'em. Not even the fellow who offered me fifty quid. Fifty quid! Think of it! I told Mr Prideau about that one.'

'You should have got a reward for that.'

'What? From old Prideau? That's a joke.' Realising he had revealed more of his thoughts than he intended, he looked angrily at Richard, the half-closed eye briefly flashing open. 'That's typical of you youngsters. First thing you think about is rewards. I do my duty, lad – it's what I'm paid for – and I don't expect to get . . . Oh, go on, get back to your work!' He walked away, muttering to himself, and for the rest of the day looked at Richard with contempt, as though he had exposed the previously hidden and most despicable side of his character. The overseer was never particularly genial towards any of the other employees in the department, but he seemed to harbour a special hostility to Richard, deep-rooted, without any of the geniality that had lain beneath Mr Renshaw's cursing.

After he had been working in the crape department for some nine weeks, Richard happened to fall into step with Mr Hill one evening as they both left the mill.

'Ah, my young friend! And how are you enjoying your new position?'

'Very well, thank you, Mr Hill.'

'I am glad to hear it. And what of the formidable Joseph Jolly? How do you find him?'

'All right.'

'All right?' Mr Hill's eyes twinkled. 'Those words seem somewhat lacking in enthusiasm. Come, you may speak frankly to me. We are old friends, are we not? And this conversation is entirely confidential.'

'I don't understand it, Mr Hill. Although he never says so, I think he's quite satisfied with my work, but he never misses an opportunity of making life as miserable for me as he can. He doesn't shout at me like Mr Renshaw used to do – I wish he would sometimes – but he treats me . . . well, he treats me like dirt.'

'And what is your answer to this?'

'I try not to let him see that it bothers me. But it does. I don't understand it.'

'You said that before, Richard. Shall I impart my theory to explain his attitude? Very well. Mr Prideau is a somewhat ruthless man, who treats his workers with consideration only so long as they can perform adequately whatever he requires of them. If they cannot do so . . .' He raised his hand and brought it down in a chopping motion. 'What remains for them, especially if they are elderly? The workhouse, Richard – that admirable but much-to-be-avoided institution. Sooner or later it will be the fate of many of us, and it is my belief that your Mr Jolly, rising sixty now, sees the prospect advancing rapidly towards him.'

'Why? He's a good overseer. He can do all the jobs in his department better than anyone else there.'

'Yes, but *labuntur anni*, as the poet says – the years are slipping by.'

'Time's wingèd chariot,' said Richard.

Mr Hill nodded happily, wondering whether any other of the employees at Prideau's could have quoted Andrew Marvell to him, even with so familiar a line. The boy was undoubtedly exceptional. 'Joseph Jolly can see a day coming when his powers will begin to fail. Moreover – and I have come at last to the point – I'd wager that he thinks that you are going to be his successor. Why else should he have been told to train you in every aspect of the work, to teach you all his skills? That is the mainspring of his hostility towards you, if I am not mistaken.'

'Is that really what Mr Prideau has in mind for me?'

'It may be. I am merely surmising. If it is, it would not be for some years yet – you are still a mite too young to be an overseer, you know. However, I have not finished with my analysis of Mr Jolly's motives. We all have a besetting sin, Richard. Yours, I think, is ambition – I've seen that in you ever since the day you arrived here with that note supposedly written by your mother.' He glanced at Richard slyly to see the effect of this remark. 'I take it she has forgiven you?'

Richard grinned sheepishly. 'I think so.'

'Good. Now, as I was about to say, in my belief it is envy which drives Joe Jolly, and you, my dear fellow, have aroused in his breast an excess of that regrettable emotion.'

'Why should he envy me?'

'Goodness me, for all sorts of reasons. I shall not list them all, because your head would swell, and it is quite big enough already. But to start with, you are young, which he is not. You are a well set up man, which he is not. You are popular, which he is not. And you are assiduous and quick to learn new skills. That is enough to make anyone envious.'

'If that is all . . .' Richard began, smiling.

'No, Richard, I am not sure that you should dismiss it so lightly. I told you once that Jolly could be a redoubtable enemy. I repeat that warning. Be on your guard.'

'What against?'

'How should I know?' Mr Hill paused for a moment. 'You must not let him upset you. People like you, who are popular and get on with the whole wide world, always find it hard to accept that others may be impervious to their charm. When they meet hostility such as Jolly evidently demonstrates towards you, it sometimes knocks them off their balance. Don't let it happen to you. When off your balance you are at your most vulnerable.' He chuckled. 'Enough of my pearls of wisdom. How is that paragon among landladies, Mrs Plackett?'

'She is well. A little . . . plumper, shall we say?'

'Indeed? Perhaps she is "resolved to grow fat and look young", as the poet Dryden has it. Kindly give her my most reverential obeisances.'

'I don't suppose she'd know what to do with them.'

Mr Hill laughed. 'You're right, Richard. My kind regards, then.'

As they parted, Richard asked, 'What is *your* besetting sin, Mr Hill?'

The little man considered gravely for a moment. At last he said, 'Loquacity, I should think.'

CHAPTER THREE

The greeting which Richard received when he arrived home on a Sunday morning in August, 1860, was particularly warm, for he had not visited his family during the previous month, having been unwell for some weeks with a persistent stomach upset. Fortunately, it had not been bad enough to make him miss work, but he had felt somewhat daunted at the thought of walking all the way to Brentfield and back. After reassuring his mother and sisters that he was fully fit again, he told them the exciting news that he was now working in the crape department. 'I can't tell you anything about it,' he said, 'because it's all secret, but it's the most important work that is done at Prideau's. I'm earning more money, and . . . and one day Mr Hill thinks I shall be the overseer of the crape department.'

His mother and sisters were naturally delighted, and asked him a hundred questions about whether he enjoyed the work, and whether it was difficult, and what his workmates were like, and what exactly Mr Hill had said. And they praised him and congratulated him, and laughed at his imitation of Joe Jolly.

'That's enough about me,' he said at last. 'What's been happening here?'

'Nothing much,' his mother said. 'As you can see, we are well.'

Richard thought that she looked tired, but the girls were blooming, and Mary, in particular, seemed to be bursting with good health.

'The only thing that *has* happened,' Elizabeth went on, 'is that Mr Harcourt has had a slight stroke. He has to rest, and he's not been seen at the mill ever since it happened. Young

Mr George is in charge for the time being.'

Richard glanced at Mary. 'What's he like as a master?'

'All right,' she said, her eyes cast down.

'They say his father's worried sick about having to leave it all to him,' Frances said. 'They don't get on.'

'You mustn't repeat gossip,' Elizabeth told her.

'But it's true. He doesn't care about work. Whenever he's supposed to be inspecting the looms, he spends the whole time leaning over the girls and pressing against them, and pinching their bottoms.'

'Hush!' Elizabeth said.

'It's true, Mama.'

'Nevertheless, we do not wish to hear it.'

There was a brief silence, and then Mary said brightly, 'There's a new foal down in Newman's field, Richard. Come and see it.'

'He's only just got here,' Elizabeth said. 'He doesn't want to go walking all that way. Besides, you must lay the table.'

'Frances can do that. Come on, Richard.' She seized his hand. 'Please.'

Richard recognised the urgency in her plea, and allowed himself to be pulled outside. When the door of the cottage had shut behind them, he asked, 'What's the matter?'

'Wait till no one can hear us.' They walked on a little way. The road was empty, but Mary seemed to have difficulty in speaking. At last she said, 'I'm going to have a baby.'

He gazed at her in shocked amazement.

'You needn't look so mazed,' she said angrily. 'It's true.'

'Are you sure?'

'Yes.'

'How do you know?'

'Don't be a fool, Richard. Women always know.'

'Have you told Mama?'

'No, I daren't. She'd . . . I don't know what she'd do. She doesn't even guess. I a'n't been sick in the mornings, or anything.'

'Is it George Harcourt's?'

'Whose else would it be?'

'I warned you. You said you could take care of yourself.'

She began to cry. 'Don't go on at me, Richard. It wasn't my fault. I didn't let him. He forced me. He hit me.'

Richard felt almost sick with anger. 'When did it happen?'

'Nearly six weeks ago.'

'Have you told him?'

'No. I a'n't spoken to him since. I've tried, but he won't walk with me. I can't talk to him about it when there's others there, and I can't get him on his own.' Mary laughed, a bitter sound. 'Anyway, it wouldn't be no use. You said yourself he wouldn't marry me.'

He did not know what to say. They walked on, reached Newman's field, and turned for home without so much as a glance at the foal.

'You'll have to tell Mama,' Richard said.

'She'll know soon enough. Everybody will. I'm sorry, Richard, but I had to tell someone – I just had to.'

'I haven't been any help.'

'You have. Talking about it makes it easier, somehow. But don't say anything when we get home. Talk about the foal.'

'I didn't even notice it.'

'It's a chestnut filly.'

Back at the cottage, Mary chattered gaily about the foal, and Richard did his best to emulate her. Normally, he loved the hours he spent with his family, but this visit, after the happy beginning, turned into an agony. Elizabeth noticed that he was often silent, but put it down to his recent illness, and questioned him probingly about the food that Mrs Plackett gave him.

Even while he was answering her, his mind was filled with thoughts of Mary. It was not merely a matter of the shame that would attach to her, and indeed to the whole family, but that for some weeks she would be unable to work, and even when she returned to the mill would receive lower wages than those paid to her more virtuous, or fortunate, sisters. That was one of the penalties exacted upon unmarried mothers, and it would sadly affect the family's finances just when there would be another mouth to feed, another body to clothe. His new wages would help, but if Mary went back to work, who would look after the baby? Richard glanced at his mother. The burden would fall on her, reducing her own earning ability.

It was a relief when it was time for him to leave. He kissed his mother and Frances, and gave Mary a special hug, hoping it would convey his love and concern. When he left the cottage he started off towards Franton, but once the others had gone back inside, retraced his steps, giving the cottage a wide berth, so that he would not be seen, and made his way to The Grange. 'I want to see Mr Harcourt,' he told the maid who answered his knock.

'Who is it? I'll see if he's at home.'

But he had already pushed past her, ignoring her cries. He could hear music coming from a room on his left, opened the door, and found himself in the drawing-room. In that first moment he was conscious of a large, richly furnished room, and of the faces which suddenly turned towards him. Mr Harcourt was sitting in a big armchair, while his wife and two of the girls occupied a sofa. Although it was many years since he had seen him, Richard recognised Tom instantly, and beside him was his brother George. Seated at the piano was a young girl of about his own age, with ringlets of striking dark chestnut hair, and eyes which drew Richard's gaze for an instant. He had not seen her before – perhaps she was a friend of one of the girls. Beside her stood another of the Harcourts' daughters. All were in evening dress, and he was astonished by the ladies' bare shoulders and their huge skirts.

'What is the meaning of this?' John Harcourt demanded in fury. His speech was a little hesitant, almost slurred. 'How dare you burst in!' With some difficulty he pulled himself to his feet, leaning heavily on a silver-topped cane.

'I couldn't help it, sir,' the maid wailed. 'He pushed past me.'

'Very well, Ellen. You may go.'

Tom, who had been nearest to the door, followed the maid out.

John Harcourt looked at Richard. The blue eyes gazed

fearlessly back at him. A good-looking youth, he thought. 'Well? I am waiting for an explanation of this intrusion.'

'I beg your pardon, sir,' Richard said. 'I was afeared you wouldn't see me.'

'Impudence!' Mrs Harcourt said.

'I am Richard Goodwin, sir. My father worked for 'ee.' The flat Essex accent was stronger than usual.

'Yes. I remember him well.' This must be the boy who had run away to work at Prideau's. 'What is the trouble?'

'My sister Mary is going to have a baby. She a'n't married.'

'Remember where you are!' Mr Harcourt said. 'There are young ladies present.'

'They've heard of babies afore.'

'That is impertinent,' Harcourt growled. 'Your sister has only herself to blame. It is of no concern to me.'

'Not when your son give it her?'

The effect of his bombshell was instantaneous, but it seemed to Richard as though everything were happening in slow motion.

Mrs Harcourt gave a shriek of horror. 'Cover your ears, girls, cover your ears!'

They did as they were told. Out of the corner of his eye, Richard could see the girl who had been playing the piano. Although she too had obeyed Mrs Harcourt's instruction, he thought he could detect amusement in her eyes. He glanced back at George Harcourt. His face had gone red, and he was looking apprehensively at his father. John Harcourt himself took two slow steps closer to Richard, lifting his feet and then putting them down again without bending them. Richard's gaze focused for a moment on the boots. They looked new, and quite uncreased, and somehow his mind registered that this must be because of the strange, awkward walk that Mr Harcourt's stroke had forced upon him.

'My son? Which son?'

Richard said nothing, but pointed at George.

'He's mad!' George shouted. His expression changed to one of relief as he looked beyond Richard to the door, where Tom Harcourt now stood, flanked by two menservants.

'Throw him out!' George cried. 'Throw him out!'

Mr Harcourt put up his hand ineffectually, as though to stop them, but the two men swiftly bundled Richard out of the room and across the hall. Tom hurried ahead of them and opened the front door. 'Throw the bastard out, as hard as you can!'

The men grinned, picked Richard up between them and hurled him through the air. He fell sprawling on to the gravel of the drive, skinning his elbows and knees, grazing his hands.

'And if you ever come here again, you'll get the same treatment,' Tom called. 'Or worse.' The door slammed shut behind him.

Richard picked himself up gingerly. He was not seriously hurt. He had been a fool to come, he thought. He might have known that he would achieve nothing against the wealth and power of the Harcourts. His grazes smarted painfully, but he tried to ignore the discomfort as he walked slowly away from the house, wondering what was happening in that great drawing-room. No doubt George was denying his responsibility for Mary's condition, telling his father that she was a slut who would, and did, grant her favours to any man who showed interest. Richard cursed himself – he had probably made things worse.

As he limped back to Franton, he went over and over the scene at The Grange, reliving it and torturing himself with every word and action. Even the amused glance of the girl at the piano seemed a bitter mockery.

The next day, on her way home from work, Mary saw George Harcourt waiting for her.

'So you're in the family way, are you?' he said. There was a kind of contempt in his voice.

'Who told you?' she whispered, terrified that everyone might know her secret.

'Your precious brother. He tried to put the blame on me, but I'm not taking that – not after all those other fellows who've had you.'

'You were the only one. You know that.'

'I know nothing of the sort. Anyway, you'd better get rid of it.'

'Get rid of it? How?'

'Oh, for Christ's sake! You can't be that innocent. Go to old Mother Winspear. It'll only take half an hour.' He pulled his hand from his trouser pocket. 'Here. Here's a sovereign. That's what she charges, they tell me.'

Before she could protest, he pushed the money into her hand, and hurried away. The coin seemed to burn her flesh. Mary stood looking after him, dizzy with the thoughts running through her brain. Perhaps he was right. If she got rid of it, her mother need never know – no one need know. She wished she had not said anything to Richard.

Old Mother Winspear lived in an isolated cottage some distance outside the village. As a child, Mary had been frightened of her – she was a witch, they said, and could put a spell on you and turn you into a toad. She certainly looked like a witch, and she mumbled to herself, but she was probably harmless enough.

Mary made up her mind. If George was right and it would take only half an hour, she could go to Mother Winspear straightaway, and make some excuse for her lateness when she eventually reached home.

The old woman opened the door at once, as though she had been waiting behind it for Mary's knock. 'Come in, dearie. Come to see Granny Winspear, have you? What is it, then? A love potion? Or want your hand read?'

Mary shook her head.

Mother Winspear looked at her for a moment, and then, abandoning her wheedling tones, said harshly, 'Oh, like that, is it? Been a silly girl, eh? Cost you a golden sovereign, that's what. And you'll swear on the Book you'll never breathe a word of it. Don't want to get me in trouble, do you? I'll see your money first. Give it you, did he?'

'Who?'

The old woman cackled. 'How should I know? Whoever landed you with what you come to get rid of, eh?'

Mary silently handed over the sovereign. Mother Winspear brought out a Bible and swore her to secrecy, and then led her into the bedroom of the cottage. Placing an old stained quilt upon the bed, she told Mary to take off her undergarments and lie down. Trembling with fear, looking with horror at the filthy quilt, Mary did so.

Mother Winspear gave her a short piece of rope. 'Bite on that if it hurts. It'll only be a moment or two.' She saw Mary's panic-stricken blue eyes staring at her. 'Scared stiff, ain't you, dearie?' She laughed. 'A moment of pleasure, a moment of pain – the one follows the other. You just close your pretty eyes, and it'll soon be over.'

Mary felt the old woman's hands on her body, and then something cold entered her, probing, sharp. She bit on the rope to stop herself from crying out. And suddenly a searing pain struck through her, and the scream that she had been trying to choke back escaped from her lips.

'Bite the rope! Bite the rope!' the old woman commanded harshly.

But Mary continued to scream as the sharpness dug into her, each movement an agony. Then suddenly it was gone, leaving just a dull ache, and the warm liquid dripping from her. She realised then that the stains on the quilt were blood from other girls who had come to old Mother Winspear for her ministrations.

The woman muttered something under her breath. Mary opened her eyes and looked at her. She was grim and unsmiling. 'Up you get, my girl. Off the bed and on to this chamber-pot. Come on, come on! Quickly!'

'What's the matter?'

'Nothing's the matter. You're going to bleed and get rid of the little bit of trouble, ain't you? But there's no need to bleed all over me best quilt.'

Mary squatted over the chamber-pot beside the bed, aware of the blood flowing steadily from her. She felt sick and dizzy. The room reeled about her, and she clutched at the bedclothes for support. When she regained consciousness, she was lying on the bed again.

'Lie still a moment,' said Mother Winspear. 'You'll be all right.'

The pain throbbed in her abdomen. She could feel a thick bundle of cloth between her legs. She knew that time must be passing, and every minute away from home would make it more difficult to explain to her mother what had kept her, but she felt too weak to move. She closed her eyes and slept for a little.

She awoke to find Mother Winspear trying to dress her. 'Lift your hips, dearie, so's I can get your drawers on you. That's it. Time to go now.' Her voice was high-pitched and anxious. 'You'll bleed a bit – only natural – but I put some clean rags there, and your drawers will hold 'em up. Stop afore you get home – the bleeding'll be over then – and make sure you throw the rags away. Don't want anyone to see 'em.'

When Mary got off the bed she felt as though her legs would not support her. 'I don't think . . . I don't think I can walk home.'

'You got to. Can't stop here. And remember you swore a Bible oath. As for me, I never see you in my life afore, and you never come near this cottage tonight nor any other night. You got that? Eh?'

Mary nodded, and the old woman hurriedly pushed her out of the cottage and shut the door behind her.

How she got home, she never knew. She had to stop to rest every few steps, her eyes blinded by tears, the pain nagging in her belly. Twice she dropped to the ground, and lay there sobbing, until she could summon up strength to drag herself on. At least she did not have to go through the village, where someone would surely have seen her, but as she walked along the rough, uneven paths through the fields, each stile almost insurmountable, the journey seemed endless.

Just before she reached the Franton road, she crawled behind a hedge, took down her drawers and removed the bundle of cloth that Mother Winspear had placed between her legs. She almost fainted at the sight of it, sodden with blood. Without the cloth, walking was a little easier, but her terror grew as she felt the blood slipping down her legs, warm and sticky in her shoes, dropping in great gouts on to the road, leaving a trail behind her.

She died before Dr Wood arrived. Elizabeth had sent Frances running to get him as soon as she had seen Mary at the cottage door, her face grey with pain and loss of blood.

The doctor examined the lifeless body. 'An abortion,' he said. 'Who did it?'

'An abortion!'

'Of course. You knew she was pregnant, I presume.'

'No. No, I did not.'

'Sit down, Mrs Goodwin. It's been a shock for you, I know.' He waited for a moment. 'Did she say anything before she died?'

'Only that she was sorry. Nothing more.'

The doctor sighed. He was almost certain who had performed the clumsy operation. Mary was not the first to die at the hands of old Mother Winspear – some years before there had been a similar case – but her victims had not named her, and no evidence could be obtained from her more fortunate clients. He did not care about those – it was no crime in his eyes to stop another unwanted child from entering a world in which it would endure a life of misery. But when the operations went wrong . . .

Elizabeth sent word to Richard through a neighbour who happened to be going to Franton the following day.

He came, horrified. 'What did she die of, Mama?'

'A haemorrhage. A woman's complaint.'

'Something to do with the baby she was going to have?'

Elizabeth's eyes widened. 'How do you know that?'

'She told me, last Sunday.'

'She told *you*?'

Richard guessed what the question meant. 'Aye,' he said gently. 'We always told each other our secrets.'

Elizabeth looked at him with hurt in her eyes. After a while she asked, 'Did she tell you who the man was?'

He nodded. 'George Harcourt.'

She stared at him for a moment in disbelief. Then she began to weep, and awkwardly he put his arms about her, conscious suddenly that she was looking to him for strength and comfort.

He stayed the following day for Mary's burial. Back in the cottage afterwards, Elizabeth busied herself feverishly, cooking, cleaning, dusting and polishing. When she drew a pail of water and began to scrub the floor, he said, 'Leave it, Mama. Sit down and rest.'

'I can't. I can't.' She continued the frantic scrubbing.

The afternoon wore on miserably. Frances, always a quiet, withdrawn girl, sat with a book on her lap, though whether she was reading or only pretending to do so, Richard was not sure. The tense atmosphere in the cottage seemed stifling, and he got his hat.

'Where are you going?' his mother asked. 'You're not going back to Franton yet, are you?'

'No, Mama. Just a walk.'

He went down to the mill, and sat on the grass by the edge of the road, knowing that he might be there a long time. In his father's day, Mr Harcourt had always left the mill at six o'clock in the evening, though the workers would not finish for another two hours, but whether George Harcourt would follow a similar routine, he did not know.

Having no watch, he was uncertain of the time, but earlier than expected – he guessed it could not yet be five o'clock – he saw the Harcourt trap coming down the hill. It pulled up in front of the main entrance, and soon after, Mr Harcourt himself appeared, leaning on his stick, slowly lifting each foot in turn and replacing it as he made his painful way to the trap. Two of the mill workers were with him.

Richard came forward. 'Mr Harcourt.'

John Harcourt glanced at him, and quickly turned his head away.

'Sir, I must speak to you.'

The little group had reached the trap. The driver got down and helped the two workers to lift Mr Harcourt into his seat. Richard went up to the side of the trap. 'Mr Harcourt, my sister is dead.'

'Drive on!' Harcourt said, staring straight ahead.

'But, sir –'

'Get away!' The driver turned, flicked his whip towards Richard, and jerked on the reins.

Richard put his hand to his cheek. He remembered young Tom Harcourt's whip. That had been of string, but the driver's was a leather thong. There had been a brief searing pain, but it was the sight of blood on his fingers which spurred his determination now. He began to run after the trap, already some way ahead. He saw Harcourt turn to watch him, and then the driver used his whip on the horse until it broke into a fast trot. Although he could not keep up with it, Richard followed. The Harcourts had to be made to listen, and perhaps it was better to speak to Mr Harcourt than to George.

By the time he reached The Grange, the trap was just moving away, empty, making for the stables at the rear of the house. Presumably John Harcourt was already indoors. As Richard went forward, the front door opened, and the two servants who had thrown him out on the Sunday emerged to bar his way, and at the same time, the driver returned, straining to hold back a large, ferocious-looking dog. 'Clear off!' the man cried.

'I've *got* to see Mr Harcourt.'

The man came nearer, and the dog, growling, lunged forward, its teeth closing on the cloth of Richard's trouser leg. Using all his strength, the driver hauled back on the leash. The cloth tore. 'Lucky bastard,' the man grinned. 'Might 'ave been a lump o' your flesh. Now, git off, afore I let 'im loose!'

Richard turned, defeated. He forced himself to walk slowly down the drive, scorning to turn to see whether the man would loose the dog. As he went, he swore to himself that one day he would be revenged. The enmity that he had felt towards Tom Harcourt was nothing, a mere childish anger. This was a different matter. The Harcourts had shamed and murdered Mary, and one day they would pay for it.

George Harcourt was not seen in Brentfield again. The family let it be known that Mr Harcourt had recovered sufficiently from his stroke to take full control again, and that Mr George had emigrated to America. The villagers were quick to put two and two together and to connect his sudden departure with Mary Goodwin's death. Their frequent meetings had not passed unnoticed; no doubt he had got her in the family way, and sent her to Old Mother Winspear. The only strange thing was that he had gone away instead of staying and brazening it out. It would have been a nine days' wonder, swiftly forgotten – except, of course, by the Goodwins. But, as everybody knew, Mr George and his father were at daggers drawn, and maybe that explained it.

George Harcourt left Brentfield before dawn on the day after Mary Goodwin's funeral. The village gossip would have been greatly fuelled had it been known that, when she opened her cottage door later that morning, Elizabeth found a purse lying on her doorstep. It contained five golden sovereigns. She said nothing of it, but after seeing Frances off to the mill, walked to The Grange, and left the purse outside the great front door. She did not knock, but walked slowly home, praying that the Lord would remove the bitterness from her heart.

It was difficult, however, to think kindly of the Harcourts when, two days later, Frances arrived home in tears, with the news that she had been dismissed.

'Why?' Elizabeth asked. 'What had you done?'

'Nothing, Mama. They wouldn't tell me why. One of the girls said it must be because of Mary.' She began to cry again.

As Elizabeth comforted her, she thought that this additional blow was almost too much to bear. 'Love your enemies!' she told herself. 'Love your enemies!' But how would they manage? Perhaps if Frances were to stay at home and help she could increase the amount of washing that she took in – but she knew well that extra work was just not available.

In despair, she sought consolation in counting her blessings. Thank God that William had built the cottage himself, giving her the security of a roof over her head. Thank God too for Richard, who passed to her almost all that remained of his wages once he had paid Mrs Plackett for his board and lodging.

Yes, thank God for Richard – it was only he who could keep her and Frances from the workhouse.

John Harcourt was at his wits' end. If only George had not had to be shipped off to America, he might have been here to find a way out of the mess, instead of lying dead after some drunken brawl. It seemed only yesterday, yet it was nearly six years ago now. As for Tom, marriage to Sarah Collington should have brought him to his senses, but though she was a fine girl, with a will of her own and a great deal of character, she had not succeeded in changing Tom, who was more interested in carousing and wenching than in settling down to work.

Everything had gone wrong after John's second stroke, a year ago. It had been a mild attack, but had left him more easily tired than before, and for months he had been forced to leave the running of the mill to the overseers and to Tom's incompetence. And the news of George's death had been a tremendous blow, just when he had been thinking of writing to tell him to come home, now that any scandal attached to the death of the Goodwin girl had long faded. He had missed George more than he would ever have imagined possible. They had always bickered, but he really loved the boy, infuriating though he could be – loved him more than any of his other children. Since the letter about George had come, he had been a prey to the blackest, the deepest of depressions.

Of course, if he were really honest with himself, he had to admit that the mill had started to go downhill soon after his father's death. He was not the man Frederick Harcourt had been, and there was no point in pretending otherwise. After all, his father was a self-made man who had created his own prosperity.

Frederick Harcourt had begun his career as an errand-boy, but by the time he was thirty, he owned his own draper's shop. Then he decided to go into manufacturing, making silk ribbons and other simple fabrics in contrast to the elaborate patterned silks imported from the Continent. He hunted until he found a small silk-weaving concern which he could afford to buy, taught himself the craft, and began to build up the business. For several years he ploughed back all his profits, expanding the mill, buying new machinery, employing more workers. It was a decade before he was ready to take money out for his own purposes, and then he built The Grange, a large and luxurious mansion with every modern convenience, and quarters for a large staff of servants.

At the age of fifty-five, Frederick Harcourt died, worn out by his own unrelenting appetite for work. His son John inherited a prosperous mill and a considerable personal fortune. For some years everything went well, the mill ran itself, the customers continued to send their orders, and John soon decided that there was little need for him to supervise the business on a day to day basis. Instead, he devoted himself to the management of the family's investments, and to a little dabbling, on the estate surrounding The Grange, in farming of a gentlemanly kind.

Good advice was readily available to him, but John Harcourt was one of those men who listen only to what they want to hear. If a loom broke down, he might decide arbitrarily to replace it, despite being told that it could easily be repaired; when purchasing new machinery, he would make his own selection, ambitiously ordering equipment which would not fit into the space available, or which the declining order book could not use to full capacity. In the same way, he invested large sums of money against the advice of his stockbrokers, and though one or two of his ventures had brought him a swift profit, most had failed. Moreover, in pursuit of a quiet life, he could refuse his wife nothing, and her whims and excesses had meant a constant expenditure on new furnishings and decorations for The Grange, on expensive clothes for herself and the children, often worn once and then discarded, and on the most extravagant dinners and parties and balls at which her one aim was to outdo their friends and acquaintances.

All of which had brought John Harcourt, in this June of 1866, to his wits' end. He had spent the whole of the day working out exactly where he stood, and the results were worse, far worse, than he had expected. The fortune he had inherited had dwindled almost to nothing, he had been forced in the past few years to borrow substantial sums and was now being pressed for repayment, and above all the mill was failing. Faulty goods, erratic deliveries and increasing competition had driven away all but the most loyal customers, and the mill in any case needed substantial capital investment. Had he been younger, and had not had two strokes, and if George had been alive, John Harcourt told himself, he would have made an effort. As it was, inescapably, in a few weeks' time he would have to declare himself bankrupt.

He thought about that. It was an intolerable prospect, especially since Lottie would be no help. She would simply go into hysterics at the thought of having to sell her jewellery, dismiss the servants, and give up all the luxuries of her life. He could imagine her now, ranting and screaming at him between bouts of the vapours, promising a future of interminable reproaches and bitterness. She was a foolish, frivolous woman, and any affection between them had vanished long since.

He thought of his children. Thank God two of the girls were married – that had cost him a pretty penny too – but Jane was still at home. Well, she could look after her mother, he supposed. Yes, he could see Jane as a long-suffering doormat for Lottie to tread on.

That left Tom. He would certainly not be capable of restoring the family fortunes and the mill. The boy took after his mother, there was no doubt of that – interested only in enjoying himself. Of course, he had a certain charm when he wanted to use it, which was presumably why Sarah Collington had agreed to marry him. No doubt her parents had suggested the match in the belief that the Harcourts were wealthy and that their daughter would be well provided for. John Harcourt smiled bitterly at that.

He thought again of George. Sometimes he believed that George was the only person he had ever truly loved. That was why he had sent him to America, sure that he was responsible for what had happened to Mary Goodwin, and determined that not the merest breath of scandal should touch his son and heir. And all he had succeeded in doing was to send him to his death. He wept a little.

Perhaps if it had not been for the depression which George's death had brought to his mind, or if he had not overheard Dr Wood talking to Lottie as he lay on the bed after the second stroke, he would not have had the courage for what he had decided to do. But the doctor had said, 'You will have to face it, Mrs Harcourt. He could have another stroke at any time, and his chances of surviving it are not of the best. Of course, with careful nursing, and complete freedom from anxiety . . .' They had moved away then, and he had heard no more of the conversation. Freedom from anxiety! That was enough to make a cat laugh. He had nothing to live for – nothing. And if he was going to die soon anyway . . .

He took the gun, loaded it and pressed the muzzle to his temple.

Dr Wood, summoned as soon as John Harcourt's body had been discovered, looked at the widow, who was sitting on a sofa, sobbing hysterically. He wondered whether her grief was genuine, and decided that perhaps it was, since she was allowing the tears to run down her face without care for the havoc they were causing in the powder and paint on her cheeks. He reproached himself for an old cynic. 'I am sorry to distress you further, Mrs Harcourt,' he said, 'but we must discuss the cause of death.'

'He shot himself, didn't he? He shot himself!'

'Yes. But have you any idea why he did so?'

'No. Oh, how could I? How can you ask me –?'

'He did not leave a note?'

'No.'

'Was he worried about anything?'

'Not to my knowledge. Oh, my poor husband! No, he had not a care in the world. Surrounded by the love of his family, and a wife who doted upon him – *doted* upon him, Doctor.' She began to weep again.

'Pray calm yourself, Mrs Harcourt.' Dr Wood patted her

hand. 'I am truly sorry, but I must ask these questions. Suicide is particularly distressing – far more so than a natural death. Burial in unhallowed ground, you know, and an inquest . . . A great deal of unpleasantness, which I am sure you would not want.' He cleared his throat, and spoke carefully. 'I was wondering whether there might be some way of . . . concealing the truth of the matter.'

Mrs Harcourt's sobs stopped abruptly, and she sat up. 'What are you suggesting, Doctor? That we might say it was an accident?'

'There would still have to be an inquest. No, Mrs Harcourt. It occurred to me that it might be advisable to let it be known that your late husband had suffered a third and fatal stroke.'

She considered his words gravely for a moment, and then said, 'I see. But . . . You would be willing to say that, Doctor?'

'As an old family friend . . . why not? A small lie which harms no one, but which would save us all a great deal of vexation – and vexation, dear lady, is the last thing that I would wish for you at this sad time.' Or, he thought, for himself. The less upset she was, the less she would call him out at all hours of the day and night.

'Oh, Doctor, how kind you are, how kind and considerate.' A thought struck her. 'But what about the servants?'

'I would suggest you forbid them to discuss Mr Harcourt's death. A little . . . reward might help to remind them of your wishes. If they do talk, it can be discounted as idle gossip.'

'Oh, mercy! The undertakers!'

'I know Mr Calvert well. I will have a word with him, and I am sure you can rely on his discretion, and that of his staff.'

'I shall be eternally grateful, Doctor. It is at times like this that one realises who one's true friends are. Oh, my poor John! The grief is insupportable!' And Mrs Harcourt slid gently into a sorrow that became gradually more hysterical, until Dr Wood gave her a strong draught to make her sleep.

When she recovered from the effects of the drug, some hours later, she found consolation in summoning a dressmaker to discuss the widow's weeds, in the latest fashion, which she would have to wear, larding her conversation the while with suitable expressions of grief and desolation. Her stricken state demanded the constant attendance of her daughter, Jane, the one member of the family who felt genuine pain at her father's death, but who kept her sorrow to herself.

Since Tom was in London – an urgent letter had been sent to summon him home – and the widow was too much upset to concern herself with such matters, arrangements for the funeral were left to Tom's wife, Sarah.

CHAPTER FOUR

Sarah had known the Harcourts since she was a child. Her parents had at that time been fairly near neighbours, and the children had often played together. The friendship which had grown between little Sarah Collington and Emma, the youngest of the Harcourts' three daughters, had remained staunch, and although the Collingtons had moved to the Suffolk coast when Sarah was twelve, the girls had kept in touch and visited each other's homes regularly, and Sarah had been one of Emma's bridesmaids.

Mrs Collington was somewhat concerned about her only child. She was eager to find a rich husband for Sarah, for she would have little enough dowry, and since none of her daughter's beaux was as wealthy as a fond mother could have wished – fortunately, Sarah did not seem to be particularly attracted to any of them – she decided to take matters into her own hands. 'My dear,' she said to her husband, 'it is time that Sarah was married.'

'She is hardly more than a child.'

Mrs Collington sighed in exasperation. 'She is twenty-three, and her future must be settled. There are no suitable unattached gentlemen in the neighbourhood, so the only solution is an arranged marriage. I have been thinking about it, and I believe that Tom Harcourt would make a very good match for Sarah. The family is wealthy, and he is a personable young man.'

On the occasion of Emma Harcourt's wedding, Tom had made a favourable impression on Mrs Collington. Though not particularly prepossessing in looks, he was quite presentable, and indeed charming. If he drank a little too much at the wedding breakfast, that could easily be forgiven in someone of his age, and his willingness to dance not only with the young ladies but also with their mothers could only commend him. In fact, when he partnered her, Mrs Collington suspected that he was actually flirting a little – though very discreetly, of course.

'She might not want him,' the Colonel said.

'You are mistaken. I watched them together, and I'm sure I saw a hint of something more than friendship in their behaviour. You must write to Mr Harcourt.'

'I think we should talk to Sarah first, my dear. She should not be forced into any marriage against her will.'

Mrs Collington was confident enough to let him have his way. Sarah was sent for, and to her mother's satisfaction, put up no opposition.

'Do you mean,' the Colonel asked, 'that you are in love with young Harcourt?'

'No, Father. I cannot confess to that, but I am not sure that I believe in the romantic kind of love that one reads about in books. I have certainly not experienced it, and those of my friends who say they are in love seem to fall out of the condition as readily as into it. No, I am not in love with Tom, but I am quite fond of him.'

'Then that is settled,' Mrs Collington said quickly. 'Your father will write to Mr Harcourt forthwith. Come, kiss me, my darling.'

Later, the Colonel sought a private word with his daughter. 'You need not marry anyone, Sarah, unless you are sure that you want to.'

'Thank you, Father. But Mother is right – it is time I was wed, and Mr Thomas Harcourt will do me well enough.'

'Are you sure? You sound so . . . so cold-blooded about it.'

Sarah smiled. 'That is better than being as foolish as most of my contemporaries. You will think even worse of me when I confess another reason which attracts me to this match. Now that George Harcourt is dead, Tom is the heir, and one day I shall be mistress of The Grange. I should enjoy that.' She laughed at the expression on his face. 'Oh, I want to do something with my life! Since women are denied the opportunity of managing a business, the next best thing is to have the running of a large establishment.' She paused. 'Of course, Tom may not want me.'

'He'd be an ass to turn you down.' Dowry or not, and whatever strange thoughts she had in her mind, his daughter would be a catch for any man, the Colonel was certain of that. Quite a beauty she was, with her chestnut hair and those dancing eyes, though some might have disputed it, pointing out that her nose was too long and her mouth too generous. She had a trim figure too, he thought, neat and yet womanly.

When she had been married for a year, Sarah took stock of her situation. On the whole, she had been a fool, though she had no one to blame but herself. At first, she had not found the ardour of Tom's love-making as unpleasant as her mother's warning had suggested. 'A wife's duty is to suffer in silence,' Mrs Collington had told her. 'Men have no delicacy, my dear, but in time you will learn to accept the bestial side of their nature, however displeasing it may be to you.' Tom had proved an accomplished lover – as indeed he should have been, she thought, after all the practice he had had. But although she had known of his reputation as a libertine, she had not expected him to continue his encounters with other women, nor that he would make so little attempt at concealing them. Equally, she had not been prepared for his addiction to strong liquor. From time to time he would consume too much, and it was then that she did find his embraces, in her mother's words, 'displeasing'.

Moreover, while life in The Grange was not unpleasant, she was bored. Her father-in-law was always kind and courteous to her, and Tom's older sister Jane was a sweet-natured girl, but Mrs Harcourt Senior was not only foolish, but ruled the household like a queen, and had no intention of letting Sarah take any responsibility in it. She had approached her father-in-law once and suggested that she might be of some assistance to him in the family firm, but he had merely given a short laugh and said, 'Out of the question, my dear. You don't want to trouble your pretty head with business matters.' And yet she could have sworn that he needed help. He often looked so tired and worried, though no one else in the family seemed to notice it.

And now, after the undertaker had removed the mortal remains of John Harcourt, she hoped she might discover why he had taken his life. A quick search the previous evening had revealed no suicide note, but Sarah had determined on a more careful examination of the scattered papers and ledgers with which the desk in his study was covered. Going through them she found scores of unpaid bills, letters demanding instant repayment of loans, page after page of figures in her father-in-law's shaky, irregular handwriting, and gradually came to understand that John Harcourt had faced personal bankruptcy. She turned to the ledgers, which made it plain that the mill was rapidly approaching a similar state.

She wondered what to do. Her mother-in-law would have to know, but to tell her at this stage would only bring a fresh outburst of hysterical weeping and fainting fits. She decided to wait until Tom arrived back from London.

It was almost midnight when he came. The letter which had been sent to London had merely told him that his father was dead. Sarah ran to meet him and to break the news that John Harcourt had taken his own life.

He stared at her. 'Shot himself? But why? Did he leave a note?'

'No. But I know why. He was bankrupt, Tom.'

'What? Oh, that's nonsense!'

'I've been through his papers. He owed money –'

Tom frowned. 'You had no right to do that. And you must be mistaken.'

'No. Listen –'

'I don't want to talk about it now. How's Mama taking it? I must go to her.' Without waiting for her reply he brushed past her into the hall, and began to climb the stairs.

He was in his mother's room for hours. When he came at last to bed, Sarah tried again to talk to him. 'Not now, for God's sake!' he said. 'I'm worn out after the journey, and Mama going on and on and on. It can wait until after the funeral, whatever it is. Anyway, it can't be nearly as bad as you think – Papa never had any problems with money.'

He would not listen to her the next morning either, refusing even to look at the papers on his father's desk. 'I tell you it can wait,' he said. 'I must go to the mill, and then speak to the Rector, and I'll have to go to Franton and see the solicitor.'

Sarah spent the day in preparations for the funeral. Rooms had to be readied for Tom's married sisters and their husbands, who would of course be staying at The Grange for at least one night, vast quantities of food had to be ordered, and in every matter Mrs Harcourt, declaring herself still too distressed to make any decisions, nevertheless had to be consulted.

Tom came back from the mill. 'They're all up in the air,' he told Sarah, 'talking about the mill being shut down. I gathered them together and told them there was no question of that.'

'But there is, Tom.'

'For God's sake!' he said. 'I need a brandy.' And he stalked away.

The church was packed for the funeral, and afterwards the Harcourts and their selected guests gathered at The Grange for the ritual meal. Later in the afternoon, the immediate relatives withdrew to the library, where the family solicitor revealed the details of Mr John Harcourt's last will and testament. It had been drawn after George's death, so the mill was bequeathed to Tom, as was The Grange, though a clause decreed that he should provide for his mother and unmarried sister, and allow them to live there as long as they wished. To his widow, John Harcourt left all his investments, while each of his daughters was to receive one thousand pounds. Lesser sums were to go to St Matthew's Church and to the orphanage in Franton, and finally there were token gifts to Dr Wood and a few other close friends.

Sarah fought to stop herself from telling them that it was a mockery, that John Harcourt had nothing to leave them – no investments, no money, nothing except perhaps The Grange. When at last the solicitor had finished, and everyone stood up, smiling at their good fortune, she took Tom's arm. 'Tom, you've got to come and look at your father's papers.'

'Later, for heaven's sake!'

'No, Tom, now!'

There was such urgency in her voice that he gave in, and with ill grace followed her to the study. He glanced through them rapidly. 'There is nothing much here,' he said. 'You expect to find bills.'

'Read these,' she said, passing him the letters demanding repayment of various loans.

As he read, his expression changed. 'Oh, my God,' he said. 'It's true.' He went on to examine his father's calculations and then the ledgers, his face draining of blood as their full meaning sank in. At last he looked at her, frowning. 'What in God's name can we do?'

'I've been thinking about it, ever since I found out. There's only one thing that's untouched – The Grange. We shall have to sell it, Tom.'

'Sell The Grange? You must be mad. Where would we live? Besides, it would kill Mama.'

'She will die of starvation otherwise,' Sarah said drily. 'If we sell it, we should be able to pay off the debts, and perhaps have something left. Then we could rent or even buy a small house.'

'We could sell the mill,' he said.

'We shouldn't get what it's worth – not in its present condition. Besides, it's our one hope for the future. Any money left over must be put into the mill, to build the business up again.'

'Oh, talk sense, Sarah!'

'It *is* sense. And it's not only *our* future that's at stake, but the future of all the people who work there.'

'It will take years to make the business profitable again.'

'I've been thinking about that too,' she said. 'I've been thinking of nothing else since I discovered all this. We need to produce whatever is most in demand in the silk trade nowadays, and that means crape. Your mother's ordered yards of it. And it isn't just your mother – everybody uses it, especially since the Prince Consort died and the Queen swathes herself in it from head to toe.'

Tom let out his breath in exasperation. 'Have a little respect, Sarah, for one thing, and don't talk about things you don't understand, for another! How can *we* make crape?' His voice was full of scorn. 'It needs special machinery and experts to work it. Nobody at Harcourt's knows how to make crape. The whole process is secret.'

'Then we'll just have to find someone who knows the secret.'

'I see. We put up a notice saying, "Wanted, experienced crape-makers," and all Prideau's people come rushing to work for us.'

'You can be as sarcastic as you like, but I tell you it's our one hope. There must be dozens of people who know how it's done. We've just got to find one of them.'

'It's all airy-fairy nonsense, Sarah. I know you're trying to help, but it would be better if you'd leave it to me. Crape, indeed!'

'All right,' she said, softly, almost dangerously, 'perhaps making crape *is* a ridiculous idea, but at least let us get Harcourt's Mill working properly again.'

'And how do you propose that we should do that?'

Sarah stood and began to pace up and down, counting the points off on her fingers. 'Firstly, we must raise standards in the mill, and make sure that it functions efficiently and that the goods we produce are top quality. Secondly, we've got to review our costs, cut out all waste, and see that our profits are adequate. Thirdly, we shall have to go out and *sell* our goods, instead of just waiting for orders to come in. Fourthly, I have a strong suspicion that many of the machines need replacing; we may be able to make a start on that with money from The Grange, and when we get more cash in, we can gradually get everything up to date.'

'I must say you've got it all worked out,' Tom said, with grudging respect.

'As I said, I've been thinking about nothing else. I had an idea about the selling.' She gave him an affectionate smile. 'I thought . . . I thought perhaps it was something that you would like to do, Tom. You'd be good at it. You could call on all our old customers, and find new ones, just like your grandfather did. They'd be flattered to be visited by the head of the firm, and you could tell them that Harcourt's Mill is really back in business. You'd be bound to win their confidence – and get their orders.'

'I'm flattered that you think so highly of my abilities,' Tom said. 'But who's going to look after the mill while I'm off seeing all these customers? Who's going to raise the standards, and see that the costs are right, and decide what new machines we need?'

'I shall.'

He stared at her for a moment in blank amazement, and then burst out laughing. 'But you're a woman, a married woman – you can't do that.'

She ignored his laughter. 'Women work in the mill already, and many are married. Why shouldn't I work there too?'

'For a number of reasons.' He held up his hand in mockery of her earlier gesture. 'Firstly, because you know nothing about silk-making.'

'I can learn. Besides, the overseers are no doubt competent enough. All that's needed is to see that they do their jobs properly.'

'Secondly, the hands would never work for a woman.'

Sarah's eyes flashed briefly, but she swallowed her irritation. 'They wouldn't have to. You would still be master.'

'And thirdly, I forbid it. Absolutely forbid it! And that applies to all of these plans of yours. I don't want to hear any more of such nonsense.'

'Then will you escort your mother and Jane and me to the workhouse? For that's where we shall end up.'

She had spoken quietly, but her words stopped him as he stood with his hand on the door-handle. 'All right,' he said, after a short pause. 'We will talk about this again – but sensibly, mind. Now we had better go back to our guests –

and not a word of this to anyone, family or friends. Come.' He squared his shoulders and held out his arm for her.

As they walked back to the drawing-room, Sarah thought that she had probably won the first battle.

Having spent over six years in Prideau's crape-making department, Richard could claim a thorough knowledge of the techniques, and indeed Joe Jolly, though still treating him with undisguised hostility, now considered him his deputy. If he were ill or away from the department for some reason, it was Richard who became the supervisor.

Richard still visited Brentfield frequently, pleased that he could hand his mother a regular and more handsome sum of money. It was much needed, especially since Elizabeth was frequently unwell, her thin body racked by coughing, though she claimed that it was no more than a passing weakness.

Richard was very worried about her, especially after Frances told him that she had come into the cottage one day to find their mother washing a blood-stained handkerchief. 'Consumption!' he said, appalled.

'She said it was a cut, but she wouldn't show me the wound. I begged her to call the doctor, but she wouldn't. You're not supposed to know about it – she forbade me to tell you.'

Richard tried to find out more from his mother, but she parried all his questions, and again denied that there was anything wrong with her.

He came home more often after that, each time looking at Elizabeth carefully, trying to decide whether she seemed frailer, thinner in the face, but he could detect no change, and indeed Frances told him that her health seemed to have improved a little. 'Especially when you come home, Richard. The thought of your coming always puts new life into her.'

Sometimes, after they had eaten their midday meal, they would go for a gentle stroll if the weather was fine, Elizabeth on Richard's right arm, and Frances on his left. His mother always wanted to hear all the details of his life, and he would speak to her of Joe Jolly, and of Mrs Plackett, and especially of Mr Hill, who had become a real friend. On those Sundays when he did not journey to Brentfield, Richard frequently spent the evening with Mr Hill and his dumpy little wife. He would make his mother and Frances laugh by imitating the Hills. 'Before we have our meal, Mr Hill will say, "And what Epicurean feast have you prepared for our delectation today, Pussy-my-love?" He always calls her that. And Mrs Hill nearly always replies, "I don't know about that." I've hardly ever heard her say anything else. Once when she said it, Mr Hill said, "Come, Pussy-my-love, if you continue to reiterate your ignorance in this fashion, our young guest will have the impression that there is not a single thought in your head, whereas you and I know well that your intellect far surpasses that of your unworthy husband." And of course, Mrs Hill replied, "I don't know about that." '

Elizabeth did not laugh. 'He sounds unkind, your Mr Hill.'

'Oh, no, Mama. He is the sweetest-natured, most gentle of men, and he adores Mrs Hill. It is just that he can never resist an opportunity of turning an ironic phrase, and she, I believe, has discovered that the best thing for them both is for her to say as little as possible. They are truly content together, Mama.'

'I am glad. And that he is such a good friend to you.'

'Indeed he is. I have learnt a great deal from him.'

'He has certainly improved your speech.'

Richard laughed. 'Oh, you never give me any peace about that, Mama. Perhaps he has. We talk about all sorts of things – politics and history and science – but his great love is literature. He's like Papa, I think – ever since he learned to read, he's been devouring books. Sometimes, after we have eaten, he reads aloud to us – he loves Milton and Dryden and Shakespeare, especially the Sonnets. And quite often we talk about the business. He knows a great deal of Prideau's policies about pricing their goods, and investing, and fixing the level of wages, and things like that, and he shares his knowledge with me, though of course he doesn't tell me anything confidential. I want to learn all I can about the business, Mama. I mean to be a manager one day.'

Elizabeth smiled at his enthusiasm, and squeezed his arm.

'I only wish it could be at Harcourt's.'

'Why do you say that?' he asked sharply.

'Because I should like to have you here at home, of course. Why else?'

For a moment he had thought he must have told her of his one-time plan to gain control of Harcourt's, and exact his revenge upon the family. That was childish, and he had long since put it behind him, though he still thought often of Mary, and missed her each time he came to Brentfield. He laughed to cover his momentary embarrassment. 'Someday perhaps, Mama. Who knows?'

'And someday you'll find a nice girl, and get married.'

'Oh, not again, Mama!' He remembered how the subject had come up the previous year. The three of them had been out for a walk, and an open carriage had gone by. Seated in it were Tom Harcourt and a woman. As they passed, Richard stared at his old enemy, hardly sparing a glance for his companion, but what he did see of her struck a chord. Her eyes, and the dark chestnut hair, seemed familiar. 'Who was that with him?' he asked when the carriage had gone.

'Mrs Thomas Harcourt. They were married two weeks ago,' his mother replied, and then asked, 'when are *you* going to get married, Richard?'

'When I meet the right girl, Mama.'

She had repeated the question more than once since, but never received the answer she hoped for. Richard had not yet come across any girl he would have wanted to marry. In summer time he had escorted more than one of the young women who worked at Prideau's to Corley Wood, Franton's traditional spot for lovers' assignations, where, in secluded dells and clearings, courting couples could be alone and unobserved. Many a hasty wedding had resulted from the dalliance there. But there were ways of indulging the appetites without running the risk of an unwanted pregnancy, and Richard also realised that there was safety in numbers, and tried to share his attentions so that none of the girls could claim to be the most favoured.

'Have you ever considered the advantages of matrimony?'

Mr Hill asked him idly one day. 'They are multitudinous and frequently far from unpleasant, are they not, Pussy-my-love?'

'I don't know about that,' Mrs Hill answered.

'However, Richard, I believe I detect in you a leaning towards bigamy,' Mr Hill continued, 'and though there are some who maintain it to be the natural condition of the human male, bigamy is not only illegal, but the excess of pleasures it brings might well be too much for any man. The latest gossip at the mill links your name with both Miss Hannah Robinson and Miss Alice Burton. Is either of them your intended?'

'Neither,' Richard laughed.

'Beware, my boy. Trifling with women's affections is, like marriage, not by any to be enterprised, nor taken in hand, unadvisedly, lightly, or . . . Well, we will omit the third adverb. Am I not right, Pussy-my-love?'

'Yes, indeed you are,' Mrs Hill replied, to the astonishment of both men.

In his capacity as general manager, Mr Leadbetter was in the habit of walking each day through every department of Prideau's, stopping for a word with the various overseers. The crape workroom was last on his itinerary, and while chatting with Joe Jolly, to the latter's barely disguised chagrin, he would invariably take out a small cheroot, nipping its end off with a silver cigar-cutter before lighting it. Once he had left, the aromatic smoke wafting behind him, Joe Jolly would take out his empty pipe and suck irritably on it.

Richard, though he took care to keep well away so that he could never be accused of eavesdropping on the conversations, had watched Mr Leadbetter and Joe go through their little rituals many hundreds of times.

One June morning, after the general manager had left the department, Richard noticed the cigar-cutter lying on a bench. His first thought was to hurry after Mr Leadbetter to return it, but at that moment Joe Jolly called him urgently from the other end of the room, and he slipped the cutter into his pocket. The crimping rollers were not functioning properly, and it took Jolly and Richard over an hour to find and correct the fault. Once the machine was working properly again, the overseer sent Richard to Mr Leadbetter to report on the incident. It was his opportunity to return the cigar-cutter.

On his way, he stopped to relieve himself, and when he reached the general manager's office, Mr Leadbetter was not there.

'Gone to the crape room,' a clerk told him. 'You must have passed him on the way.'

'I went to the lat,' Richard explained. He made his report on the breakdown to the clerk in case Mr Leadbetter had not by now heard it for himself, and hurried back.

In the crape department, he was astonished to see that many of the machines had been stopped, and their workers were lined up in front of the general manager, whose face was scarlet with anger. 'Who stole it?' he shouted. 'Own up, or it will be the worse for all of you!'

Richard took the cigar-cutter from his pocket. 'Are you looking for this, sir?'

Leadbetter snatched it from him. 'You!' he said. 'I might have known it. Come with me. You too, Jolly. The rest of you get back to your work.'

'But, sir, I didn't steal it. I found it and was going to bring it to you, and then the rollers –'

But Mr Leadbetter was already marching furiously away. Joe Jolly and Richard followed. The overseer said nothing, but looked at Richard once, his lazy eyelid wide open, his upper lip drawn back to show the toothless gum. Richard was not sure how to interpret the glance – it might have been a grin of triumph.

Richard was told to wait while Leadbetter and Jolly went into the office, shutting the door. After some minutes, the overseer came out. 'You're to go in now,' he said, not looking at Richard. He took out his pipe, clamped it pugnaciously into his mouth, and hurried away.

Leadbetter was sitting behind his desk, drumming his fingers. 'Well, what have you to say?'

'I found the cutter, sir, just after you left the crape room the first time you were there. I was going to run after you, sir, but Mr Jolly called me, and then we were working on the rollers until just now.'

'You did not tell Mr Jolly that you had found it?'

'No, sir, but –'

'He informs me that he sent you here to report that the roller had been repaired. I didn't see you as I was going to the crape department.'

'No, sir. I stopped in the latrine, sir.'

'To avoid me, no doubt. Then you came on to my office. Why didn't you return my property then?'

'You weren't here, sir.'

'No, I was not. But you did not mention it to Wilkins.' He gestured towards his clerk, seated at a high desk in a corner of the room, working assiduously but obviously listening to every word. 'If your intention had been to return the cutter, you would have told Wilkins that you had it, would you not? Well?'

'I . . . I didn't think of it, sir.'

'You did not think of it,' Leadbetter repeated with heavy sarcasm. 'No, I am sure you did not.' He paused. 'I do not believe one word of your story, Goodwin. You are perfectly aware of the standards required in this mill, and of the penalties that infringement of our rules entails. Well, are you or aren't you?'

'Yes, sir.'

'Very well. I will not have thieving, and I will make an example of anyone caught in the act. You are dismissed.'

'But, sir –'

'You will leave immediately, without references, and without wages. Think yourself lucky that I do not have you charged with theft. You know what that would mean – a heavy prison sentence is a certainty.' He paused, and shook his head. 'It is against my better judgement that I treat you with leniency. There is no doubt in my mind of your guilt. I have had my suspicions of you from the very start. However, your work here has been of a high standard, and for that reason alone I shall not report this matter elsewhere. I would advise you to get out of this mill with the utmost speed, before I change my mind. That is all.'

'Sir, I should like to see Mr Prideau.'

'Do you wish me to have you thrown out?' Leadbetter put down his pen and stood up. 'Get out of this office!'

'I did not steal your cigar-cutter, sir, nor did I have any intention of doing so.'

The general manager stalked to the door and opened it. 'I will give you two seconds to get out!' he shouted, his cheeks again flaming with anger.

Richard could only obey. As he stumbled along the corridor, he seemed to be in the middle of some dreadful nightmare. How would his mother and Frances manage now? And how could he get another job? Any employer would want to know why he had left Prideau's, and without references he would have no chance of concealing his ignominious dismissal.

Anger took over from despair. For a moment, the wild idea entered his mind of returning to Leadbetter's office and launching himself at the man's throat, choking him until he admitted that he was mistaken. Then he thought of Joe Jolly. That swine had not helped. He could imagine what he had said. 'Never thought much of him, Mr Leadbetter.' He could see the overseer's left eye staring, the lips drawn back in that smirk of victory. It would be good to knock the rest of Joe Jolly's teeth down his rotten throat. But to do anything of the kind would make a prison sentence inevitable. In frustration he banged his fist into the wall of the corridor, oblivious of the pain.

He walked slowly towards the great front entrance. At least he would leave by the way he had first come to Prideau's, instead of from the back of the mill as the workers normally did.

On the way, he passed the open door of Mr Hill's office. The little man beckoned to him. 'Come in a moment,' he whispered. 'Shut the door. I was hoping I'd see you before you left. I'm sorry about this, Richard, very sorry.'

Richard nodded unhappily.

'What are you going to do?'

'I don't know. Go back home, I suppose. Try to find work somewhere. I don't know.'

'How old are you?'

'Twenty-three.'

'Despair not, Richard. Your life is ahead of you. You will find employment.'

'Where?'

Mr Hill was silent. Then he said, 'Do you need money? I am not allowed to pay your wages, as you know, and I do not have the riches of Croesus in my pocket, but I could lend you half a crown, if you want it.'

'Thank you. But, no, I'll manage.' His anger suddenly surfaced again. 'It's so unfair!' he cried. A sudden thought struck him. 'How did you know about it?'

'Mr Leadbetter sent Joe Jolly to tell me that your wages were forfeit.'

'That bastard! It's his fault, isn't it? No doubt he put the biggest knife he could find in my back.'

Mr Hill shook his head. 'No, Richard. He pleaded for you. He told Mr Leadbetter you were the best worker he'd ever had, and honest too.' As Richard looked at him in amazement, he went on, 'Wonders will never cease, as the popular saying has it. It gives me hope, Richard. If you can win over a curmudgeonly character like Joe Jolly, you can no doubt conquer the world. You will find employment worthy of your many talents elsewhere, and rise to eminences undreamed of.'

The inflated phrases did not seem amusing any more. 'I have to go,' Richard said, holding out his hand.

Mr Hill shook it. 'We shall meet again, Richard, of that I am sure. Write to me, when you have no more worthwhile occupation to pursue.'

Richard turned and left the office, and walked out from Prideau's for the last time.

It was twenty-four hours to the minute since Mr John Harcourt's coffin had been lowered into the grave in the churchyard of St Matthew's, Brentfield.

CHAPTER FIVE

Elizabeth and Frances were greatly dismayed when Richard told them his sad story, though at least they did not burst into tears, as Mrs Plackett had done. 'Cheer up,' he said. 'I shall find work soon enough. On the land, like Grandfather. Or perhaps I shall go to London.'

'To London?' Elizabeth was alarmed by the mere idea.

'Aye, to Spitalfields,' Frances said, eagerly, 'where the merchants who import raw silk are, and throwsters and weavers.'

Richard shook his head. 'No. I shan't try for a job in silk.'

'Whyever not?'

'Because soon as I showed I knew about it, they'd ask how, and then they'd want to know why I left Prideau's, and everything would come out.'

'You could pretend you didn't know anything,' Frances said. 'Start at the bottom and work your way up.'

'They'd soon find out.'

'But by then they'd 've seen how good you are, and –'

'No, Frances – it just wouldn't work.' He pulled out his purse. 'Look, Mama. I've been saving, like you always say. There's almost fifteen shillings here. I'll give you ten.'

'You'll need it yourself, Richard. We'll manage.'

His answers to Frances had been patient, but now there was an edge to his voice. 'I know what I am doing, Mama. Take it.'

Elizabeth caught the note of irritation, and recognised that he was tense and perhaps even frightened, beneath the veneer of self-confidence. She accepted the money meekly.

'Have you heard the news, Richard?' Frances asked. 'Mr Harcourt's dead. He's supposed to have had another stroke, but they say he shot himself.'

'What? Why should he do that?'

'Harcourt's is in trouble, and he was up to his eyes in debt.'

'Hush!' Elizabeth said. 'That is no more than idle gossip.'

'The Grange is up for sale. That bit isn't idle gossip, Mama,' Frances said, as her mother rapped on the table in reproof. 'Louisa Denby told me. Mr Tom called the workers together, and told them there'd be lots of changes. He said he was selling The Grange, but it didn't mean the mill would be closed, or that the Harcourts would leave Brentfield. That proves it isn't just gossip. Why should they be selling The Grange if they aren't short of money?'

Richard smiled to himself, enjoying the thought of the Harcourts finding themselves in financial difficulties. 'I wonder how her ladyship likes the idea,' he said.

'Mrs Harcourt? Probably having the vapours all over the place,' Frances said. 'They say she's been pushed into a back seat now, and that Mr Tom's wife is ruling the roost.'

'That *is* gossip, Frances,' Elizabeth said severely. 'And I will have no more of it.'

The following day, Richard left the cottage early, telling his mother not to expect him back before the end of the week at the earliest. Walking out of the village, he remembered his first journey to Franton, and marvelled at the courage of childhood which had allowed him, despite his fears of pursuit and anxieties about his forged letter, to set off into the unknown so blithely.

Spending as little as possible on food, and sleeping rough, Richard eventually reached Maldon. He had found employment for only one day on the way there, with a farmer who needed an extra hand to hoe his turnips. Richard had lacked the skill to keep up with the farm labourers, and at the end of the day, the farmer paid him his eightpence, and told him not to come back in the morning. That ended his dreams of working on the land. In Maldon he counted himself lucky to be given a job loading and unloading the barges that sailed along the Blackwater estuary, but there was no chance of permanent work, and when after a few days he was dismissed, he left the coast, and began slowly, almost aimlessly, to make his way back to Brentfield. He remembered what Frances had said – perhaps he should go to Spitalfields after all, and apply for some menial position, hiding his knowledge and skill.

He reached home on the Saturday evening.

Elizabeth could not hide her distress when he again spoke of going to London. 'It is so far away! You will not be able to visit us. I might never see you again!' She fell into a paroxysm of coughing. The attack exhausted her, and Frances insisted on putting her to bed.

In the morning, Elizabeth felt strong enough to go to church, and begged Richard to accompany her. As he knelt beside her, he knew she was praying for him, praying that he might find employment near to hand. On their way home, she was in high spirits. 'It will be all right, Richard I know it will. Something will happen – I don't know what – but something – the Lord will provide – and you won't have to go to London after all.'

Richard doubted very much whether the Lord would really have the time or the interest to intervene in his case, but he laughed, and said, 'Good, Mama. I might have known that a private word from you to the Almighty would settle everything.'

Elizabeth reproved him gently for the blasphemy, but obviously felt that the Lord would not be too distressed by this assumption of her familiarity with Him.

It was all very well, however, to smile with her, but as they ate their midday meal, Richard began to be irritated by her certainty that he had abandoned all thought of going to London. He did not want to quarrel with her, especially since it might bring on another bout of coughing, but it was difficult to remain silent, and as soon as they had finished eating, he announced that he was going for a walk, and left the cottage without replying to Frances' suggestion that they could all take a stroll when the dishes had been washed.

He decided to take a last look at Brentfield, which, despite all the years he had spent in Franton, he always thought of as home. He wandered through the village, trying to fix it in his mind. The cottages had been built almost chaotically, each unique, standing at a different angle, its thatched roof jostling its neighbours, their charm and beauty undeniable. The gently sloping green led down to the little river and the pretty, narrow bridge. He walked by the river until he could see Harcourt's Mill, gaunt against the horizon. It had a slight air of dilapidation, he thought, bearing out the rumours of which Frances had spoken.

He came back through the village, and took the road towards The Grange, remembering how he had called there to level his accusations against George Harcourt. He thought of the day he had gone with Mary to Newman's field to look at the foal. Poor Mary. George Harcourt was dead now too, and there was no point in nursing his bitterness against the family. But it was hard to forget it entirely . . .

After a while, he found himself walking along an overgrown path, and then heard, somewhere ahead of him, a woman's voice, shouting for help. He began to run, trying not to trip over the brambles.

She was sitting on the ground, a young woman, dressed in black. Her hair was dark chestnut. He recognised her immediately.

She looked at him with an expression in which relief was mixed with a hint of apprehension. 'Help me up,' she said imperiously.

Richard went to her. 'It's Mrs Harcourt, isn't it?'

'Yes. I've sprained my ankle, I think.'

'This is no path for a lady to walk.'

'So I discovered.' Leaning on him, she put her injured foot to the ground, and winced, and the colour drained from her face. 'I . . . I'm afraid I must sit again.' She sank back to the ground, her face contorting with the pain.

'I will go and get help,' Richard said.

'No. Wait a moment.' The slightly slanting green eyes opened, and gazed at him. She was puzzled. He seemed vaguely familiar, but surely she would have remembered such striking good looks if they had met before. And that was not all. His clothes suggested a working man, yet his manners and his speech, even if the flat Essex accent was strong, were almost polished. 'I've seen you before, haven't I? Where?'

'In church perhaps.'

'Possibly, but that's not what I was thinking of.' She thought for a moment, and then said, 'Oh, I remember – I was on a visit to The Grange, long before I was married, and you were the young man who came bursting into the drawing-room, with some wild accusation or other.'

'Yes. I remember you too, Mrs Harcourt. You were sitting at the piano. But it was not a wild accusation. My sister died as a result of an abortion. It was George Harcourt's child.'

She made no comment, but asked abruptly, 'What's your name?'

'Richard Goodwin.'

'Well, Goodwin, help me up again, and I will see if I can walk. I may be able to manage if I lean on you.'

After she had slowly hobbled a few painful yards, Richard said, 'I will go and call some of your servants, Mrs Harcourt. Unless . . .'

'Unless what?'

'I was going to suggest carrying you myself, but you might not wish to trust yourself to a stranger. Or you might consider the idea in some way improper.'

There was something very appealing about him, and she smiled. 'I know your name, and that you come from Brentfield, so you are not a complete stranger. As for any impropriety, that is forgivable, I believe, in my present predicament.' She raised her arms towards him, but then said, 'Wait! My crinoline! When you lift me up, I fear it will reveal more than I should like.'

Richard laughed, and when she glared at him, said, 'But I shall see nothing that I should not, ma'am – the crinoline itself will obscure my view.'

The anger faded, and her eyes twinkled. 'Oh, yes, you are right. But if we meet anyone you must set me down at once, do you understand?' Suddenly she laughed outright. 'Oh, how foolish I am to be worrying about such matters in these circumstances.'

Richard bent and picked her up. She was light in his arms,

and he was conscious of the faint jasmine-like perfume that she wore, and, as he looked down, he could see the smooth skin of her cheek and the tendrils of chestnut hair. One of his arms supported her legs at the knee, but he could feel nothing but the bulk of her dress and petticoats, and the wire of the crinoline; the other arm was around her back, his hand resting just below her breast, and pressing against his abdomen was the soft firmness of her hip. He realised the effect she was having on him, and forced himself to think of other things.

He wondered whether she had sensed his excitement, and wished to escape from his arms, when, after they had covered a few hundred yards, she said suddenly, 'Stop! Put me down on that tree stump.' But then she continued, 'Rest. We have a long way to go yet.'

'I can fetch help,' he offered again.

She rubbed at the mud on the crape flounces of her skirt. 'Ruined,' she muttered to herself.

'It will wash, ma'am,' Richard said. 'Use luke-warm water, and do not let it soak.'

'What do you know about it?'

He grinned. 'Quite a lot, as it happens, Mrs Harcourt. I probably helped to make that crape – it is Prideau's pattern, I see.'

'You work there?'

'I used to.'

'Used to? You left there? Why?'

He hesitated, but saw no reason to dissemble. 'I was dismissed.'

'For what reason?'

'I prefer not to say, Mrs Harcourt.'

'For impudence perhaps?'

Stung, he said, 'It is my concern, and no one else's.'

'I am not asking out of idle curiosity, Goodwin.' She smiled at him. 'Come, you may trust me with your secret.'

He looked into her green eyes. The eyes are the mirror of the soul, his mother used to say. What could he see reflected there? Suddenly, because her eyes told him she would listen with an open mind and judge only if convinced of the truth, he wanted to tell her everything.

When he had finished, she made no comment, but seemed to be thinking. At last she said, 'That is a long enough rest, I believe.'

He picked her up again, and as they made their way along the path, she asked, 'What are you going to do now?'

'I'm going to London, to find work there, if I can – to Spitalfields. It is the centre of the London silk industry, as you may know. Silk is in my blood, Mrs Harcourt. My father was an overseer in Harcourt's Mill, until the work killed him.'

Again she said nothing and he plodded on, feeling resentful of the way she had wheedled his story out of him, and then did not respond. She suggested once that he should take another rest, but he shook his head. Once clear of the overgrown path, he lengthened his stride, and without another break brought her to the front door of The Grange.

As help was summoned, she said, 'Go to the servants' hall. Ask Cook to give you some refreshment. You must be in need of it.'

'I was not looking for a reward,' Richard said coldly.

'If I intended to reward you, do you think that a glass of milk and a slice of cake is the best that I could offer?' Her lip curled, but again he thought he read amusement in her eyes. 'Go and wait there. Take refreshment or not, as you wish. But don't go away. I want to talk further to you.'

Richard was not certain whether or not to obey her, but decided he had little to lose by falling in with her wishes. He enjoyed the food he was given – not milk and a slice of cake, but scones warm from the oven and dripping with butter, and a drink made from fresh lemons and sugar, such as he had never tasted before – a luxury for the rich.

He spent almost an hour and a half in the servants' hall before a maid came to say that Mrs Harcourt was ready to see him. On his previous visits to The Grange, he had barely noticed his surroundings, but now, as the maid led him along corridors, up stairs, into the entrance hall, and from there to a room which was evidently the library, he was able to admire the velvet portières and window curtains, the elegant tables and tallboys that stood against the walls, the marble statues on their plinths in the niches of the hall – everything kept spotless and gleaming with polish by the busy hands of the servants.

Mrs Harcourt was reclining on a chaise-longue. 'I am sorry to have kept you waiting, Goodwin. The doctor has only just left.'

'Nothing serious, I hope, Mrs Harcourt.'

'He says it is a slight sprain only, and will cure itself quite rapidly.' She smiled at him warmly. 'I want to thank you again for your help. I trust that you were adequately supplied with food and drink.'

'Yes, thank you.'

She took a sovereign from her reticule. 'Please accept this too.'

'I enjoyed the scones and the lemon drink, but I require no other reward for helping a lady.'

'That is sheer Quixotry.' She stopped, and frowned, as though irritated with herself. 'I mean by that –'

'I understand the word, Mrs Harcourt.'

'Do you? Do you indeed? Then I apologise for underestimating you. But it is absurdly Quixotic of you to refuse a reward which is freely offered, and which has been so well earned – especially since you are currently without employment.' The green eyes studied him.

He shook his head stubbornly. 'May I go now, Mrs Harcourt?'

'No, you may not.' She put the gold coin away. 'Sit down. There where I can see you. Now, tell me how crape is made.'

Richard stared at her in amazement. 'How crape is made? I can't.'

'Why not? If you worked on crape at Prideau's, you must know how it is manufactured.'

'Of course, but I cannot tell you.'

She raised her eyebrows quizzically, and repeated, 'Why not?'

'Firstly, because, with respect, you wouldn't understand, ma'am.' He ignored the brief flash of anger in her eyes. 'And secondly, because everyone who works on crape at Prideau's signs to say he will not divulge the secret of how it's made. It's a binding undertaking.'

'I see. I am not without knowledge of silk-making, Goodwin. As for your second point, I cannot argue. Do you believe God would strike you dead and damn you to eternity if you betray the secret?'

He smiled at her. 'No – not exactly.'

'Perhaps you swore an oath on the Bible?'

'No.'

'Then whatever you signed has little force – especially after the way you were treated. It is strange that you remain so loyal to Prideau's.'

Richard thought for a moment. 'To put aside my undertaking, Mrs Harcourt, seems to me as much of a wrong as my dismissal was. My mother always taught me that two wrongs do not make a right.'

It was the second – no, the third time that he had replied almost impudently, as though he were an equal, and she knew she should reprove him sharply, and send him away. But there was something about him . . . She smiled again. 'I am rebuked on moral grounds. I admire your principles.' She sighed. 'If you won't tell me, you won't, and I shall have to find out some other way. I shall buy the secret, if necessary. Prideau's cannot keep it from anyone with a little money and enough determination. I have that determination, Goodwin. I will tell *you* a secret. The fortunes of Harcourt's Mill will be revived by the manufacture of crape.'

'Harcourt's? Making crape?'

She laughed. 'Oh, if you could but see your face! Yes, that is our intention. To succeed, we need not only to know Mr Prideau's secrets, but to find someone with experience such as yours to supervise the process. How would you like to work for Harcourt's, Goodwin?'

Richard was stunned. 'You cannot be serious. I have no references. You know nothing about me – not even if I am telling the truth.'

'I have learnt a great deal about you already.'

'How?'

She laughed. 'I pride myself on being a good judge of character, but you may put it down to a woman's intuition, if you like.' Mentally she rebuked herself for talking nonsense. What was she trying to do – charm him? Nonsense or not, something kept telling her, insistently, that Master Richard Goodwin was a gift from Providence, which she must on no account refuse. 'Now listen, I am perfectly serious. I am offering you a position at Harcourt's.'

'In what capacity?'

'I do not know yet. It will depend on your capabilities.'

It was like a dream. He heard himself saying, 'I doubt if Mr Harcourt would approve.'

Her eyes flashed her displeasure. 'I shall consult him on his return this evening, but I have no doubt that he will accept my advice.'

'I think it is unlikely, Mrs Harcourt. He has no love for me.'

'Because of your accusations against his brother, you mean? But that was years ago.'

'It was more than that. We have been – your husband and I have not been friends since we were small boys.'

She laughed once more. 'Oh, really, Goodwin, what nonsense! You are both adults now, and will surely behave as such.' She gave a little grimace of pain, and bent to rub gently at her swollen ankle. 'I need to rest. I understand that my proposition comes as a surprise. You will want to consider it carefully – sleep on it, perhaps. Return here at nine o'clock tomorrow morning. We will talk further then.'

Richard stood up. There did not seem to be anything he could say, so he gave an awkward little bow, and turned to go. He could feel her gaze on his back, those quizzical, disturbing, dancing eyes.

'Nine o'clock,' she repeated.

He looked back at her as he reached the door. 'Yes, Mrs Harcourt.' He found himself grinning, and realised that he had made some kind of commitment.

Richard went home in a daze. He reported his encounter with Mrs Tom Harcourt to his mother and sister, dwelling on the refreshments he had been given, but omitting any mention of the conversation about crape-making and Mrs Harcourt's extraordinary offer.

Lying in bed that night, he tried to clarify his thoughts. It was exciting to be given an opportunity to continue working with silk, to exercise the skills he had learnt in his thirteen years with Prideau's – assuming of course that Tom Harcourt would ratify his wife's proposition, which was far from certain. She had sounded very definite, like a person who was not to be trifled with, but he was the owner of the mill, and would surely have the last word.

The real question was whether, if the offer were confirmed, he should accept it. To do so, he would have to break his commitment to secrecy. Did the injustice of his dismissal nullify his signature on that piece of paper? Morally, the answer had to be that it did not, but in practical terms, Prideau's had forfeited any right to his loyalty. Besides, if Mrs Harcourt was right, and money could buy the secrets of the crape-making process, he would be doing Prideau's little harm.

Then of course he had to consider whether he could accept the idea of working for the business which had brought his father to an early death, and for the family which had betrayed and killed his sister.

He wrestled with the problems for a long time, without reaching a solution, and then found his thoughts drifting back to Mrs Harcourt, the softness of her body, the beauty of her skin, her perfume.

Resolutely, he dragged his mind away from her. A picture came into his mind of himself and Tom Harcourt as small boys, fighting. What had happened then had been as unjust as his dismissal from Prideau's. He told himself that he should not become obsessed by ideas of injustice, real or imagined. Had his father's early death really been caused by the Harcourts? Was it fair to blame them for what a son, now dead, had done to Mary? Should he still feel bitter because Frances had been dismissed from the mill? However many such reasonable questions he asked, the fact remained that he had sworn revenge, and the desire for it still burned deep in the recesses of his heart.

He remembered his childish ambition to reach a position of power in Harcourt's when Prideau's bought up the smaller, failing mill. If he accepted this offer and played his cards carefully and well, it was not beyond imagining that the firm might one day fall to him. A dream? Perhaps. But it was sweet to contemplate the idea of making Tom Harcourt dance to his tune. And Tom's wife too . . .

He awoke early, and stole out of the cottage. Perhaps the clear morning air would make it easier to think things through. It was already warm, and he lay in a hayfield, gazing up at the sky, watching the small white clouds move slowly across the expanse of blue. His thoughts lapsed into a hazy, dream-like confusion of undefined longings and sadnesses and hopes, and in the midst of that tangled skein of images came again the memory of a woman's form held in his arms, her face close to his, her chestnut hair brushing his cheek. He wondered what it would be like to kiss the full lips, to strip away those black garments and reveal the beauty that must lie beneath, to take her body to his.

When he went home to breakfast, his problems were still unresolved. He had intended to give his mother and Frances the impression, when he left for The Grange, that he was setting out for London, but at the last minute he could not go through with the lie. He told them that Mrs Harcourt had asked him to return, but refused to explain why.

When he reached The Grange, he was shown at once into the library, where Mrs Harcourt was again lying on the chaise-longue. 'Good morning, Mrs Harcourt. I hope your ankle is better.'

She smiled, and he noticed that her teeth were slightly uneven. 'It is vastly improved – still painful to walk on, but otherwise bearable. I thank you again for your assistance yesterday. Please sit down.' She waited while he did so, and then continued. 'Have you had further thoughts about what I suggested to you?'

'Yes, ma'am.'

'And?'

Richard had rehearsed his reply. 'I can only accept your offer if you – that is, if Mr Harcourt – will agree to certain conditions.'

'Ah,' she said, smiling. 'Conditions. We are to bargain, are we, Goodwin? As for Mr Harcourt,' and the smile faded and her tone grew colder, 'however much it may disturb your masculine susceptibilities to conduct your business with a woman, I can assure you that I speak for Mr Harcourt, and with his full authority.'

'I did not mean to offend you.'

'I simply wish to make the position clear. Mr Harcourt will be joining us later, but we have already discussed the matter.' She paused, and then said with a vehemence which surprised him, 'I know what must be done to save Harcourt's Mill, and I intend to see that it *is* done. You may have heard of Queen Elizabeth's speech at Tilbury: "I have the body of a weak and feeble woman," she said, "but I have the heart and stomach of a king." ' She smiled. 'It is the fashion nowadays to regard the reference to her stomach as indelicate – well, pooh to that! In my humbler position, I share her sentiments. I pray you therefore to abandon any thought that you are here merely to make polite conversation with me. This is a business discussion, Goodwin. Is that understood?'

'Yes, Mrs Harcourt.' Richard smiled.

'You are pleased to be amused?'

'Forgive me. I smiled in admiration.'

A blush stole over her cheeks. She took out a small cambric handkerchief and dabbed at her nose with it. Richard felt easier. She could be disconcerting in her directness, but now he felt he had restored the balance.

She regained her composure rapidly, and asked, 'What are these conditions of yours?'

'First, if I am to disclose to Harcourt's all I know about the making of crape, then I must have full control over the process here.'

'Assuming you have the knowledge and the skills you

claim, I see no difficulty in appointing you overseer of the department.'

'No, ma'am. Manager.'

She raised her eyebrows. 'Indeed?'

'An overseer supervises the workers under him, but makes no policy decisions. He checks the standards of quality, but does not set them. He makes sure that the work allocated to the department is carried out, but does not decide which work is to be done, and when. An overseer is not consulted by the owner of the mill or its directors, nor would they necessarily give weight to his recommendations.'

'Whereas you wish to enjoy all those privileges.'

'I cannot produce crape for you otherwise, Mrs Harcourt.'

She gazed at him as she considered what he had said. 'Well, what else?'

It sounded as though she had accepted his point, but he hesitated before continuing, wondering how far he could push her. 'You may think me impertinent.'

This time she smiled. 'Then I shall try to overlook it.'

'You admitted yesterday that you have some financial difficulties. What guarantee can you give that the mill will continue in business?'

The smile vanished, and her eyes flashed. 'None whatsoever. Its survival depends entirely, I believe, on our entry into the crape market. Fashion decrees that crape should be worn for mourning – a fashion to which I myself subscribe at the moment – and since most of the middle and upper classes seem to be almost permanently in mourning for some relative or other, demand is high. But whether or not we shall be successful, I cannot tell. Among other things, it might depend on your skill. Your question is less impertinent than foolish.'

Richard nodded. 'Yes. That was not really the question I meant to ask. To set up a crape-manufacturing department will be very expensive. Does Harcourt's have sufficient capital at its disposal?'

'I think perhaps that *is* impertinent,' she said. 'Such questions are for the board to decide.'

'They may be, ma'am, but I must be assured that the board

will be willing and able to spend all that is required. You cannot scrimp. If I recommend the purchase of certain machinery, or the employment of a given number of workers, there must be no attempt on your part to try to make do with less than is needed.'

'I am sure that, if you can justify any such demands, the board will support you. As for the money, I give you my word that there will be no difficulty, within reason.' She paused, and then asked drily, 'Does that satisfy you?'

'Amply, Mrs Harcourt. Thank you.'

'And your other conditions?'

'I have no others, ma'am.'

'You have said nothing about your own financial rewards.'

Richard grinned at her. 'I did not think it necessary to raise the matter. I assumed that I should be fairly paid.'

The green eyes opened a little wider, and she nodded slowly. 'A fair assumption. Of course, before we fix a specific figure, we must be satisfied that you can deliver all that you promise. After all, so far I have only your word for your ability to produce crape for us.'

'And your intuition, ma'am.' He grinned again.

Her temper should have flared, but his humour was somehow not offensive to her. She smiled. '*Touché*. And I shall not explain that to you.'

Richard equally was enjoying the duel of words. 'My ability is such that I consider myself to be worth a minimum of three hundred pounds a year – for a start.' He waited for her to protest at so high a figure.

'I shall bear that in mind,' she said coolly. 'There is something else about which *I* wish to have some assurance. You spoke yesterday – indeed, you made a considerable to-do about it – of your loyalty towards Prideau's. Your willingness to engage in this discussion would suggest that you have found a way to overcome your scruples. I am glad of that, but how can I now be certain of your loyalty to Harcourt's – especially since I gathered that you felt, and indeed may still feel, a strong antipathy towards my husband's family?'

Her gaze was penetrating, and Richard returned it frankly. 'Only by accepting my word that those considerations no longer weigh with me. You will have no reason to question my loyalty.'

'I hope not, Goodwin, I hope not.' The long-case clock in the corner of the room chimed once to mark the half hour. She glanced at it with some irritation. 'It seems to me that we have reached a point when it would be as well if Mr Harcourt were present. Be so good as to ring.' She indicated the bell-pull by the fireplace.

After the servant had been despatched to find Mr Harcourt, silence fell. Mrs Harcourt began carefully, almost obsessively, to smooth again and again, with her long, slim fingers, the ruffles of crape on the skirt of her black mourning dress.

As he watched her, he thought how extraordinary she was. Unconventional, highly intelligent, quick-thinking, outspoken, impulsive yet level-headed – the adjectives floated through his mind. There was an element of animal wildness in her. She was like a lioness, a spirited, prancing horse, a proud falcon. Could she be tamed? As soon as the word formed in his brain, he realised that an equality of spirit would be the most that she would concede to any man. He wondered about her marriage. Did she love her husband? Had Tom Harcourt developed a strength of will and an independence to match hers?

He recognised that the attraction she held for him was dangerous, especially when his whole future might be decided in this room. To stop himself thinking of her, he glanced around at the books which lined the walls. Many were richly bound in leather, elegantly tooled in gold. They were beautiful in themselves, he thought, but it was their contents which mattered. That might equally well be said of women . . . of Mrs Harcourt, for instance. He smiled inwardly. A lioness, a falcon – and now a book . . . *Shall I compare thee to a summer's day?*

His inner amusement was reflected in his eyes. Sarah Harcourt glanced at him, and quickly averted her gaze. She would have to beware. Any encouragement, and this handsome young man might interest her more than was wise.

The door opened and Tom Harcourt entered. Of medium height, his waist already beginning to thicken, though he was only twenty-five, he had much the look of his late father. He was almost ugly, and yet, if village gossip was to be believed, his looks had been no barrier to his success with women. His dark eyes were sullen as he came into the room. 'I am sorry to keep you waiting, my dear,' he said, seating himself at a prettily-ornamented gilt table, which stood beside the chaise-longue. 'I doubted my presence was really necessary.'

There seemed to be an edge to the words, and Richard glanced at Mrs Harcourt. Yes, she looked a little put out, but she replied smoothly, 'We have had a useful discussion, Goodwin and I. He has not yet finally committed himself, but he is ready, I believe, to set up a crape-making department for us, provided that we appoint him its manager, and –'

'Manager!' For the first time, Tom Harcourt looked directly at Richard. His eyes were cold.

'His reasons for asking for such a position seem sensible.'

'Perhaps I may hear them.'

Richard went through his arguments again.

'H'm,' Tom grunted, when he had finished. 'But such an appointment would be on a trial basis only. You would not expect more, I think, Goodwin. A trial period of, say, three months. After all, we know nothing of your capabilities.'

'No, sir. I could not accept that. I know I'm asking you to take me on trust, but I must be sure that you won't cast me aside at the end of the trial period, when you've learnt all I can teach you.'

'The mill has never worked in that fashion,' Mrs Harcourt said sharply, 'and I resent any suggestion that we might act in such a way.'

'In any case, Goodwin,' Tom added, 'we are under no obligation to continue to employ anyone who fails to serve us adequately. Neither a manager nor the humblest worker has a right to employment, except he earn it. On the other hand, we discharge fully our obligations towards those who work to our satisfaction.' He paused. 'I would not have thought it necessary to explain that.'

Richard still felt that he had been justified in making his point, but knew that he would have to apologise. 'I meant no offence, and of course I accept what you say.'

Tom turned to his wife. 'What other surprises have you for me, my dear? Goodwin's wages, perhaps? What have you offered? Several thousand pounds a year?'

She refused to be nettled by his sarcasm. 'Let us say that I am aware of what would be expected if all other questions are satisfactorily resolved.' She turned to Richard. 'You have still not confirmed your willingness to work for us, Goodwin. Is your mind yet made up?'

Richard did not know what to say. They were both staring at him, Tom with an expression in which he thought he read dislike and even contempt, while Sarah's eyes seemed to be telling him, 'You and I together . . . we could make Harcourt's successful again. You and I . . .' He tried to think rationally. What other prospect did he have? What was there to lose? As though it were someone else speaking, he heard himself saying, 'I should like to do so, ma'am.'

She smiled. 'Good. I am glad.'

'I do not wish to question your decisions, my dear,' Tom said, 'but I must confess my belief that we are moving somewhat hastily. Now that Goodwin has expressed his desire to work for us, it would seem appropriate to me that he should reveal something of his qualifications.' Looking at Richard, he went on, 'Tell us about making crape. Here and now. And I do assure you that I am not intending to cast you aside when – what was your phrase? – when I have learnt all you have to teach.'

Richard pondered for a moment. It was not really an unreasonable request, and in any case he need not disclose all he knew at this stage. He realised that Tom was staring at him expectantly. 'I am sorry,' he said, 'but I am wondering where to begin.'

'At the beginning, I would suggest.'

Richard flushed, and turned to Mrs Harcourt. 'Before the

silk is woven, ma'am, the thread is thrown, which is to say it is taken from the reels and twisted. It is then doubled, so that it is of twice the thickness, and twisted again. We say that the yarn has a low throw or a high throw, according to how tightly it is twisted. For crape we use a high throw, with as many as seventy twists to the inch.'

'Why?' she asked.

'I will come to that in a moment, ma'am. The thread is woven into a thin, gauze-like material, which is then crimped with a pattern of little bumps and ridges, by passing it through rollers at a high temperature and under great pressure. One of the rollers is of brass, engraved with a pattern, while the other is covered in a thick layer of paper, which has hollows corresponding to the ridges on the brass roller. As the material passes through, the pattern is pressed into it. I trust I am making myself clear.'

She inclined her head. 'Go on, Goodwin.'

Richard remembered the way Joe Jolly had explained it to him. 'If you put the material through those rollers just as it is, what would happen?'

Mrs Harcourt smiled. 'I have no idea. But I assume from the way you ask the question that it is something undesirable.'

'Silk is not spun, like wool or cotton, but is a continuous thread. If you put a sharp pressure across the weft threads, which is what the ridges on the brass cylinder must do in order to produce the pattern, they are likely to snap. So before the cloth goes through the rollers, it has to be angled. A machine stretches it taut, and then the two sides are pulled in opposite directions, one forward and one back.' He illustrated the movement with his hands. 'Some people call it biasing. When it has been done, the weft threads no longer lie at right angles across the warp, but are . . . well, angled.'

'And that stops them from breaking? How interesting!'

'The biasing and the crimping are the vital processes in making crape. Of course, it is far from finished when it comes from the crimping rollers. The fabric has to be straightened, the natural gums removed, and it has to be dyed.'

'Degumming and dyeing are hardly secret arts,' Tom put in.

'They are not done in quite the same way for crape as for ordinary materials, sir – the heat of the liquids and the time the fabric spends in the vats are crucial. You remember I said the yarn has a high throw – that allows it to receive the crimping well, and during the degumming it untwists a little, which makes the crape curl. Too much heat, too long in the liquid and it will untwist too much.'

'Can we buy a machine to do the crimping?'

'I doubt it, sir. Prideau's build their own, and their crimping cylinders are especially engraved for them. The pattern has to be quite perfect. It takes a master engraver months to produce just one cylinder.'

'What about the biasing?'

Before Richard could answer, the door to the library burst open, and Mrs Lottie Harcourt rushed in. Dressed in black, she wore a widow's cap and veil. It was years since Richard had seen her at close quarters, and time had not been kind to her, he thought. Her hair was still as black, but the rouge and powder on her face could not hide the wrinkles and the sagging skin, and gave her a raddled appearance. She was weeping noisily. 'Cruel! Cruel! To think of leaving The Grange for some poky little house! There will be no room for anything. Where will my lovely furniture go? What of my beloved statues? I tell you I shall never support it!' She sank on to a chair, and continued her sobbing.

'I am sorry. I tried to stop her.' Standing by the door was a young woman, whom Richard recognised as Tom's sister Jane. 'Plain Jane,' they called her in the village.

'Oh, oh, oh!' Lottie Harcourt shrieked. 'Was ever a woman plagued so?'

'Mama,' said Tom between his teeth, 'we are not alone.'

'Why should I care who hears me? Oh, speak to your wife, Tom. Tell her not to use me thus!'

Richard glanced at Sarah Harcourt. She did not seem in the least disconcerted, but was again smoothing the crape on her dress.

'Come, Goodwin!' Tom said, and hastily led the way from the room.

As they left, they passed Jane Harcourt, who exchanged a weary glance with her brother. The resemblance between them was quite marked.

Outside in the hall, Tom said, 'My mother is taking my father's death very ill. You will of course forget all that you witnessed.' He waited for Richard's assent, and then went on, 'I wish to hear much more concerning crape. I shall be at the mill in about an hour's time. Wait for me there, at the main gate.'

'Yes, sir.'

'I will not hide it from you, Goodwin – I am far from satisfied as to the wisdom of this whole venture.' He turned to go back into the drawing-room, and then threw over his shoulder, 'Including the question of your employment.'

CHAPTER SIX

As he walked slowly to the mill and waited in the warm sunshine, Richard called himself all sorts of a fool. Whatever Mrs Harcourt might say, Tom would make the final decision, and since Tom disliked him, he would simply milk him of as much information as he could before showing him the door. Both of them had made a great fuss about treating people properly, but he could have asked them why, if that was so, Frances had been dismissed. He would be better off making his way to Spitalfields.

It was well over an hour later that Tom arrived. 'Women!' he muttered, climbing down from the trap. 'A man is never free of women!' He turned to Richard. 'Come on. You'd better see the state of things here.' He went into the mill.

As Richard followed, he thought he could smell brandy. Perhaps it was the women who drove Tom to drink.

The mill appalled him. Prideau's had always been kept clean, its machines tended as carefully as hothouse plants, and slackness was never tolerated. But Harcourt's was filthy, the floors covered in dirt and the windows grimy, and though the workers appeared to be busily occupied, Richard could not rid himself of the belief that their activity was merely assumed for as long as their master was near.

He was also astonished to see that many of the winding and throwing mills and even the looms were hand-operated. 'I thought all the machines would be water-powered,' he said. 'Or that you'd be using steam.'

'My father installed all kinds of modern machines,' Tom replied. 'But many of them have broken down and not been repaired.'

'What happened to them?'

They went to a large room, filled with dust-covered machinery, mostly of iron, unlike the wooden hand-driven mills and looms presently in use.

'My inheritance!' Tom Harcourt said bitterly, and led the way back to his office. He sat at his desk, but did not offer Richard a chair. 'I have a few important questions for you. If we cannot purchase the machines needed for crape-making ready-made, are you capable of giving detailed specifications for their construction? These crimping rollers, for instance – are they power-driven?'

'Yes, sir. By steam. I know the size of the cylinders, the speed at which they must rotate, the pressure they must exert, the temperature at which they have to operate. I can describe all that to an engineer, and make sketches to show what is required.'

'What about the other machines – the one that angles the material?'

'When they first made crape at Prideau's, they did the biasing by hand. It could be done that way here, to begin with.'

'How much space is required? I would guess quite a lot, if the whole process is to be continuous.'

'The large shed where all those broken machines are kept would do very well.'

'H'm. So, is the whole thing possible, or is it not?' He seemed to be talking to himself, and Richard did not answer. Harcourt suddenly barked at him, 'Well? What's your opinion?'

'I think it's physically possible, sir, but there are many other things to be considered.'

'Go on.'

'There's the question of whether you can compete with Prideau's. The market for crape is immense, but it can't be filled with poor quality fabric. New machinery needs to be worked in, and people who've not made crape before have to learn the craft, so you couldn't hope to reach an adequate standard immediately. The machines will have to be ordered and built, and the engraving of the brass cylinder will take months.'

'You are saying that it will be – what? – a year before we can be in full production?'

'Yes, sir.'

'Oh, for God's sake, sit down, Goodwin. I want to know a lot more from you yet.' It was the first time that Tom's voice had been lacking in hostility. 'Supposing we go ahead,' he continued, 'get the machinery somehow, and overcome all the early problems, what then? You say the market is immense, but haven't Prideau's got it neatly tied up?'

'Their crape is expensive. They have a monopoly, and can charge what they like. I don't know your costs, but I'd be surprised if you couldn't produce crape more cheaply than they do.'

'If we undercut them, they'd simply bring their own prices down.'

'I doubt if they'd be able to reduce them as far as you could. Their overheads are immense.'

'And so is their productive capacity. Well, perhaps we should meet that problem when we come to it. But you think the market would welcome a new crape?'

'If it's a cheaper one, yes. It isn't only the rich who buy crape – almost every family in the land uses it. At a lower price we might not need to worry too much if we couldn't match Prideau's quality – though I believe we could, eventually.'

'And what is the next step?'

'The first thing is to order the machines – a crimping machine, new throwing mills and a loom – and to get a cylinder engraved. That shed must be cleared, and with respect I'd say that as many as possible of the machines in it should be repaired. Clean up the mill, get the hands to take pride in their work, and with a better standard of output, your normal business in ribbons and other plain silks would start to pick up. Then you'd be in a good position to launch Harcourt's crape.'

Richard's voice gained in enthusiasm as he talked, and Tom Harcourt looked at him, at first with amusement and then with some suspicion. 'Have you discussed that with Mrs Harcourt?' he asked.

'No, sir.'

'Strange. It's exactly what she's been telling me.' He rose, and went over to the window. 'And what's all this going to cost?'

'I don't know, sir.' He tried to work out what would be needed, remembering some of the figures that Mr Hill had given him. 'I would guess not less than six thousand pounds.' He looked at the mill-owner doubtfully, himself appalled at the figure.

Tom Harcourt's mouth was open. 'Six thousand pounds? But that's ridiculous!' He went back to his desk and sat down. 'That puts a different complexion on the whole thing. Such an expenditure is quite beyond our means. Plainly, we shall have to abandon any idea of making crape.' He paused, twiddling his thumbs as he thought. 'I have to say, Goodwin, that I have been impressed by your attitude and comments.'

'Thank you, sir.' Richard's pleasure was mixed with astonishment at this volte-face.

'It seems unlikely that we shall be able to employ you as crape-maker, but perhaps you might be interested in working for us in some other capacity. No, don't answer now. Think about it. Come to The Grange this afternoon, and it can be settled then. Two o'clock.'

His mother and Frances were stunned and delighted when he told them of the possibility that he would be working for Harcourt's, and his own enthusiasm grew as he spoke.

'It's the answer to my prayer,' Elizabeth said. 'I knew that God would not let me cry in vain.'

Though he kept reminding her that nothing was settled, Frances overwhelmed him with questions about exactly what job he would be doing, and how it had all come about. Then Richard noticed that his mother had fallen silent. 'What's the matter, Mama?'

'Why are you doing this?' she asked quietly.

'Why? Because I need work, of course, and it's the kind of work I know how to do, and because it means being able to stay in Brentfield. And I suppose it's a challenge – to help to get the mill working properly again.'

'You always said you hated that family.'

'Oh, that was years ago. I've got over that.'

'Thank God,' Elizabeth said fervently. 'Thank God. I have prayed that the hatred should be taken from your heart.'

'I can never forget what the Harcourts have done to us,' he said, 'but George and his father are both dead now. Tom Harcourt –'

'You used to hate him too,' Frances said.

'When we were children. He started off this morning as though he wanted to be my enemy, but we ended up friends, I think.'

'I'm glad, Richard, so very glad.' Elizabeth hugged him. 'God is good to us.'

He moved away and sat down, embarrassed by the pious hush which seemed to have settled over the room. To counteract it, he said brightly, 'If this all happens, I shall be a lot better paid than I was at Prideau's, and you know what that means? You'll be able to give up working, and so will Frances, and,' he added, laughing, 'you can both spend your whole time looking after me.' His real thought was that Frances would be able to take over the housework, so that his mother could rest.

When he was talking about it in the cottage, it all seemed simple, but as he walked back to The Grange once more, his mind filled with questions. What was the true reason behind his willingness to work for the Harcourts? Was there still at the back of his mind a desire for revenge? Had he been so bewitched by Sarah Harcourt that all his common sense had left him? Or was it simply an opportunity to do the kind of work he knew and enjoyed? And why had the Harcourts been so willing to offer a job to a young man without references, who had even confessed his hostility towards them? Perhaps they were desperate, impulsively clutching at straws. He could find no satisfactory answers, and decided at last that his best course might be simply to let Fate sweep him along to whatever lay ahead.

Returning from the mill, Tom Harcourt hurried to Sarah and told her with some pleasure that the idea of making crape would have to be abandoned. 'I always thought it was absurd. You let yourself be carried away by that young man's blue eyes and golden curls.'

'Don't talk nonsense!' Sarah said, rather more sharply than she had intended, suddenly remembering the way Richard had picked her up and carried her back to The Grange.

'I've offered him a job, by the way,' Tom went on. 'He's quite impressive, and even if we don't make crape, I'm sure we can use him somewhere. As long as we keep an eye on him, of course – we've only heard his side of the Prideau story. He's coming here at two o'clock.'

'You say we'd need five or six thousand to go into crape?' Sarah asked. 'It doesn't seem all that excessive to me. Perhaps it can be pared down somehow, and we should be able to get a bank loan, even if we have to mortgage the mill. I think we should talk more to Goodwin before we give up the idea altogether.'

'A waste of time.'

'Since he's coming here this afternoon, we might just as well.'

'If that's what you're going to talk about, you can do it on your own. Just don't get so absorbed in looking at Master Blue-Eyes that you forget we're running a business.'

That remark was not worthy of a reply, Sarah thought.

Richard was surprised to be received again by Mrs Harcourt alone. Lying on the chaise-longue, she smiled when he enquired after her ankle. 'It's improving, thank you. I manage to hobble about a little with the aid of my stick.' A silver-topped, ebony cane was at her side. 'But you came here to discuss business, not my health. Mr Harcourt has told me of your estimate of the costs that will face us. The total is daunting, but I am not convinced that we have to abandon the idea of making crape. How was your figure made up?'

'It was little more than a guess, ma'am. As I explained to Mr Harcourt, I have no real knowledge of the cost of machines. But one of the overseers at Prideau's once told me that their throwing mills were worth two thousand pounds apiece, and I based my figures on that.'

'We already have throwing mills. They may be in poor condition, but they can be repaired.'

'But they won't produce "doubles". You will recall that I told you the thread has to be thrown twice, doubling the thickness, and being twisted in the opposite direction the second time.'

'I remember,' she said. 'Very well – we need a new throwing machine. What else do we have to spend all this money on?'

'The crimping machine. The brass cylinder will cost in the region of six or seven hundred pounds, I believe, including the engraving, and the rest of the machine will probably be more than a thousand pounds.'

'Say two thousand in all. That makes four thousand.'

'We'll need dyeing vats, steam baths, degumming boilers. I'd say a thousand pounds for those. And since, as I told Mr Harcourt, it will be six months to a year before we can produce a saleable crape, I added another thousand pounds to cover wages during that period, and a little over for unforeseen expenses.' Richard spoke with confidence, sure that his figures made sense. 'That's not really all, Mrs Harcourt. Money is needed to repair machinery so that the quality of existing products can be improved. That seems to me essential.'

She looked at him with amusement. 'You sound as though you own the mill, Goodwin.'

'I meant no impertinence, ma'am.'

'No, I am sure you did not,' she said slowly. 'But I begin to see why you were so insistent that you should be regarded as a manager and consulted at every stage.'

The warmth of her smile sent Richard's thoughts spinning away from crape and machines and money. Their minds seemed to be so much in tune. He wished they could have been talking of more personal matters than machines and money.

It was as though she sensed what was in his mind, for the smile vanished, and her voice became almost harsh. 'Mr

Harcourt is travelling to London the day after tomorrow to discuss our financial position with our bankers. It may be possible to raise additional capital, and if he succeeds in that, we must start as soon as possible to assemble all the machinery for crape-making. For that reason, I am going to suggest to him that he should take you with him.'

'To London?'

'If I understand you correctly, the brass crimping roller will take longer than anything else to produce. The first priority, once Mr Harcourt has secured the necessary finance – and I am confident he will, otherwise I would not think of sending you with him – the first priority will be to find a capable engraver. That will be your job. I am sure there are many first-class craftsmen in London.'

'I . . . I don't know any engravers, Mrs Harcourt.'

She gave a little laugh. 'Ah, Goodwin, you are human at last. For the first time I see you unsure of yourself, at a loss. Do not worry. My husband has many friends in the London silk trade, one or other of whom will be able to direct you to suitable persons, I am sure. All you have to do is to find the best possible man for the work. Never be content with less than the best, Goodwin, whatever the cost.'

She stood up, and he rose too. Her gaze travelled over him. 'Sit down,' she said. 'I haven't finished yet. Naturally, Mr Harcourt will pay your expenses – the train fare, your lodgings. Are those the best clothes you have?'

'Yes.' He was suddenly conscious of his shabbiness.

She limped over to a bureau and unlocked it. 'They won't do. Take yourself to Franton tomorrow and buy something more suitable.' She came slowly back to him, holding out a five-pound note.

He hesitated. 'I could get clothes for less than that.'

'No doubt, but not the best. You are not buying for yourself – you are buying for Harcourt's. We may be in financial difficulties, but we must never give the appearance of penury. Take it.' When he still hesitated, she added impatiently, 'It is not a gift. It will be deducted from your wages.'

She made him feel foolish, and he said, 'Forgive me for not measuring up to your standards, Mrs Harcourt. I am only a common working man, you know.'

She looked at him haughtily. 'I do not appreciate that kind of remark, Goodwin. Please do not behave in a way which will make me change my opinion of you.'

'I'm sorry,' he mumbled.

She ignored the apology, and continued, 'Be here at seven thirty sharp on Wednesday morning. In the meantime, apart from the purchase of clothes, you may occupy yourself in preparing specifications of all the various machines and equipment which will be needed.'

'What if Mr Harcourt cannot raise the capital, ma'am?'

'Then you will be paid for your time and trouble, and we may be able to offer you employment in some other capacity.' Her green eyes gazed stonily at him for a moment. 'I have other matters to attend to now.'

She was still angry with him, and he tried to apologise. 'I have offended you, Mrs Harcourt. I didn't mean –'

Leaning on her stick, she went back to the chaise-longue. 'That will do, Goodwin. You may go.'

Richard left the room, annoyed with himself. Sarcasm, his mother always said, was the lowest form of wit, and by indulging in it he had damaged himself. Mrs Harcourt was right to be angry. She was right in all that she had said.

On the Wednesday morning, he walked once more up the long drive to The Grange, conscious of the transformation in his appearance that the new clothes had wrought. The trap was already waiting outside the big front door, and the driver tipped his hat to him. Richard returned the greeting coolly, smiling inwardly. No servant had ever shown him that much respect before.

As he went to the front door, it opened and Tom and Sarah Harcourt came out. Richard raised his top hat.

Tom hesitated, and then said, 'Oh, Goodwin. I didn't recognise you in your new togs.'

Sarah, leaning on her ebony stick, looked him up and

down, this time with approval. 'Excellent,' she said, giving him her warmest smile.

'A real transformation,' Tom continued. 'Makes him look quite the gentleman.' He turned to Richard. 'Put your bag in the trap, and get up with the driver.' He kissed Sarah on the cheek.

Richard put his small carpet bag, containing his shaving gear and his second new shirt, alongside Mr Harcourt's large valise, and climbed up beside the driver. Evidently Tom Harcourt intended to keep him at a distance – an employee, however much of a gentleman he might look, was not to be treated as an equal.

However, when they took the train at Chelmsford, Harcourt told Richard to get into the same compartment, and began to talk quite pleasantly. 'First time you have been on a train, I dare say.'

'Yes, sir.' He could not hide his excitement.

'Not the most comfortable mode of transport,' Tom said, with the blasé air of the habitual traveller, 'but fast and reliable.'

Indeed, the wooden seats were not luxurious, and the breeze which came through the carriage windows brought only smuts and the rather oppressive heat of the day. But Richard cared nothing for any discomfort as he watched the countryside flashing by. The speed seemed incredible to him. 'How fast are we going, Mr Harcourt?'

'Oh, perhaps thirty miles an hour. They are said to be making engines now which will go even faster. God knows where it will all end. Thirty miles an hour seems a very reasonable rate to me – go above that, and accidents will be inevitable. Much better if they did something about the smuts – we shall be filthy by the time we reach London. I trust you have a change of linen with you.'

'Yes, sir.'

'Good. Now, about this engraver fellow we're going to be looking for. What sort of payment shall we have to offer?'

'Prideau's engraver is one of their regular employees,' Richard replied. 'They're constantly having new cylinders engraved – changing the design to produce different patterns – so he's kept busy all the time. I don't know what they pay him, but it must be something like four hundred pounds a year. Maybe more.'

'What? But that's absurd.'

'It's very highly skilled work, sir.'

'But we're simply offering him piece-work, surely?'

'I suppose so. But he'll have to live in Brentfield.'

'Why?'

'The work will have to be supervised daily. We shall have to experiment with it, make alterations as we go along. It would be better to have him in our full employment. If we find the right man, sir, I'd like to suggest we offer him the job of engraving one cylinder, but say that we might want to retain him for other work afterwards. As for his wages, that'll depend partly on whether you can offer him accommodation.'

'Well, I can't. We could find him lodgings, I suppose.'

'And he might have a family, sir. That would affect it too.'

'Oh, God! It gets more and more complicated. I can see him already, Goodwin – a greedy little swine, with at least eight children.' He laughed ruefully.

Richard laughed too, though he was not sure what was amusing. At least Tom's friendly mood was preferable to his earlier attitude.

'Well, what are we going to offer him?' Tom asked.

It was astonishing, Richard thought – his knowledge of making crape had made him an authority on all matters to do with it. He felt an unaccustomed sense of power. 'I'd suggest we work on a rate of three hundred a year. That should mean a maximum of a hundred and fifty pounds.'

'H'm. A lot of money. Well, we'll just have to wait and see.' He paused. 'Oh, another thing, Goodwin: I intend to take Mr Leroy, our principal supplier of raw silk, into my confidence – he is a friend of long standing – but I do not want it generally known that we are entering the crape business. You look surprised.'

'Surely everyone will know before long, sir.'

'Indeed, but the longer we can keep it from Prideau's, the

better. They'll not be best pleased to see a new competitor, and even less so when they learn that one of their former employees has revealed their methods.'

Having finally convinced himself of the justice of the matter, Richard spoke hotly. 'They can hardly expect anything else from someone unfairly dismissed.'

'Well, you're not the first person to betray trade secrets, and you won't be the last, and at least you have more reason than most. Anyway, mum's the word.' He closed his eyes, and was soon dozing.

Richard was left to watch the fields rushing past. No dream that Tom might be having, he thought, could equal the strangeness of his own current experiences.

At last the train drew in at the London terminus. They walked through the great hall, which reeked of oil and coal-smoke, and out on to the forecourt, where Tom hailed a cab, telling the driver to take them to the Bell at Spitalfields.

Richard peered out of the cab windows, eager to see as much as possible of London. It was awe-inspiring. Never had he seen so many tall buildings, such a throng of traffic, nor heard such a continual clatter and babble of sound. Every prospect was filled with bustle, and each street revealed more shops and offices and houses and churches . . . and people. Thousands and thousands of them, men, women and children, well-dressed ladies and gentlemen, beggars and ragamuffins, and every class of person in between. And they were all hurrying somewhere, it seemed to him, as though infected with a desperate need for rapid and continuous movement.

The horse clip-clopped its way through the busy streets, stopping every now and then because of the press of other traffic, while the cabby cursed, and plied his whip. They came to an imposing church, of gleaming white stone. 'Christ Church,' Tom said, and then added, somewhat bafflingly, 'The area's gone down since that was built.'

The street beside the church was lined with terraces of brick houses, their plain façades broken only by doorways embellished with pillars and little canopies. The houses were not very large, and Richard was surprised when Tom pointed to one of them and said, 'That's where Mr Leroy lives. We'll be coming back there later.'

The cab trundled on a short way, and stopped outside a tall, grimy building proclaiming itself to be the Bell Inn. Tom paid the cabby, and then strode inside, leaving Richard to carry their luggage.

'Back again, Mr 'Arcourt?' the landlady beamed. 'Well, I never! Wasn't expecting you so soon. Still, you're lucky. Your usual room's free – well, not *free*, if you understand me – you still 'as to pay for it . . .' She laughed, her plump cheeks wobbling. '. . . but it ain't got no one in it. And was you wanting another room for this gent?'

'An employee of mine, Mrs Bedford.'

'Ah.' Mrs Bedford looked at Richard briefly. 'Well, 'e can go up top, then.' Slowly, she led the way up the stairs, opening a door on the first landing. 'There you are, Mr 'Arcourt. Just as usual.'

'Bring my valise in, Goodwin,' Tom said.

The room was large and quite well furnished, and the four-poster bed gave an air of luxury, despite the bare floorboards. Richard was fascinated, never having seen so well-appointed a bedroom before.

'Don't stand gawping, man. Mrs Bedford's waiting to show you your room. I'm going to wash away some of the grime of that journey, and I'll see you downstairs in a quarter of an hour.'

Wheezing and puffing, Mrs Bedford led the way up the stairs – two more flights, three, until he realised that they must be right under the roof. The room was small, and its ceiling sloped so that only at one side was it possible to stand upright. A narrow truckle bed stood along the outside wall. There was no other furniture, and Richard looked in vain for a jug and basin such as had been provided in Tom's room.

'Pump in the yard,' Mrs Bedford said, reading his thoughts. 'Wash there, if you've a mind.' She went, shutting the door behind her.

Richard looked round his small domain. At least he had a

small window set in the sloping ceiling over the bed. He managed to open it and to poke his head out. The view stunned him. Everywhere there were houses and houses and houses. Above them, he could just see the top of a great dome surmounted by a cross – that must be St Paul's – he had seen a drawing of it in one of his father's books. He looked down, craning to see the street below. There were people walking, and horse-drawn drays and the occasional carriage or cab, all looking very strange when seen from above, and he could hear the drivers shouting, the iron-shod wheels clattering over the cobblestones, and the general hubbub of the city. He could have stayed there for hours, watching and listening.

As he and Tom Harcourt walked to Mr Leroy's house, Tom was still in an expansive, friendly mood. 'Doesn't look a very prosperous area, but if you could see inside some of these houses, you'd find they're very well appointed. Beautiful panelling, especially in the older houses. They were mostly built by the Huguenots, and many of them have big attics where the weaving used to be done – well, still is in some of them – and their back gardens are often full of mulberry trees.'

'Mulberry trees?'

'Surely you know that silkworms feed on mulberry leaves?' They had reached the door of Mr Leroy's house.

'Yes, sir. I was just surprised, because I didn't think anyone kept silkworms in England.'

'They don't – at least not to any extent. The climate's not really suitable. Our raw silk comes from France or Italy. But some still breed a few worms, just to keep up the tradition. Mr Leroy does, for one.'

'I'd like to see them.'

When they entered Mr Leroy's house, Richard thought that it seemed larger than its exterior would have suggested. They were led through to an elegantly furnished drawing-room, its walls panelled in dark oak. Through the windows, the garden could be seen. Mrs Leroy, her ample form encased in a black silk dress, plentifully flounced with crape, greeted Tom Harcourt warmly, expressing her sympathy at his father's death.

Tom thanked her. 'I see that you too are in mourning.'

'When is one ever out of it, Mr Harcourt? We heard but yesterday that a distant cousin had passed away, and though we hardly knew him, of course one shows proper respect. Prideau's must be making a fortune.'

Tom smiled. 'Indeed, they must. It is on that subject, or something near to it, that I wished to speak to Mr Leroy.'

'You will find him at his office.'

'I had hoped to see him in private, if that is possible, without it becoming known that I had visited him on business. I called on the off-chance that he might be at home.'

'He will be back this evening.' Mrs Leroy looked at Richard. 'I am neglecting my duties, Mr Harcourt, and so are you. You have not introduced me to your companion.'

'Forgive me. This is Goodwin – Mr Goodwin. He expects to be joining us, to work in a position of some seniority at Harcourt's Mill.'

'I see.' Although as an afterthought Tom had added the title to the surname, Mrs Leroy was in no doubt as to Richard's social standing, and the nod that she gave in response to his bow was quite formal. She turned back to Tom. 'I vow I was quite out of sorts with you, sir, since you did not come to visit us here during your last visit to London. You shall not escape me this time. I give a small dinner party tonight, and I insist that you join us. You would no doubt find occasion then to have a private word with Mr Leroy.'

Tom hesitated. 'I am much obliged, ma'am, but it is essential that Goodwin should be with me for my discussions with your husband. Perhaps we might call to see him at some convenient time tomorrow.'

'I will pass that message to him. However, there is no reason why you, Mr Harcourt, should not also come to dinner tonight.'

'I beg your forgiveness, dear lady. Your table is surely already arranged.'

'I can find a partner for you soon enough. There is never any shortage of unattached ladies, alas.'

'I risk your wrath, but it is quite impossible. I should be

most grateful if you would consent to postpone the invitation until my next visit to London.'

There was a note of finality in his voice, and Mrs Leroy accepted defeat. 'Very well, but I regard that as a promise. Break it at your peril.' She glanced at Richard. 'You are interested in our little garden, Mr Goodwin?'

Richard had been gazing at the large mulberry tree which almost filled the garden at the rear of the house. He fancied he could see both silkworms and cocoons on the tree. 'I have not seen silkworms before, ma'am. I was wondering whether I might be allowed to examine them at closer quarters, if you would be so kind.'

'Perhaps we could spend a moment or two in the garden,' Tom suggested, 'before we take our leave.'

'With pleasure, Mr Harcourt. The weather is very clement.'

Richard had heard about silkworms since he was a small child, but somehow had always thought of them as being worm-like in appearance, whereas in fact they resembled caterpillars, greyish-white, and about three inches long. Some were crawling on the tree, munching the leaves, while others had already reached the next stage in their life-cycle, and their cocoons, like small eggs, hung by thick threads from the twigs.

'May I touch one of them, ma'am?' Richard asked. Carefully, when she agreed, he felt one of the cocoons. It was firm, almost brittle to his fingers, with just a suspicion of stickiness about it. 'Do you leave them to hatch, ma'am?'

'Those, yes,' Mrs Leroy replied. 'The moths will provide the next generation of silkworms. But some have already been gathered for reeling.'

'And where is that done, ma'am?'

'Why, here in this house. It is my elder daughter's favourite occupation, I do declare.'

'And she is most skilled at it,' Tom told him. Turning to Mrs Leroy, he said, 'Miss Leroy told me once she was hoping to gather enough silk to have a shawl woven from it. Has she yet achieved that goal?'

Mrs Leroy laughed. 'Heavens, no, sir! It will be years before she does. Still, she works away at it, and gradually her stock of raw silk is increasing.'

Emboldened both by his interest and Mrs Leroy's greater friendliness since they came out into the garden, Richard said, 'I wish I could witness the reeling. I have worked with silk all my life, but have never seen it done.'

Mrs Leroy considered carefully before she spoke. He could hardly be treated as an equal, and indeed it was somewhat strange of Tom Harcourt to have brought him to the house at all, even if he did need him when he talked to Mr Leroy. But he was a very personable young man, and seemed to know his place. And dear Isabelle so enjoyed displaying her skills, and had little other occasion to impress. 'My daughter is away from home this morning,' she said. 'However, if you were to visit us at some other time, I am sure that she would be agreeable.'

'If Miss Leroy condescends to show you her work, you will indeed be privileged,' Tom said. 'I have a number of calls to make tomorrow morning which will not require your presence, and that might be the right opportunity, if it should be convenient to Miss Leroy.'

'I should be most grateful, ma'am,' Richard said, 'to her, and to you.'

Mrs Leroy smiled. What a polite young man! He might come from a lower social stratum, but, really, he was quite engaging. 'I shall speak to her myself,' she said, 'and a message can be sent to your lodgings. I would think ten o'clock a suitable time.'

'And now we must trespass on you no longer,' Tom said. 'Thank you for your kindness in seeing me.'

'A pleasure, Mr Harcourt. And I will not forget your desire to see Mr Leroy. Dear me, that will mean another message. We shall be wearing a groove in the road between here and the Bell.' Chuckling, she led the way back into the house and rang for the maid to show them out.

As they were walking back, Tom Harcourt looked at Richard quizzically. 'You're a dark horse, aren't you, Goodwin?'

'What do you mean, sir?'

'You had Mrs Leroy wrapped around your little finger. Mind you, I prefer 'em a bit younger myself, but I reckon you could put horns on Mr Leroy any time you wanted to. Eh? What d'you say to that, you young dog?' He nudged Richard, and laughed.

Richard was at a loss. He certainly had not been conscious of having the effect on Mrs Leroy that Tom described. He tried to join in the laugh. 'I think you exaggerate, sir.'

The remark seemed to irritate Tom Harcourt, and the smile faded from his face. They walked the rest of the way in silence, with Richard asking himself why his employer had suddenly taken offence – if indeed he had. It was already early evening, and he wondered how they would fill the rest of the time before going to bed.

When they arrived at the Bell, Tom turned to him and said, 'I shall not require your company this evening, Goodwin. My advice to you is to have a meal and then retire. London can be a dangerous place for country bumpkins. Attend me here in the morning at half past eight.' He disappeared into his room.

Richard decided that after he had eaten, country bumpkin or not, it was too good an opportunity to miss, and he would go out and explore a little of the great city. In the meantime, he was ravenously hungry, and ordered the largest helpings of Mrs Bedford's steak and kidney pie, and a pint of porter. It was ambrosial. He told Mrs Bedford so, and that large lady giggled like a young girl, and said he was a handsome lad and she wished she were thirty years younger. Richard was amazed. Mrs Leroy, if Tom was to be believed, and now Mrs Bedford – two elderly ladies conquered in the space of an hour or so!

Feeling well fed and more than a little cock-a-hoop, he began his exploration. His mother and Frances would certainly expect him to visit St Paul's, and he set out down Bishopsgate and along Cornhill, past the Bank of England, so to Poultry and Cheapside. He entered the cathedral, gazing around in wonder, and his feelings of self-satisfaction suddenly disappeared. The London streets had been almost awe-inspiring, but this building, the largest he had ever been in, made him feel small and insignificant, and out of place. No wonder Tom Harcourt had talked of country bumpkins! No doubt, too, the friendliness that Mrs Leroy and Mrs Bedford had shown was due only to the fact that he was so obviously a simple countryman, amusing in his naivety.

He squared his shoulders. They could laugh at him if they wanted. He would show them one day, and he would make a start by refusing to be overawed by London. He set off again, walking along Fleet Street and the Strand, and then up Drury Lane, keeping an eye open for pickpockets. However much he tried to adopt a blasé attitude, he was constantly astonished by what he saw – the crowds of people, the shops still open and the streets filled with traffic though it was late at night. Franton had seemed a metropolis after Brentfield, but it was a mere village compared to this, and in the evenings was almost like a place of the dead, whereas here all was vibrant life.

Making his way back to the Bell, he felt a slight disappointment. Everything had been interesting, fascinating, but no adventure had befallen him. He had been accosted by a drab or two, he had lost his way and had barely been able to understand the directions he was given, because of the strange accents of those who spoke to him – but those were not adventures. He chided himself for behaving like a child. Surely it was enough just to be in London.

He passed the Leroys' house again, ablaze with lights, and wondered how the dinner party was going, and what Miss Leroy was like, and whether she, too, would laugh at him.

As he climbed the stairs to the top of the inn, he passed Tom Harcourt's room. Light seeped through the cracks in the ill-fitting door, and he heard laughter and a woman's voice. So that was why he had refused Mrs Leroy's invitation. He hurried past. It was no business of his. But how, he asked himself, could a man not be content with a wife like Sarah Harcourt?

CHAPTER SEVEN

Richard dreamed he was in St Paul's. The nave was bustling with people, like one of the busy streets he had walked. Ahead of him he could see Sarah Harcourt, and he was trying to reach her, but the distance between them never narrowed. Suddenly the crowd had vanished, and only Tom Harcourt stood between him and Sarah, and Richard drew back his fist, unmindful of the whip that Tom was brandishing. It cracked, a hollow sound which echoed sharply in the great cathedral.

'Eight o'clock, dearie.' Mrs Bedford's voice came from outside his bedroom door. 'I brung you some 'ot water.'

Eight o'clock! He had never slept so late in his life before. When he opened the door, Mrs Bedford had gone, but a small can of lukewarm water stood in a cracked china bowl on the landing. He took it in, washed and dressed, and made his way downstairs.

As Mrs Bedford served his breakfast – a great hunk of cold meat pie and a tankard of ale – she said, 'I don't usually let them as is on the top floor 'ave 'ot water, y'know. Think yerself lucky.'

'I do, Mrs Bedford,' Richard said.

'Know why I give it you?' She chuckled. 'Yer pretty blue eyes, lovey, and yer 'andsome face. I always was an easy touch for a good-lookin' feller.' She winked. 'Besides, Mr 'Arcourt won't notice a couple o' pence extra on the bill.' She ruffled his hair, laughed wheezily, and disappeared.

A short while later, Tom Harcourt came downstairs, pale and yawning. He would eat nothing, but called for brandy, which he swallowed in one gulp. 'God, my head!' he groaned. He bent over the table, resting his head on his folded arms. After a few minutes, he sat up again, his eyes clearer. 'Good old brandy,' he said. 'Give it time to work, and it'll do the trick. Now I'm off to the banker's. I've had a note saying Miss Leroy is expecting you at ten o'clock, and that Mr Leroy will see both of us at his house at half past eleven. So you stay there until I come. Mind you behave yourself. You're being given a great privilege, so don't abuse Miss Leroy's kindness.'

'I think I know my manners, sir.'

Tom flushed. 'Maybe you do. What you don't know is that Miss Leroy tires very easily. All I am saying is, remember her health is not of the strongest, and behave accordingly.'

At each hour through the day and night clocks chimed from church towers and steeples all over the city, and even the noise of the busy streets could not entirely drown their sound. As the last stroke of ten died away, Richard knocked at the door of the Leroys' house.

The maidservant led him upstairs to a small room on the first floor and at the back of the house. Inevitably, the two young women in the room, one sitting, and the other standing behind her, both wore black. Richard bowed.

'Good morning, Mr Goodwin,' said the girl who was seated. 'I am Miss Leroy. May I introduce my sister, Miss Annette Leroy? I understand that you wish to see the reeling of raw silk from cocoons.'

'Indeed I do, Miss Leroy,' Richard said, bowing again.

Miss Leroy had her mother's dark hair and eyes, but her features were so irregular as to appear almost deformed. She seemed quite small, but it was difficult to tell because of the large number of shawls in which she was swathed, despite the fact that the room was hot. Although it was a warm June day, a fire was burning in the grate. A kettle simmered on the hob.

'I fear you may find it close in this room, Mr Goodwin,' Miss Annette said. She looked positively handsome beside her older sister. 'Miss Leroy suffers much from the cold. Indeed, she is never warm.'

'I am sure I shall feel no discomfort,' Richard said.

Miss Leroy's thin hands grasped the arms of her chair. 'Help me up, Annie, dear.' Miss Annette half lifted her out of the chair, and Richard realised then that Miss Leroy was a cripple. Leaning on a stick, and supported by her sister, she made her painful way to a table near the window. 'Come over here, Mr Goodwin,' she said in her soft voice, little more than a whisper.

On the table was a tray bearing several silkworm cocoons, a jug, two large china bowls and some twigs, the ends of which had been frayed.

'As you no doubt know, Mr Goodwin,' Miss Leroy said, 'when the silkworm goes into the pupa stage it spins a cocoon of silk, moving its head in a figure of eight pattern to cover itself completely. To remove the silk we have first to heat the cocoons, so that the caterpillar inside is killed. That has already been done with these.' She spoke quickly, nervously, and so quietly that Richard had to strain to hear her words. 'Pour a little of the cold water into that basin, Annie, and fetch the hot.' Miss Annette did as she was told, slowly adding steaming water from the kettle until Miss Leroy told her to stop. 'First we have to remove the floss,' she explained, 'the loose fibres around the outside of the cocoon. Then we shall be able to find the main filament. Put eight of them in the water, Annie.'

The cocoons bobbed on the surface of the water. Miss Leroy began to poke at them with one of the twigs. After a short while, small threads began to come away on the frayed end. While she was doing this, Miss Annette was pouring water into the other basin.

'Make sure the temperature is just right, dear,' Miss Leroy said. She turned to Richard. 'When I have found the main filaments, we shall transfer the cocoons to the other basin and I can then begin reeling. The temperature of the water in that basin is critical. If it is too cold, it will not release the natural gums, but if it is too hot, the cocoons absorb the water, sink to the bottom, and are quite useless.'

When Annette Leroy had poured the water into the other bowl, and tested the temperature, she picked up a second twig and joined her sister in scratching at the surface of the cocoons as they bobbed on the water.

'Ah,' said Miss Leroy. 'There. Do you see, Mr Goodwin? I have loosened the strand on that one.'

Richard leaned over the bowl. The thread was barely visible, a tiny filament floating on the water beside the cocoon. Catching it with the twig, Miss Leroy lifted it, and took it in the deft fingers of her left hand. 'Now,' she said, 'we need another three. Some people reel only two or three threads at a time, and some use as many as five, but I prefer to work with four.'

'But you have eight cocoons in the water.'

'Yes. You will see what happens.' She continued working at the cocoons until in her left hand she held the ends of four filaments of silk. She was totally absorbed in the task, and when she next spoke, her voice seemed stronger and more self-confident. 'Now for my needle,' she said. 'That's what I call it, Mr Goodwin.' She picked up a piece of glass, shaped so that one end formed a handle, while the other had been flattened, and had in its centre a minuscule hole. 'This is the most difficult part. I have to thread these four strands through my needle. The eye is very small – it has to be – so it is far from simple to get them all through at the same time.'

'What is the purpose of the needle, Miss Leroy?'

'It removes much of the water on the threads, and since some of the natural gum is left on each strand, it makes them stick together as they pass through the hole, and they emerge as though they were one thicker thread – still very fine, but stout enough later to be thrown and woven.'

By this time, she had succeeded in threading the filaments through the glass needle, and shortly afterwards her sister completed a similar operation with the other four cocoons. Miss Leroy now placed the two needles in a stand which held them in an upright position, and took the two strands and twisted them around each other several times. She then attached the two ends separately to two frames on a hand winder, first passing them through the notches of small metal arms. Interlocking cogs would make these guiders travel from side to side as she slowly turned the handle, so that the silk thread would move backwards and forwards across the frames.

'We twist the threads around each other because that helps

to smooth them,' she explained, 'and more moisture is removed as they twist against each other and then pass through these notches on the guiders. The thread is spread out on the winding frames, which gives it time to dry, but I must wind slowly to make sure it does.'

Meanwhile, Miss Annette had transferred the cocoons to the second basin, in which the water was much cooler. With her right hand, Miss Leroy now began slowly to turn the handle of the machine, while the twig in her left hand skilfully kept the cocoons from entangling as they jiggled in the water.

Richard was fascinated. 'Is it done like this in France and Italy?'

'Indeed it is, Mr Goodwin. And in China and Japan too. Of course, they have many, many girls working at it, because you need thousands of cocoons to make even a pound of raw silk.'

'And they use twigs like that to unravel the threads?'

She laughed. 'No doubt it seems very primitive, but I assure you that it is the only way it can be done. Naturally, the girls who do this for their living are much more skilled than I.'

'I doubt that, Miss Leroy,' Richard said. 'No fingers could be more nimble than yours. It really is a quite extraordinary process.'

'What always seems to me even more extraordinary, Mr Goodwin, is how anyone could have thought of doing it in the first place. They say that silk was first made in China two and a half thousand years before Christ, and that the Empress Si Ling encouraged its manufacture, and herself invented the loom. But who first thought of unravelling the silk from the cocoons like this?'

'Don't forget the legend about that,' Miss Annette said. 'You remember, Isabelle – the story of the Chinese princess sitting in the garden under a mulberry tree, and a cocoon fell off the tree into her tea-cup, and when she tried to get it out, it began to unravel.'

Miss Leroy gave a little tinkling laugh. 'I suppose it could be true, but it strikes me as somewhat far-fetched,' she said. 'It reminds me of Charles Lamb's account of how the Chinese equally accidentally discovered roast pork.'

The winding was a long, painstaking process. Every now and then, Miss Leroy tested the temperature of the water in the bowl, and called for her sister to add more from the kettle. 'When they do this in a reeling factory, the water is kept constantly heated,' she explained, 'but my methods have to be a little more primitive.'

Richard watched in fascination as the bobbins slowly filled with the gossamer threads. At first they had been barely visible, but now he could see them taking on the matt, slightly greyish hue of raw silk.

'My hand is growing tired,' Miss Leroy said after a while. 'Perhaps you would care to turn the handle, Mr Goodwin. Be careful to do so slowly and evenly.'

He took great pains, marvelling at the strength of the tiny filaments, and at the extraordinary ability of the silkworm to enshroud itself in a continuous thread of such length. 'How long does the silkworm take to spin its cocoon?' he asked.

'Two or three days, without stopping,' Miss Annette replied.

'The outside of the cocoon becomes quite hard, does it not? How does the moth escape?'

'I am not sure, Mr Goodwin, but I have heard that it moistens the end of the cocoon in some way, softening the natural gum, so that it can push itself out.'

Richard turned back to the older sister. 'You are right, Miss Leroy – it is difficult to understand how men made many of their early discoveries, but the works of Nature are even more miraculous.'

She smiled. 'Indeed, sir. And as I work on my silk, it is my pleasure to give thanks to God for His wonders.'

Before the winding was finished, the maid returned to announce that Mr Harcourt had arrived, and that he and Mr Leroy required Mr Goodwin to join them.

Richard stood up, thanked his mentors most warmly for so instructive and entertaining a morning, and then followed the maid to a study, where Tom Harcourt was facing a desk behind which sat Mr Leroy. His chair was a large one, its back extending several inches above its occupant's head, but its width was much needed, for Mr Leroy was a round little man, even fatter than his wife. His face too was round, and his little eyes twinkled out from folds of flesh.

'This is the fellow of whom I spoke,' said Tom. 'Richard Goodwin.'

Mr Leroy waved at a chair. 'Sit down, Goodwin.' He turned back to Tom. 'Now, Harcourt, my dear chap, what is all this mystery?'

'The fact is, Leroy, I have decided to go into the crape business.'

Richard wondered whether Tom really meant it. Had he succeeded at the bank?

Leroy whistled. 'Crape! That's a bit of a departure, isn't it? I didn't know you were equipped for that.'

'We're not – yet.'

'But you know the process? It is a closely guarded secret.'

'That's where Goodwin comes in,' Tom said. He went on to explain something of the circumstances of the decision to make crape, and of how Richard had come to be employed by Harcourt's.

Leroy listened carefully, and when Tom paused, he said, 'And how can I help you? If you are looking for capital, I fear –'

'No, no. I am happy to say that I have had a most satisfactory consultation with my bankers. The capital we need will be available.'

Richard was tempted to give a shout of delight, but managed to restrain himself.

'No,' Tom continued. 'What we want is an engraver.'

'An engraver? What for?'

Tom turned to Richard. 'Perhaps you had better explain, Goodwin. You may speak freely.'

Richard contented himself with describing the process of passing the woven cloth through the crimping rollers. Whatever Tom might say, it was wiser to reveal as little as possible.

When he had finished, Mr Leroy looked at Tom. 'I don't know what you expect me to tell you, Harcourt.'

'I thought you might know someone who has used an engraver for that sort of work.'

'No. That would be a crape manufacturer, and the only one of those I know is Prideau. From what you say, you wouldn't get much help there. I can only suggest you should go to an ordinary engraving house – there are plenty in London. You might try Billington and Mason's in Leadenhall Street. Ask for Mr Billington. Tell him I sent you.'

Tom thanked him, and he and Richard left. Once they were outside the house, Richard asked, 'It's all right then, sir? The money?'

'Money?'

'From the bank, sir.'

'Oh, that. Yes, I think so. You can consider yourself engaged to run our crape department, if that's what you mean. Now, where's Leadenhall Street?'

He was clearly disinclined to talk further about his discussions with his bankers, and Richard held his peace, though he would have liked to throw his hat in the air, and dance down the street.

A long and wearisome quest followed. Mr Billington was at first greatly interested, but once it had been made plain that Tom and Richard were looking for a craftsman who would be able to spend six months or more in Brentfield, he shook his head. 'Can't be done, sir. I don't know where you will find a skilled man willing to do that.' However, he gave them other addresses to try.

Tom and Richard traipsed back and forth across the city. After half a dozen fruitless calls, Tom said, 'We shall just have to abandon the idea of employing a man in Brentfield. Given clear instructions, a firm like Billington and Mason would surely be able to do what is needed.'

'Sir, I have seen the engraver at work at Prideau's,' Richard said. 'It is a matter of constant experiment and adjustment, for which we need all the machinery, and samples of silk. It cannot be done satisfactorily away from the mill.'

'Well, we will try this last place. What's the man's name?'

'Mr Gale, sir.'

'Right. After that, if we draw a blank, we will return to Spitalfields. I am starving.'

Mr Gale was reluctant to spare them any of his precious time, and interrupted Tom before he had finished his explanations, speaking in one long hurried flow of words. 'Yes, I know the very man, the best engraver in the business, but a bit of a queer cuss, and very independent, which I know because I've offered him permanent employment more than once, but he won't take it, and says he only does work he enjoys, and, I ask you, what sort of attitude is that? Name of Alfred Bunn, and he lives at number six Earlham Street off the Seven Dials, and I wouldn't go there at night, if I were you.'

They were only a short distance from the notorious Seven Dials, the slums in which every house was a thieves' kitchen or a brothel or both, where the dregs of London's humanity lived their unhappy, crime-filled lives. Tom was quite apprehensive about entering the area, but it seemed foolish to abandon this last chance, and at least it was still broad daylight, and there were two of them.

The district was more squalid than anywhere else that Richard had ever seen. The streets were full of ordure, every building looked filthy, and an all-pervading stench made him want to retch. Bedraggled whores accosted them, villainous-looking men eyed them speculatively, and they were surrounded by a host of barefoot children, dressed in tattered rags, begging for a penny, a ha'penny, a farthing. Raucous sounds echoed off the shabby walls of the tumbledown houses – the shouts of children, the pieman calling his wares, curses, screams, drunken songs issuing from the crowded gin-shop. Pushing their way through the teeming streets, jostled and jeered at for their fine clothes, Tom and Richard fought their way through to number six Earlham Street.

At the door, an old crone was sitting, barring the way.

'Mr Bunn – Alfred Bunn?' Tom asked.

The woman looked at him blearily, and pointed upwards. She did not move, but as they edged their way past her, a skinny arm shot out, and her dirt-encrusted hand fastened around Tom's ankle in a vice-like grip. 'Gi's a copper.' The smell that came from her was indescribably foul.

'Give her a penny,' Tom whispered to Richard, holding his handkerchief to his face, his other hand in his pocket. 'If I let her see my purse, she'll have the lot.'

Richard found a penny, and gave it to the woman, who heaved herself to her feet and hurried off to the gin-shop.

Richard and Tom mounted the rickety stairs. The stench of urine and excrement almost hid the odour of decay from the mildewed walls. As they reached the first landing, a door opened, revealing a young woman. Her tangled hair fell over the shoulders of the filthy gown she wore. She grinned at them, showing a few stumps of rotting teeth, and pulled the top of her dress open to reveal her sagging breasts. She beckoned. 'In 'ere, gents, in 'ere!' She licked her lips slowly, lasciviously.

'We seek Alfred Bunn,' Tom said.

The whore's smile faded. 'Top floor, first door,' she said. 'Spare a copper for a poor gel, guv'nor.'

Richard put his hand in his pocket once more. As he drew it out, the girl snatched at the coins, and before he could stop her was running down the stairs, her ragged gown streaming out behind her. He looked after her in dismay. 'That was fivepence,' he said.

'We'll be lucky if that's all we lose,' Tom muttered. 'All right, I'll make it up to you, Goodwin. God, what a fool I was to come here! This Bunn had better be worth it.'

They climbed to the top of the house and knocked at the door.

'Go away!'

Tom knocked again. 'Alfred Bunn? Open up.'

'Who is it?'

'My name is Harcourt. I come to offer you employment.'

They heard footsteps crossing the room, and then the sound of bolts being drawn back. The door opened a little, and a long thin face peered around it. 'Sorry. Thought you were one of those whores downstairs.'

Absurdly, Richard had expected that a man with such a name would be short, fat and roly-poly, rather like Mr Leroy.

But Alfred Bunn was very tall and so thin that he looked almost as though he had been stretched on the rack and had shrunk in width as his height was extended. His lank black hair framed an angular face, dominated by a thin curving nose. He was unshaven, and the dark stubble against his sallow skin gave him a faintly sinister air.

'Come in, come in.'

The room was lit by a grubby skylight. There was a chair and, against the back wall, a low bed. On one corner of the large table was a plate with a half-eaten meat pie, a hunk of bread, and a misshapen tankard, while the rest was filled with engraving tools and a sword.

'We seek an engraver,' Tom Harcourt said. 'Mr Gale gave us your name. He said that you are highly skilled.'

'Good of him.' Alfred Bunn grinned. 'Your name is Harcourt, you said?'

'Yes.' Tom looked around the shabby room. 'Why should a highly skilled craftsman live in a slum like this?'

The engraver wrapped his long arms across his thin chest in an unconsciously self-protective gesture, one hand resting on the opposite shoulder, while the other was around his waist. 'You'll pardon me, sir, but where I live's my own business. As for being highly skilled, you can make your own judgment.' His arm snaked out briefly to point to the sword on the table.

Tom and Richard went over to look at it. It seemed impossible that such costly beauty could be found in the midst of this noisome slum. The sword, of tempered steel, gleamed in the light from the skylight. The cross piece and the hilt were simply shaped, but the blade itself had been exquisitely chased with a design of great complexity, each groove perfectly shaped, each curving line having its own symmetry. One small patch of the blade was still bare, and it was obviously there that the engraver had been working.

'Looks worth a pretty penny,' Tom said.

'That's why I keep my door bolted. Take a seat, sir.' He offered Tom the chair by the table, then turned to Richard and said, 'The bed's the only other place.' When Richard made no move, he shrugged his gaunt shoulders and himself sat on the bed, crossing his legs and again folding his arms about his torso. He seemed to be all elbows and knees. He fixed his dark eyes on Harcourt and waited.

'I am a silk manufacturer. I have work which will demand all your skill. It will be well paid. Are you willing to undertake it?'

'Depends what it is, sir.'

'Yes, Mr Gale warned me of your high-handed ways. It is no use taking that attitude with me, my man.'

'Begging your pardon, sir, and meaning no offence, I am not your man. I live where I choose, and I do what work I choose, and if you'll excuse me I'll get on with it now.'

Angrily, Tom rose, ready to walk out and leave Alfred Bunn to his own devices, but then seemed to change his mind, and resumed his seat as Richard said quickly, 'Have you ever worked in brass?'

Bunn turned his eyes on him appraisingly. He nodded.

'We require a brass cylinder to be engraved.'

'For what purpose?'

Richard explained briefly, and a spark of interest kindled in Bunn's eyes. 'How thick is the brass of the cylinder?'

'A good half inch.'

'And what sort of pattern is it?'

'There are lines, about a sixteenth of an inch wide, quite close together, the gap between them hollowed out to a depth of an eighth of an inch or thereabouts. The lines have to be quite distinctly defined, but their edges must not be sharp enough to cut the threads.'

'I do not know your name, sir.'

'Goodwin.'

Bunn unfolded himself and went to the table, rummaging around until he found a lead pencil and a scrap of dirty paper, which he held out towards Richard. 'Draw me the pattern, Mr Goodwin.'

Richard drew a few lines about an eighth of an inch apart, mostly parallel to each other, but some curving slightly so that they joined. At brief and irregular intervals a cross line linked two of the others.

Bunn watched carefully. 'How big is the cylinder?'

'Two feet long, and eight inches in diameter.'

'And it has to be engraved all over like this?'

'Yes, and the pattern has to be continuous, so that as the cylinder turns there is no visible join.'

Bunn whistled. 'That's a big job.' He sat down on the bed again, and twisted himself into a new contortion. 'What's the pay?'

'The work might take anything from three to six months,' Tom Harcourt said, and repeated what Richard had told him of the need for constant experiment as the engraving progressed, stressing the high degree of skill needed. 'I am therefore prepared to pay at the rate of fifteen pounds per month for up to six months. If a longer period should be necessary, and providing that I was satisfied with your work, you could continue at the rate of three pounds ten shillings a week.'

Richard looked at his employer in dismay. He liked Alfred Bunn, and felt instinctively that he was the sort of man they had been seeking. But with Tom in so cheese-paring a mood, the engraver might well turn them down.

Bunn gave a lopsided smile. 'I've never had a job like that before. I've a mind to take it. But not at that rate. I know what I'm worth, Mr Harcourt. The price is twenty-five, and seven pounds for extra weeks.'

'Too much.'

'It's a fair price for the best man in London.'

'You have a good opinion of yourself, Bunn.'

The engraver gestured towards the sword. 'There's my work.'

Tom sighed. 'I'll go to twenty pounds a month. On a trial basis, of course.'

'All right,' Bunn said. 'Who's going to be on trial? You or me?'

Tom pretended not to have heard. 'When can you start?'

'I have another two weeks of work here.'

'That will suit us. The cylinder has yet to be ordered and made.'

'And delivered here.'

'Good heavens, no, man!' Tom exploded. 'Was it not clear to you that the work must be done at my mill? Surely I explained that.'

'And where might your mill be, sir?'

'At Brentfield in Essex. Accommodation can be found for you – lodging with one of my other employees. Somewhat better than this rat-infested hole.' Tom glanced around. There was no sign that Bunn shared his room with anyone else, but one could never be sure how the poor lived. 'Have you got a family, Bunn?'

'A family, sir? Not so as you'd notice.'

'No wife or children?'

The sardonic grin returned. 'I think that's my business too, sir. But since you ask, I live alone.' He was silent for a while, thinking. 'Of course, that makes a difference, living away from London,' he said. 'Couldn't do that for less than twenty-five a month.'

Richard could see the angry flush on Tom's face. He stepped over to him and whispered urgently. 'He's the only one we've found, sir, and I think he's more than competent to do the work. It's a fair wage.'

Tom Harcourt succeeded in containing his anger. 'Very well, Bunn. I will agree.'

Alfred Bunn smiled, uncoiled himself and walked over to his table. 'Good. Then I'll get on with my own work, sir, if you don't mind. The sooner it's done, the sooner I'll be able to start for you. Oh, by the way, how do I get to your mill in . . . Brentfield, did you say?'

'You take the train to Chelmsford. From there you can walk.'

'And my train fare, Mr Harcourt?'

Tom laughed. The fellow was impertinent, and yet somehow engaging in his effrontery. The interview had been like a battle between them. Like it or not, Alfred Bunn must be treated in a different fashion from most of his employees. 'Refunded to you when you arrive.'

'Very well, sir. A fortnight from today.' He held out his hand to Tom, who, to his further surprise, found himself shaking it.

Bunn turned to Richard. 'I look forward to working with you, Mr Goodwin.'

As they went down the rickety stairs, Tom Harcourt said, 'I must be mad. What was it Gale said? A queer cuss? That's only the half if it! My father would turn in his grave if he thought I was offering work to such a man, and at such a price, too. I reckon he asked for about double what he's earning now.'

'He wouldn't have come for less, sir. And something tells me he's going to be the right man for us.'

It was as much of an effort to escape from Seven Dials as it had been to get to Bunn's lodgings. Once they had left those infamous streets, Tom hailed a cab. As they waited for it to drive up, he asked, 'Why do you think Bunn chooses to live in a place like that? Surely he could afford better.'

'I doubt if we'll ever know,' Richard replied. 'He's not the sort to explain much about himself.'

When they were in the cab and on their way to Spitalfields, Richard dared to ask his question again. 'You told Mr Leroy you'd had a most satisfactory consultation with your bankers, sir –'

Tom looked at him coldly. 'What is this, Goodwin? Are you taking notes of all I say?'

'No, sir.'

'It is no concern of yours. Don't get ideas above your station. I do not share with you the secrets of my business. After all, I have no reason to believe they would be safe.' Sensing Richard's indignation, he laughed and continued in more conciliatory tones. 'Come, no sulks. You had good reason to betray Prideau's secrets, and I am glad you did. We shall make crape together, and, yes, we have the money we need.'

Richard swallowed his anger, thinking that to work for Tom Harcourt would take all his patience.

Tom remained silent after that. Disappearing into his room at the Bell, he said, 'We leave at seven tomorrow morning. Don't be late.'

Richard intended, once he had eaten, to explore more of London, but felt more tired than he had expected, and decided first to take a brief nap. No sooner was his head on his pillow than he was deeply asleep.

He was awoken by a hammering on his door. It was dark. When he sleepily opened the door, he was astonished to see Tom Harcourt there. With him was a girl, and his arm was about her waist. She held a candle, rather unsteadily. Richard realised that both of them were drunk.

'Goodwin . . . Richard Goodwin . . .' said Tom, his voice slurred. 'Come 'n' have a drink. Come 'n' meet . . . What's your name, sweetheart?' The girl giggled. 'Come 'n' meet What's-her-name.'

'No, sir,' Richard said. 'That would be above my station.' He began to close the door.

'Then go to hell!' Tom snarled. 'Come on, sweetheart.'

As Richard listened to them stumbling their way downstairs, he wondered whether he was still an employee of Harcourt's. Tom would not forgive him lightly for refusing his invitation – if, of course, he remembered the incident . . .

Perhaps in some ways it would be as well. In any case, there was nothing to be done about it. Richard got into bed, and went back to sleep.

CHAPTER EIGHT

'Good morning, sir,' Richard said.

Tom Harcourt merely grunted. At the station he bought himself a newspaper, and read it from cover to cover during their journey. Richard had plenty to occupy his thoughts, and again enjoyed the scenery as they sped through the outskirts of London and the Essex countryside. The trap was waiting at Chelmsford station, as had been arranged before they left.

When they arrived at The Grange, Richard clambered down from his seat beside the driver and helped to lift out Tom's luggage.

Tom went to the front door. 'I can rely on your discretion, Goodwin.'

'Yes, sir.'

'Report to me tomorrow morning at the mill. Eight o'clock sharp.'

'Yes, sir. And thank you, sir.'

Tom went into the house, and the big front door closed behind him.

Richard had hoped to be present when their achievements in London were reported to Mrs Harcourt, but had to content himself with telling his mother and Frances that his appointment was confirmed, and of all the strange and wonderful things he had seen in the capital.

The next morning he was waiting outside the mill at a quarter to eight. Promptly as the church clock struck the hour, a trap bearing Mr and Mrs Harcourt arrived.

'Good morning, Goodwin,' Mrs Harcourt said, as her husband and the driver helped her down.

'Good morning, ma'am. How is your ankle?'

'Much recovered, I thank you.'

Tom Harcourt led the way to the mill, and was about to mount the stairs to his office on the first floor, when his wife said, 'Come through the work-rooms first. Don't say anything – just observe.'

They walked through the big halls. A transformation had taken place, as though a genie had been at work. The rubbish on the floor had been swept away, all the workers were busily engaged in their tasks, and even in the room full of disused machinery, three men had been set to repairing a broken loom. Everyone greeted them respectfully.

When they reached Tom's office, he said, 'How did you achieve that?'

'The morning you left,' Sarah replied, 'I called all the overseers in, and told them the mill was a disgrace, that I wanted it cleaned immediately, that machines with small faults should be repaired, and that I expected all employees to work in a disciplined fashion.'

'And they obeyed you?'

'Not at first. They were a bit sullen, and shuffled their feet, and looked at each other. Then one of them said, "Begging your pardon, ma'am, and with respect, it's Mr Harcourt we take orders from." '

'You might have expected that,' Tom said, a hint of smugness in his voice. 'Who was it?'

'I won't tell you that. I said, "Follow me," and led the way down to the work-room, exaggerating my limp. There I asked for a broom, and lame or not, began to sweep up some of the rubbish.' She laughed. 'You should have seen their faces! After a moment the one who had spoken before said, "*You* can't do that, ma'am." He took the broom from me, and set one of the men to sweeping. Within a half an hour the whole place was beginning to look tidy again. Then I called the overseers back to the office. "Well," I said, "you have obeyed me in one matter. Are you prepared to see that my other orders are carried out?" They mumbled and muttered, but the upshot was that they agreed. I have been here each day since, and you saw for yourself the result.'

'Well done, my dear,' Tom said, but Richard thought that

he was a little put out. 'I am glad to see the place in order. No doubt you will now wish to return to your household duties.'

'By no means,' Sarah replied. 'Both you and Goodwin will need to absent yourselves from the mill a great deal in the coming weeks, and for me to take control only when you are away would be confusing for everybody. If I am manager of the mill on a permanent basis –'

'We have already discussed the matter, Sarah, and –'

'I thought about it while you were in London, Tom – thought about it most deeply. Although I say it myself, I have a gift for organisation, whereas your talents, I believe, lie in your ability to impress people with whom we deal – our suppliers and our customers.'

'I am not only your husband,' Tom said angrily, 'I also happen to be the owner of this mill, and I have already decided . . .' He seemed suddenly to remember Richard's presence, glanced at him briefly, and then went on, 'We will continue this discussion in private, if you please.'

'Very well,' she said calmly. 'However, there are other matters to decide – what we do next, for instance. And that is best done now.'

Tom glowered at her, and for a few moments there was silence. Then he shrugged, and looked at Richard. 'Goodwin?'

'I think the first thing, sir, is to order the brass cylinder for Bunn to work on.'

'Yes. Give me the specifications and I will attend to that.'

'Then we need to order a new loom for the weaving of the gauze, and other equipment has to be prepared too.'

'Make me a list of the requirements.'

'Since Goodwin is the only person who knows exactly what is needed,' Sarah said, 'I think that he should accompany you to the suppliers.'

Tom considered. 'Yes, perhaps that would be as well.'

'In some cases, he might even be sent on his own.'

Unable to keep the sarcasm from his voice, Tom said, 'No doubt you have some other plans for me.'

'My dear, we have an existing business to run. We are still

producing goods, and someone has to visit the customers, revive their interest, fill our order books, until such time as we can begin the manufacture of crape.'

Tom stood up, his face grim. 'Goodwin, I think it would be as well if I were to show you the office which will be your place of work – when you are not engaged in the work-rooms, that is.' He led the way to a smaller office next door to the one they had been in. It was furnished barely, with a desk and two chairs.

'This used to be my own room,' Tom said, 'before my father died. You will find paper and pens in the drawer of that desk. You can begin by drawing up specifications for the cylinder and for everything else that will be needed.' He left, shutting the door.

The walls of the offices were too thick for Richard to make out what was being said in the room next door, but he could hear raised voices. An hour passed before he was summoned back to Tom Harcourt's office. As he entered, he noticed an angry flush on Tom's face. Mrs Harcourt had turned her head and was gazing out of the window.

In a carefully controlled voice, Tom said, 'Mrs Harcourt has persuaded me of the wisdom of her suggestions, and I shall shortly be making an announcement appointing her a director of this company, and manager of the mill. By chance, Goodwin, you were present during a part of our discussions, but I warn you that you will incur our utmost displeasure should you reveal to anyone anything of what you heard.'

'You may rely on me, sir.'

'I would hope so. You will henceforth report to Mrs Harcourt on all matters, and obey her commands as though I had myself given them.'

Sarah turned to him then. 'I want to make the position clear, Goodwin. I shall of course consult Mr Harcourt fully and at all times, and he will take all major decisions. My concern will only be with the day-to-day running of the mill. Do you understand?'

'Yes, ma'am.'

'You may return to your work,' Tom said. 'When you are

ready, come back, and we will allocate your next duties.'

Richard went back to his office. He sat for a while, wondering what it would be like to work for a woman. For someone of Mrs Harcourt's class, a woman's place was in the home, bringing up her children, caring for her husband. Women from poor families might have to work, but only in semi-skilled employment in the mill or, like his mother and Frances, in laundering or cleaning or helping with the harvest. Everyone knew that women had no aptitude for business matters. And yet, he thought, if his mother had had the opportunity, she would have managed well enough. It was surely nonsense to think that women were less intelligent than men. Some might have few thoughts in their heads, but there were just as many men who were equally or even more stupid, while other women would hold their own in every field except that of physical strength. And undoubtedly Mrs Harcourt would be numbered among them.

But supposing she should start a family? She would not have considered playing an active part in the mill if she were already pregnant, but she and Tom had been married for well over a year, so a happy event might not be long delayed.

In the meantime, he decided he rather liked the idea of working for her.

During the summer of 1866, Richard was busy from morning to night. He travelled widely, ordering the new loom, the machinery for the rolling of the crape, the equipment for other processes. He went on his own more often than had originally been planned, because during this period the Harcourt family moved from The Grange into their new home, Orchard House, and Tom's presence in Brentfield was indispensable.

On the occasions when his employer accompanied him, Richard was in no doubt that Tom no longer resented the idea of leaving his wife to run the mill. Indeed, he was always happy to be journeying. Once his business was done, he could drink to his heart's content, and spend the night in some whore's arms, which seemed to be his preferred way of life. His attitude to Richard varied; at times he kept strictly to the relationship that was to be expected between a master and his employee, but there were often days when he behaved almost as though they were friends. More than once Richard was invited to join his carousals, but though at the time Tom would curse him for his refusal, he never appeared to harbour any continuing resentment.

Alfred Bunn arrived, to Richard's relief, for he would not have been surprised if they had heard no more of the engraver. By that time the brass cylinder had been manufactured and delivered, and Richard had arranged for a small room within the mill to be set aside for Bunn. He showed him the cylinder with some pride.

'And what am I to do with it?'

'Engrave a pattern of the kind I described.'

'Then I shall need the pattern drawn. I am no artist. No, that is not true – I am indeed an artist. But I do not create the designs which I engrave. I need something to follow.'

It was a problem which had not entered Richard's mind. He went, as had become his habit, to Sarah.

'And what do you expect me to do about this?'

'Where can I find an artist?'

She shook her head. 'I know no one in Brentfield who could . . . Can you not draw the pattern yourself?'

'I could try, I suppose, but –'

'Something has been worrying me, Goodwin. I do not think Prideau's will be much troubled by our entry into their market – we are too small to be a threat to them – but if we duplicate their crape exactly, they would have legitimate cause for complaint. Perhaps you should vary the pattern on the roller, at least to some extent. Is that possible?'

Richard thought for a moment. 'I believe so. The problem is to keep the ridges on the cylinder at the right angle so as not to sever the threads, yet close enough together to produce crimping in the fashionable style. Of course, anything I draw will not be exactly the same as Prideau's design, which is far too complex to be reproduced from memory. But I will do what I can to make our pattern distinctive.'

Richard still lived with his mother and Frances in the small cottage that his father had built, but at least sufficient money was now coming in for Elizabeth to give up her work and her struggle to make ends meet. She was far from well. Doctor Wood had been called more than once, and had prescribed a richer diet, which meant that the whole family ate more plentifully and of better food.

That evening, an enormous helping of stewed meat and suet pudding filling his stomach, Richard sat at home, a large sheet of paper in front of him, doing his best to produce a pattern for the crimping cylinder. It was far more difficult than he had imagined.

Frances came over and examined his pencilling. 'Dear Richard, you never could draw, could you? Here, let me try.'

Richard ran his fingers through his fair hair. 'You might as well. You can hardly do worse.'

She took the pencil from him, sat down at his place, and began to draw. 'Is that right?'

'Yes. Yes, exactly. Oh, Frances, why didn't I think of asking you before? That's just fine. A little closer together there. And a few more places where the lines join up.'

Even with the skill that Frances brought to the task, the work was exacting, and three days passed before she finally produced a design which satisfied Richard. He took it to Alfred Bunn, who examined it minutely.

'You want it exactly like this?' he asked. 'And these lines must stand clear by at least an eighth of an inch?'

'Yes. And the sides of the hollows must be as near vertical as possible.'

'I see now why you said it would be a long job. Did you draw this?'

'No. My sister did.'

'It is well done.'

'I will tell her you said so.'

When Richard reported Bunn's compliment, Frances was

delighted. 'I'd love to see the engraving being done,' she said.

'I don't see why not. I'll ask Mrs Harcourt.'

'You'd better ask Mr Bunn too. He might not like to have a spectator.' Frances paused, and then surprised him by asking, 'Do you mind working for a woman, Richard?'

'No. At least, not for Mrs Harcourt. I'm not sure that I'd like to work for *any* woman, but she's different. There was a lot of grumbling at first, especially from the men.'

'Why?'

'Oh, they said she'd be flighty, and wouldn't stick at it, and she was much too young, and didn't know anything about silk. Well, she spends every morning in the work-rooms, learning the work. She's very quick – she's already a capable throwster, and as good as any apprentice on the looms. And she's never afraid to say if she doesn't understand anything or to ask for help. She's got a wonderful memory too – she knows every worker by name, and all about their families and everything.'

'She sounds a marvel.'

'Aye. I think they're all proud of her now. They call her "Our Missus". If anyone's got a problem, someone says, "You'd better talk to Our Missus. She'll sort it out." And she does.'

Frances smiled mischievously. 'Are you in love with her, Richard?'

'Of course not. Don't talk daft.' But he could not prevent the blush which spread over his cheeks.

Frances laughed, deciding that if Richard were not in love with Mrs Harcourt, he was giving a good imitation of having lost his heart to her.

In fact, every time he saw her, Richard felt an increasing sense of pleasure and excitement. Except when he was away, ordering some new piece of equipment or checking its construction, no day passed without a meeting between them, at which he would report progress and they would discuss the situation. When he had no real need to consult her, he often invented excuses to go to her office.

Though he did not dare to express his feelings in words,

still less in actions, Sarah Harcourt could not mistake the effect she had on him, and though she was careful to maintain a formal relationship, their conversations became more and more friendly and relaxed, and laced with laughter. She had to admit that she enjoyed their meetings as much as he evidently did, and even sometimes wondered whether she was in danger of falling a little in love with him. But the very idea was absurd. In any case, she did not believe in that kind of romantic nonsense.

Nevertheless, it really was extraordinary, she thought, how well they got on together. Who would have expected a weaver's son, with no proper education, to be so well-read, to have such good manners, to assume a position of command with such ease? She asked him about his upbringing, and he told her not only of his parents, but also of Mr Hill, whose influence upon him he now recognised to have been considerable. None of what he said really explained it, and she realised that it was his own readiness to learn, his hunger for knowledge, and perhaps too his ambition, which had moulded him. She admired him the more, after that. Even the Essex accent seemed almost an asset, giving an impression of honest bluntness.

She was certain that she had been right in persuading Tom to employ him. To take on a young man who had been dismissed for theft, and who made outrageous demands about his status, and of whose knowledge and ability they had no proof, was reckless in the extreme. But her instincts had told her, right from the moment of their first encounter when she had sprained her ankle, that Richard was to be trusted, that he was exceptional in many ways, and – this was the most bizarre thought of all – that they had been destined to meet and to play a part in each other's lives.

Their relationship might not have developed so fast had it not been that Tom spent much of his time away from Brentfield at this period, calling on customers up and down the country. He discovered quickly that Sarah was right – the retailers were flattered to be visited by the owner of Harcourt's, and were often willing to order from him, though almost without exception they explained that the trade in such wares as his had declined sharply of late in the face of foreign imports.

New orders did flow into the mill as a result of his efforts, but not at a rate which would keep it working to capacity and bring in good profits. The situation was better than it had been at his father's death, but Tom had come to see how right Sarah was in saying that they needed to enter the lucrative market for crape.

Richard dreaded each occasion when Tom returned to Brentfield. Not only did it mean that he could no longer have his *tête-á-têtes* with Sarah, but there was often a difficult interview with the owner.

The ordering of new equipment, the shifting of old machinery to make room for its installation, and the many adjustments which had to be made before each piece could become operational, all took time. And although Alfred Bunn's work on the most important element of all, the brass cylinder, seemed to be satisfactory, there might be weeks of labour, once it was finished, before the pressure was right, and the lower cylinder of the machine had been covered with paper to exactly the right thickness and of a texture that would take a sharp impression of the engraving.

Tom was invariably disappointed that Richard had not made faster progress, and showed his dissatisfaction by nagging criticisms.

'Perhaps he's jealous,' Frances suggested, when Richard poured out his troubles after one particularly difficult discussion.

'Jealous? Why?'

'I don't know, I'm sure. It was just an idle thought. Unless, of course . . .' and her eyes sparkled with mischief '. . . he thinks you're making sheep's eyes at his wife.'

'Oh, for heaven's sake, Frances! If you're going to make stupid jokes like that, I shall stop telling you anything.'

Richard had not forgotten that Frances wanted to watch Alfred Bunn at work. When he mentioned it to Mrs Harcourt, she had no objection, and neither had the engraver himself. 'So long as she doesn't keep on talking,' he said. 'Can't abide being talked to while I'm working.'

The first time that she visited his tiny work-room, he did not get up or give her any more welcome than a casual wave of his hand towards a rough stool in the corner of the room. For some time he went on working, while Frances sat and admired the sureness of his long, thin fingers and the intent concentration of his dark eyes. When he straightened his back for a brief rest, she said nothing, waiting for him to open the conversation.

'My compliments on your drawing, Miss,' he said. 'It is a pleasure to work from so clear a design.'

'Thank you.' Again she waited, but when he remained silent, she said, 'I hope you do not mind me being here. I wanted to see how you used my work.'

'If it pleases you, I have no objection. So long as you expect no other entertainment.'

It might have sounded rude from any other man, but she knew he did not intend any offence. His clothes were shabby and uncared-for, his hair fell in unruly locks, and his chin was in need of a shave. He was exactly the sort of person that Frances, brought up to believe that neatness as well as cleanliness was next to Godliness, should have found little to her taste, but she felt strangely drawn to him. Despite his confidence in his own abilities, he seemed somehow vulnerable.

When next he paused, she asked diffidently, 'I hope you are comfortable in your lodgings, Mr Bunn.'

He looked at her in surprise. 'Yes. Why should I not be?'

'It must be difficult for a single man.'

'I have a bed, Mrs King cooks my breakfast and a meal in the evening. That is all I require.'

'No,' Frances said silently to herself, 'that is not all you require. You should have a woman to *care* for you, to see that you have clean clothes and that you are well turned out – someone to mother you a little.' She blushed at her thoughts, and then, before she could stop herself, suddenly blurted, 'Perhaps you would care to come and eat with us one evening.'

He lifted his eyes to her, and it was like an electric shock coursing through her body. He seemed to be gazing into the depths of her soul, as though seeking for other motives than common courtesy in her invitation. 'Thank you,' he said, but there was no warmth in his voice. 'Perhaps. One day.'

Frances felt rebuffed, and for a moment was inclined to leave. But, she decided, it was just his manner. Perhaps he had been badly hurt once, and now wore a protective shell against the world. It would not be easy to penetrate, and she had been a fool to try to do so at such an early stage in their acquaintance. She sat silent, and watched as he continued his work.

She had been there for nearly an hour before, at another break in his labours, she got up to go. 'May I come and watch you again?'

His somewhat haggard features were unsmiling as he said, 'If you wish.' As she reached the door, he added, 'But don't expect anything from me.'

Again Frances felt her cheeks burning as she hurried out of the mill and back to the cottage. She knew instinctively that his words had not been carelessly chosen, but that he was answering, in his own way, her inmost thoughts. Had she really been so transparent?

One day when Richard went for his usual discussion with Sarah Harcourt, he found her sitting at her desk with a pile of ledgers in front of her and a worried look on her face.

'I've been going through the accounts,' she said, shaking her head.

'Charlie Featherstone has never been cooking the books,' he smiled. Featherstone was chief clerk in the counting house.

'No, of course not. But they're in such a muddle. Some of the totals are wrong, and there are crossings out everywhere. I *think* we're a hundred pounds or so better off than we thought, but I can't be sure. I understand now why my late father-in-law copied everything out himself. What am I going to do? I haven't time to keep the accounts myself, but we can't go on like this. And I can't just dismiss Featherstone. How would he live?' She seemed to be thinking aloud, rather than talking to Richard. 'I suppose I could give him a small pension. Should I do that? But who could take his place?'

'I know someone, ma'am. He works at Prideau's. I don't know whether he would be willing to come here, but I could ask him.'

'Prideau's? They'll think we intend luring away all their employees.'

'If Mr Hill decides to come to us, they couldn't stop him.'

'Except by offering him an increase in wages.'

Richard laughed. 'They're not that generous. Mr Hill told me once that Mr Prideau never objects if any of his older employees want to leave, because he can hire a replacement more cheaply.'

'And would this Mr Hill be able to do the work?'

'On his head, ma'am.'

She smiled. 'I'd rather he did it the right way up. Then talk to him about it. But don't make any commitment.'

'I shall have to go into Franton.'

'Can you drive a trap?'

'I've never done so.'

'Then . . .' For a wild moment Richard thought that she was going to offer to drive him herself, but she went on, '. . . then you'll have to walk, won't you?' And she smiled again.

The evenings were drawing in early now, and the prospect of a long walk in pitch darkness to Franton and back did not appeal to Richard. He waited until a full moon was due and the sky was cloudless, and set off at dusk, which would bring him to Mr Hill's home at just about the time that he returned from work.

Indeed, walking along the street where his friend lived, he saw his unmistakable short figure approaching. As he came nearer, although it was quite a short time since they had last met, Richard thought that Mr Hill looked older. 'Spare a penny for a poor man, guv,' he said.

Mr Hill fumbled in his pocket, and then peered closely at the beggar. 'Richard! What a surprise! Of course I always predicted that you would come to an impecunious end, but since your clothes proclaim that you have not reached such an undesirable state yet, I shall retain my penny – an economy which will no doubt delight the heart of my dear wife.' He linked his arm in Richard's. 'How are you, my boy, and what are you doing here? Not come on bended knees to beg Mr Prideau for re-employment, I trust. You cannot have partaken of food recently, so I insist that you should accompany me to my humble abode.'

'That was indeed my hope,' Richard said.

'Capital! The mistress of my household shall provide you with a crust. Now, tell me what has been happening to you, and how you are employed, and of the welfare of your mother and sister, and what you are doing here in Franton, where I never thought to see you again. I vow, Richard, here we have been together for several minutes, and you have told me nothing at all, except that you purposed to visit me. I ask you, is this silence the way to treat an old friend?'

Richard laughed. 'You have given me no chance.'

The little man looked up at him, his eyes twinkling. 'Nonsense! And here we are at my house, and you will have to postpone your narration while we greet Mrs Hill, and she recovers from her amazement. Oh, Richard, I have missed you.' He squeezed Richard's arm briefly, then opened his front door, and called, 'Pussy-my-love, a visitor!'

Mrs Hill was just as he remembered her, small and neat, her grey hair drawn smoothly back from the centre parting. Her little round face wreathed itself in smiles as she greeted him, and then hurried to lay an extra place at the table.

Richard had much to tell the Hills, and found himself still talking when the meal was over and the three of them were sitting in front of the small coal fire. They listened with close attention, and many nods of the head, and expressions of 'Bless my soul!' and 'Well, I never!'. When he had finished, Richard said, 'And now tell me about yourselves.'

'Life is little changed,' Mr Hill replied. 'I am still employed, for a mere pittance, on work which is unrivalled in its tedium. I miss you, Richard – at least when you were here there was someone to enjoy my feeble jokes.' He turned to his wife. 'Apart, that is, from you, Pussy-my-love. You have always appreciated me, have you not?'

'I don't know about that,' Mrs Hill replied, as ever.

Mr Hill gave his wonted smile. 'You still haven't told me what you are doing here in Franton, Richard.'

'I came to see you.'

'A visit to an old friend? Now I call that handsome. And right glad I've been to see you, my boy. But was that all your intention?'

'No. I will confess. I have come to discuss business.'

'Business? Have a care, Richard.' He was serious for once. 'You may owe no loyalty to Prideau's, but I am still their faithful employee.'

'How faithful?'

'What do you mean?'

'I am here to offer you a position at the mill in Brentfield.'

Mr Hill looked at him, blinking. 'Explain yourself, my boy.' He listened with great care as Richard did so, for once stunned into silence. When Richard had finished, he expelled his breath in a long, toneless whistle. He looked at his wife. 'Well, Pussy-my-love, what do you make of that? Should I consider our young friend's offer?'

Mrs Hill knew it was far too serious a matter for her stock, joking reply. She thought for some time, and then said, 'Brentfield is a pleasant village, I believe.'

'Then I should leave Franton?'

'On the other hand, we are no longer young, Mr Hill. An upheaval at our age . . . You are secure here.'

'Until Mr Prideau decides that I am too old.'

'We should manage somehow. But to go to Harcourt's . . .'

'. . . would be a journey into the unknown. I can always depend on you for wisdom, Pussy-my-love. However, it does not escape my notice that your first remark might have been termed an expression of interest.' He turned to Richard. 'And what emoluments would I receive? What generous sum does Mr Harcourt offer by way of inducement?'

In discussing the matter with Sarah Harcourt, Richard had

discovered that Charlie Featherstone was paid thirty shillings a week. 'No wonder the books are in a muddle,' he had said, and she had agreed. Richard's guess was that Prideau's paid Mr Hill almost twice that amount. 'One hundred and seventy-five pounds a year,' he said. Mr Hill's expression, he noted, showed neither disappointment nor surprised pleasure. His guess had probably been accurate.

'A reasonable offer,' Mr Hill said, calmly. 'And what can you tell me concerning accommodation?'

'There is a small cottage available at a very modest rent.'

'Well, Pussy? Does the idea of a cottage in Brentfield take your fancy?' When Mrs Hill merely blinked and gave a half-smile, he continued, 'I see that in your wisdom you are leaving the decision to me.' He paused. 'I have to confess that I am tempted, Richard. But this is not a decision that can be lightly taken. I must ponder.'

'Of course. But we need a decision soon.'

'And soon you will have it. After due consideration and further converse with the wife of my bosom, I will send you word within the week.' His eyes twinkled. 'And now let us talk of other things. You are not yet contemplating matrimony, my young friend? Is there no eligible female in Brentfield who has attracted your eyes and bewitched your heart?'

'No,' Richard replied, laughing. 'I've been too busy to think of things like that.'

'One should never be too busy to think about the more pleasurable aspects of life. Is that not true, Pussy-my-love?'

But again Mrs Hill failed to give the expected reply. 'I shall make a cup of tea before you depart, Richard.'

Mr Hill sighed in exaggerated fashion. 'What my dear wife is saying, Richard, is that the pleasures of the infused leaf are more certain than those of matrimony. Perhaps she is right.'

Later, just before Richard left for the long walk home, Mr Hill said, 'No doubt Mr Harcourt will wish to interview me. But it will be difficult. I cannot give in my notice here until I am certain of the new position, and that means I could visit Brentfield only on a Sunday.'

'In any case,' said Richard, 'Mr Harcourt is away more often than in Brentfield. You will have to see Mrs Harcourt. She is the manager. You will like her. You could not fail to do so.'

Mr Hill's shrewd eyes gazed at Richard. 'So I gathered from what you said of her earlier, more than once. She has clearly made a great impression on you.'

Richard felt himself blush. 'I will talk to her about it,' he said shortly. 'I will let you know what can be arranged.'

As he walked home, he felt annoyed with himself. His feelings for Sarah were evidently so obvious that first Frances and now Mr Hill had rapidly detected them. He must be more circumspect, he decided, and temper his enthusiasm when he spoke of her. That would not be easy.

CHAPTER NINE

When he came back from his selling expeditions, Tom Harcourt usually went straight to Orchard House, and did not appear at the mill until the following morning. One day in early October, however, he strode in and shouted at the doorman, 'I want Goodwin in my office immediately!'

When Richard arrived, Sarah was sitting beside the desk, and Tom was pacing up and down. 'How far has that Bunn fellow got with his engraving?' he demanded.

'He's done half of it, or more.'

'Well, I've sent orders for him to stop. He's to do nothing until I say so. Now, listen. Yesterday I visited Montgomery's in Norwich. Mr Montgomery's a good friend, who knows the trade backwards, and he's very discreet, so I told him our plans. "What kind of crape," he asked, "and at what price?" I said it would be just like Prideau's, with a similar design, and about threepence a yard cheaper. He shook his head, and said that Prideau's are so firmly established that a similar product wouldn't stand a chance unless it was sold for at least a shilling under their price – in other words, at a loss.' Tom paused. 'But then he went on to say that Prideau's crape is very delicate, and ideal for ladies, but that gentlemen wear crape too – mourning bands around their hats, and cravats and handkerchiefs and so on – and if we could produce a heavier material, with a broader, more masculine crimp, it might find a market. Not as big as Prideau's, but worthwhile, he thought. So that's why I've stopped Bunn. Can we produce a crape for men?'

'We can weave a thicker crape easily enough, but we shall need a new cylinder,' Richard said. 'It'll set us back a couple of months at least – maybe more, because a heavier pattern could give us all kinds of problems. We'll probably have to lessen the pressure so that the crimping doesn't cut the threads, and that may mean the impression isn't deep enough.' He shook his head.

'And a new cylinder, plus the delay, is going to cost us a lot more money,' Tom said. 'I doubt if we can afford it.'

'I don't see how we can afford not to do it,' Sarah said, calmly. 'In any case, I welcome this. We shouldn't be copying Prideau's.'

A long discussion followed. Fortunately, the improvement that Tom had brought about in the sales of their ordinary silk products meant that the financial position, though far from happy, was not desperate, and it was agreed to go ahead. A new brass cylinder was ordered, and Frances was commissioned to draw new designs. Alfred Bunn engraved small portions of these on the old cylinder, so that Richard could experiment with them. Such trials, though never entirely satisfactory, gave an indication of the results they could expect on the heavier gauze.

It was a worrying time for them all. Only Frances was inwardly delighted, for it gave her renewed reason to be present while Alfred Bunn was engaged on his delicate, absorbing work.

A few days after Tom's bombshell, Richard received a letter from Mr Hill. 'My dear Friend,' it said, 'My respected helpmeet has persuaded me that adventure is not inadmissible at my advanced age. Therefore, if Mr or Mrs Harcourt will confirm their willingness to offer me employment, and will suggest a Sunday on which an interview would be convenient, I will contrive to make myself available for it. And should our meeting prove constructive, I will thereupon hand in my notice to Prideau's (still, I must confess, with some misgivings, but with the sincere hope that neither your confidence in your humble servant, nor his in you, will be misplaced). Yrs. ever, Joshua Hill.'

The interview took place, Sarah Harcourt was impressed by Mr Hill's knowledge and competence and amused both by his style of speech and his obvious pleasure in it, and his appointment was confirmed. Charlie Featherstone accepted his retirement with good grace, and in due course Mr Hill arrived in Brentfield, and began his duties at the mill, contriving quite quickly to restore order to the firm's accounts, and indeed to reduce substantially the sums owing to Harcourt's by some of their customers.

Sarah was delighted, and praised Richard for finding such a useful employee. He received her compliments dully, preoccupied with his concern over the problems facing him. Sarah realised that she needed somehow to revive his enthusiasm. 'Cheer up,' she said. 'I know you're worried about this new crape – we all are – but I'm sure of our success. There's an air of prosperity about the mill. Can't you feel it? Everyone's working with a will, and Mr Harcourt is bringing in more orders, and you'll soon overcome all your present difficulties – I'm confident you will – and the new crape is bound to be successful.'

'I wish I could be as sure of that as you,' he said. 'I haven't found the answer yet, and even if I do, we can't be certain that the crape will sell.'

'Listen!' she said fiercely. 'That isn't like you, and I'll not accept that attitude – not from anyone. Harcourt's is going to succeed, and so are you. Tell yourself that. Believe it, as I do.'

Her determination was infectious, and he went back to his work in a happier frame of mind. Sarah continued to encourage him at every meeting, and gradually he recovered his old optimism, especially when one of his experiments at last seemed to produce an acceptable result, and he was able to tell Bunn to begin work on the new cylinder.

Sarah Harcourt began to occupy his mind more and more. As he walked to the mill each morning he would think with delight that he would soon be seeing her again. He no longer pretended that he was not in love with her. If only she had not been married . . . But what chance would he have stood? He was not of her class, as he was reminded every time she made fun of his Essex accent. He might already have risen above his station in life, but even if he were to become a director of

Harcourt's, there would still be a barrier between them.

In any case, he had no reason to believe that Sarah felt any affection for him. She was friendly, and treated him almost as an equal, but it never went beyond that. She called him 'Richard', but he would not have dared to address her as anything but 'Mrs Harcourt' or 'ma'am'. He dreamed sometimes that she nurtured a secret passion for him, which she was forced to conceal for the sake of propriety. But that was sheer nonsense. He did his best to hide his feelings from her and from the world at large.

By the spring of 1867, Alfred Bunn had finally completed the engraving of the cylinder, and all that remained was to prepare the second, paper-covered roller, which would take the impression of the engraving. The papier mâché had to be of exactly the right consistency – firm enough to be sharply indented, yet not so damp that in drying the paper would shrink or lose the precision of the pattern.

'You won't be needing me any more,' Alfred Bunn said. 'If you will see that I am paid to date, I will return to London.'

'Do you want to go?'

'Not particularly, but I have a living to make.'

Richard spoke to Mrs Harcourt. 'Prideau's have an engraver permanently on their staff, and I believe we should too. I'd like to keep Bunn on. The cylinder he's engraved won't last for ever. Besides, we should have spares, and some with different patterns.'

'Send him to me.'

Any other employee summoned by Our Missus would stand to attention while she spoke, but Bunn lolled in front of her desk, seeming as always to be over-endowed with bony elbows and knees. He listened calmly as Sarah told him that he could stay indefinitely and that there would be plenty of work for him, but she thought he was pleased. 'You can settle down in Brentfield,' she told him. 'Find yourself a wife, raise a family.' His enigmatic smile disconcerted her, and she said sharply. 'Very well, Bunn. You may go.'

Frances made no effort to conceal her pleasure at the news.

She had more than once repeated her invitation to the engraver to visit her mother's cottage for a meal, and was delighted when at last he accepted. It might have been due to the presence throughout the evening of her mother and Richard, but whatever the cause, Alfred Bunn, while remaining perfectly polite, revealed little of himself and carefully kept the conversation to the most general of subjects.

He did however, when expressing his gratitude before leaving, promise that he would come again, and Frances was left to cling to the hope that one day she would succeed in breaking down his reserve.

In the work-room where the crape was to be made, Richard had also set up other equipment. First came the steam-box, a kind of tank over which the gauze would slowly pass. It had taken many weary days to find a method of leading steam from the mill's boiler into the tank so that it would be evenly distributed and would reach every part of the material as it moved over the top. The steam would soften the material slightly, allowing it to be stretched taut.

Until they could afford to install a machine, the next process had to be done by hand. Beyond the steam-box, then, waited a team of Harcourt's best women workers, ready to seize the material on either side, and pull it in opposite directions, to bias it. The gauze, when it came off the loom, would be a yard or so wide, but after biasing would have been reduced to under two thirds of that width, and would shrink even more later.

Next, however, came the crucial moment when the silk would be fed through the crimping rollers. The brass cylinder was heated to the required temperature. Everything was ready.

Sarah and Tom Harcourt were there to watch, along with Alfred Bunn, and as a special concession, since she had designed the crimping pattern, Frances. All others, except those who were actually working on the crape, had been rigorously excluded. The process would be as secret at Harcourt's as at Prideau's. The door to the crape room was always guarded, and the machines were locked when not in use.

Richard held his breath as a short length of material was fed in. This was the first really conclusive test, a very different matter from the experiments he had conducted previously. Slowly the rollers turned, and he hurried to see the cloth emerging from the other side, examining it carefully, and with bitter disappointment.

Tom Harcourt walked over to him. 'What's the matter now?'

Richard held the cloth up to the light. 'See those tiny tears? Either the cylinder has been too sharply engraved, or the pressure is too great. Whichever it is, it's breaking the threads.'

'Can you put it right?'

'If it's the cylinder, it will be a major job to file down the edges, so I pray it's the pressure.'

'It had better be!' Tom said savagely. He stalked back to Sarah, and Richard could see him talking to her vehemently, in a low voice.

Richard bent over the crimping machine, adjusting the pressure. Joe Jolly had always said that this was the most difficult part. Even the weather had to be taken into consideration, for the dryness or moisture of the atmosphere could affect the brittleness of the threads. At last he was ready and gave the command for another trial. The room filled again with the sounds of the cog wheels turning and the smell of damp cloth and hot metal. Richard examined the silk.

'Well?' Tom asked.

'It's better.'

'Not the roller, then?' Alfred Bunn was naturally anxious.

'No.' He turned to the others. 'It needs very careful adjustment, and it's going to take me some time. I'll call you when we're ready for the next trial.'

For some hours Richard and his workers tried different pressures on the rollers, until he was getting consistently better results. He was still far from satisfied, and decided that the fault now lay chiefly in the texture of the gauze. The thread was very highly twisted in order to give a good curl and to take the heavy crimping. He did not want to change that, but he thought that the answer might be to experiment with a slightly more open weave.

For the moment, however, he could call the others back. Conscious of Tom's scowl, Richard explained that the crape would still be far from perfect, but that he would demonstrate the next stage in the process, in which the cloth passed from the rollers to be steeped in a solution of tannin, heated to near blood temperature. The action of the liquid would cause the gauze to contract again, and as the material was reduced to less than half its original width, it would assume the characteristic curled appearance of crape.

'It's surely not going to be as narrow as that?' Tom asked, his tone still critical.

'No,' said Richard. 'We'll hang it up to dry and cool, and then we'll reverse the biasing. That will bring it back to a width of just under thirty inches.'

'And then?' Sarah asked.

'We have to dye it black, before the last process of all. After it's been through the steeping and the dyeing, all the natural gum will have gone, and it will have the sheen that we look for in the ribbons and other materials we make here. But crape needs a dull, matt finish. So we put the material through a bath of thin starch and glues. The crape comes out still soft and workable, but with a bit of extra body to it, and it's lost the sheen.'

Tom's foot was tapping irritably. 'How soon will you have samples ready? I can't sell it until we have something to show.'

'I don't know. We shall have to try various weaves, and different pressures on the rollers. I doubt if I'll have anything for you in less than a fortnight. It may take longer – maybe a month.'

'As long as that? For God's sake, Goodwin, you don't seem to realise how urgent this is!'

'Rome wasn't built in a day,' Sarah said. 'You've done very well, Richard.'

'Come to my office, Sarah,' Tom said curtly. 'You too, Goodwin.'

When the three of them were alone, Tom said, 'First of all, my dear, I would prefer it if you did not contradict me in public. You may be satisfied with what Goodwin has done, but I am certainly not. Before we began this whole enterprise, we made careful estimates of the time it would take to get into the production of crape, and the amount of capital we should have to invest. Both estimates have already been exceeded. And now we have additional delays and, no doubt, further expenses.'

Flabbergasted by his unreasonable attitude, Richard wondered what had got into Tom. 'We should have been on time, sir,' he said mildly, 'if we had not decided to produce a heavier crape.'

'You don't have to tell me that. I am beginning to wish we had never considered manufacturing any kind of crape. The business in our standard silks is picking up well, and if we concentrated on that, we'd be back in profit all the sooner.'

'But, my dear,' Sarah said, 'that is sheer fantasy. You've done wonders, but you said yourself that the trade has declined substantially. As things are, we should be lucky to break even.'

'I'm not so sure. Still, we've embarked on this wild scheme of yours, and I suppose we must go on. But I am not at all satisfied.' He turned to Richard. 'You will have to speed up your experiments, Goodwin. I can't wait another month. Nor can I afford to pay the staff in your department while you go through all this trial and error. You've taken advantage of me, and I won't have it any longer.'

'Sir –' Richard began to protest.

'Yes, you have. You're supposed to be an expert, but as far as I can see, you're using guess-work most of the time. Well, guess-work isn't good enough. I want results, and I want them within a week. If that is beyond your capability in normal working hours, then you must work overtime. Moreover, if you fail to produce adequate samples within the week, I intend to deduct a day's pay from your wages for every day that you are overdue. Perhaps that will show you that we are not in business for you to take advantage of my generosity.'

'Sir, I do not believe that I have done so.'

The anger in Tom's voice increased. 'Don't bandy words with me! Get back to your work!'

'Mrs Harcourt will tell you, sir, that –'

'Mrs Harcourt will tell me nothing. I am the owner of this mill. My wife may be more susceptible to you than I am, but you will not hide behind her skirts.'

'Tom, please!' Sarah interjected. 'This is unworthy of you.'

'Get out, Goodwin!' Tom shouted. 'Get back to your work, and remember what I have said!'

As Richard left the office, he could barely contain his own anger. Tom Harcourt's moods were always unpredictable, but nothing had prepared him for such an onslaught. In the past months, happy in his work, he had almost forgotten his ambition to be revenged on the Harcourts, to own the mill, to be master over Tom, but now it all came rushing back.

He thought of Sarah, wondering what was being said between them. She would no doubt stand up to Tom, but how far would she dare to go in Richard's defence? Would the quarrel signify the end of her power within the mill? For the hundredth time he asked himself how she could support marriage to such a man. Perhaps she was actually in love with him – there was no accounting for the strange affection that women often appeared to have for the most unattractive of husbands.

He went back to the crape department, and gave orders for the looming of a new batch of gauze, with a slightly looser texture.

'What's up with 'im?' one of the women weavers asked her work-mate after Richard had gone to tinker with the crimping rollers. 'Jump down your throat as soon as look at you. That's not like 'im.'

'Reckon it's 'cos the Master's back,' her friend replied. ''E can't make 'is sheep's eyes at Our Missus now the Master's around.'

Richard gave his subordinates no cause during the next week to speculate on his interest in the mill owner's wife, driving them harder than ever before, and himself hardest of all. There were so many variables – the weave, the amount of bias, the heat of the rollers, their pressure, the temperature and the ingredients of the steeping liquid and the dye – and trial after trial had to be made. Often he worked late at night, when all the workers had gone home and only the night watchman was there to see that no intruders entered the mill. He grew pale and irritable, and there were dark rings of fatigue beneath his eyes.

One afternoon, Sarah Harcourt summoned him to her office. 'You cannot continue like this, Richard. You will make yourself ill.'

'I am simply carrying out Mr Harcourt's orders, ma'am,' he said, coldly. 'His samples must be ready when he comes back next Friday.'

'Will they be ready?'

'I believe so. We are almost there.'

'Good. But if you are not finally satisfied, you must not hesitate to take more time. I doubt if Mr Harcourt will really make any deductions from your wages. He does not always mean what he says.' She blushed. It was the first time she had made any comment to him about her husband. 'I won't keep you from your work,' she said hastily. 'I am confident that you will succeed.'

Her concern and her continued belief in him gave him new heart once more, and he returned to the crape department determined to justify her faith.

The following Friday morning he completed the dyeing and stiffening of the latest of his experimental lengths of cloth, and hung it up to dry. He was almost certain that this time he had got it right, and it was torture to wait until the crape could be handled and examined. At last he dared to finger it gently. It should really have hung for several more hours to complete the drying process, but at any moment Tom Harcourt would arrive back at the mill. Richard took a pair of shears and cut a yard or so from the material. Carefully he checked it, and then hurried with it to Mrs Harcourt's office. Trying not to let his excitement show, he handed it to her. 'Be careful,' he said. 'It's still not quite dry, and it's a little sticky.'

Sarah Harcourt took the crape over to the window, holding

it gingerly by the edges. She looked at it in silence for long moments, turning it this way and that, holding it up to the light, now stretching it slightly, now letting it fall in folds. Then she turned to Richard, who was standing close beside her. 'It looks splendid. Are you satisfied with it?'

He nodded happily.

'Then I congratulate you.'

'I hope Mr Harcourt will be pleased.'

'Pleased about what?' Tom had entered the room at that moment. He had stopped just inside the door and was staring at them both.

'Welcome back, Tom,' Sarah said. 'I hope you had a good journey. Richard has just brought me the result of his latest experiment. It looks quite perfect.'

'So you managed it in time, Goodwin. I thought you might if given the right incentive.' He went over to where Sarah was standing. 'Is that it?' He touched the gauze. 'It's sticky!' he said, in some disgust.

'Yes, sir. It's not quite dry. You'll notice that the pattern is quite distinct from anything that Prideau's make. The crimping is deep and firm, and the cloth has a good matt finish.'

Richard had the impression that Tom had not heard what he said. He was gazing at the crape. Then he seemed to recall himself, and turned back to Richard. 'What will happen to it when it's in the roll? Will it lose its curl?' His voice sounded taut.

'Not to any great extent. Rolling will naturally flatten it a bit, but the crimping is permanent enough to withstand anything but a very hot iron or very hot water.'

'And you can maintain this quality?'

'I believe so, sir.'

Tom seemed to have difficulty in concentrating. He looked at Richard angrily. 'I asked you if you could maintain the quality.'

'Yes, sir.'

He thrust the sample of crape back at Richard and sat down. 'Next week I shall call on Mr Montgomery. His reaction will be crucial. If he is satisfied, I shall send word immediately, and production may begin.' He looked at Sarah, and gave her a thin smile. 'I shall send you further instructions as I continue my visits, and you will of course obey them with your usual wifely submission.' He turned back to Richard. 'I shall need exact costings, Goodwin, and to know how quickly we can meet any orders we receive. I will see you at ten thirty tomorrow morning. That is all.'

'Will you not congratulate Richard on his achievement?' Sarah asked mildly.

Tom frowned. 'He has done what he is paid for, and he is well enough paid, in all conscience. There is no certainty yet that we can sell this product of which you both seem to think so highly.'

Richard left the room, his pleasure in his achievement tarnished. Why should Tom Harcourt have adopted this curmudgeonly attitude?

Had he been an invisible spectator in Sarah's office, he would have had his answer. When the door closed behind him, Tom remained silent for a brief while, and then suddenly burst out, 'Your infatuation with that fellow becomes more evident each time I see you together! I would remind you that you are my wife.'

Sarah's eyes flashed in anger. 'And you have no cause to speak to me in those tones. I am not infatuated with him, nor has he at any time behaved with less than the utmost propriety.'

'I've a damned good mind to dismiss him.'

'Don't be such a fool, Tom, and please don't swear.'

'A fool, am I? Why should I tolerate him any longer? We know the process now. We can do without him.'

'Of course we can't. Oh, Tom, I've no patience with you when you're in this mood. Once and for all, you have no cause to continue this vendetta against a man in whose skill our future prosperity lies. And I mostly strongly resent your suspicions of me. I am and have always been entirely faithful to you, which is probably more than you can say.'

'Then, by God, behave like a faithful wife! Come here! Do

I not deserve at least a kiss when I return?' Pulling her to him, he kissed her roughly, in an embrace which, she felt, held no affection, but only a desire to dominate and hurt.

After a moment, she broke away from him. 'You reek of spirits,' she said. 'You're half drunk. I might have known that was what it was.'

'Half drunk am I? And tonight no doubt I shall be even more drunk. But wait until then, my dear – wait until then!'

Mr Montgomery was delighted with the sample of Harcourt's new Mourning Crape for Gentlemen, and placed a substantial order. Other customers were equally enthusiastic, and Sarah was able to tell Richard to produce as much of the material as he could, and in the shortest possible time.

For the next month, Richard and the workers in the crape department strained their utmost to fill the stream of orders that Tom Harcourt brought in, and to overcome the dozens of minor problems that arose. It was an exciting time, though they were all aware that their efforts might prove to be fruitless if the public did not buy the crape. But surely so many retailers could not be wrong in their judgement.

Tom Harcourt bubbled with optimism each time he returned to the mill. He was pleased to forget all his previous criticisms, claimed to have been certain of success all along, and managed a grudging 'Well done!' to Richard. But even he showed some anxiety when he left, early on a Saturday morning in September, four weeks after the delivery of the original order, to call again upon Mr Montgomery and other retailers.

It was late in the afternoon when he came back to the mill, jubilantly waving the batch of large repeat orders he had received.

Sarah insisted that Richard should be called to the office to hear the splendid news. 'We must have a celebration dinner tomorrow,' she said. 'Richard must join us, don't you agree, my dear?'

'Goodwin?' Tom's tone indicated shocked surprise.

Hastily Richard said, 'I greatly appreciate your invitation, Mrs Harcourt, but I have already arranged with Alfred Bunn and Mr Hill that if Mr Harcourt brought good news they would join us at our table.'

'A capital plan, Goodwin,' Tom commented.

The following weeks were filled with frantic activity. A new loom was ordered, extra hands were hired, and many of those who had until now been working on the traditional Harcourt silks were re-trained for the production of crape. Alfred Bunn was set to engraving a second brass roller, for it would clearly be essential to increase their output. The future seemed assured.

Early on a Monday morning in November, a carriage drew up outside the mill. A boy who was employed to run messages knocked at Sarah's door. 'Mr Prideau to see you, ma'am.'

CHAPTER TEN

'I understand that Mr Harcourt is away,' Prideau said.

'Yes. Perhaps I can help you. I am a director of this company, and its manager.'

Prideau looked at her with admiration. A fine figure of a woman. Her hair glowed with dark copper, and those striking, slightly slanting eyes gazed at him fearlessly. She knew how to dress, too. Her dress was of bottle-green alpaca – she must recently have come out of mourning for her father-in-law, he thought – with the newly fashionable small crinoline, the skirt looped up to show an underskirt of paler green.

He bowed. 'Then I will say what I have to say to you, ma'am, trusting that you will convey the gist of my remarks to your husband.'

'Of course. Won't you please sit down?'

He eased his considerable bulk into a chair, placed his hat on Sarah's desk, and then from an inside pocket of his coat drew out a short length of crape. 'This is fine crape you are producing, Mrs Harcourt. I will not beat about the bush – I would like to know how Harcourt's learned the secret of crape manufacture.'

'I am glad you approve of its quality, Mr Prideau. Praise from you is praise indeed.'

He raised his bushy white eyebrows. 'You have not answered my question, Mrs Harcourt.'

Her heart was pounding so loudly that she felt sure he must hear it, but outwardly she maintained her calm. 'I think, sir, it is a matter which both my husband and I would regard as confidential.'

'Oh, come, Mrs Harcourt. I am fully aware that one of my former employees has been largely concerned in the production of this material.'

Sarah smiled sweetly. 'Then you did not need to ask, did you? Yes, an employee who was dismissed by your company, Mr Prideau, and on more than somewhat flimsy grounds, I understand.'

Prideau had not been altogether displeased to learn on his arrival that Tom Harcourt was away, and that he would be able to speak only to Mrs Harcourt, expecting to meet some fluttery female whom he could soon browbeat into the vapours. But there was far more pleasure in a battle of wits with a strong adversary, and this woman would clearly be much less easy a victim than he had thought. He stroked his beard. 'Well, we will not argue about the rights and wrongs of the case, Mrs Harcourt. Loyalty from one's employees is always to be hoped for, but can seldom be guaranteed.'

'Loyalty has to be earned, Mr Prideau. I have no doubt of Goodwin's commitment to Harcourt's.'

Dammit, she knew how to put a fellow at a disadvantage! 'Let us leave the subject, Mrs Harcourt. I do not believe in weeping over spilt milk.' He fluttered the little piece of crape again. 'Your crape is selling well?'

'We are not dissatisfied,' Sarah said. Her heart had stopped beating so frantically, and she was beginning to enjoy the interview.

'So I heard, so I heard. However, you will not be surprised to learn that I do not entirely share your satisfaction.'

Sarah opened her eyes wide. 'I am indeed surprised, Mr Prideau. A business as large and as profitable as yours can scarcely be concerned by so small a rival as Harcourt's.'

'Large oaks from little acorns grow, Mrs Harcourt, as I well know myself.'

Sarah laughed. 'I am delighted that you expect our expansion to continue. But I still cannot believe that you see us as a threat to your own prosperity.'

'I have no fears for the future of Prideau's – none whatsoever. But I am . . . unhappy, shall we say? . . . to see a part of our market taken from us. You will surely understand that.'

'Is it really a part of your market? You do not manufacture crape of the same texture as ours.'

Prideau could not but admire her. She seemed to have a ready answer to his every point. He settled back in his chair and spread his hands over his corpulent stomach. He might disconcert her yet, by ending the sparring and launching a sudden attack. 'I will come to the point, Mrs Harcourt. I am prepared to make an offer to purchase your mill.'

It did take her aback. 'To purchase the mill?'

'At a fair price, of course.'

She recovered quickly. 'How interesting, Mr Prideau. Do go on. I confess that I am very curious. What, for instance, would you plan to do with the mill? Close it down? I would be sorry to hear that, and so of course would all our employees, who depend upon us for their living.'

'No, I have no such intention. I would guarantee continued production here, and employment for your work force.'

'Including the young man we spoke of earlier?' There was amusement as well as a challenge in the green eyes.

He answered smoothly. 'I would consider his case carefully, but you could not really expect me to be predisposed in his favour.'

'I suppose not. However, that is an irrelevant consideration. Tell me, Mr Prideau, what do you consider to be a fair price for the mill?'

'What would you say to fifteen thousand pounds?'

Sarah appeared to consider. 'Not enough, Mr Prideau. Not nearly enough.'

Prideau frowned. 'I had not envisaged more, but I might be prepared to go as high as twenty.'

She smiled. 'I must not play cat and mouse with you. Harcourt's is not for sale – not at any price.'

'I take that you will convey my offer to your husband.'

'His reply will be exactly the same as mine. I am sure he will be – amused at the thought.'

'I have made a serious proposition, Mrs Harcourt,' Prideau snapped, 'and I expect it to be treated seriously.'

'It will be. I apologise if my answer seemed flippant. Only recently Mr Harcourt and I discussed the possibility of an approach such as this, and decided that we would not sell, however large a sum we were offered.' It was not true, but she was certain that Tom would never agree to a sale now that the future of the mill seemed assured. 'After all,' she added brightly, 'your interest confirms our belief in our success, does it not?'

Prideau did not reply. He raised his eyebrows twice in rapid succession, and said, 'Then I have an alternative proposal, Mrs Harcourt – a merger, a partnership. Our two concerns could amalgamate.'

'By which you no doubt mean simply the acquisition of a controlling interest in Harcourt's. That would be equally unacceptable. My husband and I are determined that our mill shall remain fully independent.' She stood up. 'I thank you for the honour of your visit, Mr Prideau. I have enjoyed our conversation. Naturally, I shall inform Mr Harcourt fully of your proposals, but I fear you have had a wasted journey, and on such a cold day too.'

Prideau rose. Although his voice remained calm, the redness of his cheeks betrayed his anger. 'I am sorry you take this attitude, Mrs Harcourt. If your husband should think differently, my offers of purchase or merger will remain open. If, on the other hand, this is your final word, you need not think that I shall be content to let the situation continue or worsen.'

'I hope I am wrong in thinking that you are threatening us.'

'Business is business. We shall undoubtedly enter the market for this kind of crape ourselves.' He threw the swatch of material on to Sarah's desk. 'Perhaps in a few months' time you will be more ready to discuss the matter sensibly.'

Sarah rang the small hand-bell on her desk. 'Then it is a threat. Let me tell you, sir, that I refuse to be intimidated. If you seek war, then we shall defend ourselves, and do not think that we are incapable of doing so.' She went to the door and opened it. 'Good day, Mr Prideau.'

The messenger boy appeared in the doorway, and angrily Prideau stumped out. Sarah went back to sit at her desk. She was trembling and felt almost faint with anger and alarm.

She sent for Richard and told him what had transpired. 'It

was only to be expected, I suppose. What do we do?'

'We mustn't lose our heads,' Richard said. 'We have a little time in hand. It will take them several months to engrave a crimping cylinder, to experiment with the weave, to get everything right, and during that time we have to establish ourselves as firmly as we can with our customers.'

'What do you think Prideau's tactics will be?'

'He might threaten to cut off supplies of their ordinary crape if the retailers continue to order ours, but that would probably be his last resort. I think he'll start by doing everything he can to undercut us – even selling at a loss.'

'Can you cut our costs at all?'

'Probably not without reducing the quality. We mustn't do that.'

Sarah tapped a pencil on her desk, in an irregular rhythm. 'We need a council of war. Fortunately, Mr Harcourt is due home this evening.' She thought for a moment, and then said impulsively, 'Come to dinner, Richard, and bring Mr Hill. We can discuss it then.'

'Are you sure that will be all right, ma'am?' Richard asked.

'Of course. Why should it not be? We can take the time we need without interrupting work here. We will eat at eight o'clock.'

It was Richard's first visit to Orchard House. Much less imposing than The Grange, the square Georgian building was nonetheless impressive. Inside, the rooms were well proportioned, but the vast amount of furniture that had been brought from the mansion made them seem smaller than they really were. At the same time, Richard thought, they had a friendlier, more homely atmosphere.

Sarah was not there when he and Mr Hill were shown into the drawing-room. Tom Harcourt greeted them and introduced them to his mother and his sister Jane. He was evidently not too pleased that his wife had invited two of his employees to dinner, and barely spoke further to either of them during the short period before the meal was served.

Mrs Harcourt Senior, still dressed in black and wearing her widow's cap and veil, played the gracious hostess, and deciding that Mr Hill was more suitable in age than Richard as a partner for conversation, summoned him to stand before her. 'And where do you live?' she asked.

'In a humble dwelling, ma'am, which may well have escaped your notice. It is called, by a quaint conceit of an earlier occupant, Sunbeam Cottage.'

'I know it. I know it well. It stands next to the forge, does it not? But it is a very small cottage. I would not think for instance, that you had room for a pianoforte.'

'Indeed, ma'am, we could not accommodate such an instrument. Fortunately, we do not feel the lack, since neither Mrs Hill nor I could play if we had one.'

'How curious,' Mrs Harcourt Senior said. 'No pianoforte. One does forget how the poor live.'

Mr Hill would have liked to tell her that the poor had no difficulty in remembering their poverty, but contented himself with a brief smile.

'After dinner my daughter shall play for you.' Mrs Harcourt called across the room, 'Jane! After dinner you shall play for Mr Hull.'

'No, Mama,' Jane replied. 'After dinner our guests will be discussing business with Tom and Sarah.'

'Oh, yes. How very tiresome.' She fanned herself rapidly. 'Well, you must come another time. My daughter is a quite brilliant pianist.'

'Yet I'll warrant she cannot outshine her gracious mother,' Mr Hill said, hiding his insincerity with a warm smile and a little bow.

'Oh, how charming. You must indeed visit us more often, Mr Hall.'

Jane had turned back to Richard to resume their conversation. 'My sister-in-law tells me the new crape is much in demand, Mr Goodwin.'

'It would appear so, Miss Harcourt.'

She wished that she could think of something brilliant to arouse the interest of this attractive young man, or even to put him a little more at his ease. She looked up at him. He really was very handsome.

Richard realised that he had been discourteous in answering so briefly, and wondered what topic of conversation he could introduce. 'Are you interested in reading, Miss Harcourt?' he ventured.

Her eyes lit up as she smiled, transforming her face and making her almost pretty. He noticed her even white teeth, and the gleam of her black hair against her pale skin. She was slight of build, and small-boned, and her pale pink dress made her look fragile and almost child-like, as though she had not fully grown up.

'Indeed, yes. I am a voracious reader, and one of the library's most regular customers. And you?'

'I have little time nowadays, Miss Harcourt. But my parents brought me up to love books. May I ask if you have a favourite author?'

'I dote upon Miss Austen's novels. You know them? Oh, you should. Oh, what a treat lies before you! Start with *Emma*, Mr Goodwin. Many people prefer *Pride and Prejudice*, but *Emma* is my favourite.'

'I shall remember it, Miss Harcourt.'

At that moment Sarah appeared, resplendent in turquoise taffeta, and called them all to the dining-room.

Richard was unable to resume his literary discussion with Jane Harcourt, since conversation at the table was entirely dominated by Mrs Harcourt Senior, who barely stopped to take breath, while at the same time contriving to consume a large portion of the excellent roast beef. At the conclusion of the meal, she and Jane retired, and the others returned to the drawing-room.

Tom Harcourt brought with him a brandy bottle and glass, and poured himself a liberal measure, but did not offer any to either Richard or Mr Hill. 'You both know, I believe, of Mr Prideau's visit,' he said. 'And now we are to discuss the matter, so I am told, and formulate our defence. Perhaps we had better begin, Hill, with our current costings and profit margins.'

'Yes, sir. I brought some notes with me.' Mr Hill pulled a small bundle of papers from his pocket. 'The gross profit on the crape is in the region of thirty per cent, though I must beg you not to hold me responsible for the ultimate accuracy of that statement, made as it is at a time when production is barely in its stride.'

'How does that figure compare with Prideau's?' Sarah asked.

'Appreciably lower, ma'am. They make over forty per cent. On the other hand, if we can increase our output, there is no reason to suppose that we could not match them.'

'But it means, does it not?,' she continued, 'that if they start undercutting us, it will be virtually impossible at present for us to reduce our prices in line with theirs?'

'We should be making more money,' Tom said. He turned to Richard. 'I seem to remember you saying that our overheads would be so much lower than Prideau's that we should be much more profitable.'

'That was before Goodwin joined us, my dear,' Sarah said. 'He knew nothing of our circumstances then. Even if our profit margins were higher, we shouldn't be able to match Prideau's if they begin a war on prices.'

'I don't see why not.'

'For two reasons: firstly, because they produce so much more than we do, and secondly, because they do not have our debts to pay, nor our desperate need to replace our old machines.'

Tom raised his eyebrows briefly, and poured himself a second glass of brandy.

Mr Hill gave a little cough. 'Might I make a suggestion, ma'am?'

'Please do.'

'Faint heart never won fair lady, they say. At the moment the market for Gentleman's Mourning Crape is exclusively ours, and until Prideau's begin to sell a product similar to our own, I would suggest that we unhesitatingly raise our prices, and by a substantial amount.'

'But surely that will inhibit our sales.'

'I do not judge so, ma'am. The orders coming in indicate that demand is already high and is rising – a situation which has long been recognised by astute men of business as the occasion for increasing both prices and profits. We shall bring in money to pay off our debts and possibly even build up some reserves, and so put ourselves in a stronger financial position if competitive prices are forced upon us.'

'What is your opinion, my dear?' Sarah asked Tom.

Tom's mind had been far away. 'Eh? What?'

'Please go over it again, Mr Hill,' Sarah said, trying to keep the impatience out of her voice.

Once he understood the proposition, Tom argued fiercely against it, claiming that their customers would be antagonised. 'Besides,' he said, 'when Prideau's start selling their crape, they'll be able to undercut us not by pennies, but by shillings. Especially if, as I suspect, they start by selling at a loss in order to get the market away from us.'

'My friend Goodwin suggested they might do that, sir,' Mr Hill said, 'but I doubt it. Long acquaintance with Mr Prideau has taught me that he has a deep-rooted aversion to selling anything without making a profit on it. Should he one day consider disposing of his immortal soul, he would outdo the devil in his bargaining.' He turned quickly to Sarah. 'Oh, I beg your pardon, ma'am – that is no sentiment to express before a lady.'

'Continue, Mr Hill,' Sarah laughed. 'I am sure you are right.'

'Well, ma'am, first of all I should emphasise that as soon as Prideau's enter the market, we should revert to our present price. That would make the differential a matter of pennies only. Now, let us suppose that they do price the new crape below cost. They would do so for a few months at the most, after which Mr Prideau would begin looking for profits again. Moreover, if he set a really low retail figure, he would have little alternative but to reduce prices on his other products to bring them into line, and that I am sure he would not want to do.'

'In short,' Sarah commented, 'if we can survive during the

first months of his entry into our market, eventually we should find ourselves competing more equally.'

'You express my beliefs with a clarity and brevity which I wish I could emulate, ma'am.'

'I wish he could too,' Tom muttered, and yawned.

'Your advice is excellent, Mr Hill, and I thank you,' Sarah said.

Tom drained his third glass of brandy. 'It all smacks of desperation methods to me.'

'The situation *is* desperate. Prideau wasn't joking when he made his threat. I think we should at least try the idea out on a few of our customers. Ask their advice, Tom. Flatter them.'

'You don't need to tell me how to deal with our customers. I am not a complete fool, though you appear to think so.' He stood up. 'It is time these men left. I am tired. You forget that I have spent the whole day travelling.'

Richard and Mr Hill rose, thanked their hosts and made their departure as quickly as they could.

On the way to their homes, Mr Hill said, 'You know, my friend, I am grateful to you for persuading me to join you – Brentfield is delightful, and the work at Harcourt's is decidedly to my taste. But, between ourselves, it will be an unhappy day when Mrs Harcourt elects to retire from the business.'

'I agree. But if she left, he wouldn't necessarily be in charge.'

'Who else? You, Richard?' Mr Hill chuckled.

For a moment, Richard was tempted to reveal the extent of his ambitions, but even to such a friend he could not be completely frank. 'Of course not,' he replied, laughing. 'I just meant that he might not be capable.'

'Ah, you refer to the demon alcohol, no doubt. Our master is indeed somewhat over fond of the distillation of the grape.'

'The sooner he drinks himself to death, the better, as far as I am concerned,' Richard said.

'I would not like this to be known to my wife, who is a lady of high Christian principles, and on whom I rely to intercede on my behalf with the Almighty, but, Richard my boy,' Mr

Hill lowered his voice to a dramatic whisper, 'I believe that I agree with you.'

Mr Hill's pricing suggestions were put into effect. The increases were accepted by the trade with little resistance, most retailers being happy enough to enjoy their own improved profits, and sales to the public were scarcely affected.

Christmas came and went, and in the first months of 1868 money began to flow into the mill, and most of the bank loan was repaid. The crape department was working to capacity, and when the flow of orders grew, additional staff were trained and a shift system instituted so that longer hours could be worked. A parallel system was set up alongside the original, ready to go into production once Alfred Bunn had completed the engraving of a new cylinder.

Prideau's attack started in April. The retail price of Harcourt's Crape for Gentlemen had been increased in two stages to five shillings and sixpence a yard, but now Prideau's announced their new line at one and sixpence less.

'We should reduce ours to three and sixpence,' Tom said.

'No,' said Sarah. 'Prideau knows that four shillings is an economic price, and that we can match it. He has evidently decided not to fight on prices, but hopes to wipe us out by his strength in the market-place. We'll come down to our original four shillings, the same as his, and rely on our customers' loyalty, and your efforts, my dear.'

'I still think we should undercut him.'

'No. We must fight by providing the best possible service – quick deliveries, maintenance of quality, and good relations with our customers.'

The impact of Prideau's competition was felt immediately. Orders declined dramatically, and though some customers remained loyal to Harcourt's, Tom was in the depths of gloom. 'We might just as well pack up,' he said.

'We're not beaten yet,' Sarah told him, though she herself was near to despair.

* * *

On a Saturday in early May of that year, Joe Jolly's employment at Prideau's Mill came to an end. It was sooner than he had expected, and it all stemmed, be believed, from that day when he had tried to defend young Richard Goodwin against the charge levelled by Mr Leadbetter. The general manager had been his enemy ever since, and no doubt had persuaded Mr Prideau that Joe's useful service to the company was over. Bastards, they were, both of them!

He did not bear any grudge against Richard. Indeed, in a curious way, one of the things he resented most was that he was now relinquishing the crape department to a new overseer who had less talent than Richard had in his little finger. God only knew what a mess he would make of things.

Joe took a last look round the empty crape room. He would miss it when he and his wife were living in the workhouse. He would miss his pipe too – there would be no money for tobacco. He took it out and filled it, and then, in defiance of the rules, felt for his matches. Why should he wait until he was outside? He struck a match, lit the pipe, shook the match to extinguish it, and dropped it to the floor. Then he stumped out.

Later that evening, the night watchman smelt burning, which he traced eventually to the crape department. Smoke was billowing from beneath the door, which was of course locked. He took an axe and broke through, revealing an inferno of flames. The efforts of the fire brigade proved fruitless, and the crape department was totally destroyed, leaving nothing but a tangle of twisted and useless metal among the ashes. The disaster was only mitigated for Prideau's by the fact that they had recently set up a crape-making plant at the mill in the Midlands, but its output was small and confined to the lighter materials.

Joe Jolly was as shocked as anyone, but he felt no guilt. His match had been quite dead before he threw it down. He was sure of that. It must have been an accident. When questioned, he reported that everything had been in order when he left the crape room for the last time.

Although everyone at Harcourt's could not but rejoice at

this fortuitous removal of their competition, Sarah wrote to Prideau to express her genuine distress. 'Rivals we may be,' her letter said in part, 'but not enemies, and I would not have wished to hear such horrifying news. I trust that your great company will soon recover from this devastating blow.'

Prideau's reply came swiftly. 'Madam, I thank you for your letter and your sympathetic remarks. Our tragedy is your good fortune, of which you will no doubt take advantage, and for that I shall not blame you. In the circumstances I am more than ever interested in the acquisition of your mill, and would be prepared to discuss the possibility of a substantially improved offer. Yrs. faithfully, Jas. Prideau.'

A polite reply was sent to the effect that Harcourt's attitude remained the same as when the matter had first been broached.

Sarah went to the crape department, and asked Richard to call all the workers together. She told them what had happened at Prideau's, and then went on. 'It may seem almost miraculous for our competitor to be removed from our path in this way. But his absence will be no more than temporary. It is essential for us to make every effort during the next few months to establish Harcourt's so firmly in the crape market that when he returns in strength he cannot harm us. That means each one of us working harder and with greater care and precision than ever before. I myself shall do everything possible to make Harcourt's Mill prosperous, and I know that with your help I shall succeed.'

They cheered her.

Once again the mill's activity became hectic. Alfred Bunn completed the second crimping cylinder, and began work on a third, with a new and distinctive pattern which Frances had devised. They wondered whether to go in for the manufacture of lighter crapes, now that Prideau's stranglehold had been broken, but Sarah was against the idea. 'Let us establish ourselves firmly in our own speciality,' she said. 'To start other kinds of production would demand a huge expansion, and we are not ready for that – yet.'

Richard agreed. 'I couldn't cope with more than we're doing now.'

She laughed at him. 'Why, Richard, I never thought to hear

you say that. I thought you could cope with anything.' She turned away. 'But you're right of course. I worry about you sometimes – you drive yourself too hard.'

'You do too.'

'It's in my nature, I suppose. We're two of a kind, you and I.'

It was almost impossible not to go to her and take her in his arms but somehow he stopped himself. 'I must get back,' he said, and left the room quickly.

Sarah was not the only one who worried about Richard's health. His mother watched him anxiously as each night he came home late, ate a hasty supper and went straight to bed, rising early the next morning to return to his work. Even on Sundays he would often go to the mill – unless he fell asleep in his chair, which was not natural in one so young. If he did not take more care he would wear himself out, and become as much of an invalid as she was. She was so short of breath, and dependent more and more on Frances. She worried about Frances too. The girl was pining, because she had lost her heart to that engraver, and it was obvious that he did not return her love.

Alfred Bunn had joined the family for Sunday dinner quite often. Sometimes Mr and Mrs Hill had been invited too, and a jolly time they had all had, laughing at Mr Hill's drolleries, and at the by-play between him and his long-suffering wife.

Despite the close friendship between them, Richard had always hesitated to call the little man by his Christian name. And then one day he had dared to say, 'Come warm yourself by the fire, Josh.'

'Mr Hill, please. No one ever calls me anything else.'

'But Joshua is your name?'

'I believe so. I use it so rarely that I am never quite sure. Even Mrs Hill calls me "Mr Hill".'

Alfred Bunn, on the other hand, allowed a greater familiarity, but maintained an almost total silence about his life before he came to Brentfield, and indeed spoke very little. It always surprised Richard, for he seemed to remember him as quite loquacious on the first occasion that they had met, in the squalid room in Seven Dials. Perhaps it was the presence of women which embarrassed him. Alfred was always pleasant enough, and polite, but he seemed to distance himself from them.

Poor Frances, Elizabeth thought. Still, at least she had the consolation of being able to work with the man she loved. Now that the firm was prosperous again, Sarah had insisted on formalising Frances' position and paying her for her design work.

Richard had also received an increase in his pay, and nowadays the family could always eat well, and afford little luxuries from time to time. Richard often tried to persuade his mother to move from the cottage, saying that they could afford to take a house in the village, and live in somewhat grander style. But Elizabeth always refused to contemplate such an idea. At least while her two remaining children were unwed, there was no reason to change.

In the early Spring of 1869, Alfred completed his work on the new crimping cylinder. The idea had been to produce a gauze which was embossed with a much bolder pattern, but which, since the thread was less highly twisted, would not have so much curl. Its production gave Richard a number of problems, but they were finally overcome, and Harcourt's were able to present a new crape to the trade. It was well received, and was soon selling steadily, though their original design continued to be more in demand, partly because they had maintained its retail price of four shillings a yard, whereas the new crape was sold at four shillings and sixpence, a price justified by its slightly richer appearance.

Abandoning the ruins of his mill at Franton, Mr Prideau had extended his premises in the Midlands. Tom, who had passed by on one of his selling trips, reported that the new mill was vast – much bigger than the factory which had been destroyed. He had been able to take a close look while it was still in course of construction, and had been awed by the size of the work-rooms, the modern design of the whole building, and the imposing railings which surrounded its grounds, with great iron gates in which the name 'Prideau' had been impressively wrought.

Evidently their competitor would be back before long, stronger than ever. The Harcourts had, however, little fear. The past few months had firmly established them in the market, and they felt confident that they would retain the larger part of their trade.

So it proved. Prideau's ascendancy over all their rivals in the lighter crapes was soon resumed, but although they also produced the heavier materials, most of the customers continued to stock the Harcourt designs, and since public demand was increasing daily as the custom of going into heavy mourning grew more widespread, the competition was barely noticeable.

Richard's work seemed endless. Although he had now trained three overseers to a point where he could trust them to work satisfactorily on their own, there was always so much to do that he had never a spare moment. Sarah was equally occupied, and as a result they met far less often at the mill. Instead, she had taken to inviting him to dinner at frequent intervals. Tom seemed to have accepted the fact that Richard was a regular visitor, and Sarah was careful to ensure, when Tom was absent, that she and Richard were adequately chaperoned.

Richard always enjoyed his visits, although it meant listening to Mrs Lottie Harcourt's foolish chatter and hearing again and again her complaints about the cramped conditions in which she was forced to live.

'I cannot understand my son and daughter-in-law, Mr Goodwin,' she would say to him confidentially. 'We could easily afford a domicile in keeping with our station, now that the mill is so successful again, but they will not hear of it. I have asked and asked, but they are deaf to every plea. How can they be so unfeeling? They know how much I suffer in this wretched Orchard House – "Orchard Hovel" it should be called. Oh, I know I should not speak of them in such terms to a mere acquaintance, but I have known you ever since you were a little boy and have always regarded you most highly.'

Richard would smile inwardly at that, and turn, when he had the opportunity, to talk to Jane, whose conversation interested him far more.

After they had eaten, while Mrs Harcourt and Jane played endless games of Bezique, he would usually discuss business with Sarah. That was the real pleasure, just to be with her – a pleasure dimmed only when Tom was of the company.

In some ways, his success as a salesman seemed to have mellowed Tom, and he was much more friendly, though it still apparently never occurred to him to offer Richard a measure from the brandy bottle which was always at his side. Often, by the time that Richard left, Tom would be almost incapable, and Richard would walk home miserably, sickened by the thought of that drunken sot sharing a bed with Sarah.

The summer of 1869 passed, and as, on an evening in September, Richard made his way to Orchard House, he was struck by the beauty of the countryside. The autumn had come early that year, and in the last light of day, the trees were painted in gold and red and russet brown. Richard was not one of those who found it a sad season, and as he inhaled the crisp air, he felt a glow of contentment. A pleasant evening lay ahead. Sarah would be there, and Jane too.

But after dinner, Tom was more offensive than ever. 'Come to bed, Sarah,' he demanded, his voice slurred. He staggered over to her, and seized her arm. She shook him off, and he went back to his chair and unsteadily poured himself another brandy, slopping his liquor over the carpet. Soon he drained his glass, and repeated his command. 'Come to bed.'

Sarah looked at Richard, her face an expressionless mask. 'I think perhaps you had better go, Richard.'

Although the night was chilly, Richard stopped in Brentfield to lean on the bridge and watch the waters of the river flowing gently along. 'Oh, God!' he cried inwardly. 'If only she were free . . . ' He berated himself for a fool. Sarah cared nothing for him except as a business colleague, and even if she had loved him, would never dream of leaving her husband.

Women in her position did not behave like that. She might have been unconventional enough to become 'Our Missus', but that was not a matter for scandal, as a break with marital tradition would have been.

For the thousandth time he told himself that he must forget her. But how could he? 'By taking a wife,' a voice in his head said. He laughed aloud. Where would he find a wife? Where was there a woman who could possibly drive Sarah from his mind and heart?

It was then, to his surprise, that he thought of Jane Harcourt.

CHAPTER ELEVEN

Over the next several days, Richard thought a great deal about Jane Harcourt. He was very fond of her. Their conversations had ranged over many subjects besides books, and he had found that their opinions and ideas usually coincided to a pleasing degree. True, she did not excite him as Sarah did, nor did he think of her constantly, and ache to take her in his arms, but he was much attracted to her, and the affection he felt was indeed of more than a brotherly nature.

Was that a sufficient basis for marriage? Since Sarah was for ever beyond his reach, he could think of no one else with whom he would consider sharing his life. And he needed to marry – not just because he was twenty-six, and it was time to settle down, but because only marriage could release him from his longing for Sarah.

From the back of his mind he brought out the other thought – the cold, calculating thought which he did not wish to acknowledge as a true motive: marriage to Jane would mean an alliance with the Harcourts, perhaps a directorship, and certainly a step towards the realisation of his ambitions.

No, that did not enter into it. Had she been a shrew, or as foolish as her mother, he could not have contemplated making her his wife. However desirable membership of the Harcourt family might be, he could never bind himself to a woman he despised or disliked. But far from that, he was even, he told himself, a little in love with her. Was it possible to be in love with more than one woman at the same time? He remembered Mr Hill talking of bigamy, and saying that some people thought it was the natural condition of the human male. That had been a joke, of course, and in any case, the love that he felt for Jane was not to be compared with his passion for Sarah. Nevertheless . . .

And what of Jane herself? Would she accept a proposal of marriage from someone like him – a worker at the mill, who lived in a tiny cottage, and had no money or position to offer her? The Harcourts would undoubtedly be opposed to the match, but it was possible that she would ignore them. He was not sure of her age, knowing only that she was older than Tom, which would make her thirty or thereabouts. She must believe herself to be firmly on the shelf, and might not be unwilling to take the opportunity of marriage with someone of whom she was fond, whatever her family said against it. And Richard felt certain that she *was* fond of him – which brought him again to his first question: was a mutual fondness a good enough recipe for a successful partnership, if passion were lacking?

He put the thoughts away. There was no hurry.

The next time that Richard visited Orchard House, it was as if Mrs Harcourt Senior had been reading his mind. Overhearing Jane talk of some romance she had borrowed from the library, she said, 'I have no patience with these novelists, filling the heads of young girls with such nonsense! Life is not like that, Mr Goodwin, I do assure you. Oh, in our salad days we indulge ourselves in passions of the heart, but we come to understand that true love grows out of fondness and affection. Why, the best of marriages frequently begin with little more than respect and regard on either side.' She took her handkerchief from her reticule. 'Mr Harcourt and I were a case in point. When we married we scarcely knew one another, but oh, the love that grew between us! We adored each other, and no one knows, Mr Goodwin, how much, how very grievously I miss my dear, dear husband.' She sniffed, and dabbed at her eyes, recovering rapidly, however, when dinner was announced.

Richard was unusually silent that evening. Even if her grief were false, and all her opinions somewhat suspect, perhaps there was some truth in what Mrs Harcourt had said. He looked at Jane again, and felt a surge of desire as he imagined himself taking her delicate frame into his arms, and making love to her.

'Richard! You're not listening,' Sarah said. 'Day-dreaming

about crape and your machines, no doubt. We can talk business later. Now we are having a civilised conversation.' She turned to the others. 'He eats, sleeps and dreams the mill. It's a good thing for Harcourt's that he does, but really, Richard, there is a limit.'

'I am sorry.'

'What he needs,' Mrs Harcourt Senior said, 'is a wife. It is time you married, Mr Goodwin. Have you never thought of matrimony?'

Richard glanced involuntarily at Jane, who blushed. Hastily he tried to cover his embarrassment. 'Frequently, ma'am, but I have always been afraid to ask in case you should reject me.'

Mrs Harcourt gazed at him in astonishment. For one dreadful moment he thought that she was about to take his joke as a serious proposal of marriage, but then she laughed, and said, 'Oh, you are a naughty boy to be such a tease, Mr Goodwin! Suppose I had taken you at your word? But, seriously, it is time for you to accept your responsibilities, and take a wife.'

'I will give it my most serious consideration,' he said, smiling.

The more he thought about it, as the weeks went by, the more attractive Richard found the idea of marriage to Jane. She really was the most charming of companions, and he suspected that she would really blossom once freed from her mother's dominance.

The chances of speaking to Jane on her own were few and far between, but a fortnight before Christmas an opportunity came. Neither Sarah nor Tom nor Mrs Lottie Harcourt attended morning service at the church that Sunday, since all three were suffering from colds, and because the roads were icy and treacherous for a horse and trap, Jane had come on foot.

As they emerged from the church, Richard left his mother and Frances talking to the Rector, and went to Jane. Raising his hat, he asked, 'May I accompany you to your home, Miss Harcourt? Perhaps you should take my arm – the paths are so slippery.'

'That is kind of you. But your mother and your sister . . .?'

'They will be able to help each other. I have already told them that I intended to offer you my assistance. You see, there is something I particularly wish to say to you.' He gave her his arm.

After they had walked along a short distance without speaking, Jane said, 'You had something to say to me, Mr Goodwin?'

He took a deep breath. 'Miss Harcourt, you must be aware of the high regard I have for you.' He found it difficult to continue.

'Yes, Mr Goodwin . . .?' Her voice was a mere whisper.

'I . . . I want you to do me the honour of becoming my wife.' He felt her hand tighten momentarily on his arm. 'I know that I come from a humble background, and I cannot offer you –'

'Hush!' She was silent then, as she tried to still the pounding of her heart. At last she said, 'Our differing backgrounds mean nothing to me, Mr Goodwin, but I had not expected this, and I . . . I need time. Will you allow me to delay my answer?'

'Of course. For as long as you require.'

An embarrassment lay between them as they walked the rest of the way to Orchard House, and neither spoke. When they reached the door, Richard said, 'Can you say when I may expect an answer, Miss Harcourt?'

'Soon. I will send you word. Soon, I promise.' She looked up at him and blushed. 'Thank you . . . thank you for escorting me home. It was most kind.'

After lunch that day, Jane, taking advantage of a pause in the conversation, suddenly said, 'I have something of importance to tell you all. I am going to marry Mr Richard Goodwin.'

There was a stunned silence.

'What?' Tom exploded.

Mrs Harcourt Senior gave a little shriek. 'Goodwin? Richard Goodwin?'

'He has dared to propose marriage?' Tom asked.

'Yes. This morning.'

'And you have accepted him?'

'No, but I intend to.'

'You cannot! I forbid it! I shall not give my consent.'

Jane looked at him calmly. 'I am of age, Tom. I had hoped that you might be happy for me, but if you do not approve, I shall marry him nonetheless.'

'But he is a . . . a workman.'

'He is rather more than that, I believe,' Jane said. 'What is of greater importance, he is a gentleman.'

'I suppose he told you he loved you.' There was a dangerous note in Tom's voice.

'I believe I have his affections, as he has mine.'

Lottie Harcourt's mind was in a whirl. It was hardly a suitable match, but it had always been her ambition to see all her daughters wed, and even a bad marriage was better than none. Besides, she could not help liking Richard. There had been that trouble when he was young, but nowadays he was always polite and considerate, and he had done a great deal for Harcourt's. In any case, who was Tom to lay down the law to Jane in that way? He might be the nominal head of the family, but in such a matter as this he should look first to his mother's opinion. 'I am so delighted for you, my dear,' she cried. 'Oh, come and kiss me, Jane! You do not understand, Tom, the dictates of a woman's heart. What does his position matter, if he is honest and true, and if he loves Jane, and she loves him?' She found her handkerchief, and began to weep. 'If only your dear father could have been alive to hear this happy news.'

Jane went to her, in some astonishment at this unexpected approval, and was enfolded in a damp hug.

Tom looked at Sarah. 'And do you share this rejoicing?'

Sarah's first reaction had been a sudden twinge of jealousy. Absurd, she told herself, when poor Jane had plainly doted on Richard for so long; but for a wild moment she thought how joyful it would be if she were now in Jane's shoes. She knew only too well to whom Richard's heart had truly been given. Perhaps he had turned to Jane as an escape from the forbidden enchantment that she herself exercised on him. She told herself not to be a fool – he had probably fallen out of love with her, and in love with Jane. And again jealousy stabbed at her.

Tom's question brought her back to the present. 'I think it is for Jane to decide whether the match is suitable or not.'

'You realise what lies behind it? If he marries into the family, he thinks to improve his position at the mill.'

'How dare you, Tom!' Jane flared. 'I know that such a thought has not entered his head.'

'It says little for your sister's charms if you believe that to be his motive,' Sarah said.

'Did you ask him why he wanted to marry you?' Tom went on.

'No.'

'Then do so. Not that I think he is likely to confess the true reason.'

'No more. Tom!' Mrs Harcourt said. 'You are destroying your sister's happiness. Sarah is right – this is a matter for Jane to decide. If she should listen to any advice, it is that of her mother, and for my part I shall be delighted to welcome so handsome and well-mannered a young gentleman into our family.'

Tom refilled his brandy glass. 'All right. I shall say no more. But don't say I didn't warn you, Jane.'

'When is the wedding to be?' Mrs Harcourt asked.

'I haven't thought of that yet,' Jane replied.

'And where are you going to live?' Tom asked. 'In their cottage, alongside his mother and sister? An elegant establishment for you.'

'Oh, Tom, why are you being so unkind?' Jane began to cry.

'You can live here,' Sarah said.

'With Tom being horrid to me and to Richard?' Jane said tearfully. 'That's the last thing I would want. I am going to my room. I have a letter to write.' She ran out.

Tom shrugged and drained his brandy. 'She's a blind little fool.'

'I forbid you to say another word to her,' his mother said. 'You should rejoice for her. They are perfectly suited. He may not be quite of our class, but we do well to remember that Mr Harcourt's father was merely a haberdasher, at one time – though a very high-class haberdasher, I am sure. In any case, I have never been one for the snobbery that is so prevalent nowadays. He will make her very happy. It is a true love match – and there is no surer foundation for a marriage than that.'

Tom had fallen asleep in his chair. Mrs Harcourt chattered on, oblivious of the fact that he was snoring gently. Sarah looked at him with distaste. Whatever Richard's motives, whatever his station in life, at least Jane was not marrying a drunkard.

That same afternoon, a maid brought Jane's letter to the Goodwins' cottage. Richard hesitated before opening it. If she had accepted him, he was committed, irrevocably, and for a moment he was seized with panic at the idea of having put himself into such a position.

'My dear, dear Richard (the first time I have called you that, except in my heart),' the letter began. 'I am honoured by your proposal of marriage, and as you must have guessed already, I accept with joy, promising, dear Richard, to be all that you could desire in a wife. You have made me so very, very happy.

'It had been my hope that you might call upon us this evening, but it pains me to tell you that my brother does not view our betrothal favourably (though Mama and my sweet sister-in-law support me most lovingly), and it might be best to postpone the visit. I assure you that Tom's disapproval, unjustified as it is, does not alter my joy at the thought of becoming – I hardly dare write the words – Mrs Richard Goodwin.

'I beg you to come for luncheon on Sunday next, by which time I am sure that Tom will be reconciled to our happiness. Come at one thirty – we shall have an opportunity to speak to each other before we eat at two.

'My fondest love to you, my dearest Richard. Your adoring Jane Harcourt.'

Richard's doubts were swept away. Tom's opposition was only to be expected, and if Jane loved him so much, then he had indeed made a wise choice. He told his mother and Frances his news.

Elizabeth Goodwin was astonished, but delighted, and wept and laughed and hugged him until a paroxysm of coughing seized her. Richard and Frances had to help her to her chair and fetch the medicine that Dr Wood had prescribed, which sometimes eased the coughing, but offered no cure. 'You will marry soon, Richard?' she whispered. 'I should like to cradle a grandchild before I die, and there is little time.'

'What nonsense, Mama! You have years of life before you.'

She smiled sadly.

Richard turned to Frances. 'Will you not congratulate me?'

'Is it truly what you want?'

'Yes. Yes, of course it is.'

She kissed him. 'Then I congratulate you with all my heart and wish you every happiness.'

When Richard next saw Sarah at the mill, she too gave him her good wishes. Did he imagine it, or was there a reserve in her manner? Her smile seemed forced, and she gave him a strange, penetrating look. He could not meet her gaze, and dropped his eyes.

When Richard entered the drawing-room of Orchard House the following Sunday, Jane was standing, waiting for him. She wore a gown of crimson silk, which he had not seen before, more flamboyant than the dresses in pastel shades which she usually affected. Her head was lowered in shyness, and he thought that he had never seen her looking so charming. He went to her and took her hands in his, marvelling at the delicacy of her fingers, and the tiny wrists. 'My own sweet Jane.'

She looked up at him, and her eyes filled with tears of happiness.

'May I kiss you?' he asked. He was surprised by her response to the pressure of his lips. Her arms twined around his neck, and she pressed her body against his. Her mouth tasted of honey, he thought, and his nostrils were filled with the fragrance of the lavender perfume which she always wore.

'Dear Richard, I love you so much.'

Her face alight, she was no longer Plain Jane, he thought, and desire stirred in him. 'I love you too, my dear,' he replied. And it was true.

Although his declaration and the ardour of his embrace had removed all doubts from her mind, it was only fair to tell him, Jane believed, of Tom's cruel insinuations about his motives in asking for her hand. But how to do so? 'We have so much to talk about,' she found herself babbling, 'and luncheon will soon be ready, and Mama will take over, and I shall scarce have another word with you.'

'And what will your brother have to say?'

She smiled at him. How considerate of him to have brought the subject up of his own accord. 'He has withdrawn his formal opposition to our marriage – I believe we have Sarah to thank for that – but I know he still disapproves of it.'

'No doubt he considers that you are marrying beneath you.'

'I told him I cared nothing for that. But I will be frank with you, my dear – he suspects you of marrying me solely in order to advance yourself at the mill.' There, it was out. She waited for his reply, anxious when he did not respond immediately.

'It would be foolish and untruthful,' Richard said carefully, 'to deny that I have considered what marriage into your family may mean in terms of my position.' Her face went pale, and he continued quickly, 'But I swear to you that I would never have asked you to be my wife for so cold-blooded and mercenary a reason.'

Relief flooded through her, and she reached up to put her arms around his neck, but he stopped her and went on, 'Nevertheless, my dear, I did consider it, and I was right to do so. Any man of sense who thinks of marriage must look to the advantages and the problems that it may bring. Without advancement, I could not keep you in the style I would wish. But though our marriage may hasten my promotion, I would not accept it if I did not think that I have in any case earned it.'

'Indeed, you have, Richard. Harcourt's would never have survived without your efforts, I am well aware of that.' She pulled his head down and gravely planted a kiss on his forehead. 'Oh, Richard, thank you. I value the honesty of your reply.'

He kissed her again, increasingly enchanted by her fragility, the warmth and softness of her flesh, the sweetness of her lips. Childlike in some ways she might be, but it was a woman that he held in his arms.

At last they broke apart, and he asked, 'When shall our wedding be?'

'Oh, soon, Richard, soon! As soon as possible.'

He laughed. 'Such wantonness!'

She blushed, but was saved from having to reply by a knock at the door. Sarah had come to summon them to table.

Richard had first to greet Jane's mother and brother. Mrs Harcourt was effusive and tearful. 'You have brought me much joy in my declining years.' She paused to allow him to murmur the expected protest at that phrase. 'Take care of my daughter – cherish her, and may you have a lifetime of happiness together. If you are half as devoted as my dear late husband and I were, you will indeed be a fortunate couple.'

Tom said, 'Well, Goodwin, we have to welcome you to the family, I understand. It is a development that I had not expected, but Jane has persuaded me that it is one which I must accept with good grace.'

'Thank you.'

'Come,' said Sarah. 'Luncheon is ready. We have a cold collation, Richard. I trust it will be to your liking.'

'I'm sure it will, Mrs Harcourt.'

'Oh, I think we should use our Christian names now, do you not agree, Tom?'

Tom did not reply.

Once they were seated at the table, Mrs Harcourt Senior began her inquisition. 'When *is* the wedding to be, Jane? Such a pity Christmas is too near – I always consider Christmas Day a very suitable occasion for a wedding. Do not tell me, I beg, that you are planning on a long engagement.'

'Oh, there is no hurry, Mama,' Jane said, off-handedly. 'I had thought of the year after next at the very earliest.'

'Oh, but Jane – ! Oh, you are teasing me, wicked minx. You see, Richard, what a naughty child this is that you are to wed. You will have to exert your authority, I fear. The year after next – whatever next! Come, Jane, answer me seriously.'

'Would you approve of the third Sunday in February, Mama? Could you restrain your passion until then, Richard?'

'Jane, you will be the death of me!' Mrs Harcourt gasped. 'That is a most immodest remark. Whatever will Richard think?'

Jane laughed. 'He will be less shocked than you, Mama.'

'This is no subject for levity,' Mrs Harcourt said sharply. 'But February will do admirably, if it is acceptable to Richard.'

'Whenever Jane wants.'

'Then that is settled,' Jane said. 'Now, what is next on your list of concerns, Mama?'

'Really! Your tone is impertinent, miss! I am merely expressing a mother's fond interest.'

'Perhaps I may put the next question,' Tom said. 'Where do you propose to live, Goodwin? You can hardly expect to take Jane to your cottage.'

Richard found it difficult to answer. Everything depended on what his future status at the mill was to be and whether he could look forward to a substantial increase in his income, in which case it might be possible for Jane to become mistress of a home in keeping with her upbringing and position in society.

Sarah rescued him for the moment by saying, 'There is no reason why you should not live here, at least until you have settled yourselves.'

'That is no way to begin married life,' Mrs Harcourt Senior said. 'A bride needs an establishment of her own.'

'I did not have one,' Sarah said.

'Well, no . . .' Mrs Harcourt was momentarily flustered, but then continued, with an air of triumph, 'but you were marrying *into* the Harcourt family – that made all the difference. Besides, five of us in this poky little house – it does not bear thinking of.' She turned back to Tom. 'But I have the solution to all our difficulties. Now that the mill is prosperous again, Tom, you must, you really must buy back The Grange, and then Jane and Richard can live here. It is small indeed, but quite suitable for newly-weds, I think.'

'The Grange is not for sale, as far as I am aware,' Tom said. 'In any case, I do not intend to return there. It is far too old-fashioned and inconvenient, and very costly in upkeep. However, I am in fact intending to build a new house for you and Sarah and myself.'

'A new house? Where?'

'A small site is available a little beyond The Grange – a couple of acres. I've had a preliminary discussion with the architect.'

'You said nothing to me,' Sarah said.

'I wished it to be a surprise.'

'And have you already put this house up for sale?' she asked, with some asperity.

'I do not intend to sell it.'

'Then where will the money come from?'

'We have sufficient funds lying idle in the bank.'

'The mill's money? But we cannot spend that. That is our reserve.'

'Against what?'

'Against the need for new equipment, against expansion, against a hundred eventualities. We cannot spend that money.'

'I assure you that we can.'

Sarah looked at him evenly. 'I do not agree. The whole idea is ridiculous.'

'It is not ridiculous,' Tom said coldly. 'It solves all our problems. Did you not hear what Mama suggested? Jane and Richard shall live here in Orchard House – without charge, of course.'

Mrs Harcourt Senior, Jane and Richard had been silent during this exchange. Astonished, Richard still did not speak, but Jane exclaimed, 'Tom! Oh, how generous!' and her mother clapped her hands and cried, 'The very thing! You see! You all scoff at me – don't deny it – I am well aware that you consider me a foolish old woman – but I can still think more clearly than any of you. It is an excellent plan.'

Sarah sat tight-lipped, angry blotches of colour on her cheeks. 'If you mean that it is the kind of plan which is calculated to bring us once more to the edge of bankruptcy, then you are right.'

Mrs Harcourt blinked at her for a moment, and then began to sniffle.

'Sarah!' Tom exclaimed. 'Remember we are not alone.'

She turned to him. 'Richard is to be part of the family now. Why should we spare him our disagreements? I am sure that he and Jane are grateful for your concern for them. Perhaps they are surprised too, since previously you were so –'

'Sarah, no!' Jane interrupted.

'No, you are right. I will not say what I was going to. But this idea is madness. Of course it is good of you to wish to provide a home for your sister and her husband-to-be, and had you planned a larger house where we could all live, I might concede the wisdom of the thought. But to keep Orchard House too means finding the whole cost of a new one. It will be ruinous, literally ruinous.'

'Have you quite finished?' Tom asked. 'Then let me remind you that whatever your position in the business may be, I am still the owner of Harcourt's Mill, and the head of this family. I have decided, and that is an end to it.'

Sarah put down her napkin and pushed back her chair, but then seemed to think better of it. 'Perhaps, after all, we should talk of this later, Tom.'

'Indeed we will.'

The rest of the meal was eaten in silence. Embarrassed by the quarrel, none of them had much appetite, except for Mrs Harcourt, who recovered sufficiently to plough her way resolutely through the courses. Tom waited until his mother had finished her last mouthful of the trifle, liberally laced with sherry, which was one of her favourite puddings, and then said, 'Mama, Jane, perhaps you would take Goodwin with you to the drawing-room. Sarah and I have certain matters to discuss.'

Once in the drawing-room, Mrs Harcourt conducted what was virtually a one-sided conversation. Richard was silent and Jane answered in monosyllables, but she seemed quite unaware of their lack of response, and the never-ceasing prattle flowed on and on and on.

It was over an hour before Tom and Sarah joined them. Mrs Harcourt stopped in mid-sentence as they came in. In the silence, Sarah sat on a sofa, and Tom went to stand in front of the fireplace. He looked at Sarah bleakly. 'Everyone is waiting to hear what has been decided, my dear. Perhaps you would care to tell them.'

She raised her head proudly. 'Mr Harcourt has persuaded me of the excellence of his plan. I am, I hope, a dutiful wife, as you must be, Jane, and I apologise to him and to you for my intemperate arguments at luncheon.' She smiled, and stood up and went to Jane to embrace her. 'This will be your home, my dear, and happy may you be in it.'

'And you, Mama,' said Tom, 'shall have a mansion to delight your heart.'

The tension had disappeared from the room. Jane ran to her brother to hug him, and Richard stammered his thanks, and Mrs Harcourt launched herself on a speech of excited satisfaction, larded with sentimental references to her late husband, and details of what she would require in the new house.

Richard longed to go to Sarah to tell her how much he admired her. She had accepted her defeat with immense dignity. That smile as she finished her statement must have cost her a great deal.

When the initial excitement had died down, Tom said, 'I greatly doubt whether our new house will be ready by February, Jane. I should like to suggest a short postponement of the wedding, so that you can take full possession of Orchard House immediately thereafter.'

'Oh, yes, Tom. If Richard will agree.'

Richard smiled. 'I shall try to suffer the delay courageously.'

However frustrated and angry Sarah might be, she concealed

her feelings beneath a mask of gaiety, and the afternoon and evening passed happily in a discussion of plans for the new house and talk of the wedding. Richard wondered whether anything would be said about his future position within the family business, but Tom did not mention it, and he could not bring the subject up himself.

As he walked home that evening, he thought over the strange events of the day. Why should Tom have decided suddenly on such generosity? Not, surely, solely out of concern for his sister. Nor could the plan to build a new mansion have been devised simply to silence his mother's complaints about Orchard House. There was only one answer: he had been determined to demonstrate that his word was law, both in his own house and in his business. And for whose benefit was this demonstration, if not for Sarah's? Now that he had finally and firmly put his foot down, Richard wondered whether there would be other moves to diminish her authority, to take from her the control she had exercised so well?

He was pleased by the idea of living in Orchard House, but his delight was tempered by the certainty that Sarah was right. Harcourt's might be thriving at the moment, but silk was never a stable commodity, and at any moment the market might go into a quite unpredictable decline. If that happened, they would need every penny of their reserves.

CHAPTER TWELVE

Tom Harcourt was pleased with himself. He had won the argument with Sarah conclusively, and she could never again doubt that her power was merely on loan, granted by him. He had no wish, however, to take over the day-to-day running of the mill – the freedom he enjoyed on his travels, the liquor and the women, were not to be abandoned for a dreary routine in Brentfield – and Richard's fears of change were consequently unfounded. The mill continued to run as before, except that orders flowed in ever faster, and even Sarah was forced to admit that the cost of building Tom's mansion no longer threatened their solvency.

By the Spring of 1870, the house, which Tom had already decided to call 'Harcourt Place', was rising rapidly. Midway in size between The Grange and Orchard House, it was to be a four-storey building of red brick in the Gothic style, with four large reception rooms, six bedrooms, and – unheard-of luxury – two bathrooms, in addition to servants' quarters. It seemed likely that they would be able to move in by midsummer, and Richard and Jane's wedding was fixed for the first week in July.

Richard looked forward to living in so impressive a residence as Orchard House, however poky it might seem to old Mrs Harcourt, although it would mean leaving his mother and Frances behind in the cottage, which gave him some concern. Elizabeth was increasingly frail, and the burden of looking after her fell heavily on Frances. He spoke of it to Jane, who said immediately, 'They must both come and live with us. There will be plenty of room, and I shall be able to help Frances to look after your mother.'

Although fond of Jane, Elizabeth Goodwin was far from

pleased by that idea. 'Leave the cottage?' she exclaimed in dismay. 'Why, I have lived here all my life – at least, since I married your father. I cannot leave now. Oh, no, Richard, don't ask me to do that.'

'But, Mama, we should be able to look after you properly, and Jane will be able to relieve Frances sometimes, and there will be servants too. You must think of Frances, Mama – she is wearing herself out.'

'But I am sure I am not a burden to her. She never complains.'

Richard could scarcely believe that his mother, always kind and considerate of others, should have become so selfish. No doubt sickness had changed her. It took weeks of patient argument before she finally, and with ill grace, agreed.

Frances, on the other hand, was happy, not only at the prospect of help in tending her mother, but at the thought of living in a house which would seem like a palace. 'It is so good of Jane,' she said. 'I love her already, Richard – she has such a sweet nature.' She looked up at him. 'You love her too, Richard, don't you? Really love her, I mean.'

'Of course I do. Why do you keep on asking such a silly question?'

Frances was not sure why she asked. Perhaps because she was so sure that he still longed for Sarah Harcourt. His feelings for Sarah were an ineradicable part of him, just as she was possessed by her love for Alfred Bunn. Instead of replying, she asked, 'Shall we still be able to have Alfred and Mr and Mrs Hill to visit us?'

'Of course. Why should we not?'

'Jane might not approve. You will have to consider her in all things.'

'But not who I choose to be my friends. Jane will enjoy their company as much as you and I do, I am sure. But even if she disliked them, she would welcome them for my sake. After all, she will promise to love, honour and *obey* me.'

Frances giggled. 'Oh, Richard, are you going to be a stern, horrid husband?'

'Naturally!'

* * *

By the middle of June the building of Harcourt Place had been completed, and Tom and his family moved in. They were delighted with it, although Sarah had continued to protest over Tom's extravagance as he ordered the costliest materials and every modern luxury, including parquet flooring and a dumb waiter to convey their food directly from the kitchen to the dining-room. He had also insisted on leaving their old furniture behind at Orchard House, and purchasing new, saying that it would be a poor start for Jane to face her with an empty, cheerless home.

Richard was torn between gratitude and the feeling that he would have preferred to make his own arrangements and start his married life with his own new possessions around him, though how he could have afforded to do so, he did not know. His salary had been increased a few months previously to four hundred pounds a year – a substantial amount, but barely enough to provide for himself, his wife, his mother and Frances, and for servants and the upkeep of a large establishment. He had been waiting ever since the announcement of the engagement for something to be said about his position at the mill. Tom Harcourt had, however, remained silent.

On the eve of the wedding, Tom commanded him to come to Harcourt Place after work.

Tom was affable. 'Well, tomorrow is your great day, eh? No doubt you know of Mr Punch's advice to those about to marry – "don't!". My father always used to enjoy that joke. But you are probably not to be deflected now.'

Richard laughed dutifully.

'Sit down, man, sit down. Since you are about to become a member of my family, no doubt you have been expecting some alteration in your position at Harcourt's.'

'I am not marrying your sister in the hopes of preferment.'

'Come, no high-flown sentiments, please. You will not deny that you have wondered whether this marriage would bring you some – what shall we say? – some benefit in your finances and your status.'

'If I should be given any advancement, I hope it would be

on merit. I think I can claim to have played a part in the mill's present prosperity.'

'It is precisely because of your achievements, rather than because you are marrying my sister, that your salary is to be increased to seven hundred and fifty pounds a year, though I have also had in mind your need to maintain the position in society to which Jane is accustomed.'

'It is very generous. Thank you.' It was more than he had expected.

'Now we come to the question of your position at the mill. I am sorry if it disappoints you, but I do not feel it would be appropriate yet to appoint you a member of the board. You do not look surprised.'

'No. I could hardly expect that.' He had previously come to the conclusion that Tom would not welcome any weakening of his own power, or the possibility that he might find himself facing an alliance between Sarah and Richard, whose views on the conduct of the business seemed so often in accord and in opposition to his own.

'I have, however,' Tom continued, 'decided to offer you further responsibilities. Mrs Harcourt will remain manager of the mill, but I have been concerned for some time at the burden she carries, and have persuaded her that you should relieve her of some of her present duties.'

So, thought Richard, despite earlier appearances, after winning the battle over the building of Harcourt Place, Tom had indeed decided that Sarah's power should be substantially reduced in the running of the mill too, and had merely been biding his time.

'In future,' Tom went on, 'you will not trouble her with day-to-day problems, reporting to her only in the event of a serious breakdown or anything involving a policy decision. You will be entirely responsible for the hiring or dismissal of labour, the arranging of shifts, and like matters, and not only for the crape department, but for the mill as a whole.' He cleared his throat. 'You may interpret this as evidence of my belief in your capabilities, and of the trust that I place in you. I look to you to increase the efficiency of the mill, and to lessen the strain on Mrs Harcourt. Your daily interviews with her, for instance, can largely be dispensed with.'

In addition, then, he was to be kept away from Sarah as much as possible. But why? Surely not because Tom suspected them of a liaison – he had no justification for that. Perhaps he was indeed afraid that they might plot against him.

'I understand,' Richard said.

'Then I will keep you here no longer – you have other matters to fill your mind, and I must attend my married sisters and their families. Your new duties and your increased emoluments will begin on Monday. We shall meet tomorrow.'

'Yes. And I thank you again.'

St Matthew's Church was full for the wedding. Jane's mother, her two married sisters, with their husbands and children, and Tom and Sarah filled the first two pews on the bride's side. Richard had hired a carriage to bring his mother and Frances to the church, without which Elizabeth Goodwin would not have been able to attend, so unwell had she become. A small bowed figure, heavily wrapped despite the warmth of the day, she tried vainly to stifle her constant racking cough.

Behind the families, almost the whole population of Brentfield crammed every seat, taking their places according to their station in life, as was only proper: first, personal friends and well-to-do social equals of the Harcourts, then some of the more senior employees at the mill, such as the Hills and Alfred Bunn, and tenant farmers and the like; and finally, the common people, the weavers and other workers and their families, and such servants as could be spared from Harcourt Place and Orchard House.

Although it was warm, rain had been pouring down since dawn, and the interior of the church became as humid as one of the work-rooms at the mill as steam began to rise from the damp clothing of the congregation. The rain could not, however, dampen Jane's happiness. She smiled at Richard lovingly as he made his responses, but her own vows were barely audible. That again was just as it should be – a bride must needs be shy on her wedding day.

After the service, the newly-weds were driven back to Harcourt Place, where the wedding breakfast would be served to members of the immediate family. Elizabeth Goodwin had to be taken home. She insisted that she would manage on her own, but only when a neighbour had agreed to look after her would Frances consider stepping back into the carriage to be swept off to Harcourt Place.

Tom enjoyed playing the benevolent host, and even brought himself to shake hands with the groom and to call him 'Richard', both for the first time. But Richard thought he could detect an insincerity in the words of congratulation, and his suspicions were confirmed when Jane's married sisters and their husbands were no more than frigidly polite. Tom had doubtless given it as his opinion that Jane was marrying beneath her – and that was the least that he might have said.

Richard did not care. His only concerns on this day of happiness were anxiety for his mother's health, and the fact that he could see Frances standing on her own, ignored by the Harcourts. He could not go to her, for his new mother-in-law, more outrageously painted than ever, insisted at the moment on holding him and Jane by the hand, alternately weeping hysterically and protesting her joy. Then he saw Sarah go to Frances, smiling, and talk to her and bring her to sit by her side. 'Oh, Sarah,' he thought to himself, 'you're worth all the rest of them put together.' He glanced at his bride, with an unreasoning fear that she might have detected his disloyal sentiment.

The party continued until the evening, and then Richard and Jane left to spend their wedding night in their new home at Orchard Place.

Silent with embarrassment, Jane merely nodded when Richard suggested that she might like to prepare herself for bed before he came to their room. He gave her half an hour before he climbed the stairs, took off his clothes in the dressing-room adjacent to the bedroom, and donned his nightshirt.

He could see nothing of her but a small, frightened face, peering at him from above the bedclothes. He climbed into the bed and took her gently in his arms. She was trembling. 'My wife,' he said, 'my very dear wife.' He made no attempt to kiss her, but simply held her until at last the quivering died away.

'Don't hurt me, Richard. Please.'

He kissed her then. She did not respond, and he realised that he had to overcome her fear and that his love-making would need to be slow and patient. His lips moved to her eyes, her cheeks, her neck. The skin of her face was soft but dry, as though covered with the finest, softest down, and it tasted faintly of the lavender she used. Only after some while did he risk untying the bow at the neck of her nightdress, and slipping his hand beneath the fine cambric to caress her breasts. She flinched, but he was persistent and gentle, and was rewarded at last by the first stirrings of her desire. Gradually, very slowly, he moved his hand down to explore her belly, her thighs, the soft curls.

She was so tiny and fragile, he thought, and he would have to be careful, later, not to crush her beneath his weight. Her hips were as narrow as a boy's, and yet her breasts were firm and pointed, and there was nothing boyish about the soft flesh of her thighs.

They had both been silent, but now she whispered urgently, 'Kiss me, Richard. Kiss me.' For a moment he wondered if she meant . . . But she was bending her head towards him, her lips open. She pressed herself against him, and he could feel the burning heat of her body. Soon his mouth and lips and tongue became demanding, and as she accepted his passion, his fingers moved once more between her legs.

'Now, my dear one,' he whispered, 'now you will truly become my wife. Do not be afraid. I shall be gentle.' Lying above her, he sought entrance, and thrust, and broke through.

She cried out in pain, biting her lip, and turning her head away. His movements continued, gently at first, until the swirling, all-consuming sensation began to rise in him, and he drove faster, and arched his back, and cried out in the ecstasy of release.

For a few moments he seemed to enter another world, but when he came to himself again, and looked at her, she was gazing at him, her eyes huge in their proximity to his. There was wonder in her expression, a strange kind of astonishment. 'Are you . . . are you all right?' she asked.

He laughed. 'I'm very, very happy.'

'You must forgive me,' she whispered. 'I . . . I did not know what . . . what to expect.'

'Did you not know what happens between a man and a woman?'

'No. How should I?'

'I . . . I thought perhaps your mother would have explained.'

She did not reply, seemingly wrapped in her own thoughts. Then she asked, 'Did I give you pleasure, Richard?'

'The greatest pleasure I have known.'

She smiled then, and kissed him, but as he moved again in her, could not stop herself from giving a gasp of pain.

Gently he withdrew, and turned to lie beside her. 'Did I hurt you very much?'

'Only a little. I . . . I did not know that becoming a wife was . . . like that. Oh, Richard, I do not mind if it hurts, if it gives you pleasure.'

'It will not always hurt.'

'Dear Richard, I love you very much.'

'And I love you, Mrs Jane Goodwin.'

Soon he fell asleep, but Jane lay awake, feeling the soreness still, wondering what exactly it was that he had done to her, and thinking that Richard must consider her a little goose to be so ignorant and untutored. In the marriage service he had said, 'With my body I thee worship.' Was that what it meant? Was what he had done his form of worship? But how had he known what to do? Perhaps all men knew instinctively. Or perhaps he had . . . An image of Sarah swam into her thoughts, but resolutely she banished it. Sarah was a married woman, and faithful to Tom, of that she was sure. She knew when she first met Richard that he was infatuated with Sarah – any woman would have seen it – and even since their engagement, once or twice she had caught him looking at her, in a strange, sad way. But she would not think of Sarah – only of Richard and herself, now one flesh, and of Richard telling her that he loved her. He stirred in his sleep, and she smiled contentedly. Perhaps she had exorcised Sarah from his mind.

On the Monday morning after the wedding, Richard began work in his new position at the mill. He was glad now that he had fewer occasions to meet Sarah, and grateful to be free at last from all those feelings for her which had given him so little peace of mind. He enjoyed too the additional responsibilities and the power he now exercised.

It was pleasant to return to Orchard House each evening to Jane's loving kiss and wifely attentions, and while they ate and sat afterwards in their drawing-room, he listened happily to her prattle of furnishings and the entertaining that they would have to undertake, and answered her affectionate enquiries about his work. And then they would retire to the joys of their bedroom.

It had been arranged that they should have Orchard House to themselves for close on two weeks before Elizabeth and Frances came to share their home. On the evening of the Friday which had been arranged for the move, Richard found Jane in great distress. 'Your mother is very poorly, my dear,' she said. 'Dr Wood is with her now.'

As she and Frances arrived at Orchard House, Elizabeth had suffered a major haemorrhage. 'She collapsed here in the hall,' Jane continued. 'Blood was just pouring from her mouth each time she coughed. I sent for the doctor at once, but I feared he would be too late. The men shifting her furniture were here, and they carried her to her room – though I do believe that Frances and I could have managed, for she is quite painfully thin and can weigh very little. We put her to bed, and she fell into a light sleep. Dr Wood would not disturb her rest, and promised to return later. He came back just ten minutes ago. I fear you must brace yourself for sad news, my dear.'

'I must go to her,' Richard said.

'No. Wait until the doctor comes out. Frances is with them now.'

Dr Wood's face, as he emerged from the sick-room, was grave. 'There is little that I can do, Mr Goodwin – little that anyone can do. Your mother's consumption is in an advanced stage, and, alas, it is now but a matter of time.'

'How long?' Richard asked.

'A few hours, a few days – at the most a week, I would say.' He turned to Jane. 'Let her rest, keep her warm, feed her nourishing broths. I will come again tomorrow morning.'

As he left, Frances came downstairs. 'She is asking for you, Richard.' She stood looking at him for a moment, and suddenly the tears welled up, and she began to sob.

Elizabeth was awake when Richard entered her bedroom. Her eyes were dull in the wasted features, but they lit up when she saw him, and feebly she stretched out her hand. Her voice was a mere whisper. 'I am sorry, Richard, to . . . cause . . . so much . . . trouble.'

'Hush! Do not tire yourself by talking.' He sat beside the bed.

'No, I . . . want . . . to say . . .' She was silent for a while, as though gathering her strength. 'I want to . . . tell you . . . how proud of you . . . Here I am . . . in your . . . grand house . . . with your dear wife . . . and Frances.'

Not knowing what to say, he squeezed her hand gently.

'Promise me, Richard . . . that you will always . . . look after . . . Frances.'

'I promise.'

Her lips curved in a sketch of a smile, and her eyes closed. At first Richard thought that she had gone from him, but then he saw that the bedclothes over her chest were rising and falling rhythmically, though the movement was so slight as to be almost imperceptible.

He stayed at her bedside for a long time, watching as she slept, thinking of the life that was ebbing away before his eyes.

She had had a small share of happiness, especially in the short years of her marriage, but she had seen much sorrow – his father's early death, the tragedy of Mary, even perhaps his own running away, had all been crosses for her to bear. And then to be forced to leave the home she loved . . . Yet if she were truly proud of him and his achievements, perhaps she had already forgiven him.

Silently he prayed – for Frances, for himself, above all for his mother's departing, immortal soul. But, he told himself wryly, it was in little danger. So upright, caring and God-fearing a woman as Elizabeth Goodwin did not need his prayers. She would be welcomed in Heaven, and a crown of glory would be hers for ever and ever.

She died later that evening, without having regained consciousness. Towards the end, however, when Richard came back into her bedroom to sit beside Frances, she seemed to sense his presence. Her eyes half opened, the corners of her lips moved slightly. Moments later she gave a last shuddering sigh, and was still.

After her mother's death, Frances felt herself to be an intruder in Richard's household, even though he had assured her that his home would always be hers too. The trouble was that she had so little to do now that she no longer had to look after Elizabeth. Her work for the mill was no more than occasional, and much as she would have liked to, she could not sit all day watching Alfred Bunn. Jane, proud of her new position as mistress of the household, casually waved away her offers of assistance.

All she could do was to take refuge in artistic endeavours. She went out regularly with her box of paints, producing neat little watercolours of the village and surrounding countryside. They were pretty, but she knew they were uninspired, and she was bored by them. If the weather were bad, she stayed in her room and painted still lifes. She was sick to death of bowls of fruit and fans and flowers, too.

However, it was her artistic ability which finally brought her closer to Jane, who admired her talent greatly, and one day expressed a wish for Frances to help her improve her own feeble efforts. Her draughtsmanship was excessively weak, she said, and she would dearly love instruction from so accomplished an artist.

Frances, flattered by this attention, was only too pleased to do as she was asked, and gradually the two young women spent more and more time together, and a genuine affection began to grow between them. After some weeks, Frances confessed her fear of having intruded into the household, and Jane assured her that she would be deeply wounded if Frances should ever have such nonsensical ideas again. 'This is your home, my dear, and you must treat it as such.' A thought occurred to her. 'Tell me, Frances dear, have you any special friends that you would like to entertain here? They would of course be most welcome to come and see you at any time.'

'Has Richard not spoken to you on this subject?'

Jane wrinkled her brow. 'I do not think so.'

'I thought he must have done. He and I discussed it before you were married, and he said that you would not object. And then when nothing happened, I thought perhaps you did object, and of course in that case –'

'Frances dear, I have no idea what you are talking about.'

'Oh, I'm sorry. You see, when my mother was alive and Richard was living with us, we used sometimes to have Mr Bunn and Mr and Mrs Hill to join us at the table.'

'I believe I met Mr Hill once. He came to dinner when Tom and Sarah were living here – before I was married – he came to discuss something about the business.'

'It used to be such fun, Jane – we would laugh and laugh. Mr Hill is so very droll. But . . .' She tailed off.

'But what?'

'Well . . . they are not of your social standing,' she mumbled.

'I have no patience with such nonsense!' Jane exclaimed, sounding, Frances thought, a little like her mother. 'If they are friends of yours, then they shall be friends of mine.'

Frances clapped her hands with delight, and hugged and kissed her sister-in-law.

Alfred Bunn and the Hills were duly invited to dinner. All three seemed somewhat subdued by the comparative grandeur of the house, and the fact that their hostess was still a Harcourt, even if she wore a wedding ring and had changed her name. Richard was surprised that Mr Hill should be so ill at ease. After all, he had visited Orchard House before, and had been his usual self. Perhaps it was that he had come in a business capacity then, whereas this was a purely social occasion.

As for himself, although at the mill, despite his promotion and link with the owners, his attitude towards his colleagues had not changed, now, surrounded by the trappings of wealth and position, he too felt awkward. This formal dinner was not at all the same as the friendly meals they had shared in the cottage.

Of them all, Jane enjoyed the evening the most. She liked the visitors. They were quiet, but charming. 'We must invite them again,' she told Frances.

'It is good of you to say so,' Frances replied. 'I am not sure that they would wish to come.'

'Whyever not?'

'I think they felt a little out of place, overawed.'

'Oh, what nonsense! Then they must certainly come again, and get used to us and our ways. Especially,' Jane went on, 'Mr Bunn.' It had not escaped her notice that Frances had gazed at the engraver throughout the evening. She waited for confirmation of her suspicions.

Frances said nothing, but, to her annoyance, could not prevent herself from blushing.

'You are fond of him, are you not?' Jane said. 'Come, my dear – no secrets between us. I am sure he is a fine man.'

'Indeed, Jane, I am fond of him.' The colour flooded her cheeks again. Suddenly she felt she could speak more openly. 'You should see him at his work – such a fine craftsman. And he is so . . . so *gentle*. That woman he lodges with does not look after him properly. He cares little for himself, and he needs –' She broke off. 'Oh, Jane, now you know all the secrets of my heart. What a foolish creature you must think me!'

'I do not think you foolish at all. Oh, my dear, thank you for telling me this. Now we are truly sisters.' Impulsively she put her arms around Frances and hugged her. 'And do you think he is fond of you? He seemed most interested in all you had to say, and I often noticed him looking at you with – well, I almost felt it was with affection.'

'I don't know,' Frances replied. 'I have thought sometimes that . . . But he has never said anything, never given me any indication . . .'

'Perhaps he is shy. Some men are, so Mama told me. Indeed, she said once that Papa would never have proposed to her if she hadn't put the idea into his head. Perhaps you should let him see your sentiments more clearly – perhaps even speak, in the most roundabout way, of course, of marriage.'

'Oh, I could not do that. How could you suggest such a thing? It would be unmaidenly.'

'In two years' time, it will be a leap year, if you could wait till then.' Jane smiled merrily, but was instantly contrite as she saw Frances' expression. 'Oh, my dear, I am not making fun of you, and I do understand how you feel. Naturally you have qualms at such an idea, but you must do something – you cannot let your chance of happiness simply slip away.'

Frances thought frequently of what her sister-in-law had said.

The person whose friendly relationship with Richard had most changed since his marriage was Sarah. She missed her daily discussions with him, and when they did meet their interviews were much more formal than before. From time to time Richard and Jane were entertained at Harcourt Place, or themselves gave a family dinner, but Sarah could never have a *tête-à-tête* with Richard on such occasions. If they started a conversation, within a few moments Tom seemed to sense it, and would come to stand beside her, or would call out from across the room.

She would have gone mad, Sarah sometimes thought, if it had not been that the mill was so busy, and Tom was away from home more often than he was there, and she and Richard were so occupied with their respective tasks. It was absurd and, worse, immoral, she told herself. She was a respectable married woman, and Richard a happily married man, and she had no business to be constantly thinking of him. But how could she help it when Tom behaved so outrageously towards her?

The outside world saw little of their relationship. In public, Tom was usually polite, and sometimes even appeared to be affectionate. Some were aware that he took too much liquor, and a few knew that he was something of a womaniser, and could guess at his activities when away from home. But many a man drank and strayed from the path of virtue, yet could still be regarded as a devoted husband, whose wife was fortunate to have no more than that to complain of.

Even his mother did not realise that Tom's marriage had become more and more of a mockery, nor suspect how much Sarah dreaded the moment when they would retire to their bedroom.

Some evenings he was so liquor-sodden that he would fall on the bed, still fully dressed, and lie there snoring until morning, or if somewhat less incapable, would allow her to help him undress and get into bed, and again would instantly fall asleep. Those were the good nights.

Every once in a while, however, when he had not drunk so much as to be beyond desire, he would lock the door, and while he undressed recite with relish and the vilest of language every detail of his exploits with the whores who shared in his debaucheries when he was away from home. She would put her hands over her ears, but he would pull them away, crying, 'No, you shall listen!' And he would continue with his filth.

The first time it happened, Sarah looked at him with contempt. 'Is this the only way you can get . . . ready?' she asked. 'Do you have to excite yourself like this with your whores?'

He swore, and hit her. 'I get a damn sight more from them than you give me! They enjoy it.' He hit her again. Sarah screamed, but their room was away from those of the rest of the family, and the walls were thick, and they both knew that her cries would not be heard. She had not taunted him again like that, but simply endured the degradation.

It always ended the same way. 'Why can't I get you in pod?' he would bellow. 'God knows I do my part often enough, poor sport though it is. It's not *my* fault – there are plenty of by-blows around to prove that Tom Harcourt's a man. But nothing up *your* spout, my fine barren lady, no "interesting condition" for *you*. Well, I'll not give up. I'll get a son on you yet, by God!'

And he would force himself upon her, ignoring her whimpers of pain and humiliation, until, spent, he would roll away from her bruised body, and drift swiftly into brutish sleep.

CHAPTER THIRTEEN

Once Richard was safely, and apparently happily, married, Tom's attitude towards him mellowed. Although there could never be any certainty about his moods, he was usually much more amiable, and seemed to respect Richard's skills.

Richard had, in turn, to admire Tom's success. At first it had surprised him, but that was because he had so often been aware of the worst of Tom – he had seen him in his carousals, he had suffered his anger and contempt, and above all, he had pictured him in the role of a cruel and vicious husband. And still in the recesses of his mind was the old dislike which he had never finally buried. Nevertheless, he could not but admit that Tom had done wonders for Harcourt's.

Perhaps the secret of this success lay partly in Tom's mercurial character and his ability to assume any role he wished. For Harcourt's he contrived somehow always to be at his best, whatever his physical condition after the previous night's drinking and whoring. Although he had taken on salesmen to travel the country, he still called regularly on the more important customers, and his knowledge of the market had grown so effectively that they accepted his advice readily. Without ever overselling, he could persuade those who were satisfied into placing larger orders than they had intended, and he excelled at mollifying those who had complaints. Harcourt's had never known such prosperity as in those first months of 1871.

On the first anniversary of Jane and Richard's marriage, they and Frances were invited to dinner at Harcourt Place.

'Brandy?' Tom asked, when the ladies had retired to the drawing-room after the meal. 'I know you're an abstemious fellow, but this is a day for celebration.'

When Tom had poured the brandy, and lit his Havana, he

sat for some moments watching the blue smoke curl up, absently swishing the brandy round and round in his glass. Then he suddenly said, 'As you well know, Richard, I was far from overjoyed when Jane announced her intention of marrying you. The social classes can rarely mix, and I feared for her happiness. However, the sight of her today, positively blooming, demonstrates that you have proved yourself an excellent husband.' He took another sip of brandy. 'Moreover, your devotion to Harcourt's, and the part you have played in its revival cannot be overlooked.'

Richard tried to mask his surprise. For all Tom's recent friendliness, such compliments were astonishing.

'I have decided,' Tom continued, 'and Sarah agrees, that it is time to acknowledge formally your contribution, and your membership, by marriage, of the family. I propose to appoint you a director. What do you say to that?'

'I . . . I am of course delighted. And grateful.'

Tom smiled. 'Then that is settled. I do not envisage any change in your duties at the mill, but of course your financial position will be substantially improved, assuming that the mill continues profitably. Perhaps,' he added drily, 'that will prove an incentive to work even harder for our success.'

'I would work as hard for less money than I get now,' Richard said hotly, unable to control his brief surge of resentment. 'I don't need carrots.'

'I know you don't, my dear fellow. I was merely speaking jocularly. I propose, by the way, that you should share in the net profits, after the reservation of funds for investment, to the order of twenty per cent.'

Richard could not have expected more. 'Very generous,' he said.

'That should provide adequately for Jane, and for you yourself, without unduly depriving me or Sarah or my mother. Of course it will leave you a considerable way from achieving your ambition of owning Harcourt's Mill.'

Richard tried desperately to conceal his shock. How could Tom possibly know those innermost thoughts which he had never revealed, even to Jane? He stood up, pushing back his chair. 'I have never had any such ambition. What makes you think –?'

'Calm down, my dear chap, calm down. I was joking again. You mustn't be so touchy.' He was still smiling, but his eyes were shrewd as he added, 'You are far too sensible ever to nurture an ambition which could not conceivably be fulfilled. Come, smile, my dear chap. Sit down. Finish your brandy.'

Richard resumed his seat. 'You must forgive me,' he said. 'It is not every day that one is appointed a director, and I fear that the thought of that has quite addled my wits.'

Tom laughed, and drained his brandy glass. 'Before we join the ladies, and inform them of the happy outcome of our discussion, there is one other point that I should perhaps mention. I shall have the necessary legal documents drawn up for our joint signatures; they will contain a provision that in the event of your death or if, for any reason, you should leave the mill, your share in the business will revert to me forthwith.'

'Yes. Yes, of course.'

'Good. Then we are agreed.' He stood up, and offered his hand. 'Congratulations, Richard.'

In the privacy of their bedroom, Jane threw herself into Richard's arms. 'Oh, Richard, what a delightful evening! I am so happy for you. You are pleased, are you not?'

'Indeed I am.'

'Tell me what Tom said to you.'

He began to repeat the conversation, including Tom's remark that he had originally been opposed to their marriage. 'But he confessed he was wrong. He said your happiness proved that.'

'Oh, yes! I am so proud of you, my dear, so very proud.' She kissed him, and then said softly, 'And I hope that you will be proud of me, too.'

'But I am.'

'Not now, Richard – in a few months' time.'

'I have no idea what you are talking about, my love.'

'Oh, men are so slow! I . . . that is, we . . . I sent for Doctor

Wood today to make sure. Next January, Richard, you are to become a father.'

For a few weeks Richard felt as content as he had ever been. He was twenty-eight, already a director of a successful company, and soon to become a parent. Life was very good.

He often thought of Tom's comment that he was too level-headed to hanker after control of Harcourt's. Although it had been a joke, Tom was right, and it was a waste of time to dream such dreams, quite apart from the fact that to think of taking revenge for old wounds was childish, and showed a meanness of soul. He smiled to himself. Perhaps marriage had matured him!

He had conquered too, he believed, his passion for Sarah. He no longer thought of her constantly, and could meet her without having to control the surge of desire that always used to enflame him. Yet now and then, still, he would glance at her and his heart would turn over, and sometimes when he saw her husband's hand, its back quite thickly covered in fine, black hairs, lying possessively on her arm, his gorge would rise at the thought of all that beauty of body and spirit sharing Tom's bed.

The news of the expected happy event had been most joyfully received, though Tom's face had clouded momentarily when he heard. 'Lucky dog!' he had said. 'I just wish that Sarah would follow suit. Six years we've been married, you know, and . . . Still, I am delighted for you and Jane. I shall insist on being godfather.'

Jane's pregnancy was a difficult one, and she was fractious and demanding, quite unlike her usual self. Richard came almost to dread coming home at the end of the day, knowing that, though tired, he would have to face an unceasing catalogue of complaints and self-pity. He loved Jane, he told himself, he really loved her, as though he needed by repetition to convince himself that it was true. Of course it *was* true. But if, he thought, there had been between them the passion of Romeo and Juliet, of Abelard and Heloise, then surely he would have been more tolerant of Jane's sufferings. If he had been utterly possessed by her, as once he had been by . . . But, no, he had overcome those thoughts, once and for all.

Jane's mind seemed to be obsessed during this period with a number of fads and fancies, and the one person at ease with her was Frances, who treated her with remarkable patience, even when Jane insisted on turning the conversation to Alfred Bunn, repeating over and over again her advice on that subject. 'You *must* do something about it, Frances dear. I am sure that it is only shyness and reserve which prevents him from speaking. Do forget the conventions, and tell him frankly of your sentiments.'

'I could not, Jane.'

'Believe me, Frances, this is no time for maidenly modesty. You would be so happy in marriage, as I am with my dear Richard. It will take only a little courage, and I am quite, quite sure he will not take it amiss.'

'It is out of the question.'

But Jane returned to the idea again and again, and eventually Frances began to accept the possibility that she might dare to follow this shocking advice. 'But how could I? When could I?'

'Ask him if he will accompany you on a walk one Sunday afternoon.'

'Without a chaperone?'

'Oh, pooh to that! You are of age, and would come to no harm. He would not take advantage of you. When you reach some secluded spot where none will overhear, tell him frankly how much you enjoy his company, inquire whether he does not share your pleasure, and then, when he agrees, as he surely must, ask him if he could not consider the greater joy of marital bliss.'

It sounded easy enough, but Frances still hesitated.

Then on a Saturday morning in October, when she visited the mill to discuss an improved design for a new crimping roller, Alfred surprised her by himself taking the initiative and suggesting that they should go for a stroll the following afternoon, the weather being so mild for the time of year.

'By ourselves?' she asked in shocked tones, as convention demanded.

He looked confused. 'No, of course you could not do that,' he mumbled. 'I am sorry. I should have realised.'

She laughed. 'I will come, Alfred. Of course I will come.'

Frances prepared herself with care, thankful that she was no longer in mourning for her mother, and could wear her new dove-grey outfit with the bustle. The dress was trimmed in bright blue, and there was a bonnet to match, so fashionably small that it was more like a hat than a bonnet, except for the ribbons to tie beneath the chin. She would never be a beauty, but with her hair becomingly arranged, the fringe hiding her forehead, which she always felt was too high, she knew she was looking her very best.

Since he had begged to be excused from calling for her at Orchard House, she set out to meet Alfred Bunn by a small bridge across the river a short distance outside the village. It was a warm, sunny day, and she carried a parasol to shade her from the sun. Her heart was pounding.

He was leaning against the railings of the bridge. As she came near, he straightened up, raising his hat. He too had taken pains with his appearance, and looked almost smart. 'Good afternoon, Miss Frances,' he said. That was the farthest in an intimate form of address that she had been able to persuade him to go. 'I thought we might stroll through Havant's Wood, if the paths will not be too rough for you.'

'I have on my stoutest boots,' she said, without thinking, and blushed at the indelicacy of mentioning any form of footwear to a gentleman, though he seemed not to notice her indiscretion.

They walked towards the wood. At first neither spoke, but soon Frances determined to hide her shyness, and began to talk of the delights of nature, stopping to admire the berries of black bryony or to watch a flock of redwings in a field. Alfred answered her abstractedly in monosyllables. What a strange afternoon it would be, she thought, if she gained no greater response from him – she would never be able to broach any more delicate subject.

The paths through Havant's Wood were narrow, and she had to follow behind him until they emerged on to grassland. He stopped by a gently sloping bank, and faced her. 'Would you care to sit down, Miss Frances? If you will permit me, I will spread my coat on the ground for you. I have something I wish to say.'

Slightly bemused, she nodded, and watched as he removed his coat and placed it on the ground for her. He sat beside her, wrapping his arms about his knees.

Without hesitation, as though he had prepared his words in advance, he began to speak. 'What I have to say is very difficult. It will be painful for me, and I think perhaps for you too. I want you to promise, Miss Frances, to stop me if I say anything which offends you or if you do not wish me to continue.'

Frances felt her heart beating as though it would burst through her breast. 'Pray go on, Alfred.'

He looked at her and saw the eagerness in her eyes, and turned away, an expression of pain on his angular face. 'I am impertinent enough to believe, Miss Frances, that you have taken pleasure in my company, as I have in yours. We have known each other and worked together in harmony for some time, and I have had the privilege to visit your home, and . . .'

He broke off, and paused, and something told Frances that she should remain silent and let him complete what he had to say in his own time.

After a while, he began again. 'When a man and a woman enjoy such friendship, one or other, or both, may nurture feelings of . . . of affection. If . . . if it is clear that the gentleman concerned is happy in her company, the lady may perhaps expect that one day he will express that happiness to her.'

Again he stopped, and turned to her, and she saw an overwhelming sorrow in his eyes. The look froze her joy.

'I cannot go on,' he said, almost to himself, 'and yet I must.' He seemed to be trying to gather strength. 'I must return to London. It will be better if we do not see each other again.'

'Return to London? But why?'

'Because it tears my heart each time that I see you, and know that I cannot ask you to be more than a friend.' He paused again. 'You see, I am already married.'

She nearly fainted with the shock.

For a while, neither of them spoke. Then he said, 'This is why I did not respond whenever you gave me the opportunity to speak of my past life, though I knew that your interest was more than mere curiosity. I think your brother always wondered why I lived in the Seven Dials. It is a sorry story.' He gave a brief, humourless laugh. 'I married many years ago, when I was very young. My wife and I lived together for a few months. Then she left me. Another man had . . . taken her fancy.'

The bitterness in his voice bit into Frances' heart.

'I am not sure what happened in the days immediately after that,' he went on. 'I drank myself regularly into a state of insensibility. When at last I came to, I was in the Seven Dials.' He turned away from her. 'I cannot tell you more – the story is not fit for a lady's ears.'

Frances knew he would not find peace until he had finished. She reached out her hand to his chin, gently turning his face so that she could look into his eyes. 'I shall not be shocked, Alfred. I want to hear.'

He hesitated for a long time, and then continued, 'God knows why I was still alive. I was lying in a small, squalid room. There was an old woman. She was dead. How I got there, I don't know, nor who she was. Perhaps I had had a shilling or two in my pocket, and she gave me shelter and spent my money on gin. Perhaps she died of alcohol. I can see her now . . . the vomit . . . the dirt and the stench . . .' He shuddered, and then seemed to recollect himself. 'Forgive me – I said it was no story for a lady. I dragged her body out to the street. The next time I looked, it had gone – God knows where. I went on living in that room, and when they came for the rent I paid it out of the few pennies I still had. I said the old woman had gone out and left me to pay them. No one questioned it, no one asked where she was. After a while it seemed to be accepted that the room was mine. All they were interested in was the rent, and I could pay that, because I found work with an engraver. Later, I bought the tools I needed to be independent. Soon afterwards, Mr Harcourt and your brother found me.'

Despite her brave words, it was indeed a shocking recital, and for a moment Frances remained silent. 'You stayed in Seven Dials,' she said. 'Could you not have moved away?'

'Yes. I don't know why I stayed. Perhaps it was a sort of . . . penance.'

'I don't understand that.'

'I don't think I do, either,' he said, with an attempt at a wry smile. 'A feeling that I had to punish myself for . . . for everything.'

Again Frances found it difficult to speak. 'And your wife?' she asked at last, somehow aware that this would be the most painful answer.

'I have not seen her for many years,' he replied, 'but I know she is alive. A friend of mine in London sends news of her from time to time.'

'And you still care for her?'

'No!' he said vehemently. 'No, she means nothing to me.'

Suddenly she saw hope. 'Then . . . then you could divorce her.'

'I am a Catholic, Miss Frances.' He bowed his head, and his thin shoulders began to heave, and in the midst of her own pain, she realised that he was weeping. Boldly she took him in her arms.

'Oh, God!' he cried, and let her hold him for a moment or two while he tried to control his sobs. Then he broke from her. 'I beg you to forgive me, Miss Frances. I am ashamed of myself.'

'There is nothing to forgive, Alfred,' she said with a calmness belying the turbulence in her mind. 'I am proud and grateful that you have shared your confidences with me.' She looked away from him. 'I should myself like to defy convention, and tell you of the sentiments that I bear towards you. You must already have guessed their nature. I confess shamelessly that when you began to speak, I dared to hope that you were going to ask me to be your wife.' She dropped her voice, and whispered, 'I would have accepted readily, so very readily.'

'I would have asked you, Miss Frances, had I been free to do so.'

'Then let me cast all modesty to the winds, and put the question that is in my heart. Since it is impossible for us to marry, can we not continue our friendship, and perhaps . . . develop it?' She read his refusal in his eyes, and went on, urgently, 'I beg you at least not to leave Brentfield.'

'It would be better for us both.'

'No, it would be cruel. If you have any consideration for me, you will not inflict that added pain upon me.' Until now she had kept the tears at bay, but she felt them rising, and quickly got to her feet. 'I . . . I cannot speak more of this now. I must go home.'

In silence they made their way through Havant's Wood. When they came to the river, Frances stopped. 'Please, please do not leave. I beg you.' She turned and ran from him, and the tears began to stream down her face.

Before she reached Orchard House, she stopped, and tried in vain to wipe away the traces of her distress. To her relief she was able to enter without being seen, and went to her bedroom. She flung herself on the bed, and wept again. When she had at last regained her self-control, she went upstairs to face Jane's curiosity.

'Well, my dear? May I wish you joy?' Jane peered at her in concern. 'Why, I believe you have been weeping. He did not reject you?'

Frances shook her head. 'I do not wish to speak of it. If you love me, you will never mention it again.'

Although Jane tried on several occasions to discover what had passed between Frances and Alfred Bunn, she always met the same refusal. It was not too difficult to find answers to the riddle: he might have been suffering from a terrible disease, or perhaps, under the terms of some eccentric relative's will, stood to gain a fortune provided that he did not marry, or – to pile absurdity upon absurdity, for Alfred Bunn was the epitome of bachelordom – he was married already, with a wife and eighteen children; the annoying thing was that Frances would give no clue as to which of these possible explanations might be the true one.

For some days, Frances was uncertain whether Alfred Bunn would heed her plea, or whether he had already left Brentfield. She met him one morning entering the village shop, and her heart briefly leapt for joy, and then became heavy as she realised that his presence in the village at that time of day could mean only that he had left Harcourt's, and would soon be on his way to London.

He raised his hat to her gravely. 'Miss Frances.'

'Good morning, Alfred. You . . . you are not working.'

'No. I have not been well. Your brother has kindly allowed me time off for recuperation. Has he not told you?'

'No. I have scarcely seen him. And when do you return to London?'

'Against my better judgment, Miss Frances, but since you are so set on it, I have decided to remain here, at least for a short while. But –'

Her face lit up. 'Oh, Alfred, I am so pleased.'

'But I must avoid your company for a time. The fire that burns within me will not otherwise be quenched.' He raised his hat again. 'Forgive me, I am in some haste.' He slipped past her, and with long strides was soon hurrying back to the cottage where he lodged.

He continued to work at the mill, and he and Frances met from time to time, but there was always a certain wariness between them, as though both were determined never again to lose control of their emotions. She tried hard to put him out of her mind, and, as well as looking after Jane, busied herself with good works, making jams and cakes and broths and calf's-foot jellies to distribute among the poor of the village.

Richard was slow to notice the change in her. When he did, he asked Jane what was wrong.

'I told you when it first happened,' Jane replied. 'It's a matter of unrequited love.'

'What? Oh, you mean Alfred Bunn. I thought that was over ages ago.'

Jane was exasperated. 'If you adore someone, you don't get over it as quickly as that, Richard. Well, perhaps men do. How long did it take you to get over –' She broke off.

He knew what she had been going to ask. He could not have told her, for he was not past loving Sarah yet, whatever he pretended to himself. 'What can we do for her?'

'I don't know, I really don't know. He is so pig-headed, that Alfred Bunn. Perhaps you could have a word with him.' She gave a little shriek, suddenly sounding just like her mother. 'No, you would only make things worse. It will sort itself out one day, I suppose.' Her thoughts reverted to herself. 'Get me a stool for my feet, darling Richard. Put it there. That's it. And I want some tea. I crave a dish of tea.'

He went to order tea for her. How difficult women could be. It was enough to have Jane in her present fractious mood, without having to contend with Frances too. He supposed that Alfred had turned her down. Poor Frances.

As Jane's time approached, Richard began to worry about her. Her petulance had turned to weariness, and she looked drawn. Dr Wood was reassuring. 'You must realise that this is a tiring period for her, for the child is feeding upon the mother's resources. There is no need for concern. I have seen a similar lassitude in many other cases. The joy of motherhood will soon bring the roses back to her cheeks.'

'Are you sure she will be all right? She is so fine-boned. You have only to look at her wrists.'

Dr Wood laughed. 'Goodness me, the size of her wrists has nothing to do with childbirth. She is perhaps a little narrow in the pelvis, but it is nothing to worry about, nothing at all.'

On the day that her pains began, early in the morning, Richard stayed at home, but when Dr Wood and the midwife came, they told him that it would be some hours before the delivery, and that he might as well occupy his mind by working. He went to the mill, but it was difficult to concentrate, and every knock on his office door made his heart race in case it should be news from Orchard House.

The doctor and the midwife were still there that evening.

'A somewhat difficult birth,' Dr Wood told him. 'It is only to be expected, of course. The first child is often slow to make its appearance, especially when, like Mrs Goodwin, the mother is – how shall I put it? – no longer in the first flush of youth. She is tired, naturally, but she is holding her own.'

'May I see her?'

'No, I do not think that would be wise. I will take a little refreshment, if I may, and then return to her side. Have no fear – Mrs Jones is with her, and will call me if I am needed.'

Later that evening, he came downstairs again. His face was haggard. Richard rose to meet him. 'Sit down, Mr Goodwin. You must prepare yourself for sad news.'

'My wife?'

'No, but I fear for the child. Mrs Goodwin is slightly built, and –'

'I told you that, and you said –'

The doctor shook his head wearily. 'We are not infallible, Mr Goodwin. I wish we were.'

'She is in danger?'

'She is very weak, and has no strength to deliver the child. I intend therefore to remove it by Caesarian section.'

'But that will surely kill her.'

Dr Wood looked at him gravely. 'No, Mr Goodwin, it is the one way to save her. And you need not fear that she will suffer pain. I intend to administer chloroform.'

'What?'

'Chloroform. A recently discovered drug which induces a state of unconsciousness, during which the patient feels no pain.'

'May I see her?'

'If you wish, but for a moment only.'

When Richard went into the bedroom, he was reminded for a brief, ironic moment of their wedding night, for the bedclothes had been drawn up, and all he could see of Jane was her poor, tired face peeping above them. Then he thought of his mother's death. Jane seemed to be sleeping. He went to her and took her hand.

Wearily she opened her eyes, staring straight ahead. Then

she looked to the side, and saw him. Her lips sketched a ghost of a smile, and formed his name, but there was no sound. Richard bent and kissed her brow. She was cold. Her lips moved again, and he put his ear close to them. The words came with great effort, separated by long pauses, and the whisper was so soft that he could hardly hear it at all. 'Richard . . . tell me . . . you . . . love me.'

'I love you, Jane.'

'I . . . love . . . you . . . And . . . I don't . . . mind . . . about Sarah . . .'

'What about Sarah?'

'That . . . you . . .' The final words did not come.

Dr Wood had been watching anxiously. 'That will do, Mr Goodwin,' he said. 'I am ready now. I will let you have news as soon as I can.'

Richard went downstairs, his mind a turmoil of anxiety and love and guilt and sorrow. Jane's words hammered at his brain. Had it really been so plain to her that he loved Sarah? In an agony of remorse, he sank to his knees. 'Oh, God,' he prayed silently. 'Let her live. Please let her live, and I will make it up to her.'

Frances came into the room. Awkwardly he got to his feet, and began to tell her, but he had hardly begun when the door opened to admit Dr Wood. He looked old, and defeated. As he came towards them he shook his head sadly. 'I am very sorry, very sorry indeed. I did all I could.'

'The child is dead?'

'Yes. And your wife . . . And Mrs Goodwin too.'

Richard stared at him unbelievingly. The doctor stood for a moment watching him, nodded his head slowly and spread his hands in a gesture of helplessness. Then he climbed the stairs to the bedroom once more.

Later, he and Mrs Jones came out, and left the house, but Richard was not aware of their departure. He and Frances both remained where they were, she weeping softly, he gazing blindly into space.

CHAPTER FOURTEEN

Some things were sharp in Richard's memory. He could still see the sorrowful expressions of a few of those who had come, and hear their mumbled words of sympathy, but the rest had merged into a mass of blurred faces. He could remember every moment of his walk to the mill and the work he had done there the day after Jane died, but he must also have taken some part in arranging the funeral, and of that he had no recollection. Who had obtained sufficient of Harcourt's Mourning Crape for Gentlemen to make the bands on his hat and sleeve?

Orchard House seemed empty without Jane. Recalling his irritation with her during the last months of her pregnancy, he was filled with remorse. Was it only when someone was taken from you that you realised how deeply you had cared, how much you had depended on that person?

The church was as full for the funeral as it had been for his wedding, but this time, as though in cruel mockery, the day was bright and sunny. Richard stood motionless and dry-eyed by the grave as the earth thudded on the coffin.

'How brave he is,' Sarah whispered to Frances.

'If only he could weep,' Frances said. 'He needs desperately to release his sorrow.'

But Richard's tears did not come, and when the family went back to Harcourt Place, though unsmiling, he ate and drank with the rest of them and joined mechanically in the conversation.

Mrs Harcourt Senior sobbed into her black-edged handkerchief. 'My poor Jane! To be taken so young, and with her sweet babe, too. My poor Jane!' She looked venomously at Richard. 'What brutes men are! Could he not see that Jane was too delicate for childbirth? Oh, but husbands were ever so – forcing themselves upon us with no care for the ravages they inflict. Oh, my poor Jane!'

After a while Tom Harcourt called Richard into the library. 'Sit down. Have a brandy. You need it on an occasion like this.'

Passively, Richard allowed him to pour the liquor.

'A sad day, Richard,' Tom said. 'But life must go on. Do you feel up to a short discussion of family business?'

'Of course.'

'I thought we might talk of Orchard House. I am sure it must have been exercising your mind.'

'I have found it difficult to concentrate on such matters,' Richard said. 'If you wish me to leave the house, I will of course do so.'

'No, no. There is no reason for that. You and your sister may continue to live there, though of course the house remains my property. I thought perhaps it would be reasonable to charge a modest rent. How would you feel about a hundred pounds per annum? A matter of principle, you see, rather than of money.'

Richard wondered if Tom were enjoying himself. 'Anything you say.' His voice was weary.

'I must apologise, my dear fellow – this must be very painful for you on such an occasion – but I felt the position should be regularised.' He shook his head, as though to indicate that he was no more than a puppet, dancing to the strings of Fate. 'I suggest we draw up an agreement to give you the tenancy of Orchard House in your capacity as a director of Harcourt's, for as long as you remain in that position, and at a rent to be agreed annually. That is fair, is it not? I mean,' he added hastily, 'if you and your sister should ever leave Brentfield for any reason, I would naturally want to regain possession of the house.'

'Perhaps it might be better for Frances and me to find somewhere else to live.'

'Where could you go? There's no available house in Brentfield suitable for a director of Harcourt's, and certainly not at a hundred a year. No, I won't hear of it.' He took a mouthful of brandy, eyeing Richard over the top of the glass. 'Unless, of course, you find it too painful to live among such sad memories.'

Richard was silent for a long while. He sipped at his own brandy, conscious of the fiery spirit burning his throat. Tom's offer was generous, and his conditions reasonable. Orchard House was a very suitable and convenient residence for him and Frances. However distressing the ghosts of his marriage might be, they had to be faced. On impulse he asked, 'Does Sarah know about this?'

'It was she who wondered whether you would wish to stay in a house so filled with memories of Jane.'

'That was kind of her.'

'She is ever mindful of the welfare of others. Sometimes, I feel, particularly of yours, Richard.' As though to deny the jealousy implicit in this remark, Tom went on, 'She does not forget, and nor indeed do I, how much you have done for Harcourt's.'

Richard paused again. 'It is good of you to say so. I gratefully accept your offer, Tom, at least for the time being, and of course I have no objection to the generous terms you propose. Thank you.'

'I am sure you have made the right decision.' Tom drained his glass. 'More brandy? No? I suppose we should return to the others. If I might give you a little advice, Richard, I would suggest you avoid talking to my mother. Her grief appears to have overriden her partiality towards you. She will get over it, of course, in time.'

Mrs Lottie Harcourt, however, having convinced herself that Richard had been the cause of her daughter's death, vowed she could never again look upon him with favour. 'I was opposed to the match from the very start,' she proclaimed, her jowls and her painted cheeks quivering with indignation. 'But would she listen to me? No, none of you would. I warned her. "He's not the right man for you, Jane," I said. Why, I remember when he was a small boy he once attacked poor Tom quite savagely and, needless to say, unprovoked. Of course, you've forgotten that, Tom, but I haven't. It showed him in his true colours – a nasty, vicious nature. The leopard cannot change its spots, you know.'

The first time that she spoke in this way, Sarah protested. 'You were the first to be delighted when he and Jane became engaged.' But Mrs Harcourt would admit nothing of the kind, and Sarah was forced to close her ears to what was said, as she regularly did to the gossip and grievances which poured in a steady stream from her mother-in-law's lips.

Mrs Harcourt's enmity meant, of course, that Richard was less welcome at Harcourt Place than before, and he and Frances were rarely invited to go there. They stayed at home most evenings, sitting by the fire in a companionable silence, while Frances sewed, and Richard worked or read. Gradually he overcame his sense of loss, and no longer looked for Jane on his return home or missed her lively chatter; he became used, too, to the loneliness of their marital bed.

In the early days, Sundays were the worst time, and realising this, Frances suggested that they should invite the Hills to dinner.

'And your friend Alfred,' Richard said.

'He is not "my" friend,' Frances replied sharply. 'Ask him yourself, if you must, but I doubt he'll come.'

'I thought you and he . . .'

'Then you thought wrong! No doubt Jane put the idea into your head. She was always trying to match-make on my behalf. I shall never marry, Richard – I am quite determined on that. Alfred is pleasant enough company, but I care nothing for him.' She bent her head over her sewing.

He sensed her unhappiness. 'Won't you tell me about it, Frances? We used not to have secrets.'

'There is nothing to tell. Please don't go on.' Her lips tightened into a thin line.

He wished he could comfort her in some way, but did not know how. He debated whether to invite Alfred Bunn, but finally decided against it – perhaps it would be better not to rub salt into whatever wound it was that Frances had suffered.

The Hills began to come regularly on Sundays, almost as though they were part of the family. The four of them talked mostly of people they all knew, of village matters, and sometimes of events in the world outside, but only very rarely of the mill. One day, however, Mr Hill said, 'It is discourteous to do so, Richard, on such a pleasant domestic occasion, but my concern drives me to raise a matter of business. I refer to the recent fall in orders. At least – how foolish one becomes in one's dotage! – it is not a fall, so much as a lack of increase. This is the first time since I came to Harcourt's that we have not seen a continuing improvement.'

'I do not see much reason for alarm when we are producing virtually to our full capacity.'

'You will forgive me teaching my grandam to suck eggs – though of course,' he added, his eyes twinkling, 'you are much too young and of the wrong gender to be a grandam – but our costs have risen. If that trend continues and if sales do not increase, an undesirable diminution in Harcourt's profits will result.'

'What can we do?' Richard asked. 'Workers get more money than they used to – even children are paid three shillings a week now, and that's half as much again as I earned when I started. And since the Education Bill was passed, it's far more difficult to get children anyway – they're going to school instead. I'm all in favour of that – I've never much liked the idea of youngsters having to work in a factory, even though it didn't do me much harm – but it means that we have to use adults, and they cost more. We just can't make crape cheaply.'

'Is there no process that would reduce the costs? It seems to me that the throwing consumes a vast amount in time and wages. Is it not possible to use unthrown silk?'

'No. If we did, the crape would not curl properly when it is dyed. Besides, unthrown silk would result in material with less body and feel to it. But you've put your finger on a major problem. I've been thinking about it for some time, but can see no way of avoiding the throwing, costly though it is.' Richard turned to Frances and Mrs Hill. 'We must apologise for talking shop, as they say.'

'It was for me to crave pardon, Richard,' said Mr Hill, 'and since you have usurped my privilege, I must do something in reparation. What do you say, Pussy-my-love? Shall I entertain the assembled company with a ballad?'

'I don't know about that,' Mrs Hill replied.

Richard thought further, but fruitlessly, about the possibility of reducing the manufacturing costs of crape. In any case, the company's profits were very little down, and he had enough to do without dreaming of new and impractical processes.

Increasingly, too, he found himself thinking about Sarah, and indeed was troubled at this time by a recurring dream in which she seemed to be beckoning to him, but remained always, however hard he tried to catch her, out of reach. Perhaps that was a reflection of their real-life relationship, for she gave him no encouragement. Though she was friendly whenever they met, she never allowed their conversations to become personal, and always behaved with the utmost propriety. And yet . . . and yet he could have sworn that some strange link existed between them, and that she recognised it as clearly as he did.

She was thirty now, and the added years seemed to have refined and increased her beauty. Richard tried to decide what had changed in her, but it was hard to define. Her hair was still the same glorious dark chestnut, her eyes were as brilliant, her skin as glowing. There were few lines on her face, but she had the look of a mature woman now, rather than that of a girl, and it lent her a new authority, a presence. It was visible, too, in the way she walked – with a slow dignity, a consciousness of her position, and also of her womanhood, and the knowledge, without vanity, that she had the kind of striking appearance that drew the eyes of both men and women. And yet at times she could still look as wayward and ready for laughter as a young girl, especially when Tom was away.

It was a Sunday in October of 1872, nine months after Jane's death. The summer had been hot and rainless, and after a few brief downpours in late September, the sunshine had returned and it was almost like July, the ground dry, the air balmy. Richard and Frances had been to morning service, and had nodded their respects to Sarah as they emerged. Tom was away, visiting customers in the North of England.

After lunch, Richard felt restless and suggested to Frances that they should go for a walk, but she refused, pleading exhaustion, both mental and physical, after the Rector's splendid but interminable sermon.

Richard set off on his own, strolling at a leisurely pace, allowing his mind to occupy itself with nothing more weighty than the sights and sounds around him. He felt unaccountably happy and at ease with life. Although he would have sworn that he had had no such aim, he suddenly realised that he had reached the entrance of the drive leading to Harcourt Place. An overwhelming desire to see Sarah possessed him, and he turned off the road and began to walk towards the house.

It was madness, he told himself. What could he say to justify his sudden, unexpected arrival? He rang the bell at the front door.

To his surprise, Sarah herself answered his ring. 'Richard! What brings you here?'

'I . . . I called to enquire after Mrs Harcourt. She was not in church this morning. She is not unwell, I hope.'

Sarah smiled. 'She is away, spending the weekend with friends.' She laughed. 'Richard, I don't believe it! You didn't really come to ask about Mother-in-law, now did you? Come, confess!'

He laughed too. 'No, I didn't. I think it was something to do with the Rector's sermon this morning. I felt in need of a walk, and came out, and . . . well . . . I just found myself here. I didn't mean to intrude upon you.'

'You'd better come in.'

'But you are alone in the house.'

'Oh! nonsense! There are servants here. Besides, I hardly think I need a chaperone.' She led the way into the drawing-room. 'Now, tell me the truth, Richard. It was not just chance that brought you here.'

'Honestly, I didn't plan it.'

'Then it is simply a casual social call.' She stared at him quizzically for a moment, then smiled and said lightly, 'Well, I was in need of company. Amuse me, Richard.'

'How?'

'I don't know. Tell me a story.'

'A story?'

'Yes. You are always reading. Tell me a story of love and adventure, and . . . No, tell me a story about yourself.'

'A tale told by an idiot.'

She laughed. 'Is that what you are this afternoon?'

'I don't know. Am I?' He was not sure what to make of her flippancy.

She did not reply, and there was a pause. He walked over to the window and looked out, then turned, embarrassed by her eyes on him, and pretended an interest in the photographs which stood on the pianoforte. Tom had insisted that all the members of the family should have their portraits done by this process which had become so popular.

'Oh, do sit down, Richard,' Sarah said, patting the sofa seat. 'If you won't tell me a story, at least don't wander about like a lost sheep. It makes me nervous.'

'You? Nervous? Now, *I* don't believe *that*. You're in a strange mood, Sarah.'

'Perhaps the Rector's sermon is affecting me, too. It was rather long, wasn't it?' She stretched her arms above her head.

'An hour and twenty minutes.' He gazed at her. The position of her arms made her breasts strain against the silk bodice of her dress. Her eyes were closed, the lashes lying thickly against her cheek. He noticed the tiny wrinkles at the corners of her eyes, and was suddenly filled with tenderness and longing for her. He ached to touch her, and did not know how to stop himself. He turned away, staring at the fireplace, until he felt in control of his senses once more. Then he said softly, 'I *am* an idiot, you know.'

'Why?'

'Because I want something I can't have.'

'Do you, Richard?' She lowered her arms and turned her head towards him.

There had been nothing in her voice beyond casual interest. But what lay in the depths of those magical green eyes? Mockery? Friendly laughter, such as might be proper between a married woman and her widowed brother-in-law? Indifference? No, not that – that was the one thing of which he was sure. He swallowed. 'I think you know what I want to say.'

Her voice was the softest of whispers. 'Yes, my dear, I do. I have known it for a very long time – since before . . .'

'Say it, Sarah – since before I married Jane. *And* all the time I was married to her. And now. And forever.'

She put a finger on his lips. 'Hush!'

He seized her hand and kissed it. 'I can't stop now. I have to say it, whether you want me to or not. I love you. I've loved you since the very first time I saw you, years ago, at The Grange. I shall always love you.'

'You mustn't go on. Please.'

'Why not? Because if I do you will have to confess that you love me too? It's true, isn't it?' She made no attempt to deny it, and at last he was able to release the words he had so long wanted to say. 'I love everything about you – your lips, your eyes, your hair – everything, but most of all I love you for what you are, for your courage and your honesty, and your laughter. I loved Jane too, but not as I love you, not with the passion that fills my whole being.' He kissed her hand again, and then reached out to take her in his arms.

'No, Richard, please!' But his lips were on hers, and she could not even struggle, because this was what she, too, had longed for. Her arms slid around his neck, pulling him closer, and she felt the frantic beating of her heart, and almost fainted with the joy of their embrace.

After a while he stood up, pulled her to her feet, and took her in his arms again. 'Oh, Sarah, my dearest heart, my love!'

It was easier now to abandon herself to the passion of the kiss. She could feel his body against hers, could sense the pride of his desire.

'Come!' Richard said, and began to lead her towards the door.

'No!' she cried. 'No, I can't, I mustn't!'

'Yes, Sarah, yes!'

'Tom . . .'

'You don't love him. You never have. And he doesn't love you. I adore you, and you love me.' He bent and lifted her easily in his arms.

'Richard! Richard, no!' But there was no strength in the protest.

The door was shut, and he could not open it without putting her down. He cursed inwardly, knowing that a farcical accident of that sort could give her the opportunity to repair the defences which he had broken through so swiftly.

Indeed, there was a greater urgency in her voice. 'Richard, the servants!' But she made no attempt to move away from him.

'They won't come near at this time of day – not unless you ring.' He tugged at her hand. 'Come on.'

She looked at him with something akin to desperation in her eyes. 'My legs have turned to jelly. Hold me, Richard.' And then she gave him a half-smile, and went on quickly, 'No, don't! Walk quietly, so no one will hear.'

Richard followed as they tiptoed up the wide staircase to the railed landing above. There were several doors leading off it.

'In here,' she whispered.

It was not the bedroom she shared with Tom. He shut the door, and turned the key. She was trembling, and at first was wooden in his embrace. But as his passion grew, she began to respond as ardently as before.

Her dress fastened with buttons at the back, and he tried to undo them. She turned, and let him do so until she could draw her arms from the sleeves. The dress crumpled slowly to the ground, forming a circle of green silk on the floor. She stepped out of it and stood still again for him to untie the laces of her corset. 'So many silly clothes,' she whispered.

Then she was facing him, and his hands went to her breasts, caressing them, letting his fingers slip beneath the delicate fabric of her shift to touch her soft, smooth skin. Her breath came faster, and she tilted her head back, her eyes closed, her mouth open, seeking for his.

As his tongue played with hers, he pulled the silken shift away until one pink-tipped breast was exposed. His mouth moved from her lips and fastened upon the nipple.

She gave a little moan of pleasure, but then pushed gently away from him, and moving a pace or two towards the bed, whispered over her shoulder, 'Hurry!'

His back to her, he undressed, flinging the clothes down carelessly. When he was ready he saw that she too had stripped away the last of her garments. She was lying on the bed, her head turned away from him, her eyes again closed. He stood for a moment, gazing at the beauty of her nakedness. 'Oh, Sarah, I adore you, I worship you.'

She opened her eyes, and he could see that they were filled with tears. And then she smiled through them, and held out her arms to him.

He went to her. She wore no perfume, but he could smell the clean sweetness of her musk. He caressed her, covering her body with kisses, lifting his lips from the satin of her flesh only to whisper his love. She ran her hands over his broad back, and played with the curling hair at the nape of his neck and the darker, rough mat on his chest, and then sought and held him.

Eventually she opened to his questing fingers, and moaned again as her desire grew. Gently he lowered himself over her and their bodies joined. It was different, more wonderful than it had ever been before. She did not lie passive, but moved with him, gasping with the growing sensations. And their souls were one as the glory rose and at last exploded for them both in cascading fireworks of the mind and senses. Sarah wrapped her legs around him, drawing him tighter into her very being, and cried out, burying her mouth in the curve of his neck to stifle the sound.

The throbbing, jerking pulsations slowly died away, and they lay together in a glow of fulfilment, arms around each other. Richard kissed her again – little kisses, on her eyes, her nose, her cheeks, her lips.

For a few moments she lay smiling at him in joy and contentment and love. Then suddenly a look of panic and horror came into her eyes, and she turned her head away. 'Oh, my God, what have we done? Oh, Richard, what fools we have been!'

He put out his hand, but she brushed it away. She began to shake convulsively, and he realised that she was sobbing. 'Sarah,' he said, 'don't cry, my love . . . my dear one . . . my darling . . .'

But she would not be comforted. 'Wanton! Adulteress!' she berated herself in a whisper. And then aloud she told him urgently, 'You must go. Go now. Please. Get dressed quickly, and go.'

He could not argue with her, and climbed off the bed and began to put his clothes on, grateful that she was not watching him. When he was dressed, he said, 'I can't go, Sarah – not yet. We have to . . . to talk about . . .'

'No, there is nothing to say. Except that we should never have done what we have done, should never have let a moment of foolishness force us into this betrayal.'

'It is no betrayal!' he said vehemently. 'This is our truth! I shall never regret it. It is the most beautiful thing that has ever happened, and the only foolishness is in blaming ourselves now for something which had to be.'

'God will never forgive us! Guilty passions, Richard, guilty passions.' She was silent for a moment, and then said harshly, 'Help me to dress.' She slid off the bed. 'Turn your back.'

He did so, thinking how absurd such modesty was. He could hear the soft swish of the material as she put on her undergarments.

After a while, she said, still in that cold, remote voice, 'Tie my corset laces.' He did so, and then turned away again, as she struggled into her dress. 'Now these buttons.' She sat at the dressing table then, smoothing her hair into some kind of order. Her face was pale and haunted, her eyes enormous. She stood up. 'Now go. Please.'

She unlocked and opened the door, peering out cautiously to make sure that they would not be seen. Silently they went down to the hall.

At the front door, Richard whispered, 'I can't go like this, Sarah.'

'You must.'

'But we have to talk. Walk down the drive with me. Please. I beg of you.'

She hesitated, and at last nodded.

As they walked slowly towards the entrance gates, Richard said, 'Listen. You must leave Tom, get a divorce. You could do so easily – you know you have cause.'

'Two wrongs don't make a right, Richard. If he is guilty, so am I.'

'What does guilt matter? He doesn't love you – it would be no injury to him.'

'It would be the end of Harcourt's – a scandal like that.'

'Oh, nonsense!'

'It is not nonsense. It could kill the business.'

'Is that more important to you than our love?' She did not reply immediately, and he looked at her disbelievingly, and laughed with a kind of exasperation.

She spoke quite sharply then. 'We live in the real world, Richard, not in fairyland. We have to think of the effects of our actions, and our position in life, and –'

'I see,' he said bitterly. 'That is it – I am not good enough for you, am I? You laugh at the way I speak.'

'Only in fun. I love the way you speak.' She could see the hurt in his eyes, and went on almost desperately, 'Oh, Richard, that accent is strong and true. There is honesty in it, because it is not assumed – it is part of you. I only laugh to tease you.'

'But I am not of your class.' His anger burst out. 'You don't want to give up your position, or this house, or your power at the mill. You won't sacrifice anything for my sake.'

'That is unfair – you know it is.'

He stopped and lowered his eyes. 'Yes, it is unfair. I'm sorry.'

'Class has nothing to do with it. And I am sacrificing all I hold most dear – *you*, Richard, *you*. I have to do that because . . . oh, because of other people. And I am mindful of God, too, and His wrath.'

'Our love comes from God – you must believe that.'

She gave a little shake of the head, but did not argue. They moved on for a few paces, neither of them speaking, both calmer now, until she said, 'You would have to make sacrifices, too, Richard. You would have to leave Harcourt's. It means a lot to you, doesn't it?'

'More than anything, except you.' He laughed again briefly. 'It's funny – I used to hate Harcourt's, because my father died there, and because of what happened to my sister. I used to dream of taking my revenge.'

'And now you have.'

For a moment he did not realise what she meant. Then he cried, 'No! No, Sarah! Oh, never believe that! That has nothing to do with my love for you.'

'I know.' She smiled at him, warmly, reassuringly. Then she said, 'But you still hate Tom, don't you?'

He nodded. 'Yes, when I think of him with you.'

'Don't hate him, Richard – he's not worth it. He is not . . . a good man. But I am his wife, and there is nothing I can do to alter that.'

'There is! There is! Nothing matters except us. Forget Harcourt's, forget other people – think of us, Sarah. Leave him, I beg you.'

She shook her head. They had reached the end of the drive. 'You must go, Richard. Forget this ever happened.'

'I shall never forget. I shall always treasure this day.'

Her green eyes seemed to burn into his. Her lips moved, but he could hear no sound. He thought she said, 'So shall I.'

'Then how can we behave as though there is nothing between us? How can we meet each day and pretend that we are no more than business colleagues?'

'I don't know, I don't know. Oh, please, Richard, go! I cannot bear this longer.'

'You are beautiful, so very beautiful.' He took her hands and kissed each palm in turn.

She breathed his name, then pulled away from him, and turned and moved with that strange slow walk of hers back towards the house. She did not look back, but he watched until the front door closed behind her. Then, in the fading sunlight of the late afternoon, he stepped out towards Brentfield, his head swimming with the jangle of his conflicting emotions.

CHAPTER FIFTEEN

When he arrived at the mill the next day, Richard's first instinct was to go to Sarah, but then he stopped, thinking it might embarrass her if he rushed into her room without warning. It would be better to let her summon him. He waited vainly all day, and at six o'clock could restrain himself no longer, and went to her office, and discovered that she had already left the mill, much earlier than was her habit.

The next morning, Tuesday, he knocked at her office door, and went in. She was sitting at her desk, serene and beautiful as ever.

She glanced up. 'Good morning.' The tone was frosty, and she did not smile. 'You didn't come to see me yesterday. Why not?'

'I . . . I thought you might prefer it if . . . I came to see you in the late afternoon, but you'd already gone.'

'Your weekly report is due on Mondays – you know that.'

'You didn't send for me.'

'I shouldn't have to.'

He was baffled. He remembered her lying naked on the bed, and later the soft cries she had given, her eyes full of love and contentment. Had it really meant so little to her? 'Sarah . . .' he began.

She interrupted harshly. 'Have you brought the report?'

'Yes, it is here.'

'Problems?'

'None. Listen, Sarah . . .'

'Don't forget we shall need more of Pattern C crape this week. I mentioned it on Friday, but –'

'Damn Pattern C crape! Sarah, please *talk* to me.'

She looked at him, and again her expression was bleak,

almost hostile. Then she said, 'What happened should never have happened. It is over and done with, and there is nothing that either of us can say that will help.'

'Sarah, for Christ's sake!'

'I have a great deal of work to do, and I am sure that you have too. And please refrain from swearing in my presence – especially that particular oath, which I find offensive.'

He went over to her desk. 'Sarah! You *can't* behave like this to me – you can't!'

Her eyes were agonised as she looked at him, and her voice was low and urgent. 'It is the only way I can behave to you – the *only* way, Richard. Try to understand that, and help me.'

He realised what she was saying, and was appalled. Was this to be their relationship from henceforth? He did not know how to answer her, and stood silent in front of her desk. Despair filled him. Was it really to end like this? Would he never again be able to hold her in his arms and experience that matchless joy? To live without her, to pretend that they meant nothing to each other, would be unbearable.

'Please go. Please.' Taking up a pen, she bent her head and began to write. Not until the door had closed behind him did she allow the tears to come.

On Tom's return to Harcourt Place several days later, Sarah had greeted him somewhat perfunctorily, he thought, and indeed seemed to be quite abstracted. Perhaps it was just that she had already had to listen repeatedly to his mother's report of her weekend away, which was now being recounted for his benefit, including every detail of the food she had eaten, the clothes that her friends wore, the rout – as she insisted on calling it in her old-fashioned way – which she had attended, the scandalous behaviour of the young people, and so on and so on and so on.

As the ceaseless chatter continued, Tom refilled his glass regularly and often. Sarah began to dread the moment when they would retire. However successfully she had contrived to suppress her feelings when she saw Richard at the mill, the memory of his embraces was still vibrant within her, and the thought of having to submit to Tom's coarseness and the violence of his love-making made her shudder.

'And you should see the way she does her hair,' Mrs Harcourt was saying. 'In enormous plaits looped up at the back of her head. She looked a perfect fright, if you ask me, but they say it's the latest fashion, and we shall soon all be following it. Well, thank goodness I have my cap and veil, that's all I can say, and –'

Tom could stand it no longer, and interrupted. 'Tell me tomorrow, Mama. It's time for bed. Come, Sarah.' He went towards the door, ignoring his mother's protests.

Sarah stood up. 'I'll help your mother to her bed.'

'Her maid can do that.'

'I'll stay until she comes, then.'

Tom grunted, and left the room.

Sarah rang the bell for the servant. With any luck the girl would not hurry herself, and that would give time for Tom to get into bed and fall asleep.

'Oh, how ill-used I am!' said Mrs Harcourt indignantly, but had barely begun a second description of the new hairstyle, when, to Sarah's disappointment, the maid knocked and entered. 'You go up, Sarah,' Mrs Harcourt said, content in the knowledge that the servant would prove a better audience, and would not have the impertinence to interrupt her in mid-sentence. 'Tom is waiting for you.'

In the bedroom, Tom turned as Sarah entered, and held out his arms. 'Come, a kiss for your doting husband.'

She stood where she was. Angrily he came to her, and planted a wet-mouthed kiss on her unwilling lips. The reek of the brandy made her feel sick. She knew her failure to respond would infuriate him, but she could not dispel the revulsion which kept her cold and rigid in his embrace.

After a moment or two, he thrust her away in disgust. 'No wonder you're barren – it's like making love to a gatepost. But we'll see, my fine lady, we'll see.' He began to remove his clothes.

Sarah hastened to take off her dress. It was new, and she did not want it torn. She had just stepped out of it safely when he came to her, naked, already in a state of arousal.

'Look at that, my dear, my dove, my little sweetheart! Some people say that brandy's no good for a man – but not for Tom Harcourt, oh, no! The more I drink, the sooner I . . . Don't you agree, my little darling, my sweetheart! Early to bed, with plenty of brandy, makes a man happy and healthy and randy. That's the new fashionable word – randy. You know what it means? It means I'm going to roger you, my cold snow-queen of a wife. I'm going to melt that ice once and for all.' He had been smiling, speaking in an almost bantering tone, but now he grasped her by the arm so cruelly that she cried out in pain. He fumbled at her corset for a moment. 'Get that damned contraption off!'

He stood watching her. Once the corset was loose, he ripped the rest of her clothes away, then flung her on to the bed so that she was lying on her back, her feet still on the floor. He laughed. 'That's just the way I like it.' He gave a mock bow. 'Be so good as to open those marble thighs, my love.'

Usually she complied with his orders, for it saved additional humiliation and pain, but now she could not bring herself to obey.

'Open your legs, damn it!' He grinned. 'Oh, that's the way of it, is it? I like that too.'

Sarah shut her eyes. She felt his knee forcing her legs apart, and then his hands mauling her, and the sharp pain as he entered brutally. Mercifully, it took him only a few thrusts to reach his climax, and he withdrew almost immediately. He staggered round to his side of the bed, the brandy suddenly taking effect, and within moments was snoring.

Each morning that week, as he went to work, Richard prayed that Sarah's attitude would have changed, but always when they met her look was stony and she spoke in distant tones, as though they were not even friends. He had to appeal to her again, and on the Saturday afternoon, he went to her office.

She looked up from her desk. 'Yes?'

'Sarah, please. I know what you said, and why you are

behaving like this, but we can't go on as though we were strangers. I love you, and you love me.'

She looked up then, and rose, and went to the window. 'I can't forget that any more than you can. But we must try.'

'It might be better if I left Brentfield.'

'No!'

The vehemence of her answer lifted his heart. 'Then come away with me.'

She wheeled round and faced him. 'I can't, I can't, I can't! Oh, Richard, try to understand. Don't make it more of a torture than it is already. Please, please go, and don't talk of this again. It's the only way. Then one day perhaps we can become . . . friends again.' She turned back to the window.

'Let me kiss you. Just once. A farewell kiss.'

She shook her head silently, and after a while he left her office, defeated.

The following Sunday, when the Hills came to dinner at Orchard House, Richard suggested after the meal that Mrs Hill and Frances should retire to the drawing-room. 'I have a business matter that I want to discuss,' he said.

When they had gone, Richard gave a nervous smile. 'It isn't really business. I need your advice. It's . . . not for myself. I have a friend who's in a difficult situation, and I don't know how to counsel him.' He paused. 'You see, he is in love with a married woman . . . and has reason to believe his affections are returned.'

Mr Hill nodded gravely, and waited for more.

'You will say he should forget her, but it is not easy, since they are forced to meet frequently. He has thought of leaving the district, but that would mean abandoning the lady to an unhappy marriage, with a husband who is . . . who is totally unworthy of her.'

Mr Hill seemed embarrassed, and abandoning his usual precise manner of speaking, said, 'I cannot think it wise, but has . . . your friend . . . tried to persuade the lady to leave her husband?'

'She is unwilling to do so.'

Mr Hill looked at his young friend for a moment. 'Richard, forgive me if I speak frankly. I do not think there is a "friend" in this matter. We are talking of you, are we not? Of you and Mrs Harcourt.'

There was another silence. 'Is it that obvious?' Richard asked. 'Does everyone in the mill know? Do they make lewd jokes about us?'

'No. But I have known you for a long time, and I have seen you with Mrs Harcourt. I have long suspected what your feelings for her were.'

'And no doubt you have had your advice ready in case I should ask. I can guess what it is.' He rose. 'We had better join the ladies.'

'A moment, Richard. My advice may be long prepared, as you say, but I flatter myself that it is no less worth hearing for that. I realise the extent of your unhappiness, and the situation cannot be easy for Mrs Harcourt, but if you ran away together, where would you go, and how would you live? Scandal and bitterness would follow you; moreover you would both have to abandon your work at the mill, which you love so dearly.'

'I know all that,' Richard said. 'There is no point in continuing.'

'Love can be a delicate plant. It does not always survive in such circumstances. No, you must try to put her out of your mind. Think of her only as a business colleague, the manager of the mill. Any other course will mean disaster for you both.'

'Am I simply to stand by and watch her misery?'

'You forget, Richard – Mrs Harcourt may be of the weaker sex, but she has a strength of character, a courage that is lacking in many men. I would predict that if the two of you are ever to find happiness together it will be she who brings it about. Don't ask me how. I have no idea. The ways of a woman's mind are a closed book to me. Despite my long years of conjugal bliss, I do not begin to understand Mrs Hill, let alone Mrs Harcourt. But I do know that women are wiser than we are in these matters. Follow *her* wishes, and if you cannot stifle your love, at least be patient.'

Richard rose again, his face grim. 'Let us go in.' He moved to the door, and then stopped. 'I am sorry. I should thank you. You are right, of course. I suppose I was hoping you would tell me to listen to my heart and not my head.'

'Hearts make fools of us, most of the time.'

'You won't speak of this to anyone, will you? Not even to Mrs Hill.'

Mr Hill shook his head, smiling.

Richard lay awake for long hours that night. Would Sarah really be the one to bring about their future happiness – if it was ever to be? 'We might become friends again,' she had said. That could be an indication that one day her attitude would change. But if friendship was all she had in mind, she might easily convince herself one day that she no longer loved him. The thoughts swirled in his mind, and always haunting him was the cruel, menacing figure of Tom Harcourt. He tossed and turned feverishly, dropping at last into a fitful sleep.

In the morning his mind was no clearer. All he could do, he decided, was to follow Sarah's lead, and wait, and hope.

Six weeks after the night when Tom had forced himself upon her so brutally, a visit from Dr Wood confirmed that at last Sarah was pregnant.

Tom returned home the same evening. He was in a genial mood, having secured a large order from Montgomery, and though he had a brandy or two to celebrate, he did not drink heavily. When they went to their room, Sarah told him her news.

He was delighted, cock-a-hoop. 'What did I tell you? I knew we'd do it some day. When?'

'The middle of July.'

He took her in his arms and kissed her with more tenderness than was his custom. 'How do you feel? What did Dr Wood say?'

'I am well, and he said I am strong and healthy and there should be no trouble.'

'But you must take care. Rest. You'll have to give up the mill, of course.'

'Why?'

He laughed exultantly. 'Because you're pregnant.'

'Women in the weaving sheds go on working. They go on as long as they can.'

'They need the wages. Besides, they're working women – it's different for them.'

'Why?'

Tom laughed. 'Really, my dear, I don't have to explain that, surely. They're not the same as us – more like peasants. Have the baby in the field, go on hoeing – you know the sort of thing. No, you'll have to give up immediately.'

'No, Tom, please. Nobody knows, except you and Dr Wood, and nobody else need know for ages yet. If I go on working for a month or two, it will give us time to decide who shall take over from me, and to get everything properly arranged.'

Tom continued to argue, but Sarah was adamant, and eventually he gave in, aware that a woman in her condition needed to be humoured. 'But once it begins to show, you'll have to stop.'

'We'll see. I promise I'll give up if Dr Wood says I should.'

Sarah bloomed. She suffered no morning sickness or inconvenience of any other kind. Reluctant though she was to give up her work, she meant to keep her promise to Tom, and had arranged that Dr Wood should give her regular physical examinations. On each of his visits, she asked him whether it was still reasonable to continue working.

In her fourth month, he said, 'In normal circumstances, Mrs Harcourt, I would suggest that now is the time to start taking things a little easier. You need to keep your strength up. You have several tiring months ahead of you, and childbirth itself can be exhausting to a degree. You are aware, of course, of the sad circumstances of your sister-in-law's death. However, long experience has taught me that ladies in an interesting condition are often seized by strange whims, which, unless positively harmful, are better indulged than ignored or obstructed. For the time being, therefore, and since you are in such splendid shape, I shall not oppose you, but you must leave the mill at once if you feel the least tiredness.'

In the face of the doctor's consent, neither Tom nor his mother could dissuade Sarah from continuing to work as usual. Once the news had been disclosed to her, Mrs Harcourt had launched herself into paroxysms of joy and endless accounts of how she had suffered during her own pregnancies. She marvelled at Sarah's good health, implying that it was unnatural and even indelicate to be so well, and made no attempt to conceal her disapproval of her daughter-in-law's daily visits to the mill, especially when the fact that she was with child began to be apparent.

Sarah did not care if the workers knew. There was nothing to be ashamed of, and her presence was more than ever needed, for the fall in trade that had begun some months previously had intensified. Decisions had to be taken daily about the amount of crape to be produced, the patterns to which they would commit themselves, the placing of orders for raw silk, and though Richard could have shouldered the responsibilities on his own, both he and Sarah preferred to share them.

Observing her closely as always, Richard had soon become aware of a difference about her, though at first he did not recognise the cause. Once the news that Our Missus was in the family way had run through the mill, he had to talk to her, and at the next opportunity he asked, 'Is it true, what they are saying?'

She smiled. 'What *are* they saying?'

'That you . . . that you are . . .'

'In an interesting condition? Yes, Richard, it is true.'

'Is it . . . ?' He found it almost impossible to ask the question. 'Whose child is it?'

The smile vanished, and her face was wooden as she whispered, 'Tom's, of course.'

'They say it's due in midsummer . . .'

She nodded. 'Yes.'

'I worked out that it might be . . .'

'No, Richard.'

She had moved over to a cupboard in the corner of the room, and was standing with her back to him. He knew she must be lying, and was trying to prevent him from reading the truth in her eyes. He went over to her and took her arm and gently turned her towards him. 'Are you sure, Sarah, really sure?'

She gazed back at him, the green eyes open and honest. 'Yes, quite sure. There are times when a woman can be in no doubt. I am bearing my husband's child.'

Richard had to believe her. Surprised at the depth of the disappointment which swept over him, he gazed at her, still holding her arm.

The door opened, and Tom came in. He stopped short, aware of the atmosphere of intimacy. Instinctively Richard moved to distance himself from Sarah, though as he did so he realised that it could only add an appearance of guilt to the scene.

'Forgive me for interrupting.' Tom's voice was sarcastic.

'We were discussing the need to alter the order we sent recently to Leroy's,' Sarah said. 'I did not expect you back so early.'

'So I could see.'

'Don't be ridiculous, Tom,' she said calmly, dismissing the subject once and for all. 'How have you been getting on? Any improvement?'

Tom did not reply. Slowly he took off his gloves. 'You will both be interested to know that I have come to a decision. It affects you, Richard, but I think it would be better if I were to impart it to my wife in private first.'

Sarah raised her eyebrows. 'I think we have finished anyway. Let me know if you have any difficulties with the new pattern, Richard.'

'Yes, of course.' Richard left the room swiftly.

Tom stood for a moment looking at his wife. She was a handsome woman, proud and independent. It was that independence which made her so desirable, provided he could subdue her and show her that however free and self-willed she might consider herself, he was still the master. Now at last he had got her pregnant, which would tie her down, and force her back to her proper role of wife and mother, and now was the time to put an end to her insistence on working. She had been humoured for long enough. There was another reason, too – the strongest reason of all – but he need not mention that . . .

'So what is this decision?' Sarah asked.

'I think you know. It is not only for your own good, my dear, and that of our child, but for Harcourt's. You do not wish, I am sure, to have our customers looking askance at us, criticising us.'

'What do you mean?'

'It is all round the trade. Everyone knows that you are expecting a child, and everyone knows that you are still working at the mill every day. They are saying ugly things.'

'Who are?'

'Some of our customers. Certainly many of our competitors.'

'What sort of things?'

'That Harcourt's must be in a bad way if they can force a lady in your condition to work.'

She laughed. 'Oh, Tom, really!'

'It is no laughing matter. Many people thought it strange before – now they are calling it scandalous. Some are saying, too, that I must either be mad to allow it, or cruel to force it on you.'

She did not believe in the truth of what he was saying. 'You are making it up, Tom.'

He shook his head. 'No.'

'Then it's absurd. I take no notice of that kind of nonsense.'

He tried to keep calm. 'You may not, my dear, but I must.'

'But I am well enough, and Dr Wood . . .'

'Dr Wood and I have catered to your whims for long enough. You are beginning to show, Sarah, and really, my dear, it is not decent for you to continue.'

'Pooh to that! I see no reason at all why a woman should be shut away just because she is expecting a child. It is, after all, a very normal condition.'

'There is such a thing as propriety. But I do not intend to argue. You have had your own way in everything since my father died –'

'And everything that I have done has been right.'

Tom struggled to contain his anger. 'Nevertheless, it is time I put my foot down. I am becoming a laughing stock.'

'So that's it – your precious dignity at stake. Well, I care more for Harcourt's.'

'I care for Harcourt's, and also for the child you are to bear, which is more than you appear to do. I have made my decision, and nothing will change my mind. As from today I forbid you to come to the mill. I mean it, Sarah. I forbid you, do you hear? Even you will surely not forget your wifely duties so far as to disobey.'

Sarah paled. 'Tom, please don't ask me to give up my work. It means more to me than anything.'

'Certainly more than your husband. I am well aware of that. But I am not asking you, I am ordering you.'

'But . . . but who will run the mill if I am not here?'

'No doubt your friend Goodwin would consider himself able to do so. However, I have decided that I shall take over your duties myself.'

'And who will visit our customers, control our sales? No one can replace you there. Why, our whole success has depended on your efforts.'

'You will not get round me with flattery, Sarah. Our salesmen are perfectly capable of making any necessary calls, and I shall still be able to visit the more important outlets from time to time.'

'But you know nothing –'

'You underestimate me, my dear. I know a great deal more than you imagine, and I am far from being as stupid as you think. What I don't know, I shall learn.'

Sarah considered for a moment. 'At least let me help you, Tom. Let me come here occasionally – say, once a week, or if you encounter a problem which I could help to solve.'

'No.'

She was on the verge of tears, but refused to give way to

them. 'Very well,' she said coldly. 'Perhaps you will drive me home.'

'Dawson can drive you. I have work to do.'

With all the dignity she could muster, Sarah left the office.

Tom summoned Richard. 'I have to inform you that Mrs Harcourt will not be working at the mill in future,' he said. 'As to your own position, since becoming a director you have been accustomed not only to make all decisions in those sections of the business for which you have responsibility, but also to advise Mrs Harcourt on other matters. Is that not so?'

'Yes.'

'Your directorship was granted, as you well know, in recognition of the fact that you had married into the Harcourt family. Since my poor sister's death, the relationship is somewhat changed, and although I recognise that you have served the company well, I cannot allow you the excessive freedom which you have enjoyed under my wife's aegis. In future, all decisions will be taken by myself. Is that clear?'

Richard had listened in stunned silence, but now his first thought was for Sarah. 'Is Mrs Harcourt not well?'

'As you know, she is expecting a happy event. She needs to rest.'

She must have been forced to give in, of that Richard felt sure. 'But she is still a director of the company?'

'Yes.'

'And am I?'

Tom smiled superciliously. 'I am simply rearranging your duties. I do not intend to remove you from the board.'

No, Richard thought, that would have been to expose him to rumours in the trade of trouble at Harcourt's. Nevertheless, Tom wanted to humiliate him, perhaps even to push him into resignation – but he would not succeed in that. He had lost Jane, and he had no chance of winning Sarah; his work was all that was left to him. Not that his directorship meant a great deal. Many details of the company were concealed from him – only the other day Mr Hill had hinted that Tom was drawing large sums from their capital reserves, but he had been given no official intimation of that. Nevertheless, he intended to stay as long as there was work for him to do. He thought almost ruefully of the ambition he had once cherished to become the owner of Harcourt's.

'I asked if it was clear to you,' Tom said.

'Yes, I understand.'

'I hope you do. There are going to be changes here. The whole place has become slack, and in present trading conditions I cannot tolerate that. And now I will not keep you from your work.'

The workers were not surprised that Our Missus would be seen at the mill no more. A fine lady could not work to the last possible day of her pregnancy – and it was only to be expected that Mr Harcourt would in future be more closely connected with the daily running of the business. Indeed, the wonder was that he had been content in the past to absent himself so often. They waited to see what changes he would make, and especially what place Mr Goodwin would now hold.

Apart from the fact that he seemed no longer to make decisions on the spot, they did not see much alteration in Richard's position, but the first of Mr Harcourt's new decrees caused great resentment. It came in the form of a notice pinned up in all the work-rooms: 'Female employees will forthwith cease to wear bustles and draped skirts in the mill. This foolish fashion is not only entirely unsuitable, but highly dangerous, since loose folds of material may easily catch in the machines. Any female contravening this instruction will be discharged instantly.' Each notice was personally signed, 'Thos. Harcourt.'

It was not only the absurdity of the rule – for whoever heard of a bustle or a draped skirt catching in machinery? – but the tone of the notice which upset the women. Sarah had always tried to treat her work-people as human beings, believing it was better to ask than to order. As a result, her least request had been honoured to the letter.

Tom's edict was obeyed, naturally, but with much complaining and many bitter regrets for the days when Our

Missus was in charge. He followed it with other communications forbidding 'idle chatter while engaged in your several employments', imposing more stringent penalties for lateness, and generally tightening the discipline of the mill.

Most hated of all was an edict that those involved in producing work deemed to be 'poor, and below acceptable standards, for whatever cause' would suffer deductions from their wages. Carelessness had always been penalised, but no fines had been levied if, in the overseers' opinion, mechanical failures rather than human errors were to blame. When a deputation called on Mr Harcourt to ask him to reconsider, he replied brusquely that all workers were responsible for the perfect functioning of the machinery, that the rule would remain in force, and that any further complaint would result in an increase in the amounts deducted.

Richard found himself in an embarrassing position. Tom was entitled to impose any conditions he chose, and most of the demands he made were not unreasonable, no stricter than those in other factories up and down the country. When, as frequently happened, individuals came to Richard to protest, he had no option but to support Tom. Perhaps Sarah *had* been too liberal in her approach. But Harcourt's was no longer a happy place, and despite Tom's search for greater efficiency, the level of output had declined rather than improved since he had taken command.

Richard tried to speak to him about it, but Tom immediately flew into a rage. 'I am not prepared to discuss the matter. I made it perfectly plain when I took control that I would not brook any interference. If you are not prepared to accept that –' He broke off. 'Well, we will not go into that. I expect full loyalty and support from you, Goodwin. If this decline in our trade continues, we shall certainly not weather it by allowing the continuation of the slackness which my wife appears to have fostered.'

Richard went back to his own office, and wrote a long memorandum pointing out that Tom's measures were decreasing production, and begging for a reconsideration of the hated penalties. Such measures, he pointed out, might well bring about the formation of a union among the workers and the fomentation of industrial strife. He was at pains to make it clear that he did not quarrel with Tom's wishes, but only with the way he was implementing them.

Tom sent for him. 'I have read this effusion,' he said. 'I do not intend to make any changes in my decisions. However, I am grateful to you for alerting me to a possibility that I had not considered. I am preparing a notice to the effect that any attempt to form a union in this mill will lead to instant dismissal. As for the rest of what you say . . .' He tore the memo into small pieces, and dropped it in the waste-paper basket. 'I do not expect any further opposition of this sort from you, and I give you due warning. I accept much for the sake of my sister's memory, but my charity towards you is not unbounded.'

The notice forbidding the formation of a union caused little disturbance. The workers would not have expected anything else from Mr Harcourt, and were too much in fear of losing their jobs to consider flouting his orders.

Much more serious in many ways was the situation revealed privately to Richard by Mr Hill. 'At times like these, when trade is in decline, a substantial reserve of money in the bank is no longer a luxury, but a necessity. Those companies which do not possess good reserves are forced to borrow, and borrowing costs more money, which exacerbates the problem. Alas, Harcourt's has less money in the bank than I fear we shall need.'

'I thought we were building it up. Where has it all gone?'

'Need you ask, Richard? Mr Harcourt is not the most frugal of gentlemen.'

Richard could not think what to do. If only Sarah were still at the mill. Perhaps if he could see her – it would have to be on one of those days, rarer now, when Tom had gone to visit some important customer – she would be able to talk some sense into her husband's head.

Eventually, an opportunity came, and Richard walked to Harcourt Place, and asked to see the mistress.

The maid answered woodenly, 'I'm not allowed to let you in.'

'Why not?'

'Not if 'e was away, Mr 'Arcourt said.'

The door was closed in his face.

Tom returned home that evening. During dinner, he turned to Sarah and said, 'I understand you had a visitor today, my dear.'

'No, I did not.'

'You did not see him, but a visitor called. Fortunately, I had left instructions that he was not to be admitted.' So far he had spoken in almost kindly tones, but now he let his anger show. 'What is there between you and Richard Goodwin, Sarah?'

Sarah looked at him in astonishment, and then dropped her eyes. 'Nothing. Nothing at all.'

'Then why does he call on you when I am away?'

'I have no idea. I did not know that he had done so.'

'I forbid you to see him, do you hear? Do you hear, Sarah?'

'Yes, Tom, I hear you. But I do not know why you should speak to me in this unpleasant way.'

'He has every reason,' Mrs Lottie Harcourt said. 'I've never liked that man. I don't trust him. You should get rid of him, Tom.'

'We should not forget what he has done for Harcourt's,' Tom said, 'and what he still does. His work is exemplary.' He turned to Sarah, speaking once more in the quiet tones of a reasonable man, and even smiling. 'I'm sure you would agree, my dear. All I am determined to do is to put an end to the guilty relationship which has existed between you and him, and to ensure that it does not continue.'

Sarah was almost relieved that the accusation was out. It had not been concern for her and the child, nor fear of scandal affecting the business which had been his main motive when he had forbidden her to continue at the mill, of that she was certain. It was solely to take her away from Richard that he had forced her to give up her work. She threw down her napkin and stood up. 'I will not have such accusations. There is no justification for them, and you demean yourself and me by making them. I will not stay here to be spoken to like this – and in my condition too.' She began to cry, and ran from the dining-room, praying that her voice and tears had carried conviction. How much did he know?

Tom hurried after her. 'I'm sorry,' he said. 'Forgive me, Sarah. I know there has been nothing between you and Goodwin, but I can't help being jealous. I may have treated you badly in the past, but I shall be better in future, if only you will love me a little more. Just swear to me that you don't think of him, that you won't think of him.'

'I swear,' Sarah forced herself to murmur, childishly crossing her fingers behind her back to cancel out the lie.

'Thank you,' he said, with a kind of humility. 'Then I promise I will not speak of it again.'

But later she saw him in whispered conversation with his mother, and was sure that the subject had not been wiped from his mind.

CHAPTER SIXTEEN

'Come in.'

Richard was in his office. The mill was quiet, for work had finished for the week, though the hands were still there, queuing up to draw their weekly wages.

Isaac Appleby, overseer in the weaving department, peered around the door. His face was usually florid, but today he looked pale, and his fringe of white hair stood out in dishevelled wisps around his bald pate. He was breathing hard. 'Can I 'ave a word, Mr Goodwin?'

'Of course, Isaac. What's wrong?'

Appleby put a piece of paper down on Richard's desk. 'I just bin to collect me wages. And there's this. Mr 'Ill read it to me.'

The note was brief. 'As from Monday next, May 25th, 1873, your employment in Harcourt's Mill shall cease. You will receive herewith a further week's wages in lieu of notice. Th. Harcourt.'

'I bin with 'Arcourt's since I were a nipper. Is that me reward for fifty years o'work?'

'There must be some mistake,' Richard said.

'It ain't no mistake, and I ain't the only one. It's just I was the first to 'ear, seein' me name begins with A.'

'Who else has been dismissed?'

'I dunno. More 'n twenty, Mr 'Ill says. All old 'ands.'

Richard stood up. 'I knew nothing about this, Isaac. I'll go and see Mr Harcourt straight away.'

''E's gorn to London, Mr 'Ill says. Left early 'sarternoon, and won't be back come Tuesday.'

'Then I'll see him the moment he returns. Don't worry, Isaac. I'm sure there must be some mistake.'

'What about Monday morning?'
'What do you mean?'
'What do we do? Come to work, or stop 'ome?'
Richard made a swift decision. 'Be here as usual on Monday morning. Tell the others the same.' Seeing the doubtful look on Appleby's face, he continued, 'There'll be no trouble. When he comes back, I'll tell Mr Harcourt that you have come in on my instructions.'
'Ta, Mr Goodwin, ta. If I'm sacked, it'll be the poor 'ouse for me and me missus.'
'Don't say anything about it to your wife, Isaac. No need to worry her. Tell the others not to talk about it either.'
When Appleby had gone, Richard sat thinking. Despite the reassurance he had given, he was certain that it was not a mistake, and Tom's sudden and convenient disappearance to London confirmed that view. It was typical of his behaviour since he had taken over from Sarah. Richard wondered whether she knew what had happened. Most probably not. Of course, Tom would see his advice to Isaac Appleby as open defiance. Well, he was ready for that.
When Richard emerged from the mill, he was immediately surrounded by a score of angry and despairing workers. He held up his hand for silence. 'I have already given Appleby instructions for you all,' he said. 'Do as he tells you. Nothing more can be done until Monday or Tuesday, but I will do my best then. Don't be down-hearted – it must be a mistake.' They were silent as he pushed his way through and began to walk home. He knew that few of them believed him.

On the Monday morning he went to the mill much earlier than usual. A group of men was waiting at the main gate. He recognised them as servants from Harcourt Place. 'What are you doing here?' he asked.
'Mr 'Arcourt's orders, sir.' It was Dawson, the coachman. He grinned at Richard. 'We're to stop them as was dismissed from entering of the premises.'
'Then I countermand that order!'
The man grinned again. 'No, sir, Mr 'Arcourt said we was

to take orders only from him. And 'e give us a message for you, sir. We was to tell you as Mrs 'Arcourt ain't at home.'

Richard tried desperately to control his anger. 'How will you know which workers to stop? I don't see any list.'

'Why, bless you, sir, it's all the old codgers, ain't it? We'll recognise 'em easy. They're to go home. Any who stays is to be prosecuted for trespass.'

Richard went to his office, conscious of the sneering looks which followed him. Knowing that his presence at the entrance would do no good and might make matters worse, but reproaching himself for being as much of a coward as Tom, he stayed in his room until well after all those who had been dismissed would have been turned away. Then he went home.

Frances listened in dismay as he poured out the story. When he had finished, she said gently, 'Don't be upset by this question, Richard, but tell me which angers you more – the dismissal of the workers, or the way Tom has humiliated you?'

He thought for a moment. 'Yes, you're telling me that when I confront him, I mustn't let him see that he has wounded me. I must fight for them, not for myself. But it's difficult, Frances, my God, it's difficult! How can I ignore it? Telling those fellows not to obey my orders . . . the message about Sarah . . . and the worst thing, I think, is that he didn't consult me, or even inform me, about the dismissals.'

'You've got to try to forget it. Just think about those poor men and women, and the way they've been treated.'

'Sit down, Richard,' Tom said. 'I thought you would want to see me.' He held his hand up. 'No, before you say anything, let me explain. You are aware, I am sure, of the decline in orders over the past few months, but you may not understand quite how sharp it has been. Our financial reserves have been drained, and –'

'Yes, so I believe.'

'What do you mean by that?'

'You have been drawing heavily on company money.'

'Who told you that? Was it Hill?'

'No, of course not.' Richard had to protect the clerk. 'He

wouldn't be so indiscreet. No, I had a look at his ledgers myself, one evening after he had gone home. You would not deny my right, as a director, to do so. There have been very substantial drawings to your personal account over the last couple of years.'

'Have there indeed?' Tom said in an icy voice. 'Well, we will come to that point later. I was about to explain why those notices were given out on Saturday. It is very simple. Our financial reserves, whatever the cause, are low, and if we are to survive, drastic steps have to be taken very quickly, for all our sakes.'

'We've already cut the shifts, and reduced our stocks of raw silk,' Richard said.

Tom nodded. 'Come, Richard,' he said, and his voice sounded almost friendly, 'you are far too intelligent not to know that at the same time we were increasing our stocks of finished crape. The warehouse is full. Had I been as ruthless as you seem to think I am, I should have closed down all manufacturing some time since, for a month or more, and laid off all our workers, but that would have caused far too much hardship.'

Richard had prepared himself for an angry confrontation, not the reasonable, open approach which Tom had adopted. 'Then why –?'

'Because no other course is open to me. The only way I can avoid closing down the whole mill for a period is to dismiss a few of the workers, a very few. They will suffer for the benefit of everyone else. Surely you can see that. I do not enjoy it, but needs must.'

'But why pick on men like Isaac Appleby? He's been with Harcourt's for nearly fifty years. They're all old hands, who've served you and your father faithfully – some were even here in your grandfather's time.'

'There is no place for sentiment in business, Richard. Believe me, it was not an easy decision.'

Richard could not restrain himself. 'Is that why you went off to London – because you could not face them?'

'I shall ignore that remark.'

It was unlike Tom to accept critical comments so calmly, and Richard had the feeling that he was walking into a trap. Nevertheless, he had to continue. 'They're our most loyal, most trusted workers.'

'They also happen to be among the highest paid,' Tom said drily. 'Hold your horses, Richard, and listen. I had to consider what they cost us, and the fact that most workers who've joined more recently are contracted to us for at least a year, which makes them much more expensive to dismiss than older employees who are still on no more than a week's notice.'

Richard looked at him angrily. 'But that's monstrous! And stupid. You're getting rid of all the men with the most experience.'

'The oldest, yes. They may be capable at the moment, but for how much longer? Take Eales, for example.'

'He's the salt of the earth.'

'He may be, but it doesn't stop him being long past his best.'

'Have you thought what will happen to him and the others? They've been the backbone of the company, those people, and you owe them something for their loyalty and their hard work.' Richard was almost shouting. 'I protest! I protest most strongly, Tom! You may be the owner of the mill, but this whole matter should have been considered by the board of directors.'

Tom stood, and began to pace up and down. 'I do not propose to discuss it further. The decision is made, and is final. However, I do wish to say something about your own conduct. I understand that you told Appleby and the others to come to work yesterday in direct contravention of my orders. Is that true?'

'I could not believe it was your intention to dismiss them. I thought it must be a mistake.'

'Then it would have been wiser to wait until today, and find out if it was. Fortunately, I anticipated your reaction – your head is always a little too hot, Richard – and laid my plans accordingly. I am told that you also attempted to countermand my instructions yesterday morning. My mother was right – she thought you would try that.'

'You talked to her about it?' It seemed the worst insult of all.

'Why not? My mother has a long and intimate knowledge of the mill. Longer and more intimate than yours. She sees things very clearly. She anticipated your every move.'

'And was she in favour of sacking these old employees, whom she must have known for so long and so intimately?'

Tom turned to him. 'My mother was the first to see through you, Goodwin. "Give him enough rope, and he will hang himself," she said. And you've done it, haven't you? Spying on financial matters which are none of your concern, fighting every attempt that I have made to improve the standards in this mill, inciting workers to rebellion!'

'That is an absurd –'

'Be silent! And then you have the gall to catechise me!' Twin spots of angry colour burned on his normally sallow cheeks, and a small edge of white froth appeared at the corners of his mouth. 'I will answer one more question which I am sure you are burning to ask: what did Sarah have to say? Alas, I did not consult her. I am fully aware of the regard she has for you.' A nerve in his forehead began to jump, as he spat the words out in a low, virulent tone. 'What a fool I was to let you marry my sister! It was just a way for you to get nearer to Sarah, wasn't it? You couldn't have her, so you took Jane. And once Jane was dead . . . Don't think I didn't see what was going on.'

There was enough truth in his accusations to keep Richard silent.

Tom walked back behind his desk, and picked up a pencil, playing with it as he continued. 'I succeeded in keeping you away from her, but I know perfectly well that you regard her as an ally in your treachery. She is completely under your spell and would do anything you ask.' He gave a strange kind of half-smile, and said, almost casually, 'I believe she would lie with you if you asked her. Have you asked her?'

For a moment, Richard was tempted to tell him everything.

But he had to protect Sarah. 'No,' he said. 'No.'

'No,' said Tom, 'I don't think you have. I don't think you've got the courage for that. It doesn't make any difference, really, does it? You will not deny that in your hearts you and she are both guilty of *adultery*!' The pencil suddenly snapped in two.

Richard could not meet his accusing gaze.

'I am glad you do not have the cheek to plead your innocence.' Tom paused briefly, and then continued icily, 'I intend to remove your influence once and for all. You are no longer a director of this company. You are no longer employed by Harcourt's in any capacity. You have twenty minutes in which to leave the mill. You will not return. Is that clear?'

Richard went white. 'There is no justification –' he began.

'There is every justification. You openly flout my orders, you incite my employees to revolt, above all, you cast lecherous eyes upon my wife! I am not only within my rights in dismissing you, but also in making no payment in lieu of notice.'

With nothing to lose, Richard could not sit there and let Tom abuse him. His chair crashed to the floor as he strode to the door.

'One moment,' Tom said. 'I have not finished. You will recall the terms on which your occupancy of Orchard House depends. Since you are no longer employed by Harcourt's you forfeit your tenancy. As you will no doubt realise, its sale will produce some useful capital.' He smiled sardonically. 'I have no wish to be unreasonable. I will give you and your sister a week in which to remove yourselves and your property.'

Had he stayed a moment longer, Richard would have smashed his fist into those hate-filled sneering features. Tom's words buzzed in his head as he went to his office, and gathered together his few personal possessions. He was grateful that he met no one as he left the mill, and walked quickly home.

From the drawing-room of Orchard House, Frances saw

him coming up the drive, and hurried to meet him. His very manner told her that something was wrong. 'Richard! What is it? What's the matter?'

He brushed past her. 'I will tell you later.' He went into his study. There he paced up and down, trying to sort out the maze of thoughts. He remembered his departure from Prideau's so long ago, and laughed bitterly. This was now the second time that he had been ignominiously dismissed from a silk mill! But the circumstances were very different; then he had been a callow youth, and the dismissal had been totally unjustified, whereas now he was – he had been, he corrected himself – a director, and, yes, if he looked at it objectively, Tom was at least to some extent justified.

He would have done it again, every single part of it. He could not have stood by and let Appleby and his like be thrown upon the rubbish heap, any more than he could have smothered his feelings for Sarah.

Ever since that evening when Mr Hill suggested that it would be Sarah who might somehow contrive to bring about a future for them both, he had subconsciously nurtured that hope. But now that Tom had broken her spirit, now that he himself would have to leave Brentfield, he had to face reality and the knowledge that he had lost her for ever.

If his love was doomed, at least he would fight for himself and his work. He would consult a solicitor and challenge his dismissal; he would organise a revolt among the mill-workers – they would follow him, he was sure; he would go back to Tom, eat humble pie and apologise for his faults, and then, with reasoned arguments, persuade him that he had only had Harcourt's interests at heart, and beg for reinstatement.

One by one, he discarded the plans. Tom's position was legally secure, and his ban on the formation of a union would put paid to any thought of organised rebellion; above all, he could never apologise to Tom, even if he would listen. There was no future for him at Harcourt's. He would simply have to make a new life for himself somewhere else. How, he did not know. He would think about that later. Meanwhile, was there perhaps something he could do for Appleby and the others?

Sarah, he thought – Sarah was the only hope. But how could he contrive to see her? He would be refused entry to Harcourt Place even more firmly than before. Besides, if Tom suspected Richard's hand in it, he would stifle any attempt she made to help. But supposing she could be made aware of the plight of the dismissed workers and then made a plea as though entirely on her own initiative . . . It might work.

He sat down and wrote a hasty letter, begging her to meet him secretly and as soon as possible, and promising that nothing he would do or say would embarrass her in any way. He folded the paper, sealed it with wax, and wrote her name and 'Private' on the outside, printing the letters so that his handwriting would not be recognised. He called for one of the maids, and told her to take the letter to Harcourt Place. 'On no account say who it is from. Hurry, girl! And wait for an answer.'

It seemed an age before she returned. 'They wouldn't take it, sir,' she said. 'I was to tell you that Mrs Harcourt does not wish to hear from you.'

'Did she say that herself?'

'I didn't see her, sir. They wouldn't let me in.'

'How did they know the letter was from me?' Richard asked angrily.

The girl began to snivel. 'They recognised me, sir. They know I work here.'

'Yes, of course. Dammit, what a fool I am! I should have thought of that. I'm sorry for shouting at you, Amy – it's not your fault.'

Frances, who had been standing at the door to the drawing-room, came forward. 'Richard, my dear, what is wrong? Won't you tell me?'

'Yes, you're entitled to know. It affects you too, I'm afraid. Come into my study, and shut the door.'

She let him speak without interrupting, her eyes big with dismay.

'And I can't even get a letter to Sarah,' he finished, explaining the failure of his attempt to do so.

'Perhaps if I wrote to her . . .'

'It would be the same. It's damnable! There's not a single thing I can do to help Appleby and the others.'

'What about us, Richard? It is noble of you to want to help them, but what about us?'

'I suppose the first thing is to find somewhere to live.'

'No,' she said. 'That's not important. We can go anywhere – to an hotel, if necessary. What matters is where you're going to find work. I don't know how much money you've saved, but I doubt it would be enough for you to live on for the rest of your life. Besides, that kind of living would never suit you. Have you thought what you want to do?'

'Not really. What *can* I do, Frances? The only thing I know about is silk.'

'Could you find employment in another mill?'

'Not at Prideau's, if that's what you're thinking.' He gave a little laugh at the idea. 'I suppose we could go to Macclesfield, or somewhere like that. But with my record . . . Dismissed twice!'

For a long while, neither of them spoke. Then he said, 'You know what's been at the back of my mind? Supposing I could find a small mill for sale? It would have to be very small – I couldn't afford anything grand. But I could work it up.'

Her first instinct was to express all the doubts that flooded into her mind, but she realised that Richard desperately needed encouragement. She clapped her hands. 'Oh, that would be splendid! And you could take on Isaac Appleby, and some of the others – and Mr Hill, too. He'd come with us. Oh, that would solve everything.'

'Hold it! It's just an idea. I doubt if I could find the right place, and even if I did . . . No, perhaps it would be better to go to Macclesfield, or London. I could go and see Mr Leroy – he might be able to tell me where I could find work.' Again he fell silent, deep in thought.

'You ought to eat something,' Frances said. 'You must be starving.'

'I'm not hungry. Leave me be, Frances. We'll talk about it again this evening, when I've got things clearer in my mind.'

Reluctantly she went away. After a while, Richard got out

his account books and totted up the figures. He might just have enough to buy a small mill, with the help of a bank loan if he could get one, but anything that he could afford would be likely to be near-derelict, and he would need extra capital to re-equip it. It looked impossible.

Later that afternoon, Frances brought him some tea. She tapped at the door, and getting no reply, opened it softly. Richard was asleep, bent over his desk, his head resting on his folded arms. Frances did not disturb him – the sleep would do him good. In case he should wake before it was cold, she put the tea on his desk, and tip-toed from the room.

When he awoke, Richard's head was aching, and his mouth felt dry and tasted sour. The sight of the cold tea almost made him retch. There was no fixed plan in his mind, but he felt somehow more contented, as though everything were settled. He went to his room, and splashed water on his face and rinsed his mouth. The headache was beginning to fade. He looked at his pocket-watch – it was nearly time for the evening meal.

When he went downstairs, Frances was waiting. She looked at him anxiously. 'Are you all right, Richard?'

'Yes. In fact, it's ridiculous, but I feel . . . almost happy.'

'Have you decided what we're going to do, then?'

'No. And I'm not going to think about it any more this evening. In the morning, when I've slept on it – then perhaps I'll make my mind up.'

They had just finished their dinner when the door-bell rang. A few moments later the maid announced, 'A person called Appleby to see you, sir.'

'Show him into my study.'

Isaac Appleby seemed to have aged since Richard had last seen him on the Saturday. His face was drawn. Gratefully he accepted Richard's invitation to sit down, but refused the offer of a whisky. 'I never bin one for strong drink, and I ain't a-goin' to start now, though I felt like it these last few days, I can tell you. Don't let me stop you, guv.'

Richard shook his head. 'I don't drink very often myself.

Only for the sake of company.' He knew that he was not achieving his object of putting Appleby at his ease. 'What can I do for you, Isaac?'

'Nothing. I just come to say, on be'alf of me and me mates, 'ow sorry we was to 'ear about you.'

'Everybody knows? Already?'

'We 'eard there's a notice up in the mill, as 'ow you'd resigned and no longer 'ad anythin' to do with 'Arcourt's.'

'That's not exactly true,' Richard said. 'I did not resign.'

'None of us believed you 'ad. That's why I come to see you. We guessed as Mr 'Arcourt pushed you out on account of what you done for us. It's all our fault, ain't it?'

'No, Isaac, it isn't. What I tried to do for you was part of it, but there were other things, too. I'm grateful to you for your concern. You tell everyone that, and tell them the only thing I'm sorry about is that I couldn't fight for you better than I did.'

'We should've formed a union years ago. There was talk of it, but there didn't seem no point, not when Our Missus was in charge. It's too late now.'

'It will come one day, Isaac.'

'Yeah, and pigs'll fly.' He looked at Richard miserably, and got up. 'I better be goin'. I don't want to disturb you no more. I only come to say as me and me mates are sorry, and thanks for all you done.'

'No, wait a moment, Isaac,' Richard said. 'Tell me, do any of you know yet what you're going to do?'

'It's the work'ouse for some – Sam Eales for one. Others is for goin' up to London, but I don't fancy their chances none. I'm a Londoner meself – I know what it's like there. Cut-throat place if you're lookin' for a job at my age.'

'So what are you thinking of, Isaac?'

'I dunno. Me and me missus 'ope to go to 'er sister's near Norwich, if she'll 'ave us. See if I can find work there. Quite a few silk mills in them parts, there is. The missus got the Rector to write a letter for us to 'er sister, so we're waitin' to 'ear. Mind you, it won't be easy to find a job, not when I'm more 'n sixty, so mebbe we'll end up in the poor'ouse too.'

'I wish you good fortune, Isaac. I'm sure you'll find something.'

Appleby shook his head. 'What about you, if I may make so bold?'

'I haven't decided yet.'

'Ought to start up a mill of your own, that's what you ought to do.'

'It's what I've been thinking of, but –'

'Then I could come and work for you. If you'd 'ave me, that is.'

Richard laughed. 'There's nothing I'd like more. I tell you what – if you do go to your sister-in-law, let me have the address. Then if anything comes of it, I can let you know.' Seeing Appleby's face light up, he added quickly, 'Don't count on it. I doubt if I'll have the money to start up on my own.'

They fell silent, and after a short while Appleby left.

Richard rose early. He knew what he was going to do – or at least, to try to do. He went to his study and checked his figures again. The total was not encouraging, but he refused to allow it to dampen his enthusiasm.

At breakfast, he said to Frances, 'I've made my mind up. It would be madness to think of buying an existing mill, a going concern – I'd need far more capital than I could raise, and there'd be all the problems of finding wages for a large work force, and so on. What I'm going to do is start up a small new business, with just two or three employees.'

'To make silk?' Frances asked.

'Yes, but not crape – the market's too competitive for that – ordinary silk fabrics. All I need is a shed in reasonable condition and a few machines, which I might pick up second-hand. I've just about enough money for that, I think, if I can get a small loan. And then I shall try to persuade Mr Leroy to give me credit for a few months.'

'Where would this be?'

'I don't know. Somewhere near Norwich, perhaps.'

'I thought you were thinking of Macclesfield.'

'Isaac Appleby put the idea of Norwich into my head. But it doesn't really matter where.' He paused, and then added, 'As long as it's not too near Brentfield. Somewhere well away from Harcourt's.'

Although he was gazing at her intently, Frances knew that he was seeing some other vision, and her intuition told her that it was not Harcourt's Mill from which he wished to escape, but Sarah. To break the silence, she asked, 'And what about the selling?'

'I'd have to do it myself, to start with. Find someone I could trust to keep the looms going while I was away – Isaac, perhaps. We'd begin with simple fabrics, but we could go on to make figured silks, and more elaborate patterns. That's where you'd come in, my dear – you could design them.'

'I'd enjoy that, Richard. But are you sure, are you really sure about this? It sounds . . . it sounds so . . .'

'It's a gamble, I know that, but it's what I want to do. I confess I haven't thought it all out properly yet, but . . . It sounds like a dream – that's what you were going to say, isn't it?'

'Perhaps.'

'I'm going to make it come true, Frances.'

CHAPTER SEVENTEEN

Eager to put his plan into action, Richard set off for Norwich the next morning, leaving Frances to cope with finding somewhere for them to live, and moving house, all within the week – a daunting task, but one which she accepted willingly.

When he arrived home some days later, she had good news. 'I've found us a little cottage. In fact, it's where Sam Eales used to live. He and his wife had already gone. It's tiny, and not in very good repair, but it's clean and the rent is only two shillings a week.'

'Well done, my dear.'

'Oh, Richard, it's just like our old cottage! It will be just perfect for – well, however long we need it. And how did you get on? You look tired.'

'I seem to have been on my feet ever since I left. I've seen scores of places. One or two were possible, but not what I really wanted. I'm tempted to abandon the whole idea.' He sounded very dispirited. 'Damn Tom Harcourt! This need never have happened.'

'It's not like you to give up so easily,' Frances said. 'You'll feel better when you've had something to eat, and a good night's rest.'

'I suppose so.' He sat down, yawning. 'What else has happened since I was away?'

'Isaac Appleby came to say goodbye. He and his wife left for his sister-in-law's yesterday morning. They hired a cart to carry a few bits and pieces, and tried to sell the rest. If he got work, he said, they'd manage with a bed and a couple of chairs, and if he didn't, they couldn't take anything to the workhouse, so it wasn't worth trying to save their other belongings. It was pitiful, Richard. Half a dozen people came and poked around among their pathetic things, but very little was sold. They had a bonfire afterwards, and burned what was left. Poor Mrs Appleby was weeping her heart out. I bought an old mangle and a bucket and a scrubbing brush.'

'Whatever for? We don't want them.'

'Don't be stupid, Richard. I had to do something for them. We'll just leave them here. A present for Tom.'

He smiled. 'Yes, I see. Have you seen Tom . . . or anyone from Harcourt Place?'

'No. No one. But lots of people have called. Mr Hill came just after you left. I asked him to come again this evening.'

'Good. Who else?'

'Oh, I can't remember them all. Some of the others who were dismissed, and several of the people from the mill, especially from the crape department. They all wanted to say how sorry they were.'

The expression on her face was so sad that Richard went to her and hugged her. 'Poor Frances. It must have been very trying for you.'

'Yes. And there were so many other things to do.' There were tears in her eyes. She let him comfort her, unwilling to confess that she was weeping because Alfred Bunn had not been among the callers. She had seen him rarely of late, but surely he would not let her leave without saying goodbye.

When Mr Hill arrived, he seemed embarrassed. 'This is a sorry occasion, Richard. I . . . I feel something of a traitor.'

'Why should you?'

'Well, my sympathies are with you, of course, and perhaps I should have had the courage to resign in protest at the treatment meted out to you and to those old servants of the company. Instead of which, I find myself apparently basking in Mr Harcourt's high regard – but only because I lied to him. He asked me if I had ever spoken to you about the money which he personally had drawn from the company, and I fear I put on my most innocent expression and denied it.'

'I'm glad you did. I told him I had found out for myself by

looking at the ledgers one evening after you had left work. There was no need to involve you in my arguments with him.'

'That was kind of you, Richard. But the twin roles of traitor and prevaricator are foreign to me, and my conscience is heavy. My one consolation is that nearly everyone else at Harcourt's feels much as I do. They would leave if they could – but where would they find other work?'

'Don't let it bother you. You are right to protect yourself and Mrs Hill, and Mr Harcourt is right to think highly of you. Perhaps you'll be able to stop him from making too much of a fool of himself in future.'

'You over-estimate my abilities and my influence. But even he cannot fail to be aware of the unhappy atmosphere which pervades the mill, and perhaps he will learn from it and ameliorate his harshness. He is, I think, a shrewder man than it might appear.'

'It isn't very shrewd of him to get rid of all the most experienced workers.'

'Few people in any walk of life are truly indispensable, Richard. But I have no wish to act as Devil's advocate, any more than I came here to burden you with my personal problems.' He pushed his spectacles up on his nose, and smoothed his hair. 'I shall miss you very greatly, my boy, and your dear sister too, and so will Mrs Hill. You have been most excellent friends to us. We are eager to know your intentions.'

Richard had no hesitation in revealing his plans. 'What do you think?' he asked when he had finished.

'You have several gifts, Richard – great enthusiasm, and extensive knowledge and experience of the business, and, if I may say so, a stubborn streak which will drive you to persevere whatever difficulties you may face. I have no doubt that you will succeed.'

Richard laughed. 'Now there's a splendid testimonial – especially the bit about the stubborn streak!' He paused. 'I must admit, however, to one serious concern. I am no accountant, and I shall need someone to handle that side of the business for me.'

The twinkle in the little man's eyes faded. 'You are asking me to join you?'

'Yes. Not at once, of course. When I am established. It might provide the solution to your present unhappiness.'

Mr Hill looked away, and licked his lips nervously. 'I . . . I'm sorry, Richard, very sorry. You know, I think, how much I admire you, but . . .'

Richard was surprised and dismayed. 'I was counting on you.'

'Believe me, I should like nothing more, but I have to consider that other person who has the misfortune to have united her life with mine. Although Mrs Hill made no complaint, I know she was much disturbed by the upheaval involved in my leaving Prideau's, and willing though she might have been to take me for better or for worse, I fear she might regard the idea of uprooting herself yet again as an excessive demand upon her forbearance.' He tried to smile. 'In any case, I cannot truly believe that a person of my vastly advanced years would be of much use to you. I am getting old, Richard, old and feeble of intellect.'

'Nonsense! Of course, I cannot force you. But once I am settled, I shall write to you, and if you should change your mind . . .'

Much embarrassed, Mr Hill left, again thanking Richard for his proposal and his understanding, and with repeated assurances that they would undoubtedly meet again before the Goodwins left Brentfield, so that he and Mrs Hill could make their formal farewells.

The following day, Richard and Frances moved to the little cottage, handing the keys of Orchard House to Dawson, whom Tom Harcourt had sent to collect them. They spent the weekend in arranging their furniture, and on the Monday Richard set off once more in search of suitable premises for his new business.

As he left Brentfield, he could see Harcourt's Mill, and the sight tore at his heart. He wondered what was happening there, what Tom was doing, and whether his own absence was felt, or whether he was already almost forgotten, as footprints in the sand are washed away by the new tide. He tried not to think of it.

Within a couple of days, he found at last what he was seeking – a small, disused woollen mill in Wensham, a little village on the River Yare, some twelve miles from Norwich. Built of wood, the exterior was in poor condition, with broken windows and many rotting timbers, and inside was a confusion of old and rusting machines and litter of various kinds, but it was the right size, and there was water power available, and the rent was low. At comparatively little cost, all necessary repairs could be carried out and the interior stripped and readied.

The woollen mill had finally closed three years previously, and in the intervening time, many of the villagers had left to find employment elsewhere, with the result that several nearby dwellings were vacant. Richard made a swift decision and took a lease upon a fairly large cottage where he and Frances could live. As he signed the papers for this and for the mill, he was assailed by doubts. His meagre capital was already being reduced, and major expenses were still to come. The whole plan was the riskiest of gambles.

Travelling back to Brentfield, he listed all that remained to be done. On further thought, he had decided against using second-hand machines, which would probably be old-fashioned and liable to break down. But the cost of even a single new winding machine, throwing machine and loom would make it essential to secure a bank loan. He would need cash, too, for the purchase of raw materials, and to tide him over until he was producing saleable goods. Then, however modest his beginnings, he would have to employ at least one reliable assistant. Isaac Appleby would be an ideal choice, but he might already have found work and be as reluctant to move as Mr Hill.

The first problem to tackle was the loan. He could go to a bank in Franton, but it might be wiser to travel to London, and while he was there, he thought, he could call upon Mr Leroy to see if he would accept his order for raw silk. Travel was damnably expensive, and since Brentfield was so much nearer to the capital than Wensham, it might make sense to postpone moving to Norfolk for several days, even though it meant paying two lots of rent.

There were so many question-marks about the future, so many difficulties to be resolved, that it was almost overwhelming. But remembering what Mr Hill had said about his stubborn streak, he firmly pushed the worries aside, and arrived home in a much more optimistic frame of mind.

He thought that Frances looked tired, but she was delighted with his news of the mill and the cottage in Wensham. 'When can we leave?' she asked.

'Are you so eager to say goodbye to Brentfield?'

'Oh, yes!' Tears came to her eyes. 'I didn't want to tell you, but you'll find out anyway – Tom Harcourt has forbidden anyone at the mill to talk to either of us.'

'What?'

'It's like being sent to Coventry, Richard. When I went to the shop most of the people I met just ignored me – only Mrs Hill talked to me. It was she who told me what Tom had said. I was served in the shop, but they were so rude. And then I saw Tom and Sarah.'

'Sarah?'

'They were together in a carriage. I know they saw me, but they pretended not to.'

'How did she look?'

'Well. Very well. I spoke to her later. Their trap was outside the blacksmith's, and Tom was inside. She beckoned me over. "Tell Richard how sorry I am," she said. "Give him my love." And then –'

'She said that?'

Frances nodded. 'And then Tom came out of the smith's and he shouted at her, "Didn't I forbid you to talk to that woman?" He went on ranting and roaring at her, and whipped the horses and drove off. Sarah was weeping so pitifully. Oh, Richard!' She began to sob again.

Richard had tried hard to put Sarah out of his mind, but now to hear that she still loved him, to know that she was so unhappy . . . If only there were some way of seeing her, or even of writing to her. But it was hopeless, and the best thing would be for him and Frances to leave Brentfield as soon as possible. 'I have to go to London,' he said. 'If I go tomorrow morning, I should be back on Friday evening. We'll leave for Wensham on Saturday.'

With many memories of his first visit to London, Richard went to the Bell in Spitalfields. Mrs Bedford, who did not recognise him, offered him a room on the first floor, but he refused it. 'Do you not have cheaper accommodation available?'

'Not for a fine gent like you, sir.'

'I should be happier with a smaller room. Do you not have one on the top floor?'

Grumbling to herself, she led the way upstairs, and as he had hoped, opened the door of the room he had occupied before. It looked shabbier and dirtier than he remembered, and he was tempted to change his mind, but reminded himself that it was only for one night, and that he had no money to spare for luxury. He opened the skylight and gazed out on that scene which had so fascinated him – was it only seven years ago?

As he set out for the bank the next morning, he thought how strange it was that on that previous occasion it had been Tom Harcourt who was hoping to arrange a loan, and to make arrangements for a supply of raw silk. Richard hoped that he would have similar good fortune.

Having worked out his requirements, preparing sheets of figures, he asked for an overdraft of two thousand pounds, explaining to the manager exactly why he needed that amount, how it would be spent, and what the prospects of his business were. 'I see no reason why the entire sum should not be repaid within three years, and since I have taken a pessimistic view throughout, it is more than likely that I should not have to take up the whole amount, in which case, of course, I should be able to repay you much sooner.'

'I congratulate you on the way you have set out this application,' the manager said. 'However, Mr Goodwin, you seem to have omitted one matter of supreme importance. What security can you offer?'

'Security?'

'Yes. It is customary to deposit the deeds of your house, or investments, or some item of similar value. In the event that you are unable to repay your debt, we are able to recover the moneys by the realisation of the security deposited with us.'

Never having previously had to make any such arrangement, Richard was taken aback. 'You must think me very naive,' he said. 'I had thought that the fact that for some years I have had an account with your branch in Franton would have been sufficient.'

'I am sure that our Franton office is honoured to hold your account, Mr Goodwin. I must confess to some surprise that you did not make your application there. However, I fear the answer would be the same. The bank cannot offer an overdraft without security. It is a very simple matter. You must have something which you could offer.'

Richard shook his head. 'No. I do not own a house. I have . . . have nothing which I could . . . Can you not help at all? Supposing I reduced my request substantially.'

The manager smiled. 'Well, perhaps a hundred pounds, even two hundred, but no more. And we should expect prompt repayment.'

Richard went back despondently to the Bell, and spent an hour trying to work out figures based on his existing capital. If he were to revert to the idea of second-hand machines, and if he could persuade Mr Leroy to allow him credit on the raw silk, perhaps he might still manage. But it did not look very hopeful.

The previous evening he had sent a note to Mr Leroy's office in Brushfield Street to say that he proposed to call at noon, and hoped that it would be possible to see him for a few minutes then.

Mr Leroy was seated at his desk when Richard was shown in. His hair had turned grey, but otherwise he was the same little butterball of a man that Richard remembered.

'I am grateful to you for seeing me, Mr Leroy. I trust you are well – and Mrs Leroy and your daughters.'

'I thank you, yes.' He picked up a paper from his desk. 'I am a busy man, Mr Goodwin. You will forgive me if I come straight to the point. I have a letter from Mr Thomas Harcourt, a somewhat strange letter. He seems to have suspected that you might come to see me, and advises me to have no dealings with you. Now why should he say that?'

'We parted on rather bad terms,' Richard said. His hope of successful negotiations with Mr Leroy had vanished instantly, but he was not prepared to leave without some attempt to explain the situation. 'I should like to tell you about it. May I do so, please?'

Leroy's expression did not alter as he gave a brief nod of the head. Richard told him the whole story, omitting only any mention of Sarah. When he had finished, Leroy said, 'I see. And do you consider that you acted wisely in this matter?'

'No. Looking back on it, I am convinced that I was very foolish. However, there are times when one has to act foolishly or lose one's self respect. In similar circumstances I would behave no differently.'

'H'm. Of course, I have heard one side of the story only, and I shall therefore make no judgment. Since the last time we met, Harcourt's has been extremely successful, has it not?'

'Until the present slump in trade, yes.'

'And to what extent were you responsible for its prosperity? I expect an honest answer, without any false modesty.'

Richard thought for a moment. 'I think I played a big part in it. But so did Mrs Harcourt as general manager, and Mr Harcourt on the sales side.'

'Yes, that is fair.' He paused for a moment, stroking his chin. 'I am not accustomed to being given instructions, even by old customers who are also friends, as to whether or not I should do business with any other person. I decide such matters for myself. Now, what was the purpose of your visit here?'

Richard explained his original plans, and since Mr Leroy seemed to appreciate frankness, went on to tell him of his failure to secure a bank loan, and of the revised figures he had worked out that morning.

'Then presumably you are now hoping that I will supply you with raw silk on generous credit terms. That, my friend, is not good business, either for me or for you. However, I have two ideas which I think may help you. First of all, you might be well advised to purchase your supplies already thrown. Naturally, it is more expensive than raw silk, but you would not have to purchase winding or throwing machines nor find the labour to work them.'

'Can *you* supply thrown silk?'

'To any twist that you require, and in any quantity. That brings me to my second suggestion, which is that you should buy from me in small amounts. I can deliver quickly when you need more. Of course, that too costs quite a lot more than buying in bulk, but you would keep your cash expenditure to a minimum. Once your business picks up, you can increase the size of your orders, and eventually you might want to undertake your own winding and throwing.' He smiled. 'If I were in your shoes, that's what I would do, but perhaps you should ask other people before you make up your mind.'

'I should certainly not find better advice anywhere else.' Richard felt as though all his worries had been removed, and without stopping to think, he stood up, leaned over Mr Leroy's desk, and shook him warmly by the hand. 'I am more grateful than I can say, sir. You will understand that I have much to do before I can place my first order, but I shall send it to you very soon.'

Leroy laughed. 'Steady on, my boy. First we should discuss the prices.'

'It isn't necessary, Mr Leroy. I know they'll be fair.'

'Forgive me if I speak to you like a Dutch uncle. Your enthusiasm is running away with you. My prices may be fair, but you will certainly want to know what they are before you can make any decision. You need to work out all your costs, predict what kind of profit you will make, see if the whole idea is viable. You can't just rush into a commitment of this sort without knowing everything about it.'

Abashed, Richard said, 'You are right, of course. You must think me all kinds of a fool.'

'No, I don't think that. But I am old, and you are young, and it is the privilege of the old to lecture the young.'

'In fact, I've spent a lot of time on the figures.'

'I'm sure you have. Anyway, the thrown silk, in small quantities – that is, less than a hundredweight – will cost you five shillings and sevenpence per pound.'

'As much as that?'

Leroy laughed again. 'You see – you had no idea of the cost, eh? I am sure that you will still find it possible to make a profit, since you can begin with weaving, rather than with winding and throwing, but you will have to take such prices into very careful consideration.'

'Yes,' Richard said. 'Again you make me feel very foolish.'

'That is three times you have confessed to foolishness in the course of half an hour, and that is more than sufficient for any man. Come and dine with me this evening, and reserve any further self-denigrations until then.'

'That is most kind, but I promised my sister to be back in Brentfield this evening. She is . . . in a somewhat nervous condition at the moment.'

'Indeed? These recent events must have been very distressing for her.'

'Yes. So I hope you will excuse me.' He did not want to reveal exactly why Frances was so eager for his return – that would have seemed like an attempt to blacken Tom's character still further.

'I am sorry,' Leroy said, 'and I hope she is soon recovered. Of course I understand your anxiety, but Mrs Leroy would have been delighted to see you, and so, most certainly, would Miss Leroy. She has often spoken of the young man who was so interested in her silk cocoons.'

'Please give her my warm regards, sir.'

'I will. And next time you are in London I shall not allow you to escape so easily.'

Richard returned home feeling happier than he had done since his confrontation with Tom, and was pleased to find Frances in better spirits, too. She had been busy preparing for their move, and was looking forward to leaving Brentfield as though to a deliverance.

'Have you seen any of our friends?' Richard asked. 'Or are they all following Master Tom's instructions?'

'I have seen no one. I have not been out of the house since you left. But this letter came for you last night.'

It was from Mr Hill. 'Dear Richard, I understand that you and your sister are to leave us on Saturday. Mrs Hill and I cannot allow you to go without saying "Godspeed", and therefore propose to call on you briefly on Friday evening. For reasons which you will understand, we shall wait until darkness has fallen upon the land. Your friend, J.H.'

When they came, they hurried furtively into the cottage. While Frances was greeting Mrs Hill, Richard said quietly, 'Has he really reduced you to this?'

'As we agreed on my last visit, I am dependent on him for my employment, Richard,' Mr Hill said grimly. 'I do not take pleasure in it. Nor have I forgotten your kind offer, but –'

'Did you discuss it with Mrs Hill?'

'There would be no point. Women are mysterious beings, and my dear wife is among the least comprehensible of them; nevertheless, I know with certainty how she would react to another move. So I try to avoid doing anything which may give offence to Mr Harcourt, even if I offend myself and you in the process.'

Richard nodded in sympathy. 'Write to me if life here becomes impossible for you.'

'Thank you.'

Mrs Hill wanted to hear all about the new home that Richard and Frances would be going to in Wensham, and for a while they all chatted of that and of Richard's plans, carefully avoiding any mention of the situation in Brentfield.

After a quarter of an hour, Mr Hill looked at his watch. 'I think we should be going, Pussy-my-love.'

Mrs Hill rose promptly, and they all made their farewells, with some tears and repeated good wishes and hopes of future meetings.

'If you should see Alfred,' Frances said then, 'please . . . remember me kindly to him.'

'I will,' said Mr Hill. 'I will, indeed. Yes, yes. I will.' He turned to Richard. 'We really must go. The situation borders on the ludicrous, but perhaps you would be so good as to open your door and ascertain whether we may make our departure unobserved.'

He and his wife did not look back as they hurried along the road, and Richard shut the door with sadness in his heart.

Early the following morning, there was a knock on the cottage door. Frances went to open it. 'Alfred!' she exclaimed, and called to Richard, 'It's Alfred Bunn!'

He stood on the doorstep silently, twisting his hat in his hands.

'Come in,' Frances said.

He stepped into the room. 'I have come to say goodbye, Miss Frances.'

'Have you seen Mr Hill?'

'Not for a couple of days. Why?'

'Oh, it's just that . . . I gave him a message for you last night, and I thought perhaps . . .'

'No.' He said nothing more, but looked at Richard briefly, and then back at Frances.

'You know that you risk dismissal for talking to us?' Richard said.

'I am leaving Harcourt's anyway. I am going back to London. There is . . . nothing to keep me here any more, and the mill is an unhappy place nowadays. Besides, there's little work for me. I wanted to say goodbye, and to wish you well. The last time I did see Mr Hill he told me something of your plans. I hope everything . . .' His voice trailed off.

'Thank you,' said Richard. 'I trust that you will prosper too.'

All three of them were embarrassed, standing as though frozen, each waiting for one of the others to speak or make a move. At last Alfred turned to Richard. 'Would you permit me . . .? I should like to speak to your sister in private. Just for a few moments.'

'Yes. Yes, of course. I still have some packing to do. I'll say goodbye, then, Alfred. I hope we'll meet again some day. Thank you for coming.' He shook hands awkwardly, and left the room.

When he had gone, Frances said, 'Won't you sit down, Alfred?'

'No. No, thank you. I mustn't stay.' Again he seemed tongue-tied.

'You wanted to say something to me?' Frances prompted gently.

'Yes.' Suddenly he seemed to find the courage to speak. 'I wanted to tell you that I shall always think of you, and dream of what might have been. If . . . if anything should ever happen to change my situation, I will come to you, Miss Frances.' He gave a half smile. 'But perhaps by then you will be married yourself . . . I pray for your happiness.'

'I shall wait, Alfred. I shall wait until the end of my life.'

He smiled properly then, and at the sight of the love in his dark eyes, she could not restrain herself. 'Don't go to London, Alfred! Come to Wensham with us. You could find work somewhere, and we could be together, even if we were not married. I would be your . . . your wife in everything but name.' Her cheeks burned scarlet.

He shook his head miserably. 'No. No, that would be wrong. I could never ask that of you.'

'But it would bring me the happiness you pray for.'

'No,' he said again. 'No, not that way. But I will come to you, I promise, when I am free.' He stepped towards her, kissed her clumsily on the cheek, and turned, and before she could stop him, left the cottage.

'Alfred!' she cried, as the door closed behind him. It was like the cry of a wounded bird.

Richard hurried back into the room. 'Frances, my dear, what is it?'

She went to his arms. 'Oh, Richard, Richard!' she sobbed. She felt that her heart was breaking, and yet there was a kind of joy in it too. Alfred still loved her, and he had given his promise. He might never be able to fulfil it, but she could cherish the hope until her dying day.

CHAPTER EIGHTEEN

Tom's attempt to blacken Richard's name with Mr Leroy had not been the end of his campaign of vilification. When, some months later, in the autumn of 1873, Richard began to call upon haberdashers and other retailers to persuade them to stock his wares, he found that almost all of them had been given a highly biased account of the events leading to his departure from Harcourt's; and though a few had long since formed their own opinion of Tom and were ready at least to give Richard the benefit of the doubt, they were a small minority.

It was uphill work to find a market for the simple silk fabrics he and Isaac Appleby, who had joined him with cheerful alacrity, were producing. After the first few weeks of journeying around the country, Richard began to think that he would be forced to sell the machinery he had so painfully acquired, and transport himself and Frances to London in the hope of finding work there, however humble; Isaac would once more be threatened with the workhouse.

Mr Montgomery, the man who had suggested that Harcourt's should make a heavy crape suitable for wear by gentlemen, was one of Tom's closest friends in the trade, and since it seemed pointless to risk another rebuff, Richard had not called on him. But as he was passing through Norwich on his way back to Wensham, his order book yet again almost empty, he decided on the spur of the moment to see if Mr Montgomery would grant him an interview. 'Nothing venture, nothing gain,' he told himself. Dammit, he would not be beaten by Tom's malevolence.

To his surprise, Mr Montgomery agreed to see him. He was a tall, thin man, almost bald, his long, narrow face fringed by a closely-cut grey beard. His lower eyelids drooped slightly, giving him a spaniel-like look of sadness, and his lips turned down as though, Richard thought, he had never smiled in his life.

Richard's heart sank as he entered the office. Mr Montgomery was seated at his desk, and he looked up with so cold an expression that Richard was immediately certain that he was wasting his time.

'Goodwin? Late of Harcourt's?' Mr Montgomery said. 'Yes. Heard of you. Left under a cloud, I believe. Not interested in that. Gossip. Buy what I can sell. Whoever.'

Richard smiled with relief. 'Thank you. Perhaps I may tell you my side of the story.'

'Told you already – not interested. Samples?'

Richard got out his silks. 'These are the fabrics. I can guarantee to maintain the quality throughout the runs.'

Mr Montgomery glanced at them briefly. 'No use,' he said. 'Nothing new. Get enough of this from other suppliers. Anyone buying?'

'Yes,' Richard lied. 'I've taken almost as many orders as I can cope with. I thought I'd give you the opportunity before I close my order books.'

'Don't believe it.' The spaniel eyes gazed at Richard searchingly.

Richard capitulated. 'I see that I cannot deceive you. You're right, Mr Montgomery. I confess I am very disappointed with trade reactions. But –'

Mr Montgomery's down-drawn lips twitched in what was perhaps the nearest he came to a smile. 'Not surprised. Market's glutted, fabrics like these. Need figured silks. Brocades.'

'I could make brocades.'

'Samples. Satisfactory, I'll order. Small market, steady.' He bent his head back to the papers on his desk. 'Busy,' he said. 'Good day.'

'Thank you. Thank you very much.'

Richard went home in high excitement, though he was not sure why. He knew nothing about the manufacture of brocades, and probably would not be able to produce them with the equipment he had. But if he could perhaps adapt his machines, learn the craft . . .

Isaac Appleby was examining the loom. He had been over every part of it before, cleaning and oiling and adjusting, just as he had cleaned out the dyeing vats and swept the floor and put everything in apple-pie order. He had nothing else to do until orders came in. He looked up enquiringly as Richard entered.

'What do you know about brocades, Isaac?'

'Brocades? First kind o' work I done when I was a nipper startin' out at 'Arcourt's.'

'Really? That's wonderful, Isaac!'

'It was years ago, Mr Goodwin, long afore your time, and Mr Tom's. 'Arcourt's give it up, on account o' all them foreign brocades coming into the country. It killed our trade.'

'There may be a market for it now. Can you remember how it was produced?'

'I reckon so. The warp and the weft don't criss-cross reg'lar like, the way they do with a simple fabric. Some of the weft threads goes across several warps, and vicky-verky, if you see what I mean. According to the pattern, o'course.'

'Could we make brocades?'

'Not on this loom.'

'Could it be adapted?'

'Not a chance.'

'Then if I found the money to buy a brocade loom, could you work it, Isaac?'

'Reckon it might come back to me. 'Course I'd 'ave to 'ave a pattern. We can't make no brocades just makin' it up as we go along. Why?'

Richard explained what Mr Montgomery had said. 'But it's no use, Isaac. If I bought a new loom, it would take the last of my money. I wouldn't be able to pay your wages, and I don't know what I and my sister would live on either. There's rent for the cottages, and food to buy . . .'

'Where there's a will, there's a way, ain't there?'

'I can see the will, but not the way.'

'I seen this coming. I mean, apart from this 'ere brocade

business, we wasn't getting anywhere, was we? Me and me missus, we 'ad a talk about it. I told 'er it was daft, but she says, "No, you ask 'im," and I won't get no peace if I don't. It's like this – she said as 'ow you got a room in your cottage, and if we was to move in with you . . . But I told 'er you wouldn't stand for that. It wouldn't be proper, you being the master.'

'Go on, Isaac.'

'Well, that'd save one lot o' rent. And as to food, we'd only need a few pence a week for flour.'

'We can't live on nothing but bread.'

Isaac grinned. 'We won't, not with me missus around.'

Richard thought for a moment. 'I think it's a splendid idea, and I'm sure my sister will agree.'

'You really mean it?'

'Of course I do.'

Richard bought a brocade loom, just managing to do so with the money he got from selling the existing machine and with the last of his savings. He and Isaac began work on it.

The Applebys moved into the Goodwins' cottage. Sharing with comparative strangers was not always easy, but since Richard and Isaac were out during their long working hours, and the Applebys always retired to bed immediately after their evening meal, all four of them were together for short periods only.

Mrs Appleby was a large, raw-boned woman, endowed with a seemingly inexhaustible supply of energy. Her favourite saying was, 'I speaks me mind! Take it or leave it!', and this uncompromising attitude, allied to her somewhat grim cast of features, made Frances very apprehensive at first. However, she soon discovered that a traditional heart of gold beat beneath this unpromising exterior, and friendship developed between them. They came to an arrangement whereby Frances did the cleaning and the washing, while Mrs Appleby took charge of the catering.

She had a considerable talent for procuring good food without cost. Rabbits could be snared, and fish caught, and edible wild plants picked, and sometimes hens would stray beyond the bounds of the farmyard, and any eggs they then laid could be taken without fear of a charge of theft. With the flour they bought she baked delicious, crusty bread.

The sharing of the household chores gave Frances time to work on the designs for brocades, for which Richard had asked. Once Isaac had explained the techniques involved so that she knew what was possible, she produced a number of patterns which, though simple in construction, were both unusual and charming in their use of colour.

Richard was delighted. 'I didn't know you could do anything like that. They're so unusual, and so delicate. How did you work them out?'

'I just thought of the kind of material that would please me. This one's my favourite.' It had a grey background, with a light floral pattern in black and the palest of greens, and should have looked sombre, but the balance of the colours seemed vibrant. The others were almost equally striking, and Richard felt sure that if they could produce them satisfactorily, the brocades would prove popular.

At first, nothing went right. Isaac's memories of the weaving process were misty, and only after a long period of trial and error did they succeed in producing a cloth which might be termed brocade. But it was far from good enough, and they began again, while Richard looked at the decreasing stock of raw silk and wondered whether they would ever succeed before they ran out of materials and supplies. He wrote to Mr Leroy, begging for more time to pay, and though that request was granted, he knew their debts could not remain unsettled indefinitely.

Both Richard and Isaac rose before dawn to go to the mill, and stayed there late into the night, struggling to see by the light of a single candle. Both were near to exhaustion, and Isaac often fell asleep in the middle of some task, while Richard's face grew gaunt, and there were dark circles beneath his eyes. The two women worried about them, but were ignored when they expressed their fears.

At last, in January of 1874, Richard was able to return to Mr Montgomery. He spread out his samples for an inspection which seemed as cursory as on the previous occasion. There was no sign of interest on the draper's features. Was all their hard work to have been to no avail?

'Price?' Montgomery asked.

'Ten shillings a yard,' Richard replied.

'Expensive. Nine shillings.'

'Nine shillings and sixpence.' It would still give them a good profit.

'H'm. Delivery?'

'It depends how much you want.'

'A roll of each.'

'Four weeks from now.'

'Too long. Three weeks.'

'I can't do it in the time, Mr Montgomery. There are only two of us working on it.'

'H'm. All right. Write you an order.'

His enthusiasm renewed, Richard called on other retailers, and discovered that any antipathy resulting from Tom's disparagement disappeared once he showed his samples of brocade. Everyone admired the delicate designs, everyone believed they would sell, and when he returned to Wensham that evening, he had taken more orders in the one day than he had obtained in several weeks with the more conventional fabrics he and Isaac had originally produced.

By the early summer, Richard's business was thriving. He was able to settle his debts, to resume the payment of Isaac's wages at a higher level – the Applebys moved back into a cottage in the village – and to abandon their reliance on rabbit stew, and nothing but water to drink. The only major problem was the lack of time. He and Isaac still worked an excessively long day, and even Richard realised that they could not continue at this pace. He would have to find a salesman, and perhaps someone to look after the accounts. Then he could spend more time in the mill, and relieve Isaac of part of his burden.

No sooner had he made that decision, than a letter arrived. The coincidence could only be a good omen, he decided.

'Dear Richard,' Mr Hill wrote, 'We speak of you and your dear sister often, and wonder how the world, unpredictable to mere mortals, is treating you. Rumours reach us that you are successful in your new enterprise, and we pray that they are true.

'I have some hesitation in writing this letter, but trust that you will forgive any impertinence you find in it. You were generous once to suggest that I might join you in Wensham, an offer which I refused in the certainty that my helpmeet would be unwilling to accede to such a plan. How strange are the ways of Woman! Hardly a day has passed without Mrs Hill asking me why I did not agree to accompany you, asserting that another move would be as nothing compared to the happiness we should both undoubtedly find in Wensham (if only in having escaped from Brentfield, which is far from a paradise these days).

'Of late she has become more insistent, and nothing will do but that I should write to you and ask whether, by chance, you are still in need of such inadequate services as I might provide. By now, I tell her, you must undoubtedly have engaged some young clerk of high competence to assist you, but if I should be in error in thinking this (and if, since even I must be practical, there is suitable accommodation in Wensham for us), you have but to say the word and Mr and Mrs Hill will descend upon you – to the undoubted consternation of the local inhabitants.

'I shall await your reply with eagerness, and in the meantime my dear wife joins me in sending you and Miss Frances our kindest regards. Your sincere friend, J. Hill.'

There was a postscript. 'You may not have heard that Mrs Harcourt was safely delivered of a fine son last July. Mother and child are both in robust health. The boy has been christened Edward John.'

Richard read the letter with delight, and sent a reply begging Mr Hill to make all haste in coming to Wensham. But the postscript revived all the thoughts of Sarah which he had tried so hard to suppress since leaving Brentfield. Mr Hill's phrase, that Brentfield was 'far from a paradise', made him think not simply of the mill, but of Harcourt Place. How Sarah must be suffering. Or had she found contentment in motherhood, and even a new, happier relationship with Tom? For her sake he hoped so.

Her image stayed in his mind so persistently that he decided that he must make one last effort. He wrote to her, begging her to leave Tom and come to him, for the sake of the love they bore each other. Of course she could not abandon her child, but he would welcome the boy and do his best to be a father to him. He asked Frances to address the letter, in the hope that it would not be intercepted before Sarah had opened it.

'Are you sure this is wise, my dear?' Frances asked.

'I must do it.' Before he could change his mind, he posted it, and immediately began to regret his intemperance. Sarah would not leave Tom, and should the letter fall into his hands, it would do her nothing but harm. But it was too late to stop it, and he could only hope and pray for a miracle.

A week later a reply arrived, stark in its brevity. 'If you truly desire my happiness, I beg you never to write to me again. S.H.'

Sitting at the breakfast table, Richard folded the letter and put it carefully in his pocket. He glanced at Frances. At least he had his work, and he could find a kind of happiness in that. Poor Frances. She had not told him what Alfred Bunn had said that last morning in Brentfield, but he knew that she was equally disappointed in love, and had little to look forward to other than a lifetime of keeping house for her widower brother, occasional designing for him, good works among the poor of the parish. She was already beginning to look spinsterish.

Since coming to Wensham, they had kept very much to themselves, and saw few people other than the Applebys. Perhaps Frances and he should try to make friends in the neighbourhood. It was unlikely that she would find a beau, plain and shy as she was, but stranger things could happen, and a circle of local acquaintances would help to occupy her time.

'I have been thinking,' he said. 'It is time we moved. We could buy a house.' As Frances looked at him in astonishment, he added jokingly, 'An establishment more in keeping with my position as one of Wensham's most highly respected and prosperous inhabitants. You would like that, wouldn't you?'

'Of course I should, Richard. Are you sure you can afford it?'

'Yes.'

'What made you think of it all of a sudden?'

'Oh, it has been in my mind for a long time. But it came to the fore just now because I was thinking that we have been neglecting our social duties. We should make friends in the neighbourhood – give a little dinner party now and then. But we certainly cannot do so here. It is hardly suitable for entertaining guests.'

'I would hope that anyone we invited would come for our sake, not for our surroundings,' Frances said primly.

'Of course. I accept your rebuke. But there is hardly room here for ourselves.'

Frances thought for a moment. 'Should you really buy a house just so that we can hold a few dinner parties?'

'It isn't just so that we can give dinner parties, as you know perfectly well,' he said, with some irritation. 'I thought you'd like the idea of having a proper establishment again.'

'I do. I just wonder how wise it is.'

'I've already told you once that I can afford it. Why do you keep on asking?'

'Because, dear brother, you are always telling me that you have to plough all your profits back into the business.'

'Yes, but –'

'You are not thinking clearly this morning, my dear. Was it something in that letter which distressed you?' She had caught a glimpse of the handwriting, and could swear that it was Sarah's.

'No.' He had forced an enthusiasm into his voice as he spoke of the house, but now it disappeared. 'No, that was of no importance. Just confirmation of . . . of something I had been expecting.'

Frances felt certain that her guess about the letter was right, but dared not say more.

Richard sat silent for a while. Then he said, 'I am sorry I snapped at you. You are right, of course, and it would be foolish to think of buying at this stage. But we could perhaps afford to rent a modest-sized house.'

She suspected that he had still not thought the matter through, but it might be wiser to humour him. 'Do you wish me to make enquiries?'

'Enquiries?' He seemed to be miles away.

'About properties available for rent.'

'Well, I certainly cannot spare the time.' Now his tone was irritable again.

'I know you can't, my dear,' she said placatingly. 'But you do realise that we shall need furniture too, and servants, and a thousand things besides.'

'Oh, for heaven's sake! You always make difficulties.' Richard threw down his napkin and stalked from the room.

As he hurried to the mill, he was filled with remorse. It was unkind to have behaved so boorishly to Frances. She had been talking sense, while he had had his mind full of Sarah, and had hardly known what he was saying.

He apologised to her that evening, agreeing that he had expended far too little thought on the idea of a move, and the matter was forgotten the following day in the excitement of the Hills' arrival and installation in a small cottage that Frances had found for them. The reunion gave them all much delight, and they spent a happy evening exchanging news.

'How did Mr Harcourt take it when you said you were leaving?' Richard asked.

'With something less than rapture,' Mr Hill replied. 'He enquired where I was going, and when I told him, flew into an intemperate rage and shouted that I should get out. Which I did.'

'And how is the business there?'

'It survives, that is all that one can say. I must give a modicum of credit where it is due, and agree that Mr Harcourt has behaved of late with more moderation towards his employees, but it is far from a pleasant place to work. It has not been the same since Mrs Harcourt left, and it became even worse after your own departure.'

'Have you any news of Mrs Harcourt?'

'No. They say she dotes upon her infant, whom they describe as a fine, bouncing baby. I believe that is the accepted phrase, though it always sounds to me as though the child must be constructed of india-rubber.'

Richard duly smiled.

For several weeks no more was said between Richard and Frances on the subject of a house. In any case, there was little opportunity for much conversation between them, for Richard continued to work as though possessed, and even if they entertained the Hills on a Sunday, he would talk only of business matters, leaving Frances and Mrs Hill to chat of the price of food and other such domestic matters. And often, in the middle of his discussions with Mr Hill, he would fall asleep.

Frances worried about him. He would make himself ill. The business was prospering, especially now that Mr Hill was there to deal with the accounts and other paper work, and Richard could devote himself more fully to the manufacture and sale of their brocades, but what did the success of the business matter if his health should suffer as a result?

Returning from matins one Sunday morning, she waved a piece of paper at him. 'An invitation, Richard! We are to dine next Sunday evening with the Searles.'

'Who are the Searles?'

'Most charming people. Mr Searle has, I believe, a large practice as a solicitor, in Norwich. And Mrs Searle is always very gracious if I should meet her in the village. She is a great reader, Richard – I often see her with her daughter at the lending library.'

'The parents are a young couple?'

'Oh, gracious, no! Their children are quite grown up. The two who remain at home are about our age – Miss Henrietta and Mr Algernon. I think we are really *their* guests, rather than their parents'.'

'Well, I can't go. I have far too much to do.' Frances looked so dismayed that he could not help laughing. 'All right. Then we shall go. But you must stay near me and nudge me if I fall asleep.'

The Searles proved to be as charming as Frances had said. Mr Searle, a man of medium height, with a head of thick, curling hair, peered out at the world through spectacles perched on a large, bony nose. He greeted Richard and Frances warmly, and introduced Richard to his wife, a plump lady with a ready smile, to his son and daughter, and to the other guests, Dr and Mrs Trehearne.

Henrietta Searle had inherited her mother's vivacious smile and outgoing personality. Richard was immediately attracted to her and felt almost as though he knew her already. She reminded him in some ways of Sarah, though she lacked the striking features, the glorious chestnut hair, the mystery of the green eyes. Indeed, it was difficult to call her handsome, with her square, rather heavy-jawed face and mousy hair and a nose which, while not as large as her father's, was still her most prominent feature. Then what was it that made him think of Sarah? The curve of her lips as she smiled? Rather, it was the way she listened, her eyes fixed on you, giving you her whole attention, as though you were the only person in the world.

When dinner was served, Richard was delighted to find that he was seated next to Henrietta, and that Mrs Trehearne, on his other side, did not seem to expect him to talk to her. Henrietta said, 'I believe you came here from Brentfield, Mr Goodwin. Had you always lived there?'

Spurred on by the sympathetic interest that he read in her eyes, Richard found himself telling her his story, from his humble beginnings to his present position as the owner of a small silk mill.

Mrs Searle had provided a Lucullan feast, but Richard was barely conscious of the consommé royale, the turbot in oyster sauce, the saddle of mutton, and the vanilla soufflé as he talked to Henrietta. All too soon, his hostess was announcing that the ladies would retire and leave the gentlemen to their cigars and port.

'Will you forgive me, Miss Searle?' he asked. 'I have talked only of myself. You must think me very ill-mannered – not to say conceited.'

'Not at all, Mr Goodwin. I have found it fascinating.'

'You have told me nothing of yourself.'

'I shall find another opportunity for that,' she laughed. 'Though there is little enough to tell – I am really a very dull person.'

'I do not believe that, Miss Searle. I do not believe that at all.'

She smiled, and left the room with her mother and Frances and Mrs Trehearne.

'Now, Mr Goodwin,' Mr Searle said as the door closed behind them. 'Dr Trehearne and I are most eager to hear more of your silk business, if you are willing to satisfy our curiosity.' Whether because of his poor sight, or because he was naturally clumsy, Mr Searle seemed to be one of those people whose life is constantly bedevilled by minor accidents. He had already knocked over a small ornament in the sitting-room, tripped over a rug on his way to dinner, and knocked his knife and fork to the floor, all of which little disasters had been greeted by his wife with calm amusement. Now, as he passed the decanter of port, he somehow contrived to let it slip so that the wine splashed out over Richard's shirt. 'Oh, my dear fellow, what a clumsy fool I am, to be sure! I am so sorry.' He hurried to the door. 'Martha! Martha, come quickly!'

Mrs Searle bustled into the room. 'What now?'

'A little accident, my dear. I'm afraid I have spilt the port all over poor Mr Goodwin.'

'Oh, what will you do next? You'll be the death of me with your clumsiness.' But there was no anger in her voice. 'I do apologise for my husband, Mr Goodwin. You must change the shirt at once.'

'I assure you there is no need, Mrs Searle. It will wash, I have no doubt.'

'No, the stain will not come out unless it is dealt with straight away.' She turned back to her husband. 'Take Mr Goodwin up, and let him change into one of your shirts. Give his to Tilly and tell her to soak it in borax before she washes it.'

When, with many fussings and apologies, the change of clothing had been effected, Richard and Mr Searle returned to the dining-room.

'Pour your own port, my dear chap, and then, if I have not driven all thoughts of it from your mind, tell us about your mill.'

Richard gave a brief account of the starting up of his business, minimising the difficulties, and dwelling on the success which was beginning to come his way.

Mr Searle listened with careful attention, as did Dr Trehearne, who, when the story was finished, said, 'Then all is explained.'

'I am not sure what you mean, sir,' Richard said.

'Before you arrived we were discussing the fact that . . . No, Searle, I know that your lawyer's caution would prevent you from confessing to such impertinence, but I am a blunt old medico. I offer you my humble apologies in advance, Goodwin, for any offence.' Ignoring Mr Searle's harrumphings, he went on, 'I asked where you live, you see, and when I was told, expressed some surprise. That cottage of yours must be lacking in all amenities. But no doubt you regard it as no more than a temporary dwelling-place, and now that your business is beginning to prosper, you will be seeking more commodious accommodation.'

'That is exactly what I plan to do,' Richard replied. 'And you have no need to apologise, sir. I am flattered by your interest. In any case, honest curiosity between friends – and I hope we are indeed friends – should be expressed freely and answered in the same spirit.'

'Well said, sir,' Mr Searle commented. 'Though if such a generous attitude were adopted by all, I fear my practice might suffer. We lawyers feed on offence being taken, you know.' He laughed drily. 'And now, gentlemen, I think we should join the ladies.'

Richard had hoped for a chance of further conversation with Miss Henrietta, but the other half of the settee on which she was sitting was occupied by Mrs Trehearne, and he found himself buttonholed by Mrs Searle, who again apologised about the shirt. 'I will send it back to you, laundered and ironed, Mr Goodwin. And I quite forbid your sister to wash Mr Searle's shirt, which you have kindly consented to wear. Just parcel it up and we will deal with it.'

'May I not return it myself, and collect mine when I do so, Mrs Searle? I am at work all day, my sister is frequently out, and at present we have no servant.'

'But it is all our fault, you must be put to no trouble.'

'It would not be a trouble, ma'am. Please. I insist.'

Mrs Searle glanced briefly in Henrietta's direction, and smiled. 'As you wish, Mr Goodwin.'

The party broke up soon after. As they returned home, Frances said, 'Well, Richard, are you glad we went?'

His reply surprised her. 'I have been thinking about the cottage,' he said, and told her of Dr Trehearne's comments. 'It was perhaps somewhat impertinent of him, but he meant no discourtesy, and of course he is right. We really must look for a more suitable place, Frances. As soon as we can.'

'So that we can ask the Searles to dinner?' There was amusement in her voice.

'It is quite ridiculous for a mill-owner to be living as though he were one of his employees.' He laughed. 'All right. I know how pompous that sounds. And, yes, it would be pleasant to be able to entertain the Searles.'

'Then you liked them?'

'As you say, they are charming people.'

'Especially Miss Henrietta. Oh, don't deny it – I could see that you were smitten with her. And I overheard your conversation with Mrs Searle – that is why you insisted that you should return the shirt yourself, is it not?'

His eyes twinkled. 'As Mrs Hill would say, I don't know about that!'

Frances laughed out loud.

CHAPTER NINETEEN

Frances was delighted by Richard's interest in Henrietta. At last, perhaps, he was beginning to forget Sarah.

On their return from the dinner party, he had said, 'You will wash and iron Mr Searle's shirt, will you not?'

'Of course.'

'And when will it be ready?'

'First thing on Tuesday.'

'I shall return it then.'

'Desert the mill?'

'Why not? Isaac can manage perfectly well on his own. Besides, I shall be away for a short while only.'

Frances had made no comment, but had smiled inwardly.

Bearing Mr Searle's shirt, Richard called at the house. Mrs Searle and Henrietta were in the drawing-room. 'How very kind of you, Mr Goodwin,' Mrs Searle said. 'Your own shirt is all ready for you, as good as new. May I offer you some refreshment?'

'Thank you, no. I should get back to the mill. And I must not intrude.'

'It is no intrusion. At least sit down, just for a moment, please. And how is Miss Goodwin?'

'She is well, ma'am. She sent you this note on behalf of us both to thank you for your charming hospitality on Sunday.'

'That is most kind.' Mrs Searle took the letter, but put it down unopened and suddenly rose. 'Oh!' she exclaimed. 'I must speak to Cook straight away. I quite forgot. Look after our guest, Henrietta. Will you excuse me, Mr Goodwin?'

'I am afraid that Mama is somewhat transparent at times,' Henrietta said when Mrs Searle had left. 'I confess to some discomfiture.'

'Oh, please, do not say that. I had hoped to beg forgiveness.'

'What for?'

'For talking solely of myself on Sunday, and at such length.'

'I assure you that I found it fascinating, Mr Goodwin.'

'But I quite overwhelmed you, which was not only rude, but foolish, since I learned nothing of you.'

She smiled in a self-deprecating way. 'Then if you insist, I shall tell you the facts of interest about myself. They are very few. I am the fourth of five children. You have met Algernon, who is younger than I. My older brother is a captain in the army, and is serving in the Cape, and my two sisters are married. We were all brought up here in Wensham, so you see I have no great adventures to relate. I do a little embroidery, I play the pianoforte from time to time, and of course I read a great deal. Now you know all about me.'

He smiled. 'The last bit I knew. My sister tells me that you meet sometimes at the lending library.'

'Yes. Are you a reader yourself, Mr Goodwin?'

'I have little time nowadays, but I have always loved books.'

'I am delighted to hear it. Have you read *Wuthering Heights*, Mr Goodwin? Oh, you should! It is quite my favourite novel. No, that somehow makes it sound trivial, and it is a masterpiece. On the surface it is no more than a story of unhappy love, but oh, the suffering that it holds, the power, the strength of emotion!'

It was uncanny, Richard thought, that this conversation should be so like his first serious talk with Jane. But Henrietta had a passion, an intensity that reminded him more of Sarah. He watched her as she spoke, thinking that she shared many of the characteristics both of Jane, for whom he had felt such affection, and of Sarah, whom he loved.

'I marvel that any author can know so much of the human soul,' she was saying. 'I will lend you my copy, Mr Goodwin – on condition that you will consent to discuss it with me when you have read it.'

'I shall be delighted.'

'If you will excuse me, I will go and fetch it.' She rose. 'I shall not be long.'

The door closed behind her. She was charming, quite charming, and she must surely like him a little, or she would not have made it inevitable that they should meet again. He began to pace up and down, eager for her return.

After a short while, the door opened, but it was Mrs Searle who came in. 'What, Mr Goodwin? My daughter has surely not left you alone? Oh, how rude you will think us. I do apologise for us both.'

'It is quite all right, ma'am. Miss Searle has kindly gone to fetch a book which she intends to lend me. It is called . . .' He laughed. 'There, I have forgotten already.'

'I will guess that it is *Wuthering Heights*.'

'Yes, of course. That is it.'

'It is one of her great enthusiasms. But you must not let her impose upon you, Mr Goodwin. I am sure you have many other more important things to do than to read a novel, however fine it may be.'

Richard was saved from replying by Henrietta's return. She handed him the book. 'There you are. Now promise me you will read it quickly.'

'As quickly as I can. I shall take good care of it.' He turned to Mrs Searle. 'And now, if you will forgive me, I really must go. I should have been at my mill an hour or more ago.'

'It has been a pleasure to see you, Mr Goodwin,' Mrs Searle said. 'Don't forget your shirt. The parcel is in the hall.'

'I will show Mr Goodwin, Mama,' said Henrietta.

When the door to the drawing-room was shut, Richard said, 'I wonder whether we might take a short walk, Miss Searle, one Sunday afternoon. Perhaps next Sunday, if the weather is fine.'

She smiled. 'I should be delighted. But surely you will not have read the book by then?'

'I doubt it, though I shall try. In that case, perhaps we should postpone –'

'By no means, Mr Goodwin. If we cannot talk of *Wuthering Heights*, I feel sure we shall find some other agreeable subject to occupy us. I shall expect you – when? At half past two, shall we say? I shall look forward to it. Goodbye until then, Mr Goodwin.'

Soon after their visit to the Searles, Frances found a house available at a modest rent, and they moved in and were at last able to entertain. The Searles were their most frequent guests, but through them and as a result of her church-going, Frances made a number of friends and acquaintances, and their social lives gradually became quite busy. They did not neglect the Hills or the Applebys, but had them to dinner on other more homely occasions – they would not have been at ease with the likes of Mr and Mrs Searle or the Trehearnes.

Richard and Henrietta went for frequent walks together, and talked not only of books, but of their families and friends and of Richard's business, and of wider issues such as the opposing policies of Gladstone and Disraeli, and the rise of trade unions since the Act of 1871, and painting and architecture and many other subjects. They did not always agree, and would often argue fiercely, but with good humour.

Richard enjoyed their debates, though he rarely won them. Henrietta had strong views on everything, and it was not easy to change her mind. Richard admired that trait in her character. Many men would run for their lives from an intelligent woman, but he had never believed that the female mind was capable only of coping with domestic matters. His mother had taught him that, and among the qualities that had attracted him most in Sarah were her willingness to use her brains – indeed, her insistence on doing so – and her independence of thought and attitude.

Sarah . . . Why did he keep thinking of Sarah? It was Henrietta who should be, who *was* increasingly in his mind. He liked her unconventional attitudes, including the way, for instance, she would often not wait for him to suggest another meeting, but would propose it herself.

Frances had noticed that too. 'She's very charming,' she said, 'but don't you think she's . . . well . . . that is . . .' She wished she had never begun the criticism.

'Don't I think she's what?'

'Perhaps . . . just a little . . . well . . . some people might say . . . forward.'

Richard laughed. 'I don't mind if she is.'

Frances held her peace. Her first impressions were usually proved right, but the more she saw of Henrietta the less she liked her. She was often very patronising, and when her tongue was not bridled by the presence of gentlemen, she could be quite vicious in her comments on other women. Frances sometimes wondered what Henrietta said of her behind her back. However, it was Richard's happiness that counted, and if he loved her, then Frances was ready to put up with everything else. It would be pleasant to see Richard with a wife again, and maybe one day there would be children, and . . . She really must try, Frances told herself sharply, to love Henrietta like a sister.

At times, Richard felt out of his depth with Henrietta. He listened happily to her pleasing contralto voice when she accompanied herself in some sentimental ballad, but found less enjoyment when she played Bach or Mozart. 'I know nothing about music, Henrietta,' he said. 'You must think me sadly lacking in culture.'

'I think nothing of the sort. You were not brought up to appreciate it, and have spent almost all your waking hours at work, with no opportunity to learn. I shall teach you.'

Richard's 'music lessons' gave him additional reasons for regular visits to the Searles' home. He did not always understand what Henrietta tried to tell him about sonata forms and themes and counterpoint and other mysteries, but he enjoyed the simple fact of being with her. She reminded him so much of . . . Once he even called her 'Sarah'.

'Who is Sarah?' she asked.

He blushed. 'Mrs Harcourt. You remember I told you of the part she played in giving me work at the mill. You remind me of her sometimes.'

'Is that a compliment?'

'Yes. Yes, it is. I was . . . fond of her.'

'And you still think of her?'

'No, not really,' he lied. 'I have not seen her since I left Brentfield.'

'I see. Well, I am not to be confused with anyone else. Kindly remember that, Richard.'

'Forgive me, please. It was a foolish slip. I have had so many things on my mind.'

Believing that her relationship with Richard had grown beyond mere friendship, Henrietta was disappointed when, after they had known each other for some months, he still did not propose. Perhaps he was shy, or perhaps he feared rejection, or perhaps he was still dreaming of that Sarah, whom he had mentioned once and who had obviously meant a great deal to him . . . Whatever his reason, he seemed unwilling to make a move, and she determined to take action herself.

She knew that he admired her no-nonsense attitude and the freedom of thought and speech which she allowed herself, so she had little hesitation in broaching the subject. 'Have you ever thought of marrying again?' she asked him.

Richard gaped at her. Nothing earlier that evening had prepared him for such a question, which was in any case rather more outrageous than was to be expected even from Henrietta. 'Marrying again?'

'I know I should not ask, but you must be used to me by now. I cannot abide the stupid conventions which prevent one from saying what is in one's mind, or from asking the question which interests one the most.'

Richard shook his head, smiling. 'You're incorrigible, Henrietta.'

Emboldened by the fact that he seemed amused rather than shocked, she went on, 'You will think me quite immodest, and wicked, and heaven knows what else, but I cannot help that – I have to speak as I think. You need a wife, Richard. I know you have your sister to look after you, but that is not the same thing at all.'

Richard could see where this was leading. For a moment he felt a kind of resentment that she should have usurped his male prerogative, but then his sense of humour came into play. It was ironic that she should have chosen this particular occasion to launch her attack – if that was the right word – since he had made up his mind only a few days before that, when a suitable opportunity presented itself, he would ask her to marry him. 'And where would I find a wife?' he asked.

It was her turn to be taken aback. Surely he must realise what she was suggesting. And then she saw the laughter in his eyes and the little twitch at the corners of his mouth, and understood that he had realised it very clearly, and was teasing her. 'Now that's a difficult question,' she said. 'There's Miss Barrett – no, much too old. Or Miss Ransome – much too silly. Then why not a nice widow – preferably a rich one? But I don't know any nice widows, rich or not, do you?' She smiled, and then continued, still in the same flippant way, 'Of course, there is always Miss Searle, Miss Henrietta Searle.'

'Miss Searle, Miss Searle,' he said in a reflective way. 'Too clever, do you think?' And then he went on quickly, before she could think he was criticising, 'Dear Miss Searle, dear Henrietta, I don't think you're immodest or wicked. I'm not sure about "heaven knows what else", but I will put up with it, whatever it may be.' He let the amusement fade from his voice, and spoke gently and seriously. 'What I am sure about is that you would make me very happy if you would do me the honour of becoming my wife.'

She looked at him gravely. 'You mean it, Richard?'

'I will get down on one knee if you wish. Yes, I mean it.'

'Then, yes, Richard, yes.'

And so, in the Spring of 1875, Richard paid a formal visit on Mr Searle, and asked for his daughter's hand in marriage, confessing that he had already proposed and been accepted. Mr Searle was delighted.

When Richard asked Henrietta about the date of the wedding, she replied. 'I do not want a long engagement. Next month, perhaps.'

'So soon?'

'Perhaps that would seem unduly hasty. Then July.'

'Yes, that would be excellent. It is not the haste which bothers me – it is just that I am so pressed for time at the present.'

'You work too hard, Richard.'

It was true. Ever since the beginning of their social life, he had been driving himself even more frantically, as though he needed to make up every minute spent away from the mill. Frances begged him to take on more staff, but he explained that his profit margins were so delicately balanced that to do so would mean decreasing substantially the amount of money he could take out of the business.

'Take less,' Frances said. 'We live well enough.'

'But you want a new carpet for the sitting-room, and we need a maid to live in, and we no longer live on Mrs Appleby's rabbit stew.'

'We can do without all the luxuries.'

'No,' he said. 'Not now that we have guests so often. And it is no use suggesting we should give up our social engagements. I know how much they mean to you.'

'And to you too, since you met Henrietta.'

'Yes, I admit it freely.' He nodded ruefully. 'You see, my dear, there is every reason why I should continue working as I have been doing. You need have no fears for my health. I am a little tired, but otherwise as fit as a fiddle.'

In early May, with the wedding fixed for two months ahead, Richard spoke to Henrietta. 'My dearest, I hesitate to ask you this, but I have no choice. The work at the mill is increasing every day. It is absolutely crucial that we should consolidate our success, and Appleby can't manage on his own.'

'Then hire someone else.'

'That wouldn't solve the problem. I have to be there, Henrietta.'

'You could get a manager.'

'I can't afford that yet. If I can really get the business established this summer and autumn, then everything will become much easier. As you say, I should be able to hire a manager.'

Henrietta looked at him almost angrily. 'You are suggesting that we postpone our wedding?'

'It would not be fair to you to –'

'Until the New Year?'

'Yes. It is a great deal to ask, but you know I would not do so if I could see any other course of action open to me.' He looked at her anxiously.

It was a long while before she replied. She sighed. 'Naturally, this is a bitter disappointment to me – but I cannot do otherwise than agree.'

He kissed her hand. 'Thank you, my dear one. I knew that you would understand.'

'I would, however, like to ask you one question. Can you swear to me that your concern for your business is the only reason for this alteration in our plans?'

'Of course. What other reason could there be?'

As he walked home that evening, he thought again of her question. If there were indeed no other motive for the postponement, why was it that he felt a certain measure of relief? He puzzled over it. He was not head over heels in love with Henrietta, but he was very, very fond of her, and knew that she would make him an excellent wife. Unbidden, the thought of Sarah came to his mind. He shook his head, almost angrily. 'Oh, God! Shall I never be rid of her?'

He was aware of a passer-by looking at him curiously, and realised that he must have cried the thought aloud. He strode on, his mind working furiously. Sarah belonged in the past. She was forbidden to him, and he had known that for years. It could not have been thoughts of her which had brought him the sensation of release when Henrietta had agreed to postpone the wedding. It was simply that he needed his mind and his energies free for his work. It was for her own sake, as much as anything, that a longer engagement was desirable.

Feeling calmer, he went to the mill. As he opened the door, the sound which greeted him immediately told him that something was wrong. The loom clattered uselessly. The thread had broken, and Isaac was lying across the machine, unmoving. At first Richard thought he was dead, but when he stopped the machine, he could hear him breathing heavily, almost snoring. Perhaps he was ill. Gently, aware that a rougher movement could kill him, he shook the old man's shoulder.

His eyelids flickered. 'All ri', all ri',' he muttered. He yawned, and opened his eyes. He seemed to have difficulty in focussing.

'Are you all right, Isaac?'

'What's 'appened? Why's the loom stopped?' He looked at it. 'Oh, my Gawd – the thread's broke!'

'Are you ill?'

'Ill? What d'you mean? 'Ere, I didn't fall asleep, did I?' His face went scarlet. 'Oh, Gawd, I'm sorry, Mr Goodwin. Dunno 'ow I could do such a thing.'

'Neither do I, with the racket the loom makes. Are you sure you're all right?'

'Yes, I remember – I was 'aving the works o' the world to keep me eyes open. Must 'ave dropped off. 'Ere, I'll 'ave to set it goin' again.'

There was no point in being angry. Richard knew that he had driven the man almost as hard as he had himself, and Isaac was no longer young. 'You go home,' he said. 'Get some rest. I'll see to it.'

'No. It's me own fault it's gorn wrong. I ought to put it right.'

'Do as I say, Isaac. And from now on, if you feel as tired as that, stop the loom and pack up for the night. The state you're in, you're more of a liability than a help.'

Grumbling, Isaac eventually complied with the order, and Richard worked on until the roll of brocade was finished and he could shut the mill for the night. He would just have to take on another weaver, a skilled man – and that would mean paying high wages.

The next morning, Isaac was back, apparently well rested, and very full of apologies. 'It won't 'appen again,' he said.

'I'm thinking of getting another hand,' Richard told him.

The old man's jaw dropped. 'You mean you're givin' me the sack?'

'No, Isaac, I wouldn't do that. But we need more help. You can't keep going at this rate.'

'I tell you it won't 'appen again. We don't need no extra 'ands.'

Richard did no more about it, except to tell Mr Hill to keep an eye on Appleby when he was not there to do so himself.

'The only difficulty, Richard, is that fatigue is equally likely to claim me,' Mr Hill said, with his usual twinkle. 'No, I mean it – youth's a stuff that hasn't endured, if you will forgive the paraphrase. The real problem is that the worthy Isaac follows your example and works all the hours that God, in His infinite generosity, gives us. You should conserve your own energies, Richard.'

'Oh, for heaven's sake! Not you too! I'm sick to death of people telling me how to run my business.'

He stalked out, leaving Mr Hill thinking to himself how rarely Richard lost his temper, and that he must indeed be under considerable strain to do so now.

Some weeks later, Richard made one of his periodic visits to London, to see Mr Leroy and order additional supplies. It had become accepted that he would take dinner with the family. The younger sister, Annette, had married, and now it was her mother who had to look after her crippled daughter. Richard was always amazed at Isabelle's brightness of spirit in the face of her cruel handicaps, and gratified by the interest she took in the progress of his work.

His visits also gave him an opportunity to gossip with Mr Leroy about the trade. The last time he had been at the house in Spitalfields, Mr Leroy had said, 'I fear the decline has continued at Harcourt's. I am doing far less business with them than I used to, and I am told that Mr Harcourt dismissed a large part of his work force. I don't like to spread rumours, but they say his partiality for strong liquor is getting the better of him. There are times when he does not go to the mill for days on end, and Mrs Harcourt makes brief appearances to try to keep it going. But, poor lady, her powers are strictly limited.'

'Is she well?'

'I believe so.' Mr Leroy gave Richard a brief searching look, and then changed the subject.

That conversation had taken place some months previously.

This time, part way through the business discussion in Mr Leroy's office, the silk merchant suddenly said, 'You will dine with us as usual, Goodwin?'

'I had thought of going back tonight. I am fearful of staying too long away from the mill.' He told Leroy of the incident when Isaac Appleby had fallen asleep.

'I have a special reason for asking you to come this evening. No, I won't tell you what it is, but I shall be most disappointed if you cannot be with us. I am sure you can spare one day more away from the mill.'

'Then of course I will come. Thank you.'

When Richard walked into the Leroys' drawing-room, he saw her at once. She looked tired and pale, but the dark chestnut hair was still as magnificent, and the green eyes as compelling. He was stunned, and stood gazing at her, vaguely conscious of Mr and Mrs Leroy watching the encounter, but unable to say a word.

'Good evening, Richard,' Sarah said at last, and the sound of her voice wrenched at his heart.

It took a moment for him to force himself to speak. 'I'm sorry. I did not expect to see you here. You must forgive my poor manners. Good evening. How are you, Sarah?'

'I am well, thank you. And you?'

'Yes. Yes, very fit.' Richard came to himself sufficiently to greet his hostess. 'And where is Miss Leroy?' he asked.

'She is spending a few days in Berkshire with some friends.'

'I am sorry to miss her. Indeed, I had hoped to present her with this small token of my esteem. I am right in thinking that it is her birthday next week, am I not?'

'How very kind of you, Mr Goodwin. Isabelle will be much gratified, I am sure.'

'It is Edward Young's *Night Thoughts*.'

'You could have made no better choice, Mr Goodwin. Isabelle was saying to me only the other day that she wished she owned a copy of it.'

'I wonder if she knows the story, which my fiancée told me, of James Lackington and the *Night Thoughts*?'

'I am sure that I do not. Pray tell us.'

'He was born about a hundred years ago. One Christmas Eve his wife sent him out to buy their Christmas dinner with the last half-crown they had in the world. Instead, he spent the money on a copy of this book. When he got home his wife remonstrated with him, but he maintained that he had acted wisely. "Had I bought a dinner," he said, "we should have eaten it tomorrow and the pleasure would have been soon over, but should we live fifty years longer, we shall have the *Night Thoughts* to feast on." His wife was a woman of great sense; she was convinced of Mr Lackington's argument, and said no more of the dinner.'

Mr and Mrs Leroy both nodded sagely at the end of the anecdote, but Sarah said, 'An excellent and moral tale which we should always remember, especially when someone complains of the high price of books.' She laughed. 'However, had I been Mrs Lackington, I fear I might have been tempted to hit my husband over the head with his book! I would not care to miss my Christmas dinner.'

'I agree,' Richard smiled. 'It is an amusing anecdote, but there is something a little too . . . pious about it for my taste.'

Mrs Leroy rose. 'None of us shall miss our dinner this evening, I assure you. If you will excuse me, I will see that all is progressing as it should.'

'Are you staying in London long?' Richard asked Sarah, when Mrs Leroy had gone.

'For a few days only. And you?'

'I return tomorrow.'

The stilted conversation was interrupted by a crash somewhere in the direction of the kitchen, and an agonised cry. Mr Leroy jumped up. 'Forgive me. I must see what is amiss.' He hurried out.

'Was that contrived?' Sarah asked.

'To leave us alone? No, I would not think so. But I am glad of it. May I greet you properly, Sarah?' He stood up, and went towards her.

She stopped him. 'No, Richard. That would not be wise. Please sit over there.' She indicated a chair facing her, but on the other side of the fireplace. 'Then we can talk without . . . embarrassment.'

There was a brief silence. He was willing her to look at him, but she kept her eyes averted, as though fearful that they would betray her.

'You said just now that you are well. Is that really true, Sarah?'

'Well enough. A little tired, that is all. They tell me you are prospering. I am glad to hear it. And is your sister in good health? You have found a pleasant place to live, and made some suitable acquaintances, I trust?'

'Thank you, yes. Frances is very well, and we live in a pleasant house in Wensham, and yes, we have made some delightful friends there.'

She paused briefly, and then said, 'You mentioned your fiancée just now. Tell me about her.'

He heard himself replying almost automatically. 'Her name is Henrietta Searle. She is the youngest daughter of a prominent solicitor in Norwich.'

Sarah waited for him to continue, and then said, with a smile, 'Is that all you can tell me about her?'

'She is very charming, very well read, and a most talented musician. Sometimes she reminds me of . . .' Just in time he caught himself. 'She reminds me of . . . Jane.'

'And when shall you be married?'

'Early in the New Year, I think.'

'Allow me to congratulate you. I hope you will both be very happy.'

'Thank you.' Suddenly Richard felt that he could not continue this ludicrous conversation. He rose. 'Sarah! Sarah, please look at me.'

Slowly she turned her head towards him, but her eyes were still cast downwards.

He knelt beside her. 'Yes, I am engaged to be married, but it is you that I love, Sarah – it always has been and it always will be.' Gently he reached out his hand and lifted her chin. Tears had gathered in her eyes. He went to take her in his arms. 'My dearest, my darling . . .'

'No, Richard,' she whispered. 'Don't touch me, please. Don't rob me of my last vestige of control. Richard, please do not kneel to me.'

He stood up, feeling faintly ridiculous. 'I did not know you would be here this evening. You presumably did. Did you think we could meet as strangers?'

She smiled sadly. 'No. I was foolish to stay when Mr Leroy told me you would be coming, but I wanted to see you, Richard. I wanted that very much. I know now it was a mistake.'

'Perhaps I should make some excuse, and go.'

'That would be absurd. We are not children. We must try to behave like civilised adults.'

'And make polite conversation,' Richard said bitterly, 'about the weather and our health and safe subjects like Mr James Lackington. We can always leave our eyes to say what we both want to say. Is that what you mean by behaving like civilised adults?'

'Please, Richard!'

'Then at least, while we are alone, let us talk more freely. You say that you are well, but you do not speak of happiness.'

'I have my share. My son gives me great joy, Richard. He is such a fine little fellow.'

'And what of his father? What of Thomas Harcourt, Esquire?'

She did not reply, turning her face away, but not before he had seen the pain in her eyes.

'I have heard . . .' he began. 'I have heard that he . . .'

The words hung in the air for a moment, and then she said bitterly, 'Whatever you have heard is less than the truth.' She got up, and walked away, as though she could not face him, and he had to strain to hear her. 'He is . . . vile, a brute. He is . . . he is . . . almost always in drink. Not incapable, you understand – I wish he were – it is much easier when he is incapable.' White-faced, she turned to look at Richard, and gradually began to speak more readily. 'He is selfish and inconsiderate. He has always been so, of course, but now it is worse than before – much worse. He is often ill, but will listen to no one, take no notice. He has dismissed Dr Wood, and will not let him in the house. The only person he will ever listen to is his mother – oh, how I hate her, Richard! – and she encourages every madness that comes into his mind, just as she seems to believe it praiseworthy that he should drink to excess, and that he should have . . . other women. "Men need their little pleasures," she says. "Thank God Tom is not one of those niminy-piminy stay-at-homes. I like a man to be a man!" That is what she tells me.'

Her shoulders were shaking. Richard ached to go to her, but knew instinctively that he must not do so.

'He is ruining the mill, Richard,' she continued after a moment. 'We are still in business, but it is very difficult now. We have lost many of our best workers. Sometimes, when Tom is ill, I go to the mill, and it makes me weep to see it.' For a moment she seemed unable to continue. Then she laughed bitterly. 'At this moment, he is confined to his bed, and I have come here, against his wishes, to beg Mr Leroy to extend our credit, because our situation is desperate.' Her voice faltered, and then recovered. 'He is often abusive . . . and often violent. Thank God, his violence is directed against me, and not against Edward.'

Richard could not restrain himself. He went to her, and this time she allowed him to take her in his arms. 'You must leave him, Sarah, you must! You can't go on like this. You must come to me – you and the boy.' The scent and warmth and shape of her body made his senses reel. He bent his head to kiss her neck.

She broke away from him. 'No, Richard, no. Oh, what a fool I am!' She was almost hysterical as she cried, 'We should not have met. I should not have told you these things. Oh, promise me, promise me that we shall never see each other again. I could not bear it.' She ran towards the door, but as she did so, it opened and Mr and Mrs Leroy stood looking at them.

Mrs Leroy took in the situation at a glance, and decided that the best course was to pretend to ignore it. 'Our apologies for neglecting you, my friends. All is now in order, and dinner will be served in five minutes or less.'

'We heard a . . . you had some kind of accident,' Sarah said. Her voice sounded odd, as she struggled to keep her emotions under control.

'It was nothing. The kitchenmaid dropped a soup tureen.'

'A valuable soup tureen,' Mr Leroy put in. 'But my dear wife, soft-hearted as ever, refuses to dismiss the girl.'

'Good servants are hard to find. And if I dismiss her, Cook will probably take it into her head to go too, and then . . .' Mrs Leroy chattered on, trying to fill the uneasy silence which she knew would have descended on the room otherwise.

Suddenly, Sarah said, 'Forgive me – I must get a handkerchief.' She turned to Richard and tried to smile. 'I forgot to tell you – Mr and Mrs Leroy are kindly putting me up for a couple of nights.' She left the room swiftly.

Mrs Leroy looked at Richard. 'I fear Mrs Harcourt is greatly distressed. Knowing that you were old friends, I thought it might help her to see you, which is why I asked Mr Leroy to insist on your dining with us. I trust I have not also distressed you.'

'No. No, not at all,' Richard said, hoping the lie was not too transparent, 'and I am sure Mrs Harcourt will have recovered soon. I'm afraid I was thoughtless enough to say something which upset her.'

The strained atmosphere continued. At dinner, neither Richard nor Sarah spoke, except to reply briefly to any question put directly to them by the Leroys, who tried valiantly to maintain a conversation.

As soon as the meal was over, Richard asked permission to leave. 'I must catch the earliest train in the morning, and I am rather tired. I fear I have been a less than sparkling dinner guest, and I trust you will pardon me.' He went to Sarah to say goodbye. 'Au revoir, Sarah.'

She shook her head. 'No, Richard – goodbye.' She lowered her voice. 'I am sorry. I did not mean to pour everything out in that fashion, but it helped me, a great deal. Thank you for listening.'

'Leave him, Sarah,' Richard whispered. 'Come away with me.'

She shook her head again. 'I can't.'

He held her hand, gazing into her eyes, trying to tell her how much he cared, and that they could still find happiness together. But she withdrew her hand and turned her head, and he was forced at last to go.

As he walked back to his lodgings, misery welled up in his heart. They would never see each other again. He would go back to Wensham and marry Henrietta, and she would return to . . . The prospect before her was so appalling that he tried not to think of it. He was powerless to rescue her or to do anything which would lessen her unhappiness.

When he reached Wensham the next morning, the mill seemed unusually quiet. Mr Hill came out to meet him. 'It's Appleby,' he said. 'He collapsed just as he left his cottage this morning.'

'Collapsed? He's not –?'

'No. I am not sure what complaint it is which has laid him low, but I understand that it is unlikely to prove fatal.'

'I am glad of that.' He sighed. 'It could not have happened at a worse time. I shall just have to work single-handed, I suppose.'

'Must whatever it is be done today? Appleby may be back tomorrow.'

'Of course it must,' Richard said irritably. 'We have orders to fill.' He took off his coat and began to roll up his sleeves.

'You look tired yourself, Richard,' said Mr Hill, carefully.

Richard did not answer, but went to the loom and swiftly set it in motion. It was a relief to have something to do, and his weariness seemed to drop away. A sense of well-being stole over him, and he felt alert and capable of anything, and conscious of a hundred little details around him, as though he were seeing them through a magnifying glass.

Then the sharpness vanished. The clatter of the loom was soothing, comforting, and suddenly he realised that his eyes had closed, and that he was nodding. Just like Isaac had done. He shook his head to clear the drowsiness. He had hardly slept at all, thinking of Sarah.

The screech of tortured metal woke him. An arm of the loom had sheared and had fallen against other working parts. The whole machine would destroy itself if he did not act swiftly. Still half-asleep, he did not stop to think, but plunged his arm into the loom to seize the piece of metal. A searing pain shot through him, and he screamed in agony, and lost consciousness.

CHAPTER TWENTY

Richard's right arm, between the wrist and the elbow, was badly mangled. It was fortunate for him, Dr Trehearne said, that Mr Hill had come to his aid quickly, and had had the good sense to put on a tourniquet. The doctor administered chloroform, so that his patient was spared pain while he used all his considerable skill in trying to repair the damage, but with tendons cut and bones splintered, it was likely that at best Richard would regain partial use of the arm only. He would never operate a loom again.

Dr Trehearne came down wearily to the sitting-room where Frances and Henrietta were waiting. 'He is asleep now. That will do him more good than anything else.' He turned to Frances. 'Let him sleep as long as possible. If he wakes, you may feed him a little gruel, or warm milk. I will arrange for a nurse to be in attendance.'

'Miss Goodwin and I will be pleased to share that duty,' said Henrietta.

Trehearne frowned. 'I am sure he could be in no better hands, but a professional eye should be kept upon him, so that I can be called at once should there be any change in his condition.'

'Why do you say that?' Frances asked. 'Is there special reason for concern?'

'No. But Mr Goodwin has suffered an extremely serious injury and one can never be entirely certain of the outcome.'

A nurse was duly engaged, with whom Frances and Henrietta shared the vigil in the sick-room. The doctor was pleased, the following morning, to find that Richard had slept well and was in little discomfort. By that night, however, he had become feverish, his brow was burning, the bed-clothes were soaked in perspiration, and above the bandages, the skin of his arm looked angry.

Dr Trehearne saw the symptoms with dismay. 'I fear some contagion has entered his blood. I shall require boiling water, Miss Goodwin. And you, Miss Searle, kindly go out into the street and find three or four strong young men of good character, who will be prepared to help me.'

Frances looked at him in horror. 'You do not mean to amputate?'

'That will be the last resort. I hope to cut away the infection. Unfortunately, I dare not risk another application of chloroform in his present condition, and it will be very painful. Mr Goodwin must be held still, and that will require strength beyond that of the most devoted sister and fiancée.'

While four young men from the village exerted all their strength to hold him still, Dr Trehearne cut deep into the wound and beyond. Richard screamed, and then fell into merciful unconsciousness. 'We will see what happens now,' the doctor said. 'I can but hope that I have prevented the infection from spreading. If not . . .' He sighed, and went.

For much of the next three days, Richard was delirious. His ravings were pitiful to hear, and caused Frances much distress, not only because he was so ill, but because he called constantly for Sarah, and the only person who could calm him was Henrietta. He would clutch her hand, and mutter incoherently, and then out of the rambling words would come the sharp, clear sentences which Frances dreaded. 'Sarah, my darling, you must leave Tom. Leave him, and come away with me,' or 'I love you, Sarah. I always have, and I always shall.' It seemed terrible that he should bare his innermost thoughts to her in this way.

Henrietta herself was not greatly disturbed. 'Do not concern yourself, Frances. He is not in the present – he is thinking of the past, of a time when Sarah meant a great deal to him. I know how fond he was of her. Once he recovers, he will forget her again, and think of me.'

On the fourth day, Richard's fever broke. Dr Trehearne smiled. 'He will be all right now. He will never be able to use the arm properly, but at least he has it still, which is better than a stump. He owes much to the devotion you two ladies have given him. But I need not tell you that your task is not yet over. He has to adjust to his new life. It will be a difficult period for him, and he will need help and sympathy.'

Richard's first concern, once he had recovered consciousness, was for the mill, and he insisted that Isaac Appleby and Mr Hill should be brought to his bedside.

Mr Hill came alone. 'Appleby is in the middle of a run of brocade,' he explained. 'All is well, Richard. To my own astonishment, I have become, in my dotage, the manager of a silk mill, and not, I am immodest enough to think, without success. Immediately following your accident, I went to see Appleby, who fortunately had recovered sufficiently to come back to work the next day. Having discussed the situation with him, I decided upon a plan of some audacity. The next day I went to Norwich, and there encountered an experienced weaver, Simpson by name, who was in search of employment. I took it upon myself to engage him, and also, as an apprentice, his fifteen-year-old son. Both, under Appleby's supervision, are now at work, and your mill is productive.'

'But we cannot afford –'

'Permit me to contradict you, Richard. We can indeed afford it, provided, of course, that the flow of orders is maintained. I have not yet completed the catalogue of my managerial innovations. Having found my mill-workers in Norwich, I next sought a salesman, and again was fortunate. Mr Vickers, a young man who already carries a number of lines in haberdashery, was delighted to be able to add our brocades to his samples, on a commission basis. He too is already at work for us.'

'But how did you find them?'

'The Simpsons, through the estimable Appleby's brother-in-law. I then called on Mr Montgomery, to seek his advice, and my visit happened to coincide with that of Mr Vickers.' He took off his spectacles, and polished them vigorously. 'I fear I have far exceeded my usual responsibilities, but I have made it clear to our new employees that their appointments have yet to be ratified by you. As for myself, I fear I have provoked most justly your wrath and indignation.'

Richard smiled. 'Words from the General Confession demand a Biblical response. I say, "Well done, thou good and faithful servant." Thank you, old friend. Once I am on my feet again, I shall see that you reap the reward which you deserve.' His eyes closed, and still smiling, he fell gently asleep.

Mr Hill tiptoed from the room.

As Richard's convalescence progressed, he thought about his future. There was little power in his arm, and the fingers of his right hand were bent round towards the palm, so that only with difficulty could he even hold a knife. Thanks to Mr Hill, however, his disability was of little importance as far as work in the mill was concerned. If the new man, Simpson, was capable, he would relieve Isaac of part of his burden, and in time other workers could be hired. The salesman would probably be retained, but he himself could build up the business by regular visits to the more important customers, just as Tom had done for Harcourt's. He might even try selling abroad – Frances' designs could match any on the Continent for originality and beauty. He knew now that he could happily leave Mr Hill in charge, especially with the directorship that he had decided to give him.

On the other hand, travelling had never much appealed to him, and now he was even less inclined to it. Most of all, he decided, he would like to let others take over all the day-to-day business, leaving him free to think, to plan, to invent. For years he had had in mind the idea of devising a method of producing crape directly from raw silk, instead of from the double-thrown thread, making it cheaper for the purchaser and at the same time more profitable to the manufacturer. Then there was need of a better biasing machine – those used at Prideau's had been adequate, but sometimes tore the delicate material, and could not cope altogether satisfactorily with any variations in the tension of the weaving; an improved machine would save both time and costs.

Oh, there were many ways in which he could usefully fill his time, quite apart from all the reading that he intended to do – not only the works of fiction which Henrietta loved so much, but books about silk, books about industrial practices, books about trade and politics and history. He was far too much of an ignoramus, and the enforced freedom from physical activity would give him the chance to educate himself.

And of course marriage to Henrietta would change his life. He took an early opportunity of speaking to her. 'I have been thinking, my dear. I know how unhappy you were at postponing our wedding until the New Year, but now, I fear, we must delay it further. It would not be fair to expect you to marry me in my present condition.'

To his astonishment, she reacted quite angrily. 'I will not hear of it. "In sickness and in health" – is that not what we shall be saying? Or are you trying to tell me that you wish to break our engagement?'

'Of course not.'

'Then why make such an extraordinary demand? A delay will make no difference, I fear, to the state of your arm.'

When she left him that day, he was so depressed that Frances was driven to say what had been in her mind for so long. 'You don't want to marry her, do you?'

'What makes you say that?'

She hesitated, and then abandoned discretion and told him how, in his delirium, he had repeatedly called for Sarah, expressing his love for her over and over again. 'Henrietta says that you were thinking about the past, but I believe you're still in love with Sarah.' He did not speak. 'Are you, Richard?'

'I don't know. Yes, I do. Yes, I am.'

'Then you should break it off, in fairness to Henrietta.'

'The fact that I love Sarah doesn't mean that I can't have a perfectly satisfactory marriage to Henrietta. I shall never see Sarah again. So I might as well accept Henrietta's love, and give her as much affection as I can.'

'Perhaps you're right. I suppose in the end most women would prefer that, rather than nothing at all.' And then suddenly the words burst from her. 'No, Richard, no! You're wrong! If you marry Henrietta you will be miserable, utterly miserable. I beg you to break it off.'

'How can I?'

'Confess first that you wish to do so.'

He was silent for a long while. Then at last he nodded slowly. 'But it's impossible. I couldn't do that to her.'

'Why? Because you don't want to hurt her? You'll hurt her more by marrying her. Oh, Richard, can't you see? It's been wrong from the very beginning. She set out to hook you, and she succeeded.'

'Leave it, Frances, please. I will think about it.'

The next time that Henrietta called, she saw that he was worried. Yet, though she gave him many opportunities, he seemed unable to talk about what was troubling him. In the end, she said, 'What is it, Richard? Please tell me. I know there's something on your mind.'

He looked into her eyes, and then averted his gaze. 'I am afraid that what I am going to say will hurt you very much, and I would not have that for the world. But I must speak – I shall hurt you more if I do not. I . . . I want you to release me from our engagement, Henrietta.'

Her face became ugly. She stood, and moved away from his bedside. He thought she might be crying, but when she turned back there were no tears. 'Do you really mean it?' she asked.

'Yes. I have thought about it for a long time, and . . . Yes, I mean it, Henrietta. I cannot, I will not marry you.' He felt a little flood of relief as he caught the expression in her eyes and knew that his uncompromising tone had already forced her to accept defeat.

She gazed at him, stony-faced. 'I see. Very well. But tell me why, Richard. Not because of your arm?'

'No.'

'No, I hoped you would not insult me by making that absurd excuse. Then what has brought you to this decision?'

'I . . . do not think we would be . . . happy together.'

'Oh, come,' she said. 'You can do better than that. At least tell me that your heart is another's, that you cannot live without her. It is Mrs Sarah Harcourt, isn't it? Are you contemplating adultery now?'

He did not reply. After a while, he said, 'Perhaps you would prefer it if it were believed that you were the one to break the engagement.'

'What? And have everyone saying that I deserted you because you have become a cripple? No, thank you. I prefer to be the injured party. Of course, I might sue you for breach of promise. Yes, that might be an interesting course of action. How would you like that?'

'I should not change my mind, Henrietta.'

She gave a contemptuous little laugh. 'Oh, you needn't worry. I wouldn't demean myself.' Suddenly her defences crumbled, and her eyes filled with tears. Sobbing, she ran from the room.

Richard was overcome by remorse. How could he have hurt her so? What might she not do in her grief? He called frantically for Frances, and begged her to run after Henrietta, and bring her back.

Frances shook her head. 'It wouldn't do any good. She told me what had happened before she left. She's not nearly as upset as you think. Her pride is hurt. She will soon get over it, and quite enjoy spreading scandal about us both.'

'Oh, she is not that wicked.'

'Isn't she?'

Richard continued to worry until three days later a letter came.

'Sir, It is *with relief* that I terminate our engagement, since by so doing I shall spare myself marriage to a person for whose character I can no longer feel the *least* admiration. Your behaviour has been *abominable*, but no doubt I was foolish to expect more from someone with your lack of breeding.

'It will be announced, as is no less than the truth, that the engagement has been broken by *you*, but I shall make it plain that, though the injured party, I am to be congratulated on a *most fortunate escape*.'

'I would advise you and your sister to avoid *decent* society in

Wensham – you will *no longer* be welcome among those who have tolerated you only for my sake. You will learn that a common workman who persists in masquerading as a gentleman simply makes himself *a laughing-stock*.

'Yrs. truly, H. Searle.'

Richard read the letter with a lightened heart. How right Frances had been! How could he have mistaken her character so? She might profess herself pleased to be released from the engagement, but her relief could hardly equal his own.

When he told Frances that the engagement was over, she smiled happily at first, but suddenly, to his astonishment, burst into tears.

'Why, my dear, whatever is the matter? I thought you would be pleased – as I am.'

She fell to her knees beside his chair, sobbing, and he put his good arm round her shoulders as he tried to comfort her. Eventually, she calmed down, and got up awkwardly. 'I am sorry, Richard. Forgive me.'

'But what was the matter?'

'Oh . . . nothing.'

'My dear Frances,' he said, in an almost bantering manner, hoping to make her smile, 'you cannot sob like that – why my lapel is quite drenched – and then tell me it was nothing.'

'I was feeling sorry for myself.' The tears began to roll down her cheeks again. 'Oh, Richard, what's the matter with us? Why can't we find happiness like other people do?' She struggled to regain her self-control. 'I have accustomed myself to the thought of being an old maid, of not having children – I should have liked to have children, Richard – but then, even though I knew that Henrietta was not the wife for you, I told myself that one day I might have nephews and nieces. I thought . . . I though how I could be their foolish Aunt Goodwin, who would draw pictures for them, and spoil them, and that they would . . . love me.' Her shoulders were shaking. 'I'm sorry, Richard. I'm making an utter fool of myself, and I don't know why. I'm really . . . very . . . happy for you.' Hardly able to get the words out, she ran from the room, leaving Richard looking after her in helpless amazement.

She did not appear for an hour or more, and then seemed to be her usual self.

'Are you all right?' Richard asked.

'Yes. I don't know what came over me this morning. Very foolish. It won't happen again.'

'Whatever lies before us, my dear –' Richard began. It was difficult to say. 'Whatever lies before us, you will never be alone while I am alive, and you will always be loved, deeply loved.'

She patted his arm. 'Thank you for saying that, Richard. I knew it already, but it is good to hear. And now we will not speak of it again – ever.'

Since he was still recovering from his injury, there was little opportunity for Richard to see anyone in Wensham society. The friends and acquaintances he had met through the Searles did not call, which seemed to bear out what Henrietta had said in her letter, but on the other hand, Dr Trehearne continued to treat him, though he was rather stiff in manner. Richard decided that he did not care. He and Frances would be content with friends like the Hills and the Applebys.

As soon as he could, he returned to the mill, and found it in good heart. Mr Hill was overwhelmed and delighted by his new status, in which capacity he was swift to advise expansion, persuading Richard to order an additional loom, and winding and throwing machines. Once they had been installed, Richard advertised for new employees, and was at first besieged by workers who sought employment for their children as well as for themselves. But he refused all child labour, saying that they should accept the education which was now available, and gave the parents little homilies on his own experiences as a child in a factory.

He enjoyed his new freedom, and even, in these circumstances, the travelling he undertook. He went regularly to London, to see the Leroys and other silk merchants, to discuss with them the state of the market, to choose the right time to buy his supplies. He visited many customers, too – not primarily to sell his products, but to discover what was selling well, what future trends might be, and to judge when to raise or lower his prices. And he thought a great deal about the way his brocades were made, and about the manufacture of crape from raw silk.

Since he had no crape loom, no biasing machine, no crimping rollers, he could only theorise and conduct makeshift experiments. He could test cold-water dyes, and stiffening agents which would give extra body to the raw silk, but it was not really satisfactory. On the other hand, it would have been absurd to buy all the necessary equipment simply in order to try out his ideas.

He discussed it with Mr Hill, who said, 'If I may say so, your principal need is to make up your mind.'

'I have. I know I can't afford to buy a lot of useless – well, not necessarily useless . . .'

'What if your experiments succeeded, and you found your cheap way of making crape? Would you sell the idea to Prideau's – or to Harcourt's? You'd make quite a lot of money if you patented the idea first.'

Richard hesitated. 'I hadn't really thought about that side of it.'

'It is not for me to question your veracity or your motives, and perhaps I am usurping the privileges of our long friendship to do so, but I beg leave to doubt you, my friend. I suspect that you have thought about it a great deal, and that your prime aim is to get back into the crape-making business yourself. That's what we're really talking about, isn't it? Not whether we should invest money in a series of experiments which ultimately would benefit others in the silk industry, but whether Goodwin's Mill should start producing crape. And that's what I meant when I said you need to make your mind up.'

Richard laughed. 'You always were good at putting your finger on the point. Yes, I confess I should like to make crape again. But I couldn't compete with Prideau's, or even with Harcourt's – not that Harcourt's can provide much competition nowadays. Mr Leroy tells me that they're only just keeping their heads above water. It's sad, very sad.'

'Yes,' said Mr Hill. 'Poor Mrs Harcourt.'

Richard looked at him sharply. 'What do you mean?'

'I was just thinking of all she did to build the firm up.'

'I see. Yes. Do you ever hear from anyone in Brentfield?'

'Occasionally. A young man who joined the accounts department there after you'd left became something of a friend, and writes now and then.'

Richard was silent for a few moments. Then he said abruptly, 'How is Mrs Hill?'

'I find her quite satisfactory,' Mr Hill replied, only momentarily disconcerted by the sudden change of subject. He was not surprised when Richard did not react to his little joke. 'She is well, thank you.'

'Good. Good. You must come to dinner again soon. I shall speak to my sister about it.' He went to the door. 'I must get back to work.' But he seemed in no hurry to go. 'If . . . if your friend in Brentfield should have anything of particular interest to say about Harcourt's, you will let me know, won't you?'

'Of course.'

'One must keep abreast of developments in the trade.'

Mr Hill nodded.

Richard dropped the falsely bright tone. 'I'm grateful to you. I know that you understand what is in my mind, and I appreciate the way you keep it to yourself.'

Mr Hill looked at him straight-faced. 'I will give Mrs Hill your kind message,' he said.

The letter which at last brought news of Harcourt's came not to Mr Hill but to Richard himself. He recognised Sarah's handwriting, ripped the letter open, and stared at the few words: 'I need your help. Please come to me. S.' He left at once.

He was surprised to see that the front door of Harcourt Place had been swathed in black crape. A death in the family. 'It must be old Mrs Harcourt,' he told himself. Not that she was all that old . . . Of course it could be the boy, Sarah's son, but if so, surely she would have said so in her note. No, it was bound to be the old lady. And in all probability, Tom was 'ill' again, and Sarah needed help to arrange the funeral and everything else that had to be done.

The servant led him to the library, where Sarah came to meet him. She was pale and tense, and looked more striking than ever in the deep mourning she wore. The tightly-waisted dress emphasised the swell of her bosom, the curve of her hips. She seemed about to give him her hand, but then hesitated. 'I heard about your accident. How is your arm?'

'Somewhat useless, I'm afraid.'

'I am sorry. I hope it does not pain you.'

'No.'

She went over to a settee. 'It is good of you to respond so quickly to my note. Please sit down.'

She sounded more formal than he had expected. He gave her a stiff little bow. 'I see you are in mourning. My condolences.'

'Thank you.' She stood up and went to the fireplace, and then turned suddenly towards him. 'Oh, Richard, at least with you I do not have to pretend. I am free of him now, and –'

'*Of him*? You mean it is Tom who has died?'

'Yes, of course.'

'But I thought . . .' For a moment he could not take it in. 'Tom? What did he die of?'

'Dr Wood certified the cause of death as "acute hepatitis and suspected cirrhosis of the liver". In short, Richard, Tom died of drink.' She paused briefly. 'I had been warned that it might happen – so had he – but it was not very pleasant. He was very ill for some weeks.'

'When did he die?'

'A month ago.'

'A month? As long as that?'

'I could hardly send for you earlier,' she said. 'As it is, I risk scandal now, but I had to do it, for the sake of Harcourt's.'

'Harcourt's?'

'Must you repeat everything I say?' She laughed, in an attempt to remove the irritation from her voice.

'I'm sorry, but . . . Sarah, don't you see what this means?'

'I asked you to come back, Richard,' she said quickly, 'because Harcourt's needs you. You know of the mill's decline. Now that Tom is no longer here, I intend to make it respected and prosperous again. But I cannot do it alone – I need you to help me.'

He could not believe it. She should have been in his arms, swearing her love, planning their future as man and wife; instead, she was talking of the business as though there had never been any affection between them. Ever since coming into the room, he had felt confused, as though it were all a dream, or as if some part of his brain were not functioning properly. 'I have complete freedom of action, you see,' she was saying. 'Tom's will was an old one, fortunately, made soon after his father died. If he'd written a new one, I doubt if I should be in this position now. As it is I can offer you whatever you want – your old position back, your directorship, and all the power that goes with it. No large remuneration at this stage, but once the business picks up . . .'

She stopped, as though aware that she had been almost gabbling. There was something false about the whole situation, but he felt wary of challenging her. Perhaps she was playing a game of her own devising, but if so, he had no option but to play it too – at least until she disclosed what was truly in her mind. 'I cannot leave Wensham,' he told her.

'Why not?'

'There is my own business to think of, and my responsibilities towards my employees.'

'That is important, of course, but is it the only reason?'

'Yes.'

Sarah seemed embarrassed. 'I heard, Richard . . . I heard that your engagement was . . . ended. Is that true?'

'Yes.'

'Then perhaps there is someone else to whom you are attached.'

'No, there is no one. It is simply that I am not sure that I want to return here.'

It was her turn to repeat his words in surprise. 'Not want to return here? But you must. I need you. The mill needs you.'

'Why are we talking about the mill? We should be talking about us. I love you, Sarah. And now that you're free –'

'No, Richard, please –'

'I love you, and I want you to be my wife.'

Suddenly she stood up and moved quickly to the fireplace. 'Please, Richard, I beg you . . . '

A sudden horrifying thought crossed his mind. 'Sarah, is it my arm? I'm not much of a catch. I can't expect you to want a cripple for a husband.'

'I would never think of you as a cripple. Oh, Richard, how foolish you are!'

He went to her. 'Then you will marry me?'

'How can I? I'm in mourning. Tom hasn't been dead a month yet.'

'You mean you're going to go through the whole rigmarole? Full mourning for two years, half mourning after that, and black dresses and a widow's cap for the rest of your life? For a man you loathed?'

'It is expected.'

'Since when have you cared about what is expected?'

'I have to consider our friends, our relations, everybody.'

'To the devil with everybody! Nothing matters except us.'

'You know that isn't true. And please don't shout at me.'

'I'm sorry. It's just that I don't understand.' She allowed him to take her hand, and he continued softly, 'Listen, my dear one. If it were not for these conventions, would you marry me soon?'

'I don't know.' She sounded almost distraught.

'Why not?'

'There are so many things to consider. Oh, God, Richard! I just don't know what I think about anything, or what I want to do. Oh, it's been so horrible, horrible!'

Suddenly she was sobbing desperately. He held her tight, saying nothing, believing that what she needed most of all was the comfort of his arms around her. His love for her, his sympathy, his desire to restore her happiness were overwhelming, and yet at the same time one part of his brain was thinking how strange it was that she, so strong of character

– much stronger than himself – should be simultaneously so vulnerable.

As she wept, she told him, in little bursts of muttered words, of the humiliations and horrors of the recent months, of her increasing bitterness towards Tom and his mother. 'It *consumed* me,' she whispered. 'I could think of nothing else. And then I found an anger – anger at what was happening to the mill. And I fed on my hatred and my anger, until I began to believe that I was going out of my mind. Truly, I watched myself moving nearer and nearer to insanity. I think that if . . . if Tom had not died, I might have . . .' She shuddered, and could say no more.

It was a long while before the quivering sobs died away, but at last she seemed to have regained control, and broke from his arms, dabbing at her eyes with her handkerchief. 'I'm sorry. I'm ashamed of myself for creating such a scene. And now I must . . . I must look a sight.'

'You look adorable to me.' He paused, and then said, 'Are you all right now? Really?'

She nodded, a little uncertainly. 'Yes. Yes, I'm all right.'

'Sufficiently for us to resume our conversation?'

She managed a half-smile. 'Yes. Thank you for being so patient. I think . . . I think I'm back in my right mind now.'

'Then, my darling, I will ask you my question again. No, I will change it. I have waited so long – surely I can wait a little while longer. So, whether it is now, or two years from now when you are out of mourning, or twenty years from now, will you promise that one day you will marry me?'

She looked at him gravely. 'Yes, perhaps – one day.'

He could feel his heart pounding as he kissed her. She did not respond to his caresses, but that was not surprising, he thought, after all she had been through, and when a moment or two before she had been near to hysteria.

'I love you,' he whispered. 'I loved you the moment I first saw you. I have loved you every moment of my life since that day. I shall love you to the end of time.'

She moved away at the sound of a knock on the door. The maid entered, bearing a tray with a decanter and two glasses.

Sarah gave him a glowing smile. 'You will take a glass of sherry, Richard?'

'Thank you. We must drink to our future happiness.' He poured the sherry, handed her a glass and then raised his own. 'To you, my darling.'

'To us.' Sarah sipped her drink, and then put down the glass. 'You will come back to Harcourt's, won't you?'

The question struck a chill in his heart, but he smiled and said lightly, 'I do believe that's the only reason you've agreed to marry me.'

'It needn't be for ever – just until Harcourt's is on its feet again.' She paused. 'I thought . . . What's your ambition, Richard?'

'I don't think I have one – except to marry you.' He laughed. 'Yes, I have. I want to make crape from raw silk without throwing it. And I think I know how I can.'

'Tell me.'

'I don't want to talk about that now.'

'No, please – I want to hear.'

'Well, I was looking at the brocade loom in my mill. The threads don't criss-cross each other regularly, you know, and I thought that if we could weave a gauze with some of the wrap threads very slack, and others taut, then that would give a permanent crimping effect.'

'Have you tried it out?'

He smiled wryly. 'I haven't been able to. I haven't got the machines.'

'You could try it here. You could do anything here. My God, Richard, if you succeeded, what that would mean for the mill!'

'Yes,' he said, looking at her almost as though he had never seen her before.

Sarah laughed. 'You surprised me when you said that was your ambition. I always thought you wanted to be master of Harcourt's.'

'What an absurd idea! How could I ever have aspired to that?'

'Don't lie to me, Richard – don't ever lie to me. I saw it in your eyes right from the start.'

He smiled, a little sheepishly. 'All right. Yes, it's true. It *was* my ambition for many years. I told you once how I hated the Harcourts. I used to dream of becoming the owner of the mill, and taking my revenge on them. I'm not sure how. By humiliating them, I suppose, and dismissing them from the company. And then, as I got older, my work began to mean more and more to me, and I wanted to own the mill not for revenge, but because I loved it so much.'

'And you still do.'

He considered. 'No, I don't think so. Tom killed that.'

'You would love it again if you came back. The mill is yours to own if only you'll take it.'

'No, my dear. I have my own business now.'

'You could put a manager in charge of it. And you could go there regularly to see that everything is all right. And here you could do your experiments, and –'

He shook his head. 'No. I'll tell you what I *will* do. I'll spend as much time as I can spare here – help you to get the mill back on its feet, and perhaps I'll have a chance to see if I can make crape in a cheaper way – and then, when we are married, we will sell Harcourt's and move to Wensham, and make our life together there.'

There was horror in her expression. 'Sell Harcourt's? How can you suggest that?'

'Prideau would buy it. Your people here would be protected, the mill would continue.'

She paused. 'You said just now you loved me, Richard. Do you love your business more than me?'

'I could ask the same question.'

She did not reply. Then she gave a little laugh. It sounded false, and it seemed to him that the look in her eye was somehow calculating. 'We are going too fast,' she said. 'We need to think about it, discuss it at our leisure.' She got up and rang for a servant, then came back to sit beside him. She took his right hand, and caressed it. 'Tell me about your accident. How did it happen?'

He related the story briefly.

'It must have been very painful.'

'Yes.'

'Can you use your arm?'

'After a fashion. I manage. My writing is rather illegible, I fear.'

'Poor Richard,' she said.

'Are you sure you don't mind about it?'

'I only mind for your sake, not my own.'

'Truly?'

'Truly. I told you, we must never ever lie to each other.'

There was a knock at the door, and a maid entered.

'Go to the nursery, Eliza,' Sarah told her, 'and bring Master Edward down to me here.'

When the girl had gone, Sarah turned to Richard again. Gazing into his eyes, she said, 'I did lie to you once, Richard. Only once, I think. Do you remember that day when you came to me when I was pregnant and asked whether it was your child that I was carrying?'

He nodded.

'I told you it was Tom's. And that was a lie. I knew perfectly well the child was yours. I lied to you and I lied to Tom. I don't think he ever knew the truth, but he may have suspected – Edward has few of his characteristics, and there are no blue eyes in his family or mine.' She smiled. 'I think it is time for you to meet your son, Richard, don't you?'

He did not know what to say, and gaped at her in bewilderment.

Sarah laughed, enjoying his astonishment. 'Of course, you will understand that he is far too young to be told of his relationship to you.' She paused, and then said in a more serious tone, almost to herself, 'Perhaps it would be better if he were never told.'

'If you wish,' Richard replied, still too stunned even to think of questioning the matter.

A moment or two later, the knock on the door was repeated, and the maid came in, leading by the hand a small boy. He would be three or four, Richard thought. He was so like his mother that it was uncanny – the same dark chestnut hair, the same shape of face, the same full lips.

As soon as Edward saw his mother, he broke free and ran to her. 'Mama!'

Sarah lifted him in her arms. 'Look, Edward,' she said. 'Here is your Uncle Richard. He's come to see you.'

The child glanced at Richard, the blue eyes suddenly apprehensive.

'Hello, little man,' Richard said.

Edward turned his head and buried his face against Sarah's shoulder.

'You mustn't be shy, my pet,' she told him. 'Say "hello" to Uncle Richard.'

But the boy was not to be persuaded, and clung more tightly to her. She tried again, and he began to cry. 'Never mind, my darling. You shall go back with Eliza, and Mama will come to see you soon.'

When the maid had taken Edward out of the room, Sarah said, 'I'm sorry, Richard. He's always shy with strangers, but he'll be all right once he gets to know you.'

'He's a fine boy.'

'Yes, he is. He's very intelligent, and he has a sweet nature. One day he'll be the master of Harcourt's Mill.'

All at once he saw, as clearly as though she had confessed to it, exactly why she had sent for the boy at that point, and why she wished to conceal the truth about his parentage. The mill was at the centre of her life and her desires, and Richard realised that she meant to bind him to Harcourt's with the knowledge that it would one day be his son's inheritance – an inheritance which would perpetuate the Harcourt name, the Harcourt traditions.

The thought which had been hovering at the back of his mind ever since she had first greeted him that morning, suddenly burst into a flash of total comprehension. She did not love him, not truly and deeply. If she cared at all, it was not for himself, but for the master craftsman, the silk maker – a pawn to be manipulated in the game she was playing.

And then the terrible knowledge came to him that he did not love her either. The person he had adored for so many years, and had thought was at last within his grasp, was not this Sarah. Perhaps the Sarah he had carried in his heart had never existed, but was only a dream, a shadow.

The real Sarah had agreed to marry him, but had she any intention of keeping her word, or was it simply another ploy to bring him back to Harcourt's? In any case, if she did eventually become his wife, he realised now that there could be no true happiness for either of them in such a marriage. How blind he had been.

He felt numb, unable to think clearly in the face of this devastating revelation, as though a part of him had been cut away. Sarah was talking, but he could not distinguish her words for the confusion in his mind. She was laughing at him, no doubt believing that it was the sight of Edward which had reduced him to a dazed silence.

He tried desperately to pull his thoughts together, and then suddenly knew what he had to say. He stood up. 'It won't work, will it, Sarah?'

'What, my dear?'

'It won't work for us to marry.'

He could have sworn that there was relief in her eyes, but she gave a little cry, and then said, 'But I need you, Richard, I need you.'

He could not keep the coldness from his voice. 'I've already promised that I will help you to build Harcourt's up again, and I will keep that promise. And if I find a way of making crape from unthrown silk, then the rights in the process will belong half to Harcourt's and half to me. I think somehow I owe you that. With luck, that will mean great prosperity ahead for both of us, and young Edward will inherit a thriving mill – and a fortune.' He took her hands in his, and, with an effort, continued in a lighter, more affectionate tone, 'As for ourselves, why, my dear, we shall simply be good friends, very good friends. But not husband and wife.'

For a long while Sarah did not speak. Then she said, 'Yes, Richard, perhaps that would be best.'

As he travelled back to Wensham later that day, Richard went over in his mind all that had happened. The first shock had passed, and he was able to think rationally about Sarah. He understood her at last, and sympathised with her, but though he would always be fond of her, that heart-tearing passion had vanished for ever. He smiled wryly to himself – it was almost like the merciful release at the end of a long and painful illness.

He felt a contentment that he would not have thought possible. He was eager to see Frances again, and Mr Hill and Isaac Appleby, and to start living a life in which he was no longer haunted by that dream which had plagued him for so long. He would enjoy helping Sarah at Harcourt's, safe in the knowledge that he could always escape back to his own world. But he would not marry again. He would never let himself be trapped by the likes of Sarah, or Henrietta. No, he would live quietly and happily with Frances. Unless, of course, he should meet a reincarnation of sweet, undemanding Jane. Ah, then . . .

And suddenly a different thought struck him. During the time he would spend in Brentfield, he would get to know his son. And when the boy was older, he would bring him to Wensham to stay for a month or two every year. Sarah would not deny him that pleasure. And he would teach his son everything he knew. Edward would one day be the finest silk maker of all.

Richard smiled.

By the author of
THIS SIDE OF HEAVEN

Street Song

EMMA BLAIR

Susan's parents had wanted a son . . . and they did little to hide their disappointment with her. As soon as was decently possible they packed her off to boarding school.

If only they could have known . . .

Because in the tradition-bound Scotland of the 1920's there was no place for a woman like Susan. But she was determined to find one – even if it meant beating her wealthy parents at their own game . . .

STREET SONG – Emma Blair at her best . . . a passionate saga.

GENERAL FICTION 0 7221 1941 0 £3.50